Gill Alderman was [...] with two daughters and four [...] husband in County [...] in micro-electronics r[...]lly acclaimed *The Arch*

By the same author

The Archivist

GILL ALDERMAN

The
Land Beyond

Grafton
An Imprint of HarperCollins*Publishers*

Grafton
An Imprint of HarperCollins*Publishers*
77–85 Fulham Palace Road,
Hammersmith, London W6 8JB

Published by Grafton 1992
9 8 7 6 5 4 3 2 1

First published in Great Britain by
Unwin Hyman Ltd 1990

ISBN 0 586 21368 6

Set in Baskerville

Printed in Great Britain by
HarperCollinsManufacturing Glasgow

For my mother and father with love
and in homage to
the Arctic explorer, Knud Rasmussen (1879–1939).

I have always been a great frequenter of circuses... If only we writers could write as these people move, if only we had in our style the inexhaustible resources of their vigour, their almost fluid suppleness, their undulating grace, their mathematical precision; if only we could control our words as they do their movements, we should be great writers.

Barbey d'Aurevilley

CONTENTS

Acknowledgement

Thanks, as always, to my continuity man.

Author's note.

The Folk of the Land Beyond obviously owe their existence to the Inuit (Eskimo) of Greenland and to other indigenous Arctic peoples. I have used the following genuine Inukitut words:

imaqa: probably not.
qu: probably.
quvit: trousers.
Nigerdlit: the people who live nearest to the South West Wind.
Orquordlit: the people who live in the lee of the South West Wind.
Avangnardlit; the people who live next to the North Wind.
Akunarmiut: the people who live between the winds.

Six Romany words occur:
gajo: one who is not a gypsy.
dukrame: I tell fortunes.
rai (rye): gentleman or lord.
chiv: a blade.
poshrat: a vagabond of dubious character, not a true gypsy.
chabo: child.

The verse on page 57 is adapted from a traditional Inuit song; the quotation on page 144 is from 'The Cap and Bells' by W.B. Yeats and that on page 306 from 'Inversnaid' by Gerard Manley Hopkins; the quotations which head each section and that on page 180 are from *Greenland by the Polar Sea* by Knud Rasmussen, translated by Asta and Rowland Kenney (William Heinemann, 1921) and the short passage about circus and writing skills the words of Barbey d'Aurevilley, a nineteenth century Parisian dandy, first quoted in *Les Goncourts* (1889) by Alidor Delzant.

Prologue

Once upon a time there was an undiscovered continent. No one lived there. There was no food, no shelter, no water and no warmth; the land was frozen and the snow which covered it never thawed.

This land surrounded, contained and covered the North Pole. It became a magnet, a lodestone which drew people to it as surely as the magnetic pole moves the compass needle. To discover snow and ice southern peoples made arduous journeys, which exercised their minds and bodies. Below the unproductive surface they found rocks and minerals which exercised their greed and ingenuity. The colonists came next and imposed their will upon the place; they tried to make order out of the unorderable and to improve an environment which was already as finely balanced as a diamond hanging from a single hair.

They named the country Hiberna because it was at the end of the world. But Hiberna was the final prize. Noiro encircled it, hard to miss. Some discoverers stayed there, others passed on; no one could avoid it for it lay across their path.

Noiro begins with the island of Imaqa and ends with its neighbour, the island of Qu, for it is a necklace which passes around Hiberna and around Guna herself, and its end is its beginning and its beginning its end. Halfway along it lies Sowash, one of the Amber Islands; nearby are Hairete, Malpogak, Vai and Demender, beads on a string. Some say that Hairete is the most beautiful island on Guna; others make claims for Eye in Lutreia, and the coral atoll of Diademe. Arne Shakla preferred Sowash, which has an ugly name but many compensating beauties. When the thaw prevented her from travelling on the ice, she would set up camp at Toul, on Sowash's southern coast. Here, she could look towards the world from whence she came while she enjoyed chilly outskirts of the world she had discovered, a wave-washed inlet of shingle, tussock grass and frost-formed rock where nothing intruded beside seals, birds, and the ever-present wind.

Shakla belonged to a third category of travellers: the lone single-minded explorers who went north to discover themselves. They always had ready excuses, reasons for their journeys like Expedition, Scientific, or Geographical. There were many explorers, but Arne Shakla and Panon Anak-Ho are Guna's foremost. The first claimed to have discovered the strong current which flows south from Hiberna through the Ilmiti Ocean and dies upon the southern coast of Mahkrein; the second, beside the heroic achievement of locating the invisible pole, claimed to have discovered the Folk before Shakla.

The Folk say they have always lived in the north and that such discoveries have no more relevance than the formation and dissolution of individual snowflakes. They were Shakla's friends and they respected Anak-Ho, but Hiberna and Noiro had been there all the time, and belonged to everyone and to no one. The continent and island chain had been named already, though no one from the south would acknowledge it. To make sure of their claims, the people from the south gave Hiberna and Noiro yet another name: the Land Beyond.

The discoverers, colonists and explorers mapped, measured and analysed the north; yet it constantly surprised them. The Folk said that they alone understood its wide open spaces and its hidden, wilderness spirit.

It is certainly true that the Folk lived in Noiro and Hiberna for many millennia and that they were able to survive the harshest winters – until more of them died than were born. Then, they did not cry out although, with their small bodies and determined expressions, they had all the pathos of a lost child in a market place. They required help, though they did not ask for it. Collections were made in public places and governments promised funds. Those sometime colonists, the Eririan Sineinians, blew the trumpets and sounded the drums of their superior culture and mounted a rescue operation.

The Folk, those who remained, under a hundred nomadic Fishfolk, a group which had lived by fishing in summer and in winter by hunting, were grateful to their saviours. After all, they were in no state to protest. The Sineinians began to educate them and gave them proper work, which earned money. They built a research station and encouraged the conception and birth of a great many children.

Yet, in the same way that Toul was wilderness and haven, there was paradox in the education of the Folk. They could not be taught everything; and they must remember what they had left behind them. The Sineinians gave them new knowledge and taught them about things they used every day but had never know the names of: Mathematics, for example, and Language. The education programme was extensive but, even so, there remained a few universal fundamentals the Folk had never heard of, such as William Shakespeare, Haibeg's Theory of the Transference of Matter Through Space and Time, Harlequin and Columbine, Mandelbrot and Julia Sets, afternoon tea and the circus.

WHITE

I must go to those people.

Knud Rasmussen, *Greenland by the Polar Sea*

It was night. It was always bloody night—

She smiled into her cup. The coffee she had drawn from the dispenser not ten minutes ago was tepid. The bitterness came through like grains of aspirin on her tongue.

—at this time of the year, it was night all day and each hour followed the next without notice: no shadows, no sunset; no calm, limitless twilight.

Cold coffee, cold comfort; and it was cold outside, too cold for her warm body and too cold for the green and bronze tussocks which carpeted the islands in summer. Delicate flowers had given way to flowers of ice. She sipped and let the sour liquid wash around her mouth: the coffee filled nose, mouth and throat with its aroma, and the first sip was like the first thought of the day, clear and untainted.

She looked up. The moon had set long ago. Up here, in the Land Beyond – well above the temperate latitudes, fast in the pack ice, in the mouth of the North Wind. . . up here, they called Eshtur, Usht', a harsh exhalation, a whisper uttered through the teeth. It made her think of the nursery and her first nana: shush! She had lived here, in Traumesse, for eight years and was still unable to suppress her urge to correct that hissing, babyish, sound whenever she heard it. Usht', Eshtur – the moon, my lady, she thought. Even she has declined and set. Several artificial satellites travelled these skies, false stars amongst the unvisited and inhospitable stars, but the Folk had no name for them. Tyft: their word for star was like a kiss, a tender greeting to the guides by which they had navigated when they were free.

Most of their words sounded like the language of an infant, pretty groups of phonics on trial, words for tasks like mending and earning, words for essentials like eating, Mother, sex – not words to build theories with, and proofs; not for global communication, literature, government. Their childish words made a dying language which their children had to be taught in the classroom.

Sentimentality was with her, in the ascendant. While she blamed it on the dream which had troubled her at three o'clock and robbed her of sleep, she knew that the

3

tenderness which invaded her when she thought of children and the Folk had begun in her own childhood. Snow and the North wind had blown into her nine-year-old mind in a curious way, tearing away the twin veils of innocence and sobriety and fixing there a desire to see Noiro. Aunt Jest had given her an old tape on which the epic tales of the Explorers were retold and, in the same month, Cousin Bel had come home, the soft cadences of her native speech alive with these same, magical and onomatopoeic words: Ushtaim, Matoq, Ipiqitarod. . .Cousin Bel had brought her a doll dressed in skins, a little Fishfolk woman, one of the ones the Folk made for sale to tourists and those scientists, miners, and government agents who had to work in the frozen North.

The stars made it all worth while, littering the sky for twenty-four hours in deepest winter, brilliants, diamonds, jewels for all.

The Fish swam in the southwest, its outline as clear as one of those stellar plans in which the stars are joined like a child's dot-and-line puzzle into the picture of a heroine or beast; Aanori, the star which made its eye, stared without blinking. Ikbik, the great Fish, named for the green pelagic pike which had been landed here in Sowash before Traumesse was built or even an architect's dream: Ikbik, asexual, primordial, cold – She liked to look at Oma who ate her long and scaly body from the tail, curled in the sky in a gigantic ring, the metaphor for life, and futility. The photographs she had taken of the constellation last month had shown her nothing but difficulties, the individual stars separate dots of light, disparate pixels which would not join up. She had been minded to tamper with the old artform: fix her enlargements in the eye of the computer and enhance the imagined serpent at the expense of truth. The light which had entered the lens of her camera that night had come so gently out of space and brought her only the picture she had seen herself, the faraway flares of gases burning: the stars. She had believed she would make a profound discovery if she studied that light and let it into her mind.

4

And there, in the long night, the picture she had wanted to make had vanished and become, on the film, the picture she did make, the one that was already there.

She dropped her coffee cup into a bin and knelt upon the stark and purple-shadowed floor which imitated the hill outside; she lay down upon her back, looked up, and let the starlight enter the pupils of her eyes.

Between her warm body and the bitter cold outside, the glassy dome which protected her, the circular room, the tropical plants, the telescopes and the coffee machine, was an interpolation no greater than the window of a starship, or a permanent corrective grafted into an imperfect eye. It was heated from within and automatically washed. Robot crawlers wiped it, clean as a whistle, even in the eye of the storm.

The ice and the long winter day might prevail, and the snow, picked up and carelessly tossed by the bitter North wind, might make the darkness cold purgatory but in the midst of it, around the edge of the dome, grew a close ring of moonflowers which revelled in the transmitted warmth, always in flower and white like the snow. When summer came, they turned yellow. You could see that golden circle from the air when the ice had broken up and the light returned, an unsought and lovely blessing, a bonus and visible sign. Buried Traumesse, despite the investigation, the learning and the planning, despite the long, cold war of 4502 itself and the subsequent treaties and entreaties, the excavation and building begun eighty years ago, had modified its environment, though in the subtlest way. One gold ring, three reflective domes and a forest of slender aerials on rocky Skaa, close by Sowash, were the only signs of its invasion.

The ice sang to the woman, its piercing groans relayed into the Viewdome where she heard it with impunity. She lay still and watched the far away stars. The wailing of the ice-floes lulled her and, presently, she fell asleep.

Her name was Ang Semo. Her parents in naming her had no thoughts of anguish or angst, although the intense spasms of pain Ang felt when she tried to impose the normality she

5

feared upon her wayward body were real enough, and she was more aware than many of her humanity. Ang was an old-fashioned Nenian given name: no doubt her parents hoped their daughter would be as honest and uncomplicated as the monosyllable. As for Semo, her mother had told her that it came from an old word for counsellor, a word from the first millennium when the loose, elected, parliaments which had coalesced and become the Council of Nations and Noiro, had begun. Later, in school, Ang had looked up the word in an etymological dictionary and found that her mother had told her the truth, the mother who, suitably, was employed as a counsellor to the bereaved.

Ang's own career, which had begun with a post-grad secondment, here, in Traumesse, was a success. She played upon the touchboard of the mainframe graphic with such virtuosity that the mundane dreams the Establishment manufactured became things of such beauty and quality that they topped the ratings everywhere. She had earned her status of Artistic Director and she kept at bay the Northern Disease, unalloyed despair, which had caused her predecessor to retire at thirty-nine. Lalla Arveida had gone from Traumesse under a figurative cloud and, in the distant tropics, found literal warmth and personal ardour in painting in unctuous resins, in many lovers and one child. Her annual letter to her one-time pupil seemed a burst of this new, and better, life's sunshine penetrating the winter darkness.

When Ang woke, the sky was still a star-filled black bowl. There was no sign from heaven to mark the dawnless morning. It was five o'clock. In Sollar Kein, if her mother woke, she would know that there were only two more hours of darkness; here, in the North, there would be no dawn until another month had passed, a rapid and ungracious sunrise half an hour before midday with sunset following close upon its heels. There was no daily rhythm like the one she had learned in childhood with its morning, afternoon, twilight and night, the chapter-headings of a familiar book. But eventually the long day would come, six months with minimal night, culminating in a midsummer without a midnight, when the Folk asked the Establishment

6

gynarch to intercede for them and pray to Mahun that Eshtur would not always be a thin pale disc in a sunlit sky; that life would not end because Oma, their Mother, could take no rest.

It was quite clear to the anthropologists and to the educated opinion which followed them, that Oma and Mahun, the great and universal deity, were one and the same being.

Spiritual concerns, the need for approval from above, had governed the Folk long ago when they had travelled and fished the seas; the prayers they asked for were an odd instance of the racial unconscious and superstition combining to produce insurance against sleepless nights. Their days, now, were filled with dreams: with the dream of wealth, and the dream of safety; with dreams of comfort, learning and love. If these were not enough, then they could turn to the construct sagas on the screen and find there dreams already made. Each day they manufactured and packaged dreams for the rest of the world and saw the six letters of the Establishment logo with its linked triple wings, suggestive of the oneness and threeness of life, stamp out their cultural identity.

This anarchic thought was new to her, no more than a year old. She saw it as a symptom of the Northern Disease; one she could control with reason.

She had not dreamed, asleep upon the floor; yet, the dream which had visited her in her bed was still with her, a hangnail, a loose tooth to jiggle. Strange that she, the maker of dreams, should be troubled by a dream. She lay still, her hand on her belly, imagining her womb to be an empty purse. She felt the dream worrying at her, bathed in a sea of melancholia because she had no daughter. Intervention? Implantation? She had considered and rejected them. Her affliction prevented them; she had an inbuilt infirmity which closed all routes.

The dream baby had been perfect, a thornless rose, warm as the breast it sucked at; like that breast, part of herself. But the random programmes of her sleeping brain had turned it into a seal whose eyes were full of tears and, after that,

7

to a cancer she nourished with her blood. She shuddered, rubbed the sleep from her eyes, and lay still.

She had not been home for three years; her short leaves had been spent walking on Sowash and, once, in hiring a Folk skiff for a trip to Hairete where, in the clear light of Blue, the moonflowers had made golden carpets on the cliffs and the bird-mountain at the island's southern end had been as noisy and as crowded as a city, the gulls stacked up in their tenement nests. She was hoarding the long leaves, until she had a year's-worth, when she would go south, to the Highlands.

She had not been home for three years because, last time, Cousin M had come up from the country (ostensibly to buy clothes) had captured her and carried her off to eat oyfish at Lara's. With the dessert – a spoonful of chilled frangipane dissolved in her memory – came the questions.

'Not many men in Sowash, Ang, apart from the Folk?'

'A few hands, on leave between ferries.'

and

'I expect you have considered Universal?'

'It's not the same, Em: they deal in facts not fictions.'

'You could switch careers?'

'I'm good at my job.'

'Dear Ang, I don't decry. . .but you are twenty-nine and if you want a natural pregnancy – '

Silence, frangipane, the last crumbs.

'You must have met suitable men?'

'One or two.' (Oh, the anguish of parting from Tobin; Pior's kisses.)

The oval dish she had eaten from was finest bone, the silver heavyweight. The pink-shelled oyfish had lain upon the dish like rare organs discovered by an anatomist's knife, exotic, exquisite and very dead. Cousin M's vintage breasts rested on the table-edge and challenged her.

'Has Mother been speaking to you?'

'No, my dear.'

'Perhaps we could ask the waiter for the bill?'

He had come at once, prompt in answer to Cousin M's raised finger, slim and pale in his black clothes, his blond hair slicked back, deferential, obsequiously charming. She would have preferred to eat at Zack's, where the waiters wore shorts and smiled generously at the customers. He presented the bill in its neat blue folder, the silver lettering, 'Lara' on it shiny as the knives and forks, the bill inside written in longhand on white paper. It was a very expensive restaurant. The waiter retired and, instead of reaching for the bill, insisting, arguing about her share, she had rested her chin on her hand and watched him. He had seen her watching him. They played a little game of cat-and-mouse while Cousin M arranged money on the salver and calculated the correct percentage for the tip. Lara only accepted cash: no wafers, no credit. Her cuisine depended on imports, out-of-season vegetables, fresh fish from the tropics: therefore, her customers were select.

The waiter returned to serve them with slim glasses of palest ichor: on the house. Lara herself smiled and bobbed at them from behind the glass panel of her counting-house.

Ang had drained her glass, opened her bag and put down twenty redbacks for the beautiful waiter. Cousin M smiled bleakly and replaced them with a silver ten.

'Your mother would love a grandchild,' she said. 'Efemy will get the house: you don't want that to happen.'

The house had become a counter, but she did not take it up. Her home. The grey town house with its tall windows: a valuable piece of property. The smell of the clipped box trees on either side of the front door came suddenly to her, wet, after rain, the scale altered because it was a picture from her childhood and around her the flagged courtyard stretched away. . . And she realised that she didn't care about the house. Efemy would take care of it, better care than she, away in Traumesse. . .she cared about her photography; she wanted to see the metamorphic bluffs in the Central Highlands; she cared about her job, and the Folk.

'Well?' said Cousin M.

Ang had answered her as if she were making a reasonable request for pleasant diversions in the afternoon city.

'Let's see some of my pix: the Chocolate Box is showing the compilation from last year. Then I'll buy you cream cakes for tea.'

The 4621 series of 'Greed' had been a winner. Her characters had walked unscathed through the dramatic traps she had set for them; the series even had a happy ending, in the soft focus of which enough doubt had been cast upon the motives of the leading character to provoke discussion, to make people talk and the critics hum, to lead them expectantly toward a new series – the one they could access now, three times each day to catch the maximum, their appetites whetted so that, when the cube set was issued and the new merchandise, it would be snapped up.

Watching Siloe and Jannl tread elegantly through her fractal landscapes and meet in the infinite locations of the charmed cities of her imagination that afternoon in the comfortable tea-room in Sollar, she had known disappointment and felt the critics' rub. The dramas were not meant to be strung together and shown as a whole; each was complete in itself, each led into the next in a series of planned stages as elegant as Haibeg's classic proof of the transference of matter through space and time. And, throughout, Cousin M had whispered and clapped, caught up in the drama onscreen yet distanced enough to remark at the parallels between the fiction and Ang's own life. Ang had bent her head over the tea table and the headache which had been imminent all afternoon bore down upon her, squeezing her temples in its vice. M had stroked her arm and murmured, offering calculated amounts of sympathy; and an analgesic.

'Dear girl,' she had said, 'I do hope I haven't upset you.'

The pastries, brimming with whipped cream, had finally silenced her cousin who could not speak with her mouth full. Delightedly, had Murali poured cream on cream, watching the opaque stream obliterate the chocolate whorls and crayberry coils on her cake as if she deserved a reward, a measurable return for all the milk she had produced to nourish her children, her foster-daughters and her nieces and nephews.

Ang found her hand at her breast, the fingers plucking at one nipple, vainly seeking to uncover the sensation she denied herself. It was all a dream, a bad dream. She stood up and straightened her clothes, pushed her hair from her eyes. It was too late to go back to bed and, at nine, she had a difficult interview to conduct with one of the Folk: Salter Bren, Loading Operative One – and a craftsman. He would put it another way: 'Salter, suetstone crafter and Spokesman. My job? I drive a loader.'

Ten white steps led up to the glass of the dome. She was warm and indolent, sleepy again, and they looked like steps cut by a crazy mason in the ice of a berg. The marble steps which led up to the International Peace Monument in the hills outside Sollar were not so steep. She walked slowly up them and, as she mounted higher, the bleak prospect outside revealed itself. The landscape she had taught herself to love wore a mask; every year the bald beauty of its winter face astonished her. Before her, the white hillside sloped gently down, the snow upon it hiding the irregularities and tussocks; the smooth slope ran gently down and out and an uneven grey line marked the clifftops. The sea had gone; where it should have tossed and fretted was frozen gloom. Far away, at the limit of her vision, a ripple in the dusk was water, flowing freely and fast along the centre of the Sound where the Shaklian current made a turbulent race which could not freeze.

Everything out there was white, or deepest blue, the colours she had mixed on her computer palette to make Siloe's ball gowns in the disappeared days before she got the Arts Directorship. More money, more responsibility, which meant toward the job, never oneself or one's integrity; and less art. These days, she was chained to the touchboard which was her fortune.

The stars glittered over the ice, for ever burning, never sentient, never knowing what febrile spirits the Folk had given them. She peered out at the snow and the dark and distant plain that was the sea, trying to summon a blessing from the wilderness.

11

She blinked and saw on that indeterminate brink, slow movement, a determined progress across the frozen sea. The surface, she knew, was pitted and windworn but the animals moved as easily over the ice-foot as across a summer meadow: icedeer, heads alternately raised to scent the air, lowered to snuff the ice. They were searching for food, any food: moss they could uncover, bare twigs they could chew; even seaweed. She could not see them clearly and, torn between the desire to see them more closely and the fear of losing them altogether, she hesitated; and turned and ran along the top step to the telescopes. They all pointed at the sky and she swung one hastily down, twirling the focus nut.

The deer were – there! The leader had turned inland, an old hind whose hair was yellowing with wear and age. She raised her head. She was blind in one eye and the corona of hair which surrounded her face stood out in the freezing air. Oh, Salter should see this! She would tell him – what was the tradition? When the icedeer show, then. . .no, she had forgotten. The two stags walked on either side of the herd, keeping watch. In the centre, last year's fawns were white as the snow itself. Once upon a time, the Folk shot these noble animals, ate them and made clothing from their skins; before that, they trapped them, tumbling them indiscriminately into concealed pits, carving them up, using every bone and sinew: sledge-runners, spoons, jewellery, knife-handles, thread, fishing traces. Before that, they drove whole herds to extinction over the steep cliffs of Hairete.

The prehistoric carving she had bought in Sollar before she ever heard of icedeer showed a woman of the Folk sitting, rotund in her deerskins, on a sailsledge. Her child peeped out over her collar, his tiny head haloed by a ring of icedeer hair.

The women of Traumesse, her heirs, were also hardy. They worked in the lines; they learned and practised traditions, new and old; they gave birth regularly and easily; their children were strong. In the clinic, the graph which showed the regeneration of the Folk was a beautiful soaring line which threatened to run off the chart.

The icedeer were hidden from her by the blue line of the cliff.

She looked at her watch. It was two minutes to six: she watched the digits flash and change colour and, when they were black again and stood still upon the hour, she turned away from the wide sky and the snow beyond the dome, crossed the arena under the stars, opened the door and stepped into daylight. In the body of Traumesse the lamps shone as bright as day. She stretched her arms above her head and yawned; and walked slowly down the green-walled corridor to her unit, her career, status and the colleagues she was beginning to find wearisome, obsessed as they were with the great experiment of Traumesse. Doctor Wireloom was remote in manner, but diligent; the anthropologist, Eda Voran, was keen as mustard and Carey Aleph and Ander Voran, who tended the computer, tedious in a different way, always sending her chocolates or liquor in the hope that she would respond.

She would be happy if the interview with the Spokesman went on all day.

Salter Bren's hair was slicked back with grease. He smelled of musk and vetiver and wore an earring, a style copied from the ferryhands, who were Eririans from Habin and ahead of the fashion. He had a powerful body which he usually displayed in a vest but now, for the interview, he had put on his working clothes, neatly-pressed coveralls. She knew he had asked to see her and nothing more. She was curious, a little flattered – but cautious; she had only basic training in Folk stewardship.

'They tell me you collect carvings,' he said, and cleared his throat.

'I've two, that's all. The old ones are very expensive.'

He cleared his throat again. He did not know how to begin. She helped him.

'Are you worried about the number of carvings being exported?'

He shook his head.

'No – souvenirs. They don't mean a thing.'

She smiled. It helped.

'I am worried,' he said, 'I might lose my touch – we all might. Ten hours Traditions a month isn't enough. There's too much to learn, much too much to take in. What if we can't remember, what then?'

He had come to her, she realised it now, because she wasn't a scientist or a manager but an artist, someone like him who was supposed to be sensitive to the needs and moods of others. Salter did not know – how could he? – that she had two techno degrees as well as her doctorate in Computer Art; but he knew that she was, if not a manager, in direct control of thirty people. Because he knew she made photographs and owned two suetstone carvings, he saw her as an ally, a route to the goal he was finding it hard to define.

'Listen, Salter – Bren,' she said, using his given name. 'Something happened last night which might interest you – as a carver, I mean. Nothing to do with your job, or Education.

'I couldn't sleep. I got up and went into the Viewdome to look at the stars; then, just when I was ready to leave, I saw icedeer, far out, near the water – twenty-seven of them. Their herd-mother was very old, blind in one eye. Her corona was frozen – it stuck straight out, all round her head.

'They turned inland. Maybe we could get permission to go up and see them.'

The last statement seemed to amuse him. She had hoped for awe – excitement, at least.

'You want to feel the cold?' he muttered. 'You want to go out there? A Sineinian upside in White?'

She watched him puzzle over her story. She lit a cigarette, offered him one; smoked.

'Icedeer,' he said, very low. 'The deer come in when the ice is ripe.'

That was it, the saying.

He was delving into Tradition, running it through his mind like an old drama, stopping the playback here and there.

'Thaw'll come early, ' he said, 'In the dark. But the deer: they turn inland and follow the shore. Ulbeg's too steep for them. They come ashore at Forso, up the beach, follow the path. . .they'll walk right up to the dome, it's the highest point.'

'So they will!'

She inhaled deeply. The taste of tar and smoke had woken her; in the shower, dressing, putting up her hair, she had felt limp and oppressed. But she could do nothing about the deer. She might get a picture or two, through the glass; but the animals were outside amongst familiar hardships, and she in shelter as distant from them as if she watched them on a screen.

'I should like to see them,' said Salter Bren, shyly.

'I can't make rash promises,' she said. He had status and a position in the tribe. He was a Spokesman. Possibly. 'But maybe. When does your shift start?' She rushed on, gave him no time to reply. 'You don't need my permission to go to the Viewdome.'

'I'll go there now,' he said, half-rising from the edge of the narrow office chair where he had perched, neat as a gull in his lavender plumage.

'Wait, I'll come with you. What time did you say?'

'Two.'

'Oh, fine. One moment.'

She paused to leave a message for her secretary on the link. She scanned the screen: junk mail, posters, one to be answered, a memo from Wireloom in red.

She walked along the corridor with him, striding out now, the executive, the professional, her grey suit solemn beside the ling-bloom colour of his coverall. She was used to the Folk; she liked and respected them; she admired their neat and nimble industry usurped as it was by their service to her nation. But they, respectful and correct, their natural vivacity muted by her grey persona, almost always kept a polite distance from her, the Sineinian intruder. Their formality of speech and loquacious body-language emphasised their charm, the impression they gave an outsider of precocious innocence. This, and their ready smiles, white as malpog

15

ivory, had endeared them to the conservationists who first worked among them. In Nenian they were fluent, exact, and unforthcoming. Good children, uniformly dressed, they were diligent in the classroom and on the lines. The interview with Salter Bren in the seclusion of her office had been intimate by comparison with this silent walk, the little carver an armslength from her, keeping pace. She towered over him, although she was not tall. Neither was he a dwarf, his small body well-made, almost burly about the shoulders and upper arms and developed in the gym; no more, alas, in hauling sailsledges and heaving on shrouds in a blizzard. He was not a reader, though he used words well when he spoke, and his carvings were – very good, she judged, but not excellent; certainly not masterpieces. She knew nothing about his mind. It was a difference of scale, this disparity between them, of horizons and schooling, of upbringing; of race. The Folk were treasure trove. They had been endangered; now, they were safe.

The miracle was, that she was part of it, that she was helping them.

Once, on holiday in a vibrant and blazing otherworld far from the snow, she had visited the greatest archive, the ancient and continuing collections of the Sacred City. The air-conditioning had chilled her sweating face, while the vastness of the building and its octagonal geography bewildered her. In a small, dark gallery she had come upon a photograph taken by Shakla on her second expedition in 1950. It was embalmed in a plastic. A reading lamp released a brief burst of light which allowed her to examine the picture and read the short tragedy pencilled on the back. A man, a woman, a child, a tiny baby were immortalised there, in the decaying emulsion: a family of Folk, Snowfolk. They had walked across the ice for the three months of White, trudging south, in search, like the icedeer, of food. In the North, where the cold wind began, was nothing but snow and they had begun their journey late because the woman was in labour. 'Redbeads Susu, aged 23: placenta was retained.' Shakla's neatly-written coda hinted at other hardships.

They were uncivilised people, these Snowfolk. A raw placenta would have been a feast for them; a raw placenta expelled on to the ice would not have festered as it did inside the warm cavity of the woman's body.

She smiled from the photograph and her new baby peeped from her collar just like the suetstone child; but the husband stared at the camera as if there was nothing in his mind but falling snow, and the face of the child who held his hand was pinched and bleak and had deep craters around the eyes. They had died: mother, baby, child. Their man had hanged himself from the rooftree of the expedition hut because of it. And the Snowfolk were extinct.

In her small collection, she kept and treasured a facsimile of the photograph. Its sepia tones echoed the sombre tale it told. She thought a colour print would have revealed less, concealing the fortitude of the woman under the bright light reflected from the snow, hiding the pain, emphasising the red and blue beadwork on her tunic. All tragedies should be photographed in sepia, so that the agony was fixed and the bright hues of normality removed; so that the shadows, stretching out from the solids which blocked the light, were emphasised. Death, too, took the light from life.

'Doctor Semo,' said the little man, his sing-song voice scratching at her mind, 'Hmm – What time is it, please?'

'It's almost ten.'

He sunk into himself again and she noticed the creases already developed in the young flesh of his face. He would be marrying soon, she remembered, leaving the free life of a bachelor for the solidity and enforced companionship of marriage: eating together, playing and sleeping together. She had put a fifty into the collection box one of the girls hawked round. 'Thank you, Doctor. We're buying them china.' A quaint bob, and the girl was gone with her prize. Angle Fenner, was it, or the other plump one, Spinner, from QC? Not Gaby, though she was usually given these tasks -

The given name was always applied to Gaby: in this Ang did not transgress. The girl was the pet and mascot of her line, her wide grin like the soul of friendship emanating from the Folk through this, their irreverent and untypical representative. Friendship with a Sineinian was scarcely allowed; intimate relationships were absolutely forbidden. Yet Ang was pleased to be walking the corridors and squares of Traumesse this morning with Salter Bren. His presence transformed the plain day. Underneath that dour exterior he must be as excited as she.

They left the morning bustle behind them and took the lift. In the green corridor, the man unbent again and spoke to her. His innocent remark that this was an odd way to be spending his free time and that he should be taking breakfast with his friends delighted her.

He pushed open the Viewdome door. The yellow daylight of the lamps flooded into the chamber and coloured the floor and the tier of steps. Then the door swung to and they stood in twilight under the stars. Tern sparkled. The washers had been over and the glass was so clear that Ang felt she might reach out to grasp the stars. Their position in the sky had changed since five and they looked huge, a brilliant arrow pointing north. She saw that Salter Bren had stiffened, his whole body one taut, questing line and she caught the thrill herself and the relief – for the quarry was near, the long wait almost over, the kill at hand and the hunter alert. But they stood in a technological Diold, the climate eternally temperate summer. All they lacked were the hyacinth waters of the Trench beating softly below the sunny corniche at Ama and the vines in the hills. . .Here, safe inside Traumesse, under the dome, they were protected from the dark morning and the cold at minus thirty above them, privileged voyeurs like tourists viewing the icefields from a skimmer. The would-be hunter could hear nothing through the glass but the Viewdome's inbuilt system relayed the deer's every breath to him. Their inspirations boomed.

Ang's smile of resignation vanished as she watched him: the little man was acting out his fantasy.

He moved slowly up the steps, and she followed him, keeping her head down. He moved gracefully and while she watched and followed him she remembered how her mother's cats would change in an instant from langorous beauties into stealthy predators: all for a moth, or a fly.

When her eyes were level with the topmost step, she saw the deer and wished she could see through the eyes of Salter Bren and feel the ancient blood-lust. The deer were wild, magnificent, beautiful, free, every superlative: what must they be to him, one of the Folk? There was a programme in his genes, somewhere an inherited pattern to be passed on and one day used; a need to be out there in the snow, upside with the deer, an equal in the hunt for food. One of the stags was looking directly at her. He was chewing, munching on a white garland of moonflowers. Swags of them hung down amongst the hair about his mouth. To the animal their human heads must be two more inexplicable and inedible objects in the white expanse, like the telescopes, the coffee machine, the plants –

'Would they recognise the plants?' she hissed.

'They're eating the plants. Those are moonflowers.'

'No. The glicidias.'

'I think so. Green, brown, purple – all food. But don't worry: they can't get in.'

He was silent for a long time after that. She could hear him breathing softly; once, he sighed. The two perfumes he wore and the sweat he exuded made her giddy. It was a smell she associated with the bars and daash-houses of Sollar. If he went out there, the deer would scent him and run for miles.

She began to ask him technical questions. 'How do you kill them?'

'You only kill one, or two – enough to provide. The spearhead, or the bullet must go directly into the brain – aim there, you see, above the eye where the corona thins a little and the horn is brittle.'

'And do you have to eat them raw?'

'Once, we did.' (She noticed he did not say 'they'.) 'Before we learned about fire. The hindquarters are the best cut, and the kidneys. We say "Red Kidney: Red Blood." Deermeat and kidneys make courage run in the veins of the Folk.'

'How do you stop the lookout deer seeing you and warning off the rest?'

'That's easy. You get there before they do and hide upwind.'

She wondered how he would cope. If there was some cataclysm, some disaster, and they all found themselves out in the snow. She thought she would be safe in his party.

One of the fawns was being suckled by its mother although it was nearly as big as she and only the purity of its white coat distinguished it from the adult. It nuzzled under her flank. The herd-mother was keeping watch, her blind eye toward her family, her good eye looking out across the snow, to the icefields of the sea from whose frozen eddies a troupe of vair might erupt; or a carrion bear. Her frozen corona had thawed in the warmth from the dome and swept down over her bony withers to touch the snow. Another doe – the corona of hair was fuller, softer, than that of the stag – stopped grazing and stood back from the bank of flowers; she changed places with her grandmother, lifted her head, pricked her small, round ears. The old doe grazed.

'No good, that one,' said the man, 'Tough: bitter flesh.'

The stag they had seen first moved closer. His horns were longer than the other's. He did not seem to see the glass and then, when the soft grey pad of his muzzle was against it, he put out his tongue and licked the smooth solid as if it were the crusted surface of a salt-pan in the kjarr.

Ang Semo and Salter Bren discovered that they had grasped each other's hands in their excitement and delight.

'I'm sorry,' she said, drawing back, embarrassed.

'So sorry.' His sallow face was flushed.

She supposed it would make a tale to tell his friends. He would boast, make the accidental contact seem deliberate.

The spell was broken. She had ten episodes of 'Greed' to view and approve. She had a mountain of tasks to scale before she could be herself again, alone with the eye of the camera. Outside, the deer continued to eat moonflowers in the dark Noiran winter. Ang slid down three steps and stood up.

'I must go,' she said. 'What was it you came to ask?'

Salter Bren turned his head.

'It was a question about the length and scope of the rehabilitation programme.'

'Make another appointment with my secretary when you are ready to ask it. Goodbye.'

As she opened the door – a crack, enough to squeeze through – she looked back. The man crouched there, oblivious, blind and deaf to everything but the icedeer which pressed, huge white rugs, up against the glass. Several of them were licking it, searching vainly for salt, confused by the transparent hillock which stood in their way. They could clearly see the snowfield continuing beyond and they shoved and shouldered the glass. The intoxication returned. She wanted to run, to dance, tell everyone. He must see them upside in the snow, be among them; so must she. It would take days for a permission, maybe a week; they would have to verify in Sollar, send someone, send a team. . .

Bren went into the canteen. He looked around, studying the crowded tables and the heads bent over portable screens. He nodded to several men, smiled at the women: he knew them all but saw no one wise enough to take his burden from him. For years he had enjoyed the enclosed winter life and gone carelessly about from work to leisure and back to work again; every day, an hour or two of worrying with file and scriber at the small green blocks of suetstone had given him a different space on which to look. He would never be the same again. The great white wilderness had opened for him. The North had struck out and broken him open.

Nearly twelve. He was too late to take breakfast, much too late for Cait and the others. She would probably scold him. Ah, well.

He sat on one of the stools at the long counter. Someone had left a cube-wrapper in the trash and he unfolded it and smoothed it out. He laid it down on the stool beside him and pressed the red menu button. One of Traumesse's saccharine voices spoke to him.

'There is melon,' it said, 'from Mahkrein: Honeyheart, Banded Planet, and Anak-Ho which means "without equal" in the language of Cheron.'

Nothing equals a good roast, he thought and, Why do they give you a lecture with everything? He could see dishes of the fruit laid out ready in the kitchens, green and gold skins topped with lush pink flesh like the inside of Cait's mouth, sweet flesh, a dish as inappropriate to the season here, upside on Sowash, as lipstick on a man. Melon: tropical intruder. No.

'We have ice cream: Strawberry, Vanilla, Chocolate, Passion-fruit, Mango and Crayberry.'

Icecream? In White, when upside it was cold enought to freeze the salt sea?

'Hot coffee from Ineit?'

'Sweet dates from the Tayaal?'

The counterhand took his order: malpog soup, rinds. The dusky hours he had spent under the dome flooded his mind. In here under the bright lights, swathed in the indistinct chatter of the diners, he felt the wound the deer had given him. And Ang Semo, spilling her emotions out of her grey shell – he would have to see her again, spit out that question, get rid of the itch that was troubling him; but she would do nothing except file a memo, and she could do nothing about the deer. They would soon go away, when they had eaten all the flowers, scraped a bit and uncovered the dead tussock, eaten that. If the wind kept up, they could travel with it down to Hairete, get into the col and graze the lichens. Ang, Dr Semo in her grey designer suit with its expensive lapel brooch and her soft, shiny shoes. A Sineinian: what could she be but a slicker full of enthusiasm, without stamina? But she worked at her job. She was good. So did he; so was he. The loading was so easy and the driving no problem. He had time to plan new carvings while he worked the line.

The soup came. It was too hot to drink. He dipped into the bowl of crisp, fatty rinds. Too much salt.

While he ate, he stared at the wrapper he had retrieved from the trash-tray. It was designed as a keepsake, a poster memento of the last series of 'Greed'. On it Siloe, the audacious paragon of the sagas, reclined gracefully, her blonde head propped on a small white hand, her long legs exposed, the neat inverted cup of her sex more than just a hint of shadow and line. Behind her, her lover, Jannl, looked out; not at her but at the burgeoning garden he had cultivated, his hand on her shoulder – almost on her breast – evidence of his interest, his proprietorship. It was curious how the stories turned everything upside down. Wish-fulfillment, that was the term. There was no harm in it. He couldn't imagine ignoring Cait while he gazed at – what? – his loader stacked with gaudy shrinkwrapped packages of dreams; into the dreamscene on her screen; at the furniture in the double unit they would soon occupy. She would have to give him space and time for the carving, for the snowscape he had to learn and the message from the deer.

He was promised to Cait. He had to search amongst the deer, the hairy flanks and bottlebrush tails, the long horns, for her. In Blue, in daylight. After the thaw, the wedding.

Cait, although she did not have blonde hair, small white hands or long legs like Siloe, provoked him. He was relieved to find her in his imagination, solid as the counter, there. She had copied her walk from Siloe and provoked him deliberately with those bold movements. She scented her body and emphasised the shape of her mouth with red paint, the colour of her eyes with black lines and blue shadows; she tied up her brown hair in a nodding tail which showed off the smooth back of her neck and went well with her permanent expression of cheeky greed. Her hands were large and practical but they were deft about his body and she dressed them up with coloured varnish and rings and bangles on leavedays. Her legs were not long but sturdy, thick even, the legs of a woman descended from hard-working fisher stock; yet she took care of them and sometimes wore high heels which made her calves stand out and her thighs tense and hard. And underneath her pastel-coloured coveralls she had the same thrusting breasts and hungry orifice as the computer construct, Siloe. Maybe when they were married she would wear the silky gown he had bought her – in their unit, leisure times – and there would be no need for a device, creaking, rustling. . .

The wind blew south. He called it Matoq. It chilled him. Matoq began here, in the North, his birthplace the high white

23

parkland of the pole, the ice-prairie where the herd-mothers gathered for their parliaments. They had the power of life and death. Their long coats were made of feather snow and their eyes of ice. Oma had given the stags their horns.

They would not leave him alone, the deer. Why, in the ordinariness of this morning, had Dr Semo refused to answer him and given him, instead, this permanent vision of another life? It was not snow which concealed everything his people once knew well and used: it was the pale walls of Traumesse, the designer co-ordinated pastels, the relayed music, the gymnasiums, the cafes, the indoor skating-rink. Ang – the Sineinain woman at his shoulder, amazed, her grey skin split. . .the deer had witnessed the pact this strange woman had made with him.

He drank from his cup of hot broth and smacked his lips. The ancient gesture of appreciation came naturally to him but it was one which was becoming rare as his people caught foreign habits from the ferryhands and the Sineinians. The women, particularly, copied the Sineinians whom they perceived to be not only more intelligent, but more desirable than themselves. He was afraid they would catch bad diseases too, the maladies of the cities and their unbridled sex. He wouldn't want Cait tainted by the licence which overflowed into the very corridors of Traumesse from the drunken ferryhands – lending your woman to a friend, borrowing his: that was friendship, perfectly natural.

Cait would have seen the sinews in the deer, the fat and flesh, the warm white pelts. Fenner and Gaby, too, would have appreciated the thick white hair, the big hooves which could be boiled down for glue, the manifold uses of the teeth. . .Practical women, the sort to have along: managers.

Ang Semo, he thought, couldn't cook a roast over a hot fire without a team of assistants and a computer – yet, take her upside, show her the icedeer, and she would see the beauty of their clear brown eyes and their long lashes; the hollows in the bone beneath the flesh; the shapes and colours of the shadows; which way the wind blew and how it shaped the powder snow into eddies and troughs. Like him. It was hard to have come twenty-five years to discover another being with the soul of a raingoose; and a foreigner too. He shivered because the ancestors had laid hands on his spirit. The old entities, the ones who came before Oma – they had given him the answer to his question and there was no need to formulate that question in Nenian, speak it to Ang Semo and have it copied down and fed into the computer. He knew what he wanted. He knew what should be done.

He wanted the Sineinians, who had brought his people in from the cold and given them life, who taught his people their own lore with computers and classrooms, to give up. He wanted them to dismantle this place, fill it in and be gone with their lights and machinery back to Sinein. Then he could be a man. He could be responsible for his own life; he could hunt and Cait could fish; he could teach the children they would have. His happiness was no part of the rehabilitation plan. "In due time," the treaty said, "when it shall be agreed between the Spokeswomen and men representing the Folk and the Confederative Government of Sinein and those signatories to the Memorandum drawn up by the Council of Nations and Noiro whose names are here appended: Annalat M'unah, Sacred City of Mahun and the Five Provinces; Hayla of Hayna; Tikan Voal Chacma, Cheron; Magrethe Tallin, Sinein" – he might not be allowed to learn Reading, but he had a good memory. All the Folk did. Pike had known all the lays.

He was warm. Down here, no one felt the frost. He wondered, for a brief and worrying instant, if he would be able to cope with the cold upside, were he to find himself there.

Soon, he must go to work, divest himself of all these fancies, and become what he was here, an operative in the dream factory, stacking and loading the boxes of cubes, removing them to the Outward store on his truck. It required a soberer frame of mind than this. What was he, after all? A tame aboriginal. The wild ones were all dead. He wondered if the Sinenians, when the time was right for the release, in two or three hundred years' time, would hold classes in forgetfulness. Or how would the Folk forget the warmth of the shelter in which they had been seduced, and the countless toys and comforts which blinded them there?

The colourful poster was trash again, clenched like a ball in his hands. On any normal day he would have whistled and skimmed it across the room at some easy target: Rower's head, perhaps or Sailmaker's broad back. He placed the rough ball on the counter and flicked at it with finger and thumb so that it rolled unsteadily and fell to the floor.

At the nearest table, the Sineinian redhead sighed with such passion that he started. He glanced. A kiss was in progress on the screen of her portable, a mini-saga or a thirty-second tease, seven square centimetres of osculating lips, silk, velvet, teeth, tongue – it wasn't Jannl kissing those perfect lips. There was hair, just a hint, the thin line of a moustache: now who? He affected indifference toward the construct sagas but he had to admire the plotlines – and the technique.

Ang Semo was their author! He tried to imagine why. The passionate tales were as trashy as the poster: colourful, nonsense. She was pale, face, skin, hair; she buried her feelings like all southerners. The endless tales were trash and yet they contained the matter of life – love, marriage, children, work, death. And, while she made elaborate pictures with the computer, public pictures of such detail you could never get to the bottom of them (and so quickly gone, passed over in a flash to leave an impression, a prevailing colour) she made secret pictures with her black box. He had seen just one of her photographs, the familiar landscape of Sowash displayed – no, not displayed, hidden – in a corner of the chapel. Glass and a gilt frame cut it off from him: a view of the island from Skaa, a flat sea mirroring the cliffs so that they seemed to continue below it, symmetrical and black; and all around the clear water.

He sipped his hot soup, letting the liquid raise a sweat which would have been welcome upside. Here, in the heart of Traumesse, it was an indulgence he allowed himself before each shift in White, knowing how Matoq kissed the buried town – twice-buried, once in granite and composites, once in snow – knowing how the whiteout covered his home until the thaw. The thaw would come early. Om was stirring: the deer had told him that. The back of his neck prickled. He saw the snow melting, drip after drip, and water running down over the frozen-hearted land into the sea, where the ice was mush on treacherous broken cakes and small leads opened up enough to take a body and swallow it. He pictured the decay of the ice and the broad stretches of salt water it became.

Then day would come and the immense view across the Sound to Sair and Clash would be revealed for anyone who had a spare ten minutes to look: a white prairie breaking up, giving way to the sun and the current which carried the ice away. The Sineinians had given the current the name of an explorer but he used the proper name: Om. Pike had died in it, the victim of Om's wayward temper, falling from the prow of his skift. Now, perhaps, his bones rested at the bottom of a warm sea, washed there by the swift waters, at peace with transparent fish swimming between them and the electric eel coiled in the hollow of the pelvis.

The old picture, the wobble and cry, the horror of the infinite moment when Pike lost his balance was still bright. He must have been ten, or eleven; Caulker was twelve, yes, the Fish Supper afterwards was more of a wake, he'd had his first liquor there, dreamed of hard ice and Pike, fishy now, trapped beneath it, fins not fingers scratching at the underside of the opaque ceiling above him.

Upside now, the icedeer grazed and here, below, he had eaten and, doubtless, Ang Semo too had broken her fast on some of the same imported food. On her excessively neat desk was a small carving of a fat and naked woman squatting over a bucket. It did not look like Art. She had tapped the ash from her cigarette into the little bucket and grimaced. He, crouching on the edge of the plastic chair as uncomfortably as the woman on the bucket-rim, had not smiled either; now, he did so, and laughed out loud. She wasn't all ice, then.

Once, years ago, on the last day of Tern when the ice was about to break up, he had looked through one of the optics and seen Ang Semo out there : a bent and dogged shape clutching a camera in hands mittened like bears' paws. The strong wind punched her and she staggered.

He had focused on her face and seen her disbelief and fear. The smoky blue eyes were narrowed and the even features contorted. He heard afterwards that she had been severely disciplined and deprived of her leave for a year. But that was all. She had kept her status. A liner or a hand would have been sent down to Refuse.

She wasn't all Sineinian.

That was it: some hot blood in her, the legacy of a ruthless ancestor. It made her cry after the wind.

He finished his soup and paid for it with a credit, the light, shiny coin he was paid in and which could only be spent in Traumesse, on the Rest and Recreation island of Hara, or set against a catalogue debit.

The malp might come now to be with the deer, big yellow teardrops a long way away, hauling themselves over the ice, hauling and diminishing into the whiteness until the eyes hurt and, crossing to a screen, you could see with the eye of an optical imager, malp hauling themselves over the ice, hauling and diminishing into the whiteness until the eyes hurt. The old ones had hunted them too and flayed and flensed them: fat, sinew, skins, meat.

On the empty beaker, cupped in his hands, was printed a long list he was unable to read. It was the table of ingredients, a recipe born in a nutritionist's laboratory: water, rehydrated onion (Sinein), tomato concentrate (Sinein), barley (SW Noiro), allspice (Mahkrein), pepper (Mahkrein), bayleaf (Ineit), Vitamins B&D, fibre, guaranteed flavouring CoNN 21, salt. No malpog.

He stood up and dropped the cup in a trashcan. It bounced and settled and lay among the other cups. The small black letters on the cups looked like midges swarming – and as much use: an irritant and a block to reality, pests to be swatted from his face. He looked down at his hands, spread them. They were broad and the ridged nails were long and cut square as he liked them. The anthropologists said it was a secondary adaptation: centuries of making nets and fixing hooks on gut in the cold had made these horny, yellow nails.

As a boy, he had played the game of greedy seaparrots, picking cone shells from the rocks. The shellfish held fast but parrots and clever boys could detach them: the trick was to pick one off when its foot was relaxed. It impressed the girls, sleight-of-hand which looked like pure strength: a child's game. There was nothing deceptive about the adult strength of his hands and nails – and his will. Suetstone was soft and the inside of Traumesse, was soft and coloured like a candybox but he, Salter Bren, was hard as permafrost. He would endure.

He had to go, to get home to the set of colourful interlocking boxes on Fourth which he called home. His bachelor unit. The Sineinians had made straight-jackets of Folk custom. Above it, on Third, was another set of interlocked boxes, the double unit he and Cait would soon call home. He had to return to the unit he had left and forgotten at eight-forty and change out of the clean mauve coveralls which, untainted by his encounter with the icedeer, unmarked by his two hours alone with Ang Semo, had clothed him, body and soul, while the deer spoke to him. He would take another suit from the pile in the locker, another one just the same, and put it on. He would wash his hands and his face and, just before leaving, spray his neck with some of that essence Cait had given him which smelled faintly of grass and made him think of sunlight and the greening of Sowash later in the year. Then he would become Loading Op One.

He walked swiftly from the canteen along the pink and winding tube which led to the stairs. His feet made no sound on the pliant composite of the treads. He ran where they were widest, close to the wall, and came out on the entresol. He liked to come this way because it seemed shorter: he was on his feet, using them, using his muscles and his lungs. In the lift, he would have expended no energy.

The cries of children floated upward from the big nursery below like the cries of young creatures, uninhibited and experimental. The sound, made him think of gulls and, after gulls, of the wide sky and the endless sea which met itself on the other side of the globe. He stopped running and leaned on the glass parapet to look down.

29

They ran like young animals: whelps, kits, half-licked cubs whose legs and feet did not obey them. They rushed about without purpose and fell over; they cried and scrambled up to continue their erratic journeys about the huge room. He sighed, and smiled at their antics because he could not remember the intense purpose of a child, the iron will to do and be. The older children, who had learned how to control their legs, ran along coloured pathways painted on the floor. Not one of them was still. From the walls birds, butterflies and big tropical cats smiled on them and Bren smiled more.

The northern constellations were painted on the ceiling near him, far above the children. Green ropes and wires hung down and tangled in mid-air and on these artificial vines were leaves and flowers and models of hang-nests and their builders the sun birds; there were stuffed linsangs and tamarins, plastic silktail monkeys and heavenly blues. He thought it was all lovely, better for a child than the cold upside; he had grown and played there himself and he remembered particularly the bright red colour of the ivies. He looked at them now and was sad to see them still clean and shiny but faded by the intense light to a mute brown.

The pinpoint lights coiled on the ceiling glittered, Oma in little. It was stupid to put them there like that, and a jungle hanging below. He felt as though twenty-five years of sticky sleepdust had been wiped from his eyes. Tears stood in them. That was why the lights glittered so, a hundred separate points darting out from each glowing centre. He blinked and wished a neighbour might happen along, old Catch from next door or Netmender Falk with his wink and the two rogue patches of hair on the backs of his hands; he wished for a friend to comfort him. All that came was a reaction born of his own body. He broke out in a muck sweat and his heart pounded as if he'd just stepped down from the treadmill apparatus. Fear: adrenalin: flee. In a way it was a comfort, this readinesss in his body – but it was meant for real danger, flying before the wind, your sail bellying, or standing your ground while your stick flew about you, thumped and thwacked and got each hungry vair before it launched itself and fastened its teeth in your meaty legs.

The moulded glass of the parapet had made deep marks on his palms. He wiped away the sweat and breathed easily again. Once, in an Education lecture, the instructor had talked of claustrophobia and bothy fever. Maybe it was a touch of that. He looked at his watch and fiddled with the knobs. He held it close to his ear to hear the chimes. He had plenty of time. An hour still.

His unit was warm like everywhere else, and it was quiet. He stood by the bathroom sink and peeled off his coverall. He washed. He found the clean suit and put it on.

And there he was: Salter Bren, Spokesman and First Loading Operative, ready for work at two. He couldn't be bothered to find the essence: the cleaners tidied everything away. But he unlocked the top drawer of his dressing chest and took out a tissue-wrapped package. He laid it on the bed and opened up the paper layers, one by one.

The dress he had bought for Cait, his bride, was as filmy as the paper itself. The light passed through it. He held it up and saw his bed through a sunset mist. He had chosen the colour carefully. Not black, or red or anything vulgar but the subtly blended colours of the northern sunset. The ribbons on it were small and white as skating ice. As he held the flimsy gown and imagined Cait wearing it, his body began to worry at him, pleading for sex. His hands grew damp and he put the dress down and examined it anxiously in case it was stained. The muscles of Cait's back and the bones under them were young and strong. They were not meant to be hidden; they should not be masked in this dirty Sineinian way. He was ashamed of himself. He was an empty jug and shame poured into him. He put his hands over his eyes and bowed his body under the weight.

When the fit had passed and he had recovered and straightened up, everything was clear. He must get rid of it. Cait must not be tainted. But he could not dump it in the bin. The cleaners would find it and then his secret would be all over Traumesse. Hastily, he folded the dress and its rustling paper and stuffed it back in the drawer; locked it away.

Atluki, the simpleton, was in the corridor when he went out. Bren's guilty conscience made him start and blush. It was as quiet out there as in the unit. Atluki seemed to lurk, his plump body propping up the wall. He held a silent portable to his ear. It was useless to tell him it was meant to be watched: he preferred the sounds it made and usually he kept the volume high.

'Is it broken?' Bren asked.

Atluki gave him the shiny machine. Bren started to fiddle with the tuner, and then he noticed that the central switch had not been touched.

'You haven't turned it on!' he said, and did so. The corridor filled with noise. He looked at the box in his hands with horror. The music was unbearably loud and it issued from a tiny grille on the top of the box. He imagined it expanding from its source in a whirling cone and sweeping them both away.

'Baby baby baby,

Gimme gimme gimme

Yo' love,' said the box.

Atluki smiled patiently and took the portable from him. He stabbed at the red panel with a forefinger: off.

'What the fuck's the matter?' said Bren. The anger surged without warning as the sweat had done. 'I just switched it on for you.'

Atluki smiled his sweet, patient, smile. 'Listening,' he said, and held the silent portable up to his ear. 'Goodbye.'

Guilt washed over Bren. Not only did his secret conflict over the improper dress wring him: he had sworn at an innocent and disobeyed both the Ethic and the establishment rules. He must be ill. He felt his forehead. It was neither too hot, nor too cold; it was not sweaty or dry. He took out a handkerchief and snorted into it: no sign of a cold and his throat wasn't sore. Maybe he needed a drink. Or a holiday, that would be good – a holiday *before* the wedding. Atluki skipped in front of him and he resumed his walk.

Then something else happened that was an odd part of that odd day. A film of snow lay on the floor. His feet made prints in it and he saw old Catch came round the corner

32

and, without a word, shuffle past him as if he were totally invisible. There was no sign of the snow. How could there be, in Traumesse under the ground?

The blue bedroom was her own, a private retreat from the rest of the Needle family. Gentle music filled the room but the girl on the bed did not hear it. She was reading, her stocky body curled up on the bedcover. She twisted a strand of hair round a finger, but she was not in this room. Her mind was absent from Traumesse in Sowash where the Folk lived comfortably and worked the production lines making dreams; nor did she imagine herself wandering upside in the snow where one endless day ran imperceptibly into the next. She was in Fairmile amongst red and blue globes and glassy ziggurats, walking down a garden path which had no end. The flowerbeds were limitless and the flowers themselves had no edges. The print upon the page stimulated her imagination which played back variations of the scenes it had absorbed from the 'screen. The last word in the story was 'love'. Below it, in case you hadn't realised and hoped for more of the same breathlessly exciting stuff were, in capitals, two more words: THE END.

Cait sighed and closed the magazine. She laid it carefully down on the table beside her. A smudge marred Siloe's perfect nose, a grain of soil from the fertile garden behind her, a flake of ash from the fall fire Jannl tended, his well-proportioned body labouring in tune with the heavy fork, the leaves he was lifting a loose bundle of burnt orange, umber, scarlet; chestnut, holmoak, Kein ivy . . . the smudge took nothing from Siloe, added rather, emphasised that milky complexion, white teeth, lips as pink as rosebuds and as smooth. Were they? She, Needle Cait, had never seen a real rosebud; not a rose, not a bush, not a thorn (except on screen). Pride in her collection compelled her to remove the smudge. Gaby most likely with her everlasting candy bars, or marking ink from Fenner's plump fingers. Good friends loaded with cakes and gossip, they came often to her room. Fenner, silent in the well of her own imagination, would stay for hours poring over the fanzine

33

collection if Gaby didn't grow restless, turning somersaults in the space between the bed and the wall, breaking into the reveries with her silly walks and pratfalls. 'That Float girl,' Mu said sometimes, 'needs either a good spanking or a husband to keep her occupied.' Useless to tell Mu of Gaby's broken heart and the promise she had made last Slackwater to marry her brother-in-law. Mu was a pragmatist and a traditionalist; one forlorn and broken necklace in the tray of the Marriage Box was the only evidence that she had once been a romantic girl.

But just now, Mu and Dil were at work along with Fa, and Grand had gone down to the store. Cait and her company of dreams filled the unit.

She chose an eraser, a fat piece of rubber shaped like a heart, half of it blue, half pink, and across the centre in frivolous rubber curls the two words KISS ME. Other erasers lay with the pens, pencils and ruler in her schoolbox, plain old tools with which to begin a life on the line because (it was the First Rule of the Work Ethic) a worker must begin at the beginning and (the Second) a worker should be taught the ancient basics of Sineinian civilisation in conjunction with the use of her/his own civilisation's artefacts.

For a day or two those gaudy plastic shapes had diverted the class: FACTS, MORE FACTS, PET, MEET ME, LOVE. Others were lost. SOT had gone, HEARTLESS, and POSER. She remembered a spherical SLOB rolling across the shiny floor to be triumphantly caught by the instructor op. Softly, gently, as if she stroked her own skin, Cait applied the blue cusp of KISS ME to Siloe's blemish and restored her purity.

Inside the magazine – she turned the pages again – was the story of Jannl's Garden in Sineinian words, and pictures as bright and colourful as the networked episodes themselves, beautiful pictures, poetic words, and then more pictures, whole pages filled with full-, half-length, close-up scenes from the sagas: Jannl dancing with the broom because Siloe was late; Siloe in her ball gown; the fat and sinister nurse wheeling Madam Juh across smooth lawns, tall trees there, dappled sunlight, deep shadow; Siloe in her office,

34

Siloe at home, Siloe shopping for jewellery, Siloe on the beach, Siloe (one to colour in) in fancy dress. How could she move at all in that tight silken wrap? Then there were the products: Jannl cologne, Jannl soap, Jannl talc (for men); the Dreamtime range for women; Fairmile watches, calcs, ionisers, screens, remote-control portables, electrolysis pens (no more superfluous hair), imager cubes (send your own code for our BPROMs to interrogate); there were cosmetics, peach-toned blushers to give you pinkpale cheeks like Siloe's, scarlet lipsticks for evening, eyeliner black as a winter night in Noiro, glitter sprays (for parties: Give Yourself a Sparkle Like Siloe's), pancake, foundation, blemish cover, deodorant. . .

You could buy 3D heads with makeup, shapely plastic Siloes as white as an icedeer: she might get one for Dil to practise on, for her birthday, next year . . . she was quite sallow, Needles usually were. Gaby (being a Float) didn't need colour: her cheeks were red – crimson – to start with, her eyes shone. Too much. Of the three Gaby was the humorist, the sceptic; she, Cait was the leader, the oldest and closest to majority, yes, she was the norm, the one they copied, even untidy Fenner who couldn't fancy Jannl. Too perfect, she said, too good. I couldn't live up to a man like that. Give me a ferryhand any day or a toolmaker. Then, her laugh exploding like fireworks, like steam from the coffee-maker, like farts: Fenner farts laughs. That word alone would be enough to make them giggle – let alone Gaby. The way Gaby laughed was quite special. It began as a groan, something lively being strangled, a gurgling in her throat – until it escaped with a howl and went on rising in volume and speed while they all laughed, infected with mirth, rolled and gasped literally on the floor or sagged against the walls, panting and weeping wherever they were because of those grotesque sounds pouring out.

To think of it made her smile, just to think – but when Siloe laughed the birds sang even in Fairmile where she really lived, not the enchanted garden which was her dream and Jannl's who toiled in her mother's garden and was poor while she was so rich and a lovingcaring wholeandpowerful woman men died for the glance of. Oh, Cait could make distinction between dream and reality, what passed the time and was the time.

She blew the eraser dirt from Siloe's face and stroked the paper with one brown hand. Against the autumn palette on the page, the colour of her skin came somewhere between the holmoak leaves and Jannl's sunburned hands. Only the white faces were alien; the black lines which defined the edges of the faces and limbs were smudgy and indistinct, where the printer could not follow the jigsaw of the fractals. In fact the passion-filled eyes were overdone, overcooked – ringed in black like sea-parrots' eyes. Cait giggled.

Still, it was a lovely story. She held the magazine close against her breast.

Romantic, to give you a warm glow waiting for the after-noon shift when your man has forgotten you; when far above and outside, unseen on the periphery of reality, in the utter cold, the North wind blasts the snow which covers Traumesse.

Upside the snow was frozen. White mounds covered the grass and ling, the empty burrows of the sea parrots, the grey rock and Traumesse below it. Darkness covered the snow and every curve and hollow of Sowash herself and the view from Perimeter and Lookout toward the two bays of Ulbeg and Forso on the Reach was masked.

Somewhere out there beyond the snow was the rest of Noiro, ten thousand islands; somewhere Orso, Hairete, Malpogak and Clash, somewhere the Shaklian current racing south and the leaden seas changing from grey to green, turquoise, cyan, deepest blue, and then came the warm South, fruit, and no winter, never this, the all-smothering whiteout of the bitterest season, White, the blind and blank months, time and space upside blanched. Somewhere, life was lived beneath a bright sky and there were flowers and trees like those in Jannl's garden.

But things could be worse: she could have been born a soldier in Hayna or a hand in a silk mill in the back streets of the City; things could be a lot worse and were not at all bad because here, in Traumesse, was home, warm

and dry with everything she needed: food, drink, work,
leisure, friends; Gaby and Fenner, Mu, Fa and Dil, Bren,
majority and marriage coming, Siloe and Jannl playing out
their story every day. She could have been born elsewhere:
further north where the last islands of Noiro ran out as
they nudged the icebound continent of Hiberna where
astronomers watched ancient history in the stars; where
the Keepers of the Peace looked out for hostile starships
and rogue missiles from internecine strife in the south;
where the uraninite miners lived under the snow itself in
insulated cabins, were decontaminated, rested, and returned
to work without ever the relief of icebreak when the water
surged and oozed between the floes and the new season
began. Blue was the season of thaw, when water covered
the lowest land and vast sheets of blue reflected the sky, one
with the flat sea, seabed and drowned soil indistinguishable
beneath a polished mirror. In Blue mist rose quickly to hide
sea and land and streams ran from every tussock and hag.
In Blue, Cait's ancestors had risen from the darkness in their
bothies and gone out to prepare their nets and lines for the
fishing.

Meanwhile, she had to get ready. No use imagining things
she had never known, but it must have been, might have
been fun? hard? rewarding? bitter cold? fishing for a living
instead of packing dreams. She was deft and a section leader
on the line, deft and a bit different: it had got her the
job and the respect of the rest. Fenner sang and plodded,
marking her packages with the black squiggle which meant
'passed'. Gaby – well Gaby was different too and if she'd only
think instead of clowning . . . if only. Now, Cait packed her
magazines away between the tissues in the bottom drawer of
her chest where more prosaic things, the wedding suit, the
cutlery, the plates and dishes, the pack of contraceptives, lay.
And the big silver flask of perfume. Absurd for work but. . .
She bent suddenly, lifted the flask high and released a misty
essence from its nozzle, rubbing her nose to banish a sneeze,
smiling – surely it wasn't accidental the shape of that flask
and the tip of it where the scent came out. It was her secret,
that flask, cost a months's wages: clever to have concealed

its source. Passion, it was called, by Ardrazen of the Avenue in Sollar Kein, Golden Square in Diold and Citadel Street in The Sacred City. The girls thought Bren, in his devotion, had gone mad and bought it for her through the onshore catalogue; and Bren, she had told him it was a majority present from Grand – who knew nothing about it but had remarked that Cait's new soap smelled nice. 'Brains and beauty, that's what he'll be given,'said Grand, 'What more could any man ask?'

She had given him perfume: civet and vetiver from the Fairmile catalogue. He wore it every day for her. 'Go on, Bren,' she'd said, 'Try it. Please!' He'd tipped out two drops on a forefinger, bent his head and wrinkled his nose. The wide nostrils flared and she giggled. He looked like a horse – not that she had seen a horse but Siloe had lots.

'Smells like grass to me.'

'Well, put it on! More!'

She loved to rub her nose against his chest inhaling the Sineinian scent and his male smell together. The musk-smell excited her; of course *he* couldn't smell it, another of those wonderful differences which made women women, and men men. To please her he was content to smell like a vair on heat.

Her brains were her servant, yes, her status proved that; but her beauty was the precious commodity. It had captured Bren who (after the liquor party) had said he would like to die for her, perish bravely in icy seas to save the beauty he was getting, the beauty which (reflected here, now, in her mirror) was a little bit, if she squinted, like Siloe's. It had got her the job she wanted, that more than the cleverness, the brains, because the line was a showplace too: people came from all over to see Traumesse; the beauty pleased everyone who saw her, even oddfish like the Director passing in stately progress through the shop, and Ang Semo, an anxious acolyte at her heels, turning her head as she walked to stare. Ang Semo. One of the Sineinians; a sophisticate. She could go up, easy as a wedded woman, use her status, flourish her pass, take the ferry, fly the cruiser – buy herself a bottle of Passion on the Avenue itself. . . But SHE HAD

TO GO TO WORK and Gaby would be waiting so wash, eyepaint, lipstick, coveralls, slippers, hair, which hung to her shoulder blades, thick and dark and glossy so it had to be tied up and confined under her overall hood. A last look in the mirror. Gaby would be waiting. She was late.

Fenner, whose family name of Angle suggested stealth, leanness, and a sudden strike, but who was plump and frank, eased the narrow shiny belt with which she had improved her coverall. The loose suits looked good on Cait but made freaks and marvels of her generous haunches. She must have tightened the belt too much hurrying to be ready, rushing (hair escaping from its combs) to be the first to arrive. And now Gaby was late. It was a pretty belt, silverypink, with a star for a buckle. The pink matched her lips, the silver the tiny birds which dangled from her ears, pretty ears with narrow lobes, shell-like as they said and as Ial had whispered cuddling and stroking her in the dark, feeling her up in the close warmth under the macroscreen. Pneumatic flesh had its advantages and Ial had plunged his finger into her softness like a knife into cream cake. And thick hair: hers escaped still but (she hoped) in such a way that, as she adjusted it, she seemed to Noto passing about to shed her clothes and let down a long dark veil. But Noto, being a mechanic and a plastimorph, was indifferent to sex and he scuttled across the atrium like a crab and out of her sight.

Fenner fidgeted with her hair, coiling escaping tresses around her fingers, chewing a wispy end, anchoring a comb; for where was Gaby? One o'clock had come and gone, the time had passed, ten minutes ago, and Gaby was not here. Cait you expected to be tardy.

The snow made it gloomy. Instead of a skyful of stars shining above the atrium's glass roof the dull belly of the snowdrift yellowed in the lamplight. Like being inside a tub of ice cream. She was protected, safe from the cold without, snug in the top level of Traumesse while she waited in vain for her thoughtless friend. The plants flourished with hopeless endeavour. The hibiscuses flowered and there were

39

fruits on the pomegranate trees; but like herself they were desperate, starved of natural light.

White was the worst time. In Blue and Greening she could get out easily, walk the Perimeter, stand up on the Lookout and gaze at the shifting sea and lovely Hairete guarding the entrance to the Sound with her brown and russet flanks and rocks like sheep grazing. She could go to Forso and lie on the warm sands. When the Catch had been brought home and the Fish Supper eaten, she could stay out by the burial grounds and spend the long night awake and drinking. She liked this twilit time which was neither day nor night and she went from group to group (they all knew her) accepting a tot from the Salters, a mug of soup from the Floats, exchanging snippets of gossip with the Ropewalkers. Then full summer came and the pink skies yellowed. It was Race time. Bets were taken, guesses made, and the favourites pursued, grabbed, and dunked in the sea. This year, thought Fenner, Gaby has a chance; but she would bet on Salter Bren. The Race was started with a flag. It dipped, and the runners flew away.

Then the wind would turn cold again, spoil the warmth and bring back the midnight dusk; bring too, the Northern Lights to colour the night. It got colder still; the sun hardly showed and the sparkle left the sea. You didn't want to be out: you were happier downside.

Sometimes, as she initialled the boxes she had checked, she would dream of riches, a seat in a stratocruiser, the tree-lined streets of Sollar Kein, a husband slim as a reed and herself miraculously likewise; or she might dream of Fairmile, the Judge's palace and Siloe at work inside it. There was little of the natural world in the sagas: the pictures were like shadows reaching from Ang Semo's mind, sombre colours at that bleak time of the year. She settled herself more comfortably so that she could think about Ang Semo. A real puzzle. . .but here was Cait, smiling and sturdy in her new yellow coverall. She had made up her lips and eyes to match and she smelled of the perfume. . . she was *clever*. She had new earrings too, sunny discs decorated with black wavy lines and circles, images of the sun and sea.

'Are those from Bren as well?' Banish the envy.

'Silly. They're the ones I made on the Historic Crafts course. Don't you remember?'

'They weren't that colour.'

'Yes they were. After they were fired.'

Her own had broken in the little round kiln the instructor had brought – all the way from Diold. At the end of the course all she had was a black coil, a handful of reddish sherds and a misshapen bowl which she used now to hold her washcloth in the bathroom.

'Where is she? Gone on?' said Cait. 'Oh dammit there's Bren.'

Fenner watched the betrothed man approach. He looked fit – as he should, for he spent two hours every morning in the gym. His body, programmed by his pure genetic ancestry toward stockiness and subcutaneous cold-combatant fat, had shed its surplus and he walked lightly. The muscle concealed by his coverall would be revealed on Raceday when he had stripped and was being blessed and anointed by the '624 champion. Then she would place her final bet. His hair, she noticed, had been recently dressed, probably that morning, washed and oiled; he looked proud, as befitted a promised man. It was the kind of pride which might easily become dissatisfaction and the Sineinian clothes and hairstyle were a brittle shell about the real man. The malp tooth Cait had given him in traditional token of the betrothal had been mounted on a silver plaque which he wore on his collar beside his status badge.

'Where were you?' Cait shrilled.

'I —' His assurance dissolved. He looked guilty; he looked worried. He was not himself. He made an excuse. 'The interview went on for hours.'

'Oh.'

She wasn't even interested in hearing if Ang Semo had answered his questions, the questions he had given her in detail the night before: the lecture. How could he tell the morning's story? What could he say about the deer? He looked about him, studying the atrium, Cait, Fenner.

'Where's Gaby?' he said. His voice was breathy and anxious, as if he had a boat to catch.

'We don't know. What do you want Gaby for?'

'I don't want Gaby. Just asking.'

'What d'you think of Colomb?' Cait asked him.

'It's miles away.'

'Everwhere's miles away, unless you want a holiday on Wirra with the midges. I want to go to Hara.'

'We can't afford it.'

'We can borrow on my quotas.'

Fenner listened in silence. I'll go to Wirra with you, she thought. The picture of Bren bouncing on her ample stomach overwhelmed her and she wanted to laugh. Instead, she smiled at Cait. 'I bet Gaby's in Two,' she announced. 'She'd find the idea of us kicking about here funny.'

'She might be silly but she's not stupid. She knows we agreed to meet here, said Cait peevishly. 'We've only got ten minutes now.'

Gaby was bored. She slumped and drummed the toe of one red boot against the heel of the other knowing she had gone deliberately to Atrium 2, knowing she wanted only to annoy someone, anyone, knowing and not caring. The fish circled inside the circular pool. They had more colours than a computer palette, dozens of scintillating hues between them. They looked as though they were made of silk and they came from a far country where people wore silk to work, from Maralis in the deep south. Why didn't they put local fish in the pools – dragonets for example or electric anglers? Some people would be stupid enough to put their fingers in the water. She leaned down, held her face close to the water, and mouthed silent obscenities at the fish.

Her hair was short and thick; she liked to run her fingers through it till it stood on end, the image of disorder. She saw her shadow in the pool and the brown mask of her face adrift on the water; no features were discernible.

Work loomed, the long afternoon and half the evening. Six hours. Morning shifts were better, they did not divide the day. Six hours of collecting cubes as they spilled from the line, turning them so that the letters TRAUM were uppermost and packing them neatly into the waiting boxes.

She bet that today she would be packing blues, dramadocs for Sinein. Yesterday she had been on yellows which, filling the grey boxes like essence of sunlight, seemed appropriate to their destination in tropical Mahkrein, golden dreams for the continent of silks and beautiful men, where the exact time of any rainstorm was known and recorded in advance, where rich tourists lolled on the white beaches; where the Sacred City was and where the Sineinains did not rule. Cait and Bren should spend their honeymoon in the City! Her mind ran on the south; it was better than dreaming in sagaese, in borrowed images.

It was hard to get the truth. Lessons taught bald facts such as twoandtwoisfour or the table which began 1um is one millionth of a metre. She knew exactly, latitude by longitude, where Ineit was with its central plain, where Sinein, Hayna, Mahkrein were: but how people *lived*, that was a question no one was willing to answer. To be travelled like Ang Semo, educated, publicly articulate and a maker of dreams! She had not even the experience to be a construct programmer, let alone an artist. (Nor did she have to marry – imagine it, single at 32! Unwed and unlikely to be, unconstrained and childless.) Siri's three loved her wholeheartedly. She was glad of that because soon she would be their mother. Next month, in Floe when the ice began to move, she would be twenty and must approach Needle Mu formally to speak for Pak.

That she must be the one to speak distressed her. It was right that the woman who had, after all, to bear the inconveniences of marriage and biology, should be the one to make the selection; it was all wrong that the custom of glosit and the carefully-constructed Establishment Ethic should force her to marry the man who had been her brother-in-law. But someone had to mother her dead sister's children. There would be more, hers and his. Ribble and Taviak and little Siri were his sureties. The tests which she had completed last week proved her own viability and she had a duty to breed. She was one of an endangered race; that was why she lived in the reserved lands of Northern Noiro. Once, tourists had come to goggle at the Fishfolk and provide a cash boost to the economy. The dream factory was a modern equivalent, home, work and school buried under a natural landscape, where the visitor's perceptions of the wild beauty of Sowash and her shoals and flocks would remain undisturbed.

It was a wonder CoNN did not send them all out to make a living fishing the seas and hunting malp again; but her lessons had also taught her that stage too had passed. When it came again – if – she would be dead and her body with the land of her birth, while her soul – how could she know its destination? She liked to think of it free and blowing with the north wind. Matoq. She did not often use the old names.

The South. Thus, she might reach it, on Matoq's breath. She smiled and then, in the warm underground atrium beside the fishpond and the foreign plants, she felt her sister's presence. She was very close.

'Siri oh Siri, why did you have to die?' she cried. 'I could have married Kattaluk or Snowshoe, he's nice; or even Salter Bren, sons of first families all of them. Instead you've given me Pak. You couldn't even fade away gracefully like the fog in sunlight or die prettily like they do in the sagas. You died accidentally, horribly, messily. You frightened me.'

'It wasn't an accident. I killed myself,' said Siri, and her bright outline faded.

'I know now.' She spoke to a void and wondered to what new and lonely place her sister's restless spirit had fled.

The shore patrol had told her, sparing no detail because she was one of the Folk and could take it, that Siri's body had been washed up on the mud by Loon Point. There were teeth marks in it and pieces of flesh had been bitten off. A carrion bear? She had viewed the body in the company of her Grandmother and Mother. The meat, for that was what she had to call it to save herself from vomiting, was waterlogged and pulpy; it was clear that vair had come upon it and feasted there after the drowning yet they had all gone to the Director's office and signed statements which denied the facts. When they were at home again, they had prayed silently in the manner of the Folk, to Om and the kjarr demons; they did not go to the chapel.

One day the marrow of Float Siri's story would appear on screen. All right for Ang Semo to romanticise death and make stories from other people's sorrows: she couldn't feel, she didn't know. She was a Sineinian and could not see the lost souls which waited out their time on Sowash. No one could make a foreigner see them nor understand how the Folk respected the Old Settlements by Omi and Ulbeg, visiting them in summer and leaving gifts of food for the dead. Dr Semo went out looking for mysteries, upside into the cold and wet which sensible people avoided; everybody knew she spent her leavedays wandering the island. It was rumoured that she swam in the sea.

The shift bell rang. Well she would not go. Bugger and fuck. There were lots of bad words. She would spoil her weekly quota. It wasn't a crime yet she couldn't go home. Mu and Fa were there, sleeping after their shift; Grand was there, her younger sisters, and Siri's three children, until they were taken up to the crèche. Then Grand would go shopping and in to work for the two hours her senior citizenship permitted. The cafes would be full; in the canteen someone would see her and make a report. She had seen the drama in the all-around. Running? She had sped along the track at nine in the morning, breaking yesterday's record. There was little of Traumesse that she did not know as well as her own mind. She would play Left and Right, taking alternate roads, or Colours. One of the roads was dawn yellow. Upside, there were no roads, just the old tracks, boggy or stony depending where you were; and the smooth green circlet of the Perimeter. She had only once been on a real road, the plasticised strip which led up from the harbour to the hotel on Hara. Years ago, holding Mu's hand. They had missed the next R&R slot because of Siri. The yellow path then and pretended excitement. She left the atrium at a run because if Cait and Fenner found her they would make her go down to the line for her own good. The yellow road led her into Maritime Plaza, past the nets and reconstructed drying-racks which roofed the promenade outside the amusement arcade, and out again on the south side. It was wide with guide rails for the refuse crashers and the washers, which ran when everyone slept. Light and warmth flowed from the wall panels and the ceiling was in flower, inlaid with a mosaic of Noiran flowers, because it led to Floraliy.

She would give a little time to Floraliy before she took the road again. It was impossible not to. Flowers spilled from hanging baskets and pedestals and real palm trees grew out of the floor; those were live macaws in the branches.

The square had been designed to make her people feel at home in the world. Consequently, the lift which carried you up to the aerial walkways was disguised as a blue tower, some of the shops were hidden behind tall housefronts hung with painted balconies, while others were concealed in bothies built from real driftwood and ling. The facade of the theatre was modelled on the CoNN building in Sollar Kein.

Gaby passed the low entrance to the Folk Museum.

Most of the chairs and tables outside the Fountain Bar were empty. Two ferryhands sat there kicking their heels against the neat terracotta slabs, waiting for the thaw.

Today, she liked Floraliy. She smiled and the square glittered at her in return. The big, bold flowers were delicately scented and the current of warm air which flowed into the square, at this time in the afternoon from the West, was cool. She saw herself in the window of the bar, small, flat-faced, and fitter than any Sineinian, the picture of the Primitive on her History cube. She wouldn't grow any more. Twenty years to grow a woman, the proverb said, and twenty-five to fashion a man. It stopped you marrying an immature man. And the Sineinian contraceptive devices stopped you having a baby before you married. Instead of the old trial marriage: blood and urine tests, a speculum, dilation; Sineienian doctors poking about inside you. The penalty for an uncontrolled pregnancy was abortion. She made a face at her reflection.

The red floor ended by the palms and beyond them stretched the shiny white space of the square. Moving ways and stairs of tinted duraplastics mounted up, studded with lights whose cyclic patterns were under the control of one of the computers. They pulsed with the fervour of a jellyfish surprised by a diver's lamp.

She watched the biotronic display. Ang Semo's team, she thought, wrote better programmes for the saga titles than the algorithms which made these lights change colour. She waited for the magenta flush again; gold came next, and red. They reminded her of the fairground at Hara. The lights turned silver.

A woman carrying a bundle of paper descended the stairway. She walked carefully because she could not see the stairs or her feet. There wasn't time to flee, so Gaby watched her and wondered why she didn't use the escalator. The stills and hard spreadsheets she carried filled her arms and hid her body from the waist up. Her chin held the topmost burden, a transparent bag of dreams, in place.

On cue, thought Gaby. I won't be shamed.

Ang Semo blushed, not Gaby. She nodded her head. The acknowledgement might have been intended as a rebuke but the blush turned it into a greeting. A reply was required.

'Good afternoon Dr Semo,' Gaby said.

The Artistic Director's hair was untidy and her make-up worn. The central valley of her mouth was pale. All that remained of her lipstick were two scarlet lines which looked as though they had been added to define a more generous mouth. The mouth creased and began to smile but before the lips had been drawn back enough to show the teeth, it opened wide to form one unvoiced word.

'Fuck.'

Gaby read the silent plea and caught the slippery mass of paper as it slid towards the floor.

'Thank you very much.' Ang Semo became instantly authoritative. 'If you could just help me: lay them here and then I can get a proper hold.'

The two women faced each other across the papers they had manoeuvered on to a table. The top sheet was a still from 'Greed'. Siloe's lovely mouth smiled in the white oval of her face. Gaby smiled too. Her smile was open, the quintessence of Fishfolk charm. Her flat brown face with its red cheeks and black eyebrows was the perfect type. In the long instant while they came to terms, Ang admired its authenticity. The girl's eyes reflected the myriad lights of Floraliy and her natural intelligence shone. Ang felt her own smile falter and knew that her embarrassment showed. The expression she had hoped was friendly became the hesitant grimace of a lonely woman who would like to make friends.

Why does she look so stunned? Gaby thought. They had both invoked the same wanton deity in their separate moments of crisis, she because another tedious shift was intolerable; Ang Semo because she had dropped her load of important papers and cubes, in the perusal and understanding of which her supremacy rested, before an inferior; further confounded her position by uttering that inaudible, insensible word.

It was convenient blasphemy which, with its short explosive monosyllable, expressed the tedium of a long, dark season spent in the warm confines of this super-den; a word and a function necessary in an endangered race reserve. By the Lady, thought Ang, how I wish the ice would melt; and she stood up straight as if she really were upside and free by the dancing sea at Ulbeg. Her face closed up and she watched the waves with the eyes of her mind. The glossy paper was smooth as skin beneath her hand and the hand trembled. She felt in her pocket for her cigarettes.

The smoke screened her and the paper cylinder comforted her. Gaby wrinkled her nose: rotting seaweed, stagnant water.

'I'm on my way,' said Ang between puffs, 'home. Exhausting morning. Afternoon off. Thank you very much for your help.'

'Mè too,' said Gaby, without further explanation. 'Can you manage all that?'

'Mmm. Thanks. Just finish this.'

The skin around the blue eyes was creased against the irritating cloud of smoke and the lids, lashes smudgy with mascara, half-closed. The brief meeeting of eyes and intentions was over and Gaby, on her solitary way across the square, did not look back although she felt the lean and

48

hungry gaze of the Artistic Director on her and the plaintive message she had not managed to convey.

The road led Gaby on, ceiled now with plain panels, still yellow, still promising, a pathway like the regular course of the sun. The guide rails were silver ribbons. A sign on the wall said WOMENS TOILETS.. She read it backwards so that it lost its meaning and became a rune. She pretended to be a pilgrim, a traveller in icebound lands. Like Shakla: no, that was alien culture. Like the Snowfolk when they hunted greater malp.

The silver ribbons led her on.

When she reached the refuse point, she laughed. So obvious. The silver ribbons veered into a cavern and she followed them. The washers and crashers were parked in two rows and plastimorphs attended them. Some of them poured cleaning fluids and polishes for the shift to come into the washers' tanks; others scrubbed out the crashers, removing the last shreds of garbage; still others were washing brooms in a huge sink of steaming water. Vapour coiled about them, phantasmal beards and coronae. They grinned at her out of its depths like kjarr-sprites. At their backs, all artifice removed, was the bare rock of Sowash's heart.

Gaby smiled politely at the plastimorphs. No one was afraid of them, but they were treated with reserve. She felt pity for these reassembled and reconditioned victims of accident, whose bones had been strengthened and responses recoded to serve industry; compassion and empathy for these experimental animals which resembled herself. One of the broom-washers stepped forward and spoke to her. Beside his black status badge, the lowest, he wore an identity badge. His name was Tomat.

'Hello,' he said, like any normal person. 'We don't often get visits from one of the Folk.'

'I'm on holiday,' said Gaby. 'Do you know it's White upside?'

Tomat frowned, puzzled. He rubbed the place where the frown made creases. His hands were big and capable, his face sensitive and thin, his gestures pantomime.

'Upside,' said Gaby, pointing at the ceiling.

'Traumesse!' Now that he had the answer, he smiled.

'It's snowing.'

Another frown.

'When water turns to ice.'

'That's water.' It was his turn to point.

She abandoned the conversation, sat on the floor and swung her feet up behind her head. She scuttled about on spread out hands. Their laughter bounced off the rock: every plastimorph had stopped work to watch her and every one of them was big, strong, and male.

'Where are the women?' said Gaby, resuming her normal posture. She cupped her hands in front of her chest and wobbled them; she rocked an imaginary baby. The plastimorphs laughed again; this time she did not know why. Then one of them, labelled with his name, Aumon, came close. He slapped his crotch and hissed; in mime, he drew a knife and slashed it through the air. His fellows booed.

'Women?' he said, 'Men? We are plastimorphs. There are others in the laundry whose names are derived from the word *zombie*.'

She knew the sterile, big-breasted laundry workers and was ashamed.

'We don't remember what we were,' said Tomat firmly.

And I don't know what I am; but I'm looking for her, Gaby thought. She smiled at Aumon and Tomat, seeing as she spread her smile to include them all, the shadows of the Sineinians who, going about their daily business, had been fatally injured and lost for ever.

They must laugh again. She bowed and spread imaginary skirts; she curtsied low and swung upon her hands to walk. In the gym she had practised for hours – years – until she could bend her pliant body into any uncouth shape. She sprang and tumbled and entertained the solemn, disinherited men until they were all laughing. On her feet again, she breathed hard but kept up the show, pirouetting and bowing; she clapped them.

'Thank you,' said Tomat gravely and Aumon began to clap. Then they all clapped and some kissed their hands and

50

blew the ghostly kisses in her direction so that the shower caressed her, soft as white flowers or falling snow.

The yellow road led on. Here, she had never been and she had left the guide-rails behind. The road was wide still and well-lit. She passed a number of closed doors on which the functions of the rooms they hid were stencilled: REST, STORE, OFFICE and STACK. She could hear the computer humming its song as it sifted the polycyclic data hurled into its memory. At Sineinian eyelevel was a porthole and she jumped to see the pale metal boxes which contained the brains of Traumoose.

The ultimate door was bright and shiny like the rest but without the painted legend. Beside it were a mechanical bell-push of obsolete design and a white card in a clear holder. She read the words on the card: PIKE NEEMI. PLEASE RING. Entranced, she obeyed the request as if it were a command. Somewhere beyond the door a bell buzzed querulously and slow footsteps advanced. And now she was alarmed. She drew back from the door and jumped when it was flung open.

A little old lady stood in the doorway. The two Fishfolk regarded each other, the girl in her green coveralls and the old woman in a shabby approximation of traditional Folk costume, a beaded apron sagging over her thin chest and satin onshore blouse and hanging limply – the beads had worn off – to cover her belly and legs. Her fur drawers made concertinas round her ankles. Gaby was too surprised to laugh.

'You disturbed me at my meditations. I was minding my own business,' she said and cackled suddenly at her own joke. 'It's allright. I've finished now and I'm wiped. You're not the Carer.'

She smelled like Grandgrand Float had not long before she died, stale, ammoniac, and sweet with the flowery scent of cheap talcum powder. Gaby smiled. It had been her early-morning task to help her great-grandmother on the pot. While Grandgrand sat there straining and complaining, she had amused her by pulling faces as contorted as her

51

grandmother's under the anguish of terminal constipation.

'Good afternoon,' she said. 'I found your bell at the end of my walk, so I rang it.'

Behind the old woman towered the furnishings of her obscure unit. Dim lights showed, on every surface, a crowd of objects seeming to jostle for space: boxes, lanterns, ropes, skins and glassy floats. On the floor was a jumble of fish boxes and creels; even one cerf, still dark and weighty from long immersion in the sea. The fresh smell of it drowned out other odours and a path, clear amongst the debris, led to her chair. She gestured at the untidy display, rotating her hand as if she were about to conjure Oma from the deep. 'When I'm gone, they'll want it all for the museum,' she said. 'I'm Grandgrand Pike. Who are you?'

'Float Gaby.'

It was as if she had rung another bell, an alarm in the old woman's mind.

'Poor chick-a-biddy,' she said, 'You've been given Needle Pak to fill your drawers and bed. It's a hard task, mothering orphaned children. They used to drown them. Never mind, you'll soon have some of your own and I know the man's a good earner. As for the bed-stuff, you'll have to close your eyes and pretend he's another. It's no fun with a Needle – they stink of fish. Had to chuck 'em in the sea every Blue to get 'em clean for breeding. Why didn't you ask for Salter Bren?'

'He's Cait's. Pak's the next-best. He's only *promised*; I haven't married him yet,' said Gaby. 'But you're right. He does smell like a fish.'

'No more than me in my dotage.' The old woman gave another of her sudden cackles and pulled up her drawers, buttoning them tight with the slow deliberation of the very old. Gaby watched her. When she was properly clothed and had composed her ragged self, she presented a different image, one of shabby and primitive grandeur. Like herself, her apron was very old and much of its interlocking pattern of sea birds and fish had worn off and fallen away. Here and there a blue or white bead glinted amongst the litter on the floor. More beads hung against her thin chest, several dozen narrow crystalline strands. Her long drawers were covered in yellow stains which, in an older world, would have been fish-oil but here, in buried Traumesse, were the reminders of bodily accidents and the detritus of this new and alien world. They were made of icedeer skins and once had been as white and virgin as the frozen world upside. The violent cerise colour of her blouse was unlike any cherry ever grown. Grandgrand Pike held out an arm so that Gaby could touch the satin and appreciate its quality.

'Not a mark; not a hole,' she said. Gaby saw several of each. 'My daughter brought it back from Hara in '615. Pretty, isn't it? Pretty as your rosy cheeks: you should ask for Salter Bren.'

Gaby smiled patiently.

'Are you going to stand on the doorstep all day?' said Grandgrand Pike petulently.

'May I come in?'

'Why didn't you let me know you were coming? The place is very untidy.'

The old woman led the way into the heart of her cluttered room where a cleared space in front of her chair contained the chamber pot she had been using when the doorbell rang. With a hearty sigh, she sat in her chair. Gaby followed her after carefully closing the door so that her secrets were not displayed to the empty corridor. She moved a stone lamp and a plate on which lay a half-eaten biscuit, and sat on the cerf.

'It was Pike's,' said the old woman. 'We used to fill it to the brim with lobsters.'

It was clear that she spoke of her husband, perhaps of her father; both long dead. The smell from the pot, stronger than Pak's fishy farts, was a barrier between the two women. In it, two hard stools made islands in a small sea of urine. Gaby straightened her face which threatened to crease and make uncontrollable laughter, sat up, and looked ahead. It was one thing in your own kin but in a different family... The solution lay with her. She looked at Grandgrand Pike and caught her eye; she looked at the pot.

'Shall I – '

The old woman looked defiantly back.

'If it offends you,' she said. 'Myself, I just muffle it with a cushion until Élis comes.'

With this, they compromised. The pot, its contents stifled by a cushion, ceased to offend and Gaby, as she gingerly placed it in its hiding place beneath a cupboard, wondered if it would ever be found again. She sat down on the cerf while Grandgrand Pike settled herself deep in her chair, comfortable against the beadwork, shawls and nets with which it was draped, and began to talk. Her conversation was one-sided, for she never stopped to listen to a reply, but swept remorselessly on like the Shaklian current. Sometimes her words made sense; sometimes they didn't. It was like standing on the cliffs beyond Ulbeg after a storm and seeing the smashed boxes and broken tridents of the Amber Gatherers carried past amongst a tangle of weed dragged from their holdfasts. Two days after the storm, the sea would be calm once more with only the white heads out in the current to remind you where Om slept; where the rip Arne Shakla had discovered and measured flowed onward. Just so, with Grandgrand Pike's sentences, alternate incoherence and order. The best of them carried motley cargoes and they sailed gently into port and rested there against the quay of Gaby's perceptions, to be unloaded and examined. In the dim room, the wall lamps cast a subdued light which was reflected in the glass floats on the shelf: carmine, a biting blue, a green as rich and dense as grass in Greening, a clear crystal ball for fortune telling and the summoning of dreams. They were not the little floats her ancestors had made.

'What are those floats for?' she asked.

'The Ineiti balls? They are from Hook Grounds. The Ineitis use them on their colin nets.'

'Why don't they break?'

'There aren't any rocks there, chicken – just sand. It's where the colin come for love, each fish woman to her man.'

Gaby asked if she could pick one up. She chose the green one and, returning to her seat, made a cradle for it with her hands. Amongst the echoes of the room which it had

54

captured in its uneven surface she saw parts of her own face reflected and stretched to fit the convex surface of the globe she held, and she studied each distorted feature. Her mouth: large, the lips curving in a self-conscious smile, not good at holding in mirth or secrets. Her eyes: the glitter in them owing more to the varied excitements of the day than to the low level of light. Her chin: small but determined. Her nose: snub, even the tip flattened, two dark oval caves for nostrils. Her cheeks: plump. Her brows: emphatic. Her dimples: punctuation marks. The images coalesced and she saw herself, Float Gaby, staring intently into the green glass float with the concentration of a clown about to attempt the impossible, to outrun a galloping horse, to hold water in a sieve. She laughed and swallowed and shushed herself because her hostess, Grandgrand Pike had fallen asleep.

She was free to look about the room without restraint: perhaps find hidden treasure there. The old woman slept deeply and loud snores erupted from her open mouth.

Gaby stood up softly and moved across the room. The shelves were loaded. She picked up treasure after treasure, suetstone figures, shale whales, stumpy tundra owls won with a copper chisel from the tuff of South Noiro, and set each tenderly down again in its place, imitating the movements of the absent Carer; for every carving had been dusted. A hooded figure at the end of the top shelf reminded her of Bren. He held a staff to balance himself while he carried a heavy block of suetstone across shingle. The strap which supported the stone bit into his forehead and he grimaced; the outline of every gripping toe and nail was as plainly incised as the pebbles he trod.

She opened a box with the outline of a malpog and the head of a man. Inside it was a collection of floats carved from driftwood and painted: narwhal, minke, orca, right whale. She turned the box over hoping to find the emblem of her family, an oval float with a face, but the base was flat and worn.

A female demon grinned up at her, yellow malpog ivory, very old. In her hand the carving felt smooth and comforting though its teeth were pointed and its fearsome eyes and flat nose travesties of her own. Propped amongst the stone icedeer and shoals of ivory fish upon the lowest shelf was a mask. She started when she first touched it, for it had hair like hers, dark, dense and human. She picked it up and turned it so that she could see it clearly by the light of the suetstone lamp.

It had a scarlet face. She tilted it: a face as fiery as the sun's when she set before the six dark months; but the chin was white and each eye delineated by a star drawn in yellow and black, and down the nose there ran a toothed design of the same colours. Two round holes were the pupils of the eyes and a larger hole made the open mouth. The face was sinister and comic at the same time. A rustle made her turn her head. Mice? They knew how to enter Traumesse by ways too small and insignificant for people. The rustle came from the dimmest corner and there she saw, her eyes adjusted now, a white owl sitting in a dead tree. The owl stared at her. He did not blink. He was small, his body no longer than her hand and his tree was also a dwarf, a stunted skaa birch. The dwarf owl bobbed his head, measuring her up; he called to her, a question: 'Kwi? Kwi?'

Grandgrand Pike rustled in her chair, awake. She opened her old eyes.

'Paikwi. Chee-rup,' she said.

'Kwi,' said the owl again and took wing.

The bird used his wings like feathery sweeps and rowed swiftly across the room; his flight was buoyant, light and airy as eider down. He made no noise. He settled on the old woman's shoulder and, sidling close to her head, began to preen her hair, taking it strand by strand, between the hard and powerful mandibles of its beak and straightening every hair.

'I don't need a comb. Paikwi is my hairdresser.' said Grandgrand Pike and blinked the sleep from her eyes, solemn as the wide-eyed owl. 'You're Float Gaby aren't you?'

'Yes, Great-grandmother.' Gaby sat on the cerf again. She laid the scarlet mask upon her knees and it gazed forlornly at her with its empty eyes.

'What have you got there?'

'A mask, Grandgrand. From your shelf.'

'Looks sharp, doesn't she? That's Witto. Her face burns like Soonoo's and her eyes are the two eyes of Tern. But that's another story —

'After Witto's face caught fire she ran all over Guna looking for cold cold water to quench the flames. Snapper Fish told her it was to be found in the crystal seas of Mahkrein, Jacket Seal that such water flowed only in the underground rivers of Southern Ineit, but "Go to Noiro" said Raingoose and so Witto turned North.

'When she came to the Boatfolk's islands, everyone had gone hunting. In an inlet she found Minke Whale singing to her child. She had no time to listen to Witto although she said "There's plenty of cold cold water hereabouts."

'This is what Minke Whale sang:

'There by the promontory the boat is coming out, yayee. . .

'The boat-man's oars are red with blood, yayee. . .

'The white bone edges are red with blood, yayee. . .

'Oh, he has killed your father, yayee. . .

'Witto dived into the cold cold water. She was cross with Minke Whale. Witto swam but the water did not cool her face and she swam into the hunter's boat. He lifted his spear because he thought she was the Whale Child and she lifted her head with its great red face. The hunter laughed. He laughed so much that he dropped his spear; he laughed so much he could not stop and he is still laughing and looking for Minke Whale and her child.

'There are more stories locked away up here,' said Grandgrand Pike, tapping her head.

'Tell me.'

'In the other time I would have. Just now. . . this owl is mine. His name is Paikwi. He is the only pet on Sowash.' She twitched her shoulder. 'Off now, off,' and the owl, discomfited, flew up and made a circuit of the room before he settled once more in his tree. 'Good boy,' said the old woman, 'Chee-rup.'

Paikwi replied with a noise between a snort and a laugh and Gaby laughed because he sounded exactly like old

Catch when he'd been on liquor. But the owl, appalled at such temerity, clacked his beak for silence and uttered a long drawn hoot, a whoohoohoohoo which summoned ghosts and the mists of Blue into the room. Gaby shivered and Grandgrand Pike laughed.

'Come here, pretty one,' she said and Gaby, awed by the haze owl's voice, bowed her head before the old woman.

'Here, my girl. Closer.'

Pike Neemi lifted her old arms and took off her necklace. She hung it about Gaby's neck and the warm crystal beads rattled and whispered to each other.

'It's of no use to the dead.'

The owl, Paikwi, clacked his beak twice. 'Hear! He blesses you,' she cried, her cracked voice shrill and full of the craft of the lays and the true, Folk sagas.

Gaby raised her head. The neck of the old woman was bare, all its folds and wrinkles revealed; the many strands of beads she had passed on were heavy about her own. She turned her head to look at the owl, but he had fluffed up his feathers and withdrawn his gaze from humanity.

Gaby opened her mouth. Her thoughts remained unspoken for a key turned in the lock, light flooded the room and the hearty voice of the Carer rang out.

'A visitor,' said Élis Tailler, 'We are lucky today! I'm sorry to be so late, my dear: there are three more babies today!'

Paikwi closed his eyes. Day had come, his night. He slept.

Outside in the yellow corridor the same steady lamps burned, but when Gaby came again to Floraliy a counterfeit dusk had fallen and the square was lit by individual lamps on poles. Shadows striped the white floor and the flickering lights on the escalators were subdued, clusters of stars. Her new ornaments reflected them; people stared. She went quickly into the Fountain Bar and while she picked her way amongst the tables, searching for her friends, she held the lifeline of crystal beads tight.

They were gathered round a table beyond the umbrella plants, a close group of dark heads; talking over the day most likely, speculating about her absence. Fenner and Ial, Pak waiting for her, for ever fishy. A smile formed and fled. Cait sat by Bren who was silent in the midst of the talk. He stared into his glass, a million miles away.

'Hello, Gaby,' said Pak.

Gaby!

Bren looked up. He saw the crystal beads and blinked, his eyes alight with their trapped dazzle; he started up and took his seat again. He had some secret to tell, some awful revelation he must make – but the others claimed and questioned her. She was to be fined, a day's pay.

'I don't care!' They laughed at her bravado and only Bren and herself knew she spoke the truth. Gaby fingered her beads and told her tale. She did not expect it to be greeted with delight, a burst of chatter and planning. They would all go next time, said Cait; it was shameful the way the old traditions had gone: a mother, a great grandmother, the victim of neglect. Gaby sat sovereign amongst them.

If she was an uncrowned queen than Bren was an unrecognised king. She stared at him, comparing him with Cait's cousin, Pak. Bren, alive with his new knowledge and purpose, looked at her.

'But you haven't been told,' he said.

Rumours of the coming of the icedeer had fed the Folk all day, gathering momentum until, at the end of the second shift, the Viewdome was full as never before, with a crowd. Gaby, far away with Grandgrand Pike, knew nothing.

Bren told his tale.

'They came first to me,' he said and, as he spoke the boast, knew that he lied: their caller had been, not him, nor anyone of Sowash, but the Sineinian woman, Ang Semo. He had not thought this out, did not understand it; and he fell silent again while, around him, those voluble talkers, his own Cait and Angle Fenner, vented their opinions. He looked again at Float Gaby with her new strings of beads, looked and blushed because she was more beautiful than Cait; and then the snow blew up in his mind, clouding his reason and touching him with cold and shocking fingers. He was lost.

'Come on, Bren. Bren!' Cait's shriek.

'Bren. Are you sleeping?' Fenner's coo.

Pak slapped his shoulder.

They were going upstairs, to the Viewdome. Gaby must be shown and they must see again those silent white travellers from the back of the north wind, Matoq's envoys.

The herd mother sniffed the wind. He carried many messages. Chief among his many scents, was the stink of death. He had many voices too, one of persuasion, one of approval, several which warned of the terrors he could choose to bring, deep angry bellows. Matoq barked and breathed deep. He exhaled, and there was snow, clean and odourless, vairless, food and waterless. The wind whirled up the snow and the herd mother bent her head again and ate the flowers Matoq had provided. At her back was the strange warm pool, whose surface would not break. It gave heat and light throughout the blizzard. She stood and faced the weather patiently like the rest of the herd. Matoq might choose to take a fawn or a doe from her.

Pak clasped Gaby's hand. They could see the blizzard but they could not experience it like the deer above them, patient as stones. The snowflakes clouded the circular horizon and the deer became shadows on it; snow began to pile up on the glass of the dome. Bren was smiling. Gaby, seeing this, felt she must smile too.

'They will survive it,' Pak assured her and released her hand so that he could step forward and, mounting the steps, be close under the glass and near the disappearing deer. They were snow themselves now, bound up in it, part of its pure whiteness. The fallen snow stuck to the dome and built itself into a thick layer until the warmth of the glass got to it. It degenerated and began to slide, while more snow fell and took its place. Abstractedly, Gaby rubbed the hand Pak had held, while she watched her friends find places on the crowded steps to watch the battle of warmth and snow, of the energies of Traumesse with the winter darkness.

She and Bren were left below, in the centre of the Viewdome floor.

'What shall we do?' Gaby asked him.

'We must go on learning,' said Bren.

'Sineinian stuff?'

'That too.'

She could see that he wanted to touch the beads Pike Neemi had bequeathed her and that, when he had held and caressed the chiming strands, he would want her. He was biting his lower lip.

She was a lovely thing, cheeks flushed dark red in her excitement, poised on the brink of decision like himself. In this snowy light her beads were clear and bright as stars, and the strands on her breast, where his shadow fell, were black. They might be alone in the crowded room, for the other folk were staring at the snow on the window and hoping for a miracle, a sign from the incommunicative deer. He breathed out, expelling all the warm air trapped in his lungs in one great gust and, in that breath, consigned Gaby to whatever Om had in store for her. She could never be his. He looked up. Cait was talking to her cousin, Needle Pak, and he could imagine her excited voice, even some of the words. He looked away and smiled at Gaby.

'In after times,' he said, 'Remember this night.'

Her beautiful smile widened, and grew. 'How could I forget it?' she said and then, in exactly the coppery tones of the saga construct, Siloe, 'My own, dear love.' She laughed, swept the skirts of her ballgown up, and curtsied; she spun, she glittered.

In between the laughter and buffoonery, he was able to tell her his secret.

'They came to Ang Semo,' he whispered, 'Not me. She brought me to them.'

Gaby's impudent expression did not alter. She was still pretending, still Siloe showing off and opulent in her long dress at the ball but,

'Ang,' she said, 'What a peculiar woman she is.'

'Peculiar?'

'Yes: individual, special.'

He left her then, to whatever fool or clown the future might find her, and ran lightly up the steps to Cait.

A week ambled by. Every day Ang expected that her morning expedition to the Viewdome would end in disappointment; but the deer did not go. The supplies of hay the skimmers from the mainland dropped were devoured quickly; the animals, pressing against the warm glass, waited patiently for the next delivery. The response of other Staff members was gratifying. Even Carey Aleph showed interest and Eda Voran spent hours at a terminal calling up data on Fishfolk hunting practices.

Sollar responded promptly to her call, first with an alert on the trans-ocean link and then with a personnel drop.

'I haven't time to entertain them,' said Dr Wireloom, handing Ang a wallet of credits and security passes. 'They aren't rookies: take them to your place and give them the best. Besides – it's your party.'

The drop was imminent. On the screen a moving dot marked the passage of the skimmer as it fled, silent as a moth, across the green ocean and her numb sister, the ice. Wireloom dropped her mask enough to smile.

'You'll enjoy the company.'

Two women, Drs Noy and Mahn, were landed: one a zoologist, the other a climatologist. They came below armed with camcorders, stunkit, snow-goggles, snowclothes, a core probe and an assistant who has no part in this story. She may be imagined, ever-present in the field, speaking into her notebox, taking blood-samples from tranquilised icedeer, entering data into her recorder: the essential and invisible tasks of the uncredited technician. Elige Noy was small and intense; Undine Mahn a thin, dark sprite. They had been married for two years and each wore the other's ring. Then Undine had spent eleven months camped on the south polar pack-ice, rotating with the current, while Elige followed the migrating raingeese north. This time they had fallen on their feet: they were together on a project. Ang regarded them with suspicion while she smiled and shook their hands. The invaders smiled back and appeared glad to see her. Bring your own culture, she thought, listening to their excited chatter in the corridor. It was the Sineinian national vice. Their accents were polished and their voices clear: pure Sollar Kein, as she supposed her own must be. Gradually, while they showered and helped her lay the table and drank her wine, their accents soothed her and became the norm. She was at home again with her peers. They talked well, Undine discoursing on the neo-postmodernist Parliament House being raised in Sollar ('You must see it soon!') and Elige, whose photomaps of the raingoose path had won several awards, knew something about sheet film photography: 'Let's see your snaps.' Ang was prevailed upon and there was quiet while her monochromatic images of rock and water were analysed. Then they talked, inevitably, of 'Greed'.

They woke her in the night. She had learned the pattern of their voices and could distinguish one from the other: Elige's soft moans and Undine's breathy yelps. She sat up, the sheet caught protectively to her chest, dry inside as an old bone, and listened. We are all beasts, she thought, vair, icedeer, carrion bear. . . We squeal for joy and pain. The intercourse taking place in the next room was nothing more than the answer these particular women had found. She heard Elige speaking words of love, intimate, idiotic, and the disorder of the double bed and the stark furnishings of the guest-room were as clear to her eye as if no wall intervened. She listened carefully, wanting to learn, but when the ultimate moment came and she thought herself relaxed, sitting there loose-jointed, the sheet fallen across her thighs, she felt her own dry vagina respond with the customary spasm of pain. She reached for the light switch and a novel. The thought that they might have been female and male, that she would then have had to deal with a different threat, did not leave her until she had read the first chapter.

Neither showed embarrassment at breakfast. They talked about the deer and Undine washed the dishes while Elige unpacked the snow-gear. Then, laughing and admiring the rotund, padded jackets as they laid them out, they asked Ang to summon the Spokesman.

Bren had seen Atluki dance to his silent music in Floraliy and felt haunted. He entered the unit hesitantly and stood by the door looking steadfastly at his feet. Ang, one now in

63

conspiracy with the Sineinian visitors, offered him a drink. He was dumbfounded. He drank the shot off and found his voice: 'Thank you, Dr Semo,' gruffly. He coughed, the good child.

The three women humoured him. Elige, whose small stature was no embarrassment, drew him to the table. The liquor bottle stood on it, near a map, and he looked from one to the other. Elige, perceiving that in this situation the little man had regressed and become what she had often employed, an indigene, winked at Ang and poured another shot. Undine demonstrated the map. A large blue circle represented the Viewdome, smaller circles the two buried rooflights of the atria; the icedeer were drawn as wedges with horns. Beyond the red arc of high ground was a small square, the upper gate of Traumesse. Bren began to talk.

'When we come out – there – we can walk upright but here – is this the wind direction? Good. Here, you must wait while I go forward to look – '

The white down jacket altered him. Below, he had praised its construction and light weight. Here and now, upside, it made him a king. Below, in Traumesse, the women had led him along the coloured corridors but now they dropped behind and the only manifestation of their culture in the cold dark landscape was the reflective hemisphere of the Viewdome rising beyond the close party of deer. They crouched in the snow and watched his stealthy advance.

Ang watched him. He moved as he had done in the Viewdome, knowingly. He understood the place and the awe and trepidation she had seen in his face when he first beheld the deer was replaced by a confident expression. She began to learn: cold about her nose, pinching it; the near-panic she remembered from her crazy foray to photograph the ice-column in '620; the constant pressure of the North wind; a sweet smell of deer, dung and hay – summer leas, escaped here from Sinein, meadows, red machines and girls and men there, sunbrown men, straw-hatted, young, herself reading among the hay-bales, wishing for a lover. What in the world am I doing here? The greengold paradise faded. She saw the fields of snow. Salter Bren was close to the deer. A drift concealed him from them. The stags were oblivious though they eyed the horizon and the herd mother herself stared into the dark east where the kjarrs and the craggy Old Woman were. Above them, Tern was huge, filling a quarter of the sky.

Salter Bren stood up. Ang swallowed her shout. Beside her in the snow-hole Elige Noy vented a sigh of exasperation which she muffled in her glove. The man stood straight on the deer's horizon, clear and vertical as a pressure ridge. Every one of the animals stopped feeding and looked up, round ears pricked. But they did not flee.

And now a miracle happened. Ang remembered it as such, felicity in which she and the scientists had no power to intervene, the gift of the old dark powers these incredible people had once worshipped. The mother moved slowly to the front of her herd and shook her magnificent head. A cloud of haystalks and ice flew from her corona and she snorted it away. Then she advanced on him. She came forward fearlessly, and halted when she was no farther from him than one length of her black whiskers. She lowered her great head, bent one leg and then the other, and knelt before the man. The watchers saw him take the deer's grey muzzle in his hands and raise her to her feet again. He shouted, a great cry of triumph and exaltation: 'O-ou, O-u!'

This time, the technician sighed and Ang heard Undine's base whisper: 'He must have some bait in his pocket.' Her own sigh was one of pure awe.

The herd-mother returned to her kind and began to graze.

Ang was certain that they would have been able to move freely amongst the deer, measuring and recording but Science directed and first a stag was darted, felled and examined; next, a doe. The herd drew into itself and made the beginnings of the defensive formation called the Empty Circle.

While the essential measurements were being made – length of bone and density, size of testicles, length of penis and horns, morphology, number of hairs to the square millimetre – Salter Bren turned his back. It took Ang many weeks to lay the ghost of that sight. He stared at the frozen sea with a cold and stony face, his eyes brimming with the tears his stoicism would not let him shed. She left him and knelt with the scientists in the trampled hay, holding heavy legs and heads and the end of the tape, part of her mind a calculator, the rest with the little man. When she returned to him, not daring to utter any of the platitudes she had thought out, his face was still expressionless, but his eyes had cleared and were full of purpose. He looked at her. 'I can smell the thaw,' he said. 'It begins– listen!'

The cold stream of air flowed over her, dulling her senses. She felt the change. The air was suddenly warmer and it carried salt and iodine, the intense ghosts of summer when the seaweed rotted high on the rocks and stranded fish gasped their last and died. She felt Ulbeg strain to open and be free of the ice; she remembered how the water would flow about her and penetrate the tight floodgates between her legs. She heard the thaw begin with a dull boom like percussion artillery far away. The ice which all winter had sung to them was breaking up.

'We are free,' said Bren inexplicably.

Cries from Undine and Elige alerted them. The little man swung round and Ang turned, the brief vision of the open Sound fading. The deer had crowded round their fallen and the herd-mother was nudging the sedated doe with her nose. Undine was quick to act, stabbing the sleeping deer with darts of antidote, so that they struggled up on trembling legs, blowing steam. The herd-mother had already taken her place and the stag joined his fellow on the flanks of the herd. The four women and the hunter stood still to watch them leave, a solid phalanx marching to the coast.

The scientists watched the migration through image-intensifiers but Ang and Bren saw twilit ice, fading deer-shapes, and the glitter of the stars. The deer would leap from floe to floe across the opening leads until they saw the icefoot on the far side of the Sound. Then their mother would lead them into the race; their heavy coats and subcutaneous fat protecting them. They would be swept in minutes down the Sound until, beside the dim shores of Hairete ten miles south, they would attempt to land. Some might die, but for those who survived there was shelter and here, amongst purple lichens, moonflowers and sugar grass they would summer until Matoq, at the sullen end of the year, brought back the ice.

The women and the Fishfolk man had made separate journeys of discovery on the cold surface of Sowash. Below, where it was safe and warm, many questions awaited Bren. He put his own aside and answered the foreign women. He drank their liquor freely. Then the small woman gave him his own bottle and sent him away.

He worried at the questions the deer's homage had raised. His questions produced others, of loyalty and intent. But what could he say to the Folk? That he had seen the future? What could he, First Loader and Spokesman, Carver and Salter, do? The several persons the Sineinians had divided him into refused to unite and he warred with his selves; his head ached all the time and he found the pastel halls of Traumesse as close and stifling as a fog blanket in Blue.

The scientists, too, had many questions. The chief one, relayed to Sollar was 'Climatic variables important we stay confirm please' but 'No extension' came the instant reply and both women railed, as ineffectual against Research Commission as chained dogs.

Ang had a question for the scientists but she did not ask it until they were packed and ready to leave, waiting out the last hour before the skimmer was due.

'Didn't you feel insignificant out there, when the Spokesman raised the deer?' she asked Undine.

'Sure. You always do when you fetch up against a true primitive. But you learn to disregard your feelings: subjective judgements are useless.'

She turned away and knelt to adjust the straps on her luggage, concealing her own feelings in needless action, leaving Sowash and the mystery of the premature thaw to Ang Semo and her aboriginals.

Fifteen minutes of the patchwork ice each morning were not enough for Ang and she began to visit the Viewdome in the evening. After work there was a difference of scale and intensity within and without. Inside, the Viewdome was lively with the voices of the Folk gathered there to watch the melt. Above, in the wider universe, Guna had tilted and Tern set. The myriad stars of Oma and the Fish gave a better light. You could see across the Sound unaided.

Salter Bren was there sometimes, and a group of Needles; Float Gaby and her man; roly-poly Angle Fenner with her rustling bars of candy. It depended which shift was at leisure, A or B. Twice, Ang saw Gaby attending a wheeled chair in which sat the demented bundle of bones and rags which was all that was left of the Pike family, crooning to herself. Sometimes Ropewalker Aglit, the Spokeswoman from A was there, her eyes fast to the best 'scope; sometimes Float Gaby had captured it and, poised on tip-toe, was similarly fixed to the eye-piece, her laughter resonant. It was a salutary experience to see her discovering humour in climatic change. When Needle Cait had charge of the 'scope everyone in the dome was treated to a commentary:

'Look, blue prion. They fly faster than you run, Bren.'

'Oh, the raingeese – they're back.'

'Look, oh look, malp in the water!'

Ang stood on the top step, apart from the Folk, and used her own glass.

In the mordant light of the stars the ice sheet was sundered into crazy islands which jostled in the centre of the Sound. The current raced, warm, turbulent, bringing the melt. When the exuberant chatter of the Folk faltered, the magnified groans of the labouring ice-sheet filled the room. Ang felt its misery as if it were her own. She became silent and depressed; when she studied the latest code-scripts of 'Greed' she was tempted to murder Jannl. She might infect Siloe with a hideous cancer and watch her perfect features rot away. The desolation she had felt when Tobin left returned to haunt her.

The five rocky islands across the Sound were waking and their chilly surfaces heaved with migratory birds: Malpogak and Vair flat and brown above their raised beaches; bony Clash desolate, the basalt cliffs of its northern peninsula a set of devil-children's blocks; Demender was full of purple shadows and mountainous Sair appeared to roll and buck, afloat upon the soup of ice and water. Nearer, Orso and Wirra sparkled as their many lakes and lochans turned from shining ice to clear water which reflected the stars.

She turned to face south.

Out there, a flight away or ten days in a boat, was the flat northern shore of Ineit, where elephants and white jungle pards lived; there, to the east, home: Sinein, wide and lovely continent, Ros and Sollar, the Central Highlands rising dusty red from the plain. And here was Skaa, a little rock crowned with a ring of satellite masts, and here, full and black in the double lenses, Longbeach where she had visited the Amber Gatherers with Pior. He had kissed her gently on the mouth before he boarded the ferry which took him away for ever. His sister had sent her the photoimage of the war memorial in Alut, grey stone scribed in silver, stars and helical decorations; but all that mattered to her was his name, halfway down the long list, and the three words of slaughtered hope: 'Killed in Action', the wages of aggression and vain, stupid greed. The tears which ran down her cheeks were a symptom of the thaw outside, a wound which would never heal. They were private tears and, as she shed them, she was glad that her back was turned to the Folk. She began to worry that her tearproof mascara had failed and made dirty rivulets in the pancake on her cheeks; yet she wanted the mask to crack.

The sound-system relayed the drip drip of water falling from every stem upside.

She tried to make sense of the thaw. It had come a month early in the dark; it would end before the coming of the light. The old woman of the sea, Om of the Folk, was free to send up her flocks and shoals, her herds of malp and whale schools. Maybe this summer would be long and generous; maybe the ice would return early, locking her in and confining her to barracks, closing Ulbeg up. She longed to be at Ulbeg to see the light enhance the water. The weight and volume of this water running from the land must be immense. She feared it. She associated the thaw with sunlight and a benign warmth upon the ice, melting it crystal by latticed crystal. That this should happen in the dark while the North wind blew!

The Folk seemed to take it in their cheery stride. 'A haze owl!': she heard Gaby's bubbling voice. She looked over her shoulder and saw Salter Bren's white grin. A chuckle broke from the shawled figure of Grandgrand Pike. They shared a secret. She wondered if she herself, Ang Semo, had become ordinary and understood; like the granite island, a stony and watchful familiar whose influence was mainly for the good. The clear glass of the dome reflected nothing and she watched the land emerge from the snow and the sea become a liquid entity which cradled Sowash and herself together.

BLUE I

With every spring comes the wander-lust, and when
Nature itself shakes the yoke of winter from its shoulders the desire arises to strike camp and follow the many
birds of migration which herald summer's arrival.

Knud Rasmussen, *Greenland by the Polar Sea*

Cait sang at work and Gaby sang all day. The early thaw made them restless; production suffered and they spent credits wildly in the bars after work. But there was no bad behaviour amongst the Folk. They were polite and cheerful as ever, their unease signalled only in a mild display: they wore fewer Sineinian ornaments and the men let their hair grow. Bren was seen, wearing fur drawers, in the Fountain on Floraliy.

Blue had come, release, and the sea, reflecting the new-born and luminous gentian of the sky, held the islands delicately. The waves rolled ashore; the wind had undergone a similar change and blew steady but soft. Freed too by the change, the ferries set sail with their cargoes of dreams and their windfoils mirrored the sea's new colour.

Sometimes, the islands were obscured by fog, and haze owls flew invisible through vapour coloured like themselves. Then, the foghorns of the ferries sounded, although their pilots could see as well as an owl through their computerised eyes.

Ang saw the solemn public demeanour of the Folk towards her alter. Some of them smiled and greeted her openly. She felt that she had begun to know Salter Bren and Float Gaby. She understood why Salter Bren looked like his ancestors and no longer like a ferryhand, and why Gaby had been wandering in Floraliy on that dull afternoon in Tern when she should have been at work.

Yet Gaby herself, while she was conscious of her mother's preparations for the Fish Supper on the twentieth day of Tow (there were hooks and lines everywhere and, on the living-room table the brightly-painted floats from which her family got its name) went doggedly to work. She wanted to be upside; she wanted to renounce the line and spend all day in the sun. This unreal desire had never troubled her before; like Cait, she had gone unthinking between her repetitive work and the relief of play.

She visited Grandgrand Pike three times a week. The old woman was nearly ninety-eight. She said she wanted to celebrate her birthday with a liquor party upside in the daylight.

73

'I can't climb the Mountain these days,' she said, 'But I can look at her.'

The message came at the start of the shift, a blue and white printout plainly addressed to Float Gaby, Dispatch. She unfolded it incuriously: messages were standard, another medical, a dental check, but, 'So sorry: Pike Neemi died suddenly 2 a.m. Please come for bird. Élis Tailler, Visiting Carer.' She gulped, but did not cry. Cait, seeing her hesitate over the white paper, summoned the chargehand. She was released from work and, running, found herself free and in the yellow corridor at half-past two.

Grandgrand Pike, two in the morning: on the ebb. The proper time to die. Gaby hoped that she had gone peacefully, with her hoarded ancestral memories intact.

The room was neater and many of the artefacts had been packed away. Élis, the Carer, was sorting clothes, wonderful pied old garments covered in beads and bone toggles.

'Where is he?'

Gaby did not know what she would do with the owl, with the only pet in Traumesse, but she supposed she would be allowed to keep him. Élis gestured. The tree stood in its usual corner. She peered at the dark branch where the bird liked to sit, but the miniature birch was empty and the bird crouched below it on the floor.

'Chee-rup,' she said, as Grandgrand Pike had done. 'Chee-rup.'

The owl stared at her with an unblinking yellow eye and she did not realise, until she bent and saw how he slumped upon his striped breast, that he too had died. He looked perfect, every feather in place and his neat, curved beak ready to seize the next offering of meat.

'You've let him die!' Gaby accused.

'What?' The Carer bustled over. 'Oh dear – but maybe it's for the best. I'll get rid of it. You choose something else of hers to keep – would you like one of the lamps?'

'Yes, I would like a lamp. I'll have that one. But you must bury dead birds.'

Élis smiled and stood back. In Gaby's mind floated the white wings of gulls and terns, held stiff and sailike on the breeze and lit by the brief sun of summer. She remembered how the raingeese flew, low and fast over the waters of Mewsmere. Paikwi lay dead under his dead tree. Soon his body would rot. She could not bear the thought of his light and striated feathers, his downy feet, tipped amongst the rubbish into a lighter. She stroked his soft back and picked him up; she spread one of the long wings which, all out of proportion with his stumpy body, had lifted him from the floor in the close air of Pike Neemi's little room; she blew upon his feathers and folded his wing. Then, cradling him in her left hand and taking up Grandgrand Pike's lamp from the old and blackened cerf, she left the room.

The yellow floor and walls of the corridor had nothing to do with sunlight. They were fakes. The sun shone upside. That was where she would go, to bury the owl in the soft wet earth above the permafrost, facing south so that his spirit could fly with the wind.

She crossed Floraliy. Dr Semo was coming to meet her, this time without the usual armful of pictures, carrying only her big camera bag and walking lightly in spite of its weight. She smiled. Her eyebrows went up, almost disappearing into her sedge-coloured hair. Gaby felt that this time she should be given an explanation.

'Grandgrand Pike has died. This is her owl.'

'May I see?'

They bent their heads together over the dead bird and Ang saw what a thing of beauty it had been. In Ang's head, great birds circled, the bronze raptors of the Highlands; in Gaby's the ring of yellow moonflowers glowed. She would inter the sleeping owl beneath them, if any were left from the hunger of the deer.

Ang made a decision to speak, to confide. 'I had no idea,' she said, 'that anyone kept a bird. Did Pike Neemi have others, or this poor fellow only?'

'She had lots of things. Not birds. Things like this suetstone lamp. They are putting them all in the Museum.'

Gaby, in turn, asked her leading question.

'I expect you would like to photograph the owl?'

'I couldn't. It's dead,' said Ang Semo, fear and urban disgust in her voice.

'No deader than a rock.'

'But the sea is alive, Gaby. You know that. There is always water in my pictures. Where will you bury it?'

'I don't know yet.' (But in her mind the shining garland of yellow flowers, faces turned now to the sun.)

The Sineinian woman smiled remotely and turned away. Gaby watched her hesitate upon the white floor and turn towards the Fountain. She weighed the lamp and the owl in her hands, the suetstone oval dense and greasy, the dead bird the friend of the wind. She put the lamp in her pocket and then, with both hands free to protect the owl, she carried it up by lift and moving stair, effortlessly transcending the space between Floraliy and surface of the island, out into the light.

As she passed out of the Gate, unguarded and open now that Blue had come, she felt the longing again. She wanted to tumble and cartwheel across the tussock where the sea-smell blew in wild gusts towards her.

The moonflowers were alive. The intensive cropping had stimulated the plant and it was covered in open flowers and green and yellow buds. Tufts of white hair were caught in the creeping stems. Gaby laid Paikwi by one of these and began to dig his grave. The black soil stained her fingers and filled her nails as she scraped; rapidly, she became hot; she wiped her face and the stains transferred themselves. She took off her scarf and undid the neck of her jacket. Happiness invaded her as she scrabbled there in the sodden earth, making a grave with which to free the owl, and the beads of sweat which broke from and glistened on her brow had the same delicate translucence as the necklaces of ancient beads around her neck.

Ang Semo, emerging ten minutes later from the gate, moved swiftly out of sight behind the high Perimeter ring. The steep and bumpy hillside spread like a map before her, empty of people, hers. She did not want to see anyone, nor be seen. Up here, where the wind had a backbone and the

76

sea rolled turquoises against the horizon, she wanted the solitude which was hers whenever she closed the door of her unit. Shut them out. Here am I: alone.

The walk was the first thing to enjoy, no more brittle flats of cat ice through which the boots broke into deep holes, long squelching strides now possible on the mosses. Next, the balancing act, tussock to tussock down the hill. It never dried out. The gulls on the up-draughts over the cliff were a moving curtain of white; the courting sea parrots bowed to her. She paused upon a smooth erratic which the ice had dumped a million years ago and looked out across the lilting sea. It seemed that the water in its new mobility rejoiced as much as she did.

Here, on the cliff above Ulbeg, she felt new as the season, refreshed by the keen wind and yet old in learning as the rocks themselves and a warmer and more pliable entity, despite the infirmity, than they.

It was not hard to say which of the two coves was her favourite. Although Forso's white sands and gently-sloping shoreline were sometimes paramount and she could not rest until she had gone there, taken off her shoes and paced the hard wet sand at the water's edge, let the soft sand full of dry shards of dead weed tickle her toes and make ghostly sandals which clung with as much glitter and glamour as a pair of Ardrazen's slippers to her wet skin, Ulbeg's deeper inlet fascinated her. The rocks would be themselves again, green and black sunlit giants which waited for her at the water's edge. Every gallon and acre of blue water waited in the cold landscape for Greening; every frith and pool, the clement sea herself waited for the warmest days, no longer bound, no longer frigid. She watched the current whip up white horses in the middle of the Sound: no sanctuary out there. It carried hareng, colin and white coelenterates south, carried long scarves of kelp and their passengers, snails, squirts and keepi crabs and brought the ability to grow the crops of temperate climes to Hayna and chill streams of water to the warm seas of northern Mahkrein. Once, on long leave far from here, she had lain on the old stone jetty in downtown Roakn and, dipping her hand in the clear water, felt the cool fingers of the current reach down from the top of the world and grasp her hand. So, they said, did Mahun order life.

Such thoughts were akin to Folk credulity, she thought: delving towards our origins with unshaped tools. I can't believe. Seawater was salt because it leached minerals from the rocks; not because a legendary bread baker had been careless with her ingredients. The polychrome sea, rolling now awash with its own marvellous palette, had been explained. Salt was not white, nor pure water black; they did not combine to make cyan, indigo, cobalt, beryl, aquamarine – sea water – as the ancients believed. And the colours she saw were not revealed to birds or bears; the eyes of vair and icedeer, deficient in retinal cones, could not perceive them. And almost as far again beyond their ken were the patterns she captured in her camera of rock and water moving beneath waves of light, each medium fractured and reformed by the predictable tide.

When she came to Ulbeg, the tarunt gulls too were courting and advising all who heard them to "wake, 'wake.' Their cries rebounded from the black cliffs in a thousand echoing pieces and seemed fragmented and magnified at one and the same time by the unforgiving rock. The soft shapes into which it had flowed when it was a superheated liquid belied its mass; black ropes of it hung against billowing green curtains and there were glassy pillows at the edge of the water, bulbous shapes thrust from the fiery heart of the planet into the icy waters of the minus millenia, long before the Year One. Only one stretch of rock beyond the bathing pool appeared what it was, hard rock, a rough pavement of scoriaceous aa, the ashes the ancient eruption had thrown out.

Discovery and Science made Ulbeg wonderful: the more you knew of it, the more marvellous it was. In days long gone by there had been a Fishfolk summer settlement near the cliff. It was remembered still, and she had been told that spirits lived there. The food the Folk put out for them was eaten by the gulls.

The tarunts hurtled towards their ledges below her and, suddenly, lifting on a thermal, dropped gently to rest, alighting on the narrow ledge which was bower, nursery, roost and, too often, sepulchre. Ang stepped boldy on to the narrow cliff path and leaned out to balance her heavy bag. Once, the Folk had hung and clambered here, harvesting eggs from the nests of the gulls.

She knelt on the green rock pillows and dipped her hands in the sea. The ebbing tide pulled them away from the safety of the shore and its cold assaulted her blood gradually, starting at the fingertips, encroaching on the fingers joint by joint; beneath the water she saw her fingers as purple and wizened as the weeds which streamed below them and withdrew her hands to hide their raw wet redness between her warm thighs which imparted heat slowly until her hands stung. Once, clutching the snap camera awkwardly between a weaker, warmer left hand and her cheek, she had photographed the scarlet dominant hand stranded on her white thigh, an impotent and guilty crab which offered occasional satisfaction but was no substitute for the men she wanted and feared. In the ice-worn pool behind her, long strands of hairweed reached up to the light. Her hands had to sting, acknowledging the cold power of the sea; then she was satisfied and could turn from it to consider its gentler daughter, the quiescent water of the pool.

She dipped her hands in the confined water. After the sea, it felt warm. The hairweed floated and she imagined its caress. This was Slackwater, the first month of Blue. There was still snow in the lee of inland rocks and the tarns froze over at night: too cold to swim. Like the pool, she must wait until summer, until the brightest light could warm water in the pool and her naked body, both eager for renewal.

She paced the uneven rocks, looking for new shapes, for an accidental juxtaposition of water and petrified lava with which to illustrate her new thesis of essential waveform. And so, she happened on the symbol. She thought she knew Ulbeg, every fold of rock, each pool, the great bolster of lava at the head of the inlet up which you could clamber to explore the old summer shelters of the Fishfolk, uneven tent-rings on a wide and grassy ledge. The rock hung in swags above the abandoned boulders, an exuberant backdrop to human drama. The receding tide had left damp prints, fleeting images of itself, upon a smooth billow in the rock: as it dried and she watched the vapour coil from it she saw the carving. Water lay in it, as in a moat, but it was an incomplete circle: perhaps abandoned because of the hardness of the rock. On the south side of the island, in the softer schists, were many carvings, seals and women fishing, men with spears. This – this was idiotic, a carving in basalt crude as the broken tent-rings nearby. The angular groove of the chisel cut was unmistakable, dating it after 2000, imported steel tools. Yet, very old. The break in the circle seemed to her significant, an outflowing from the centre of things and again she found herself thinking nonsense.

It was time to set up the big camera. She opened her bag, took out the tripod sections and unfolded them; next, the camera with its soft bellows, red wood and shiny catches. The detailed work of setting it up made her forget the cold in her bones and the wind which sought to make her colder still. The antique box and its two glass eyes absorbed her; she was always careful with it: a mother with a new baby. It wasn't an original but it had been made more than a hundred years ago, one of the copies of the Gaian plate camera which had been fetched out of capsule storage for the Sollar Kein Society's anniversary and had then impressed a clutch of hobbyists with its nuts and bolts simplicity: a plain statement of function in leather and wood. She was the only imagist of her generation to see its potential and make proper use of it.

The black cloth was a hide, a small tent over her head, and she bent over the camera to concentrate her picture.

Seen out of scale through the camera lens, the reversed image of the broken circle was a curving canal, a waterway for pleasant cruises, the crystalline structure of its smooth channel like the finest marble. She fed the camera with a slide of film, unsheathed it and operated the release. Reading the light again, its pale fingers touching Ulbeg's sides, the hues and tones of Sollar in winter, she reloaded twice, took two more exposures, and dismantled the camera.

The work had made her warm and content. When every precious component was safely packed away, she knelt once more to the bitter blue sea, immersed her hands and waited while the water aged and stiffened them. The North wind blew salt into her mouth and eyes.

She shivered as she climbed from Ulbeg and began the uphill walk over Traumesse. The camera bag dragged at her shoulder; each step brought her away from the water and returned her to clocks, timetables and confinement. She kept her eyes on the uneven ground and saw the insects which ran among the stems, the scraps of sea-parrot down and their immense pied droppings outside every burrow. She stepped carefully amongst the male parrots resting between fishing flights. The tussock was bright green and the nine inches of black soil under it rich in oozing salts and wet as a bath sponge; she wondered why the parrots nested on the permafrost: they were driven to pluck their breasts bald to make their nests. They could not know how their shit made the ecosystem turn, nor the panic they caused the maintenance engineers when they strayed from their burrows into the refrigeration inlets.

She looked at the steep mound which concealed Traumesse: from here, low down, the two atrium skylights were narrow, reflective steps and the Viewdome a blue bubble. Figures appeared beside it, black and gesticulating against the light. She recognised the forthright shape of Eda Voran. Anthropologising with the natives. . . and Dorta Wireloom. They were all waving their arms at her and shouting. What were they shouting: 'Get any snaps?'; 'Fire!'; 'Help!'? Dr Wireloom's words blew away on the wind.

On Murali's farm, in childhood, she used to tag along behind a group of local boys, one with but not of them. There were ant-mounds down by the river, mighty castles of mud, and the boys poked sticks into their narrow doors until a crowd of agitated ants ran out. She was allowed to disturb the nest by the crack willow which was only waist-high and she remembered the obscene satisfaction she had got from the havoc her long stick caused. Here, her inquisitive and antisocial habits had become the goad.

The people on the skyline were a mixed group: Folk, the two Staff, Wireloom's PA and two ferryhands. None of them should have been upside at this time of day. Three figures detached themselves from the group and bounded toward her: Salter Bren, Gaby, her face streaked with earth, and Atluki the simpleton, his silent portable swinging wildly from its strap. Bren took the bag from her shoulder and hung it on his own, Gaby and Atluki took her hands, one each side; they pulled her along.

'You're cold,' said Gaby, 'You're damp!'

'But I got my pix. Rock *and* water.' The crescent canal merged in her mind with the pale facial discs of a haze owl. A basalt idol built itself on the ruins of Pike Neemi's familiar; if only she had known about the old woman and let herself experience the potency of her magic. She had not after all been shattered by time. She was a seer. A prophet. She could have foretold... That wheaten ghost, the dead owl Gaby had shown her, proved it; for to keep an owl in Traumesse was otherwise folly.

You're thinking nonsense again, Ang. And what should Pike Neemi foretell? Gaby's hand about hers was hot as fire. Without the heavy bag she could run almost as well as they. Salter Bren, who had been ahead, now stopped and waited for her.

'There's folk,' he said. 'On the shore.'

'Folk?'

'Strange folk. Not amber gatherers.'

'Folk? People?'

'Women, men and carts. A beast.'

Eda Voran put an optic into her hand. She screwed up her right eye and squinted down the tube with her left.

'By the beach at Toul.'

The stony valley sprang into focus. It was full of boulders beached, like the lone erratic above the Sound, by ice. A man was standing by one of these surrounded, as she was, by an excited crowd: twenty or thirty people. There – she swept the valley with the glass – was a horse, three; several tall-wheeled carts; a little brown and white dog; children; a small flock of chickens scattering from an open cage; a girl in a chequered dress; an elephant —

'Goodness!'

She looked at the valley-foot, where the thin grass petered out amongst the shingle and the heaving sea returned untold quantities of water to the beck. There was no boat. Briefly, she scanned the sea for one. It would take a big boat to transport an elephant. Maybe they had thought Sowash uninhabited. Bewildered, she lowered the glass. Wireloom looked annoyed; shouldn't she be puzzled too?

'Illegals,' she said. 'Must be.'

'But Director, they have an elephant; there is no boat.'

Beside her, Gaby giggled and took her hand again.

'Elephants can swim,' she said, 'It says so in my natural history book.'

'Rubbish, girl! The sea's too cold,' Wireloom snapped.

'Elephants have thick hides. And Dr Semo's hands have been in the water. Feel them!' The girl hid her face in her sleeve. Her strings of crystal beads rattled, one against the other, as she laughed.

The Director and the Artistic Director vied with each other for words to describe the situation; they seemed unable to reach a decision. Gaby thought she would welcome visitors, illegal or not. Ang's hand, smooth and cold in hers, grew warm and sweaty.

His invariable and first reaction to a slip was to swear; but he had to do this out of Aurora's hearing since the mildest blasphemy brought prayers cascading from her big, red mouth. So he swore softly, under his breath; then he shouted for Cantor.

The older man had no such inhibitions.

'Bugger it,' he said. 'Where in creation have we fetched up?' His breath was stale and tobacco-laden. Loy turned aside and breathed clean salty air.

'In the North?'

'Back of the North Wind, I'll be bound. Brass monkey territory.' Cantor detached the black weed from his lips with a sucking sound and tapped ash down the neck of his vest. The garment was a convenient receptacle and his use of it prevented the women from complaining. In the van he shared with Shiny the acrobat and the general hand, Tash, he could scatter ash where he willed.

Both men looked about them: a new land, new customs, a fresh audience. Loy touched the great boulder which now blocked his way. A moment ago his view had been of a dusty brown road crossing a dry plain, man-cactus and mesas in the distance. The valley where the circus found itself was green and wet. A chill wind scoured it and in some obscured places where the sunlight could not reach were patches of ice and snow. His company gathered about him and complained of the cold. Peach shielded his body with his long, thin arms; Dork had jumped from the van where he had lingered over his change, still clad in Columbine's chequered dress; Vixen and Prenta had found shawls to keep out the wind and the same wind stirred Aurora's multi-coloured skirts. The dwarf, Florian, looked vulnerable, a miniature man lost amongst the monoliths, his usual bombast fled. Sierra – that intrepid adventurer and taster of men – stood slapping her thighs with the handle of her rat-whip. The fortune-teller, Alluleya, plain and brown as a mouse, sat calmly on the steps of her van. Like her, the children were never fazed: 2-Sweet led an assault on the highest boulder. Zoe, confronting the sea for the first time in her little life, held up her dress and watched the water flow and spread among the pebbles at her feet.

The bantams had escaped again.

An hour ago, they had been in an Ineiti market town, shabby Verzyon, giving an outdoor show; but their experience of travelling was too comprehensive for another anachronism to trouble them much.

Loy Sen stroked his long face and felt the film of grease which lingered where his white clown's face had been. For a moment, while he let the stark landscape possess him and his body absorbed the cold, his mind swung in time. The Biggest Circus in Alut, an old stone arena which the company had filled with colour and sound; the sodden forest of Lutreia, monthly trips from one community to another, wide rafts, birdsong, mighty trees, garlands of flowers; pretty women smiling in Archaen, and the long, white road. Where was that? Did it lead to the City or away? He could remember his audience with Sondrazan Nonpareil, her grey robes and behind her an unfinished picture full of shadows, the man it portrayed looming – interlocked planes of brown, black and olive. Only one of the hands was finished, the left, which held an apple carved from ivory. He felt he should know these ghosts, that there was some connection.

And then the brown horizon swung. Funny how empty the sky was. This rock: it must have been in its lonely place a long time. Cantor was hawking and spitting beside him, staining the tall rock with his phlegm.

'Let's get them sorted. We'll soon have visitors,' he said.

They had arrived in an empty landscape. Now, they were watched. A long stasis must accompany each transition, Loy thought; this was not the first time an audience had appeared on someone else's cue. Kind of the Lady to give them a gentle let-down.

What a picture they must present! Dork, his skirts blown high, had moved up to Bluebird's head and taken her reins. He hissed and gentled her. She was puffing slightly, disoriented. Flecks of foam on her neck: not good for a rosinback, rock-steady, trusted. . . Suddenly, the elephant trumpeted and the valley rang with echoes of her strident voice. Loy looked up, following Cantor's arm. On the steep hillside, the natives were approaching at a swift trot. They looked as motley a crew as his, small people and tall ones, a couple of hefty men —

If he got up on the flat rock, he would have the advantage; though he was not sure why he should feel threatened here in what must, in all his timeless world, be empty Noiro, the Land Beyond. He stepped lightly up on its lichened summit. His ragged dungarees flapped in the wind and the cold penetrated. Quite right, Cantor, quite right.

A gaunt woman led the welcoming party. The rest followed impatiently behind, holding themselves back. The big men were burly with it: soldiers? guards? They would expect words of explanation; an introduction to his troupe. With a shock he recognised the brown people, one woman, two men: Folk, the legendary race, mostly extinct. Genetic purity was an aberration to him: it meant inbreeding, restriction, repression, and these people were being bred, bred from, like racehorses, prize dogs and Temple Dancers.

Small, too.

The little red-cheeked woman spoke first, the one with the glittering beads. Loy felt reassured: the meeting of cultures would be straightforward; it was all plain sailing now. She spoke Nenian well.

'What beautiful coveralls!' she said, delight in her voice and face. She laughed, unable to contain her mirth, and her laughter spilled over her companions so that they, the solemn man and the rube, laughed with her. Beside them, the two Sineinian officials were silent, watching. The big men grinned.

Loy looked down at his patched dungarees. He had cut the patches from one of Morn's old dresses; there were five squares in different shades of pink, tacked like flags on the blue cloth. He decided to be honest while he lined the punters along. 'Alas,' he said, and wiped the quizzical expression from his face with one broad gesture of his eloquent hands. His mouth drooped. 'When I am dressed, I am Loy Sen. I am the White-Face Clown. Look around you, at the company: we are The Democratic Travelling Circus. Here is Sierra, the Rat Queen's Lieutenant; here, lovely Columbine.'

He clapped his hands. Dork pirouetted and they all gaped at the beautiful man/woman in his snow-white dress. The illusion took hold of them: they were not sure. The lovely girl blushed and hid her face in her skirts. Then Peach cartwheeled across the cold, hard ground.

'Here is Ahlikin.'

He never could get his tongue around the old Gaian word. Peach somersaulted; his lithe body never touched the ground. Then, just as he was about to swing into a one-handed stand himself, the fat woman interrupted his

86

patter. He continued anyway and heard her upside-down on his rocky dais. The smiling Folk were as compact as fighting dogs, their feet booted in soft, coloured plastics. One of the Sineinians had blue, rain-shadowed eyes and hid her gender beneath a padded coat and spotless white trousers. He thought her forthright stance hid uncertainty. Red Cheeks interested him almost as much, her delight at discovering a circus in her barren land still shining.

'Which boat put you ashore?' the gaunt official asked.

'Ah-um.' She was neither discomfited by the elevation the rock lent him, nor diverted by the curious sight of his inverted body. Never, ever before – always the magical manifestation had happened on a lonely road, a remote and empty highway far from settlements. Should he lie? Peach was jabbering in his City argot: 'Say we flew in; say the skimmers have gone.'

'Luxury submarine,' murmured Cantor and coughed, choking on cynicism and smoke.

But Loy Sen, once more squarely on his feet, bowed deeply to her and announced in solemn tones, 'I am afraid I am unable to explain our sudden appearance but we hope we did not interrupt your dinner.'

The blonde Sineinian laughed out loud, an alto guffaw which reminded him of the gelded men who used to sing a capella in the City malls, notes for bits, the tossed coins a silver pavement when they were on song. She had no need to beg. Still laughing, but softly now, she dug in one of her coat pockets and brought out a box of cigarettes, looked up at him as though she was about to seal that important bond, a first meeting, with the offer of a cigarette; then, turning from him, she huddled out of the wind and lit one for herself. With narrowed eyes she stared through his clowning at his embarrassment. His interlocutor beckoned to her and the three Sineinian women whispered like children together.

He watched them discuss him. How could they know how little control they had over him, though he was a trespasser in their colony? If they chose to imprison him – or any of his people – sooner or later he would walk free – and find himself in some other stark or leafy land with new hours before him. The lock-up in Besemy for example, vile and stinking, old straw on the floor and an electronic print on the door: on the second night he had felt the familiar touch, the real/unreal sensation of hands on his head, and moments later walked out into the velvet lands above Diold where the circus awaited him. . .

Loy sat down on his rock and confined his anxiety to thoughts about cold and the elephant, the unrelenting patches of snow and the thinness of Zoe's ragged dresses.

Bren held the strap of Ang Semo's camera bag as if it were a tether to reality and watched the gaudy newcomers closely. They looked and smelled like himself, human, and their clothes were worn and unsuitable for the cold; they had come so quickly and inexplicably into empty Toul that he felt they must possess a great secret, some mystery they had come to share. The raw colours of their unfamiliar garments lit up the valley and he saw how delicate and subtle were the colours of the north. Bren felt no awe but disquiet began to seep, filling him up and taking him over. Thought-ache, ayenbite: more people meant more change and he would welcome that, yet– he had always wondered how the spirits moved, transcending air, light, water and solid earth; during the long sermons in chapel he tested the stuffy atmosphere for signs of the spirit dance, remembering tales as if they were reality and wishing to sing and dance himself. Oom, oof, heyaa, his heart sang then; and his toes skipped inside his boots.

The brown-faced man who had called himself White-Face stood up. The wind blew straight through his blue garment and his face looked pinched. The man tucked his hands into his armpits, Gaby claimed Ang Semo's bag, and they all walked away from him up the hill. They marched in order of importance. He was left behind to continue the talking, with Atluki and the two ferryhands to back him up.

The old man in the dirty vest spoke suddenly to him.

'How'd you like to see the elephant, chum? Bet you've nothing like her in this two-bit place – no offence, chummie.'

'In the sea,' said Bren, searching his reluctant mind for words the man would understand, 'Is the big legless beast.'

'Whale? Ah, but he doesn't come ashore; can't do tricks, can he?'

The elephant stood patiently where she found herself, only her long trunk and its sensitive, flexible, tip moving, testing the salty rocks.

She knows, thought Bren, more than this man.

'I see she has great wisdom,' he said.

He looked back, at the hill on whose uneven surface the walkers mounted up, Ang Semo white, the clown a spider beside her. Gaby had caught up. He could see her trudging beside them, her shoulder pulled down by her burden; he could imagine her quizzical expression. Above them, the sky had deepened, an aerial sea of indigo with a shoal of birds beating through it. They had long necks and their yellow feet hung down; the breadth and the rhythmical beat of their wings told him what they were, singing swans, and a moment later they spiralled, sighting Brightlink on Wirra, and he heard them call down the clear air.

Ang Semo heard the swans sing. Their voices hung, a crystal diapason, against the deep blue sky.

Beside her, the man started and looked up. 'Music!', he said, 'Those birds? Where, exactly, am I?'

'Guna's Pearls, the Amber Necklace, the Glass Illusion'' and, when he shook his head, 'the Land Beyond,' she said.

Float Gaby had heard enough:

'This is Sowash in Noiro,' she said flatly. 'You people from the south say it lies beyond civilisation – beyond life, at the back of the north wind; but we Folk know it is the centre of everything.'

Loy sat on a grey chair in a chaste grey room and waited for Dr Wireloom. On the wall in front of him a grey and white seascape without a frame gave him a prospect of receding perspectives, wave after wave after wave. An hour ago a secretary had brought him coffee and told him the Director would soon be finished.

He would have preferred a beer, something with a gentle

kick; he would have liked to taste again, just once for old times' sake, a mouthful of sweet rahi, neat and unwatered, so aromatically vaporous it burned the mouth and stuck around the teeth and tongue for a long time after, with its taste of anise and long ago. The clock on the wall told him it was eleven at night in Noiro. Did these little people and their masters never rest?

On the way in, he had passed a flock of them, as ragamuffin with their pastel overalls, bead necklaces, and unkempt hair as his people. They were misplaced too, their identities on the move; but perhaps the authorities encouraged this bizarre blending of two cultures. Somewhere in his past or future he had read a newsheet story about the rehabilitation unit of Traumesse; and the blonde had told him, her hurried sentences short bursts of eloquence between drags on her cigarette, how endangered were the little folk. He had stared intently at her because that was how she looked at him, her eyes with their cold sea colours asking questions; wide, as if she had never seen a man before. Yet she wasn't altogether attractive. Dork was prettier. She made him feel uneasy.

Red Cheeks now, called Float and Gaby, knew what he was. She was not afraid: life bubbled. She had hurried to catch up with him, the alien, and the blonde official and, after her matter-of-fact definition of his cold and windy destination, had been introduced with a trace of Sineinian condescension as a bright star – but of what? The nomadic life of the Fishfolk had been destroyed long ago and here they were, the last original people of Noiro: cheap labour buried beneath the ground with their helpful employers. How could they live without the sky?

Nothing in the room but himself, four chairs, an empty coffee cup on an empty table. The picture rolled its water through time in perpetual stillness.

He studied the idents he carried. On his left wrist was the indelible tear-mark which made him forever a citizen of the Sacred City and a Clown. He had made the tear his own, no longer a caste mark and reminder of City ways, and three black teardrops oozed from the corners of the painted eyes of Loy Sen, the white-face clown. He also had a pass from the early days of the Revolution and a warrant which had once allowed him and the troupe to pass unhindered through Ineit. Then there was the Sineinian voice scan, the paper which the brisk woman in Diold had signed, the little metal disc with the diestamp from Sy, tokens of times future and past as irrelevant and inconvenient as the varied currency the circus earned. For, travelling unconventionally as it did, he must always take care to convert the moneys into untraceable goods, or gold.

Who am I? he thought. Landless, homeless Loy Sen carrying his preposterous baggage of one circus fully equipped with tent, performers, horses, dogs, rats and elephant, around the land beyond time. Who am I, missing person or fatality, once upon a time Loy Sen, once the cousin of the fabulous and dead acrobat Amita, once Charis's man, still Zoe's father? Who is this fool in greasepaint and spangled costume? Who here will laugh at me?

He saw the round red cheeks of Float Gaby and smiled. She, too, made laughter, a natural comic, someone who could love. Already, he felt, he knew her well and she would laugh with him, an audience of one. Let the show go on!

The certain fact that they had no ship was the crux. He supposed that some kind of scanner or wing, some airborne machine of this time was searching for it and failing.

Submarine, like Cantor's feeble joke, undersea beneath the predictable tide: that would be the place, under the waves which would once and for all conceal them and obliterate the memories of their sudden entrances and spectacular exits. A home beneath the sea, a ship of bright steel which would carry and hold them all. How would they live then? By fishing from the crystal windows, by dangling bait before the luminous fish of the abyss, by hunting the lost mountains and chasms... they would have to learn to breathe again, to exist in a world where oxygen was one dissolved part of the liquid, ambient, wave.

A woman entered the room and broke his reverie. He blinked and adjusted the focus of his thoughts. It was the uneasy one, the blue-eyed smoker. She strode into the small grey room, her body stiff with anxiety and the door closed behind her, disembodied brown fingers on its rim. The long wait was over: the Sineinians had decided what to do with them. Agitation pushed him to his feet and formed the abrupt sentence he spoke.

'Where's Dr Wireloom?'

'Still in conference, I'm afraid. But she has made her decision. I can give you that.'

'Haa. . .' He sat down, and felt the overblown bladder of his expectancy deflate.

'Smoke?'

While he declined she opened her box with stained and fumbling fingers, greedy for the drug. Her lighter was a small gold cylinder, no different from those he remembered – somewhere. She held her smoke firmly in the v between the two first fingers of her right hand; sat down, easy now and confident.

'It has been a long wait,' she said. 'For you.'

The afterthought felt like kindness.

'Longer for the others down at the beach,' he said, seeing them toiling to set up in the cold.

'We sent some personnel down with coats.'

In this warm grave, she had shed her bulky coat; her jacket was black as winter and glazed like a carapace. The fabric gleamed dully against the regimented greys of the room. On one lapel was a silver badge or brooch, a metal ribbon intricately folded. She had tidied her hair and wore fresh paint; she smelled of ambergris and cultivated flowers, of smoke. She did not know how to provoke him with the paper cylinder which smouldered between her fingers and used it as a prop to support her authority. He stared at her, trying to make out the honest shapes of hips and breasts under the stiff suiting. He was baffled by his body's responses; lust asserted itself when he should be cool. He smiled uncertainly. He was slipping again, gawping at this Noiran official; brainless like his gaudy brothers, the augustes. He wanted to postpone the awful admission, make each moment last after the hours of boredom; savour the unknowing.

'Thanks, anyway,' he said.

'Speak any Noiran?'

'I'm afraid – no,' he decided and made it sound like a firm reply. Did he? He frowned and remembered that the answer was truly no. To this country, he had never been.

'Maybe you'll have to learn it. There are several dialects: takes time.'

But we won't be staying long. We shall – but no: let her and the moment speak.

'The Director says you and your people are to stay in the valley at Toul – where we found you – pending enquiries and a report. You are to be made comfortable and you may carry on with your show – with whatever it is you do. Dr Wireloom assumes it is an entertainment similar to the animal cabarets of Ros. She thinks it will provide an outlet for our spring fever. And what does that elephant eat?'

She laughed at his reply: two tons a week of fruit and vegetables, and fifty pounds of hay each day 'I think we can accomodate it,' she said, 'Especially now that the ferries are running.'

He was grateful. The sentiment nearly overwhelmed him. Another friendly gesture from this challenging woman and real tears would have flowed. He let himself relax a little but did not forget to thank her and the absent administration.

She had more.

'I persuaded them to let you stay,' she said, offering him the sentence and the deed.

He was very tired. He could feel sleep pawing at him and rumpling his clothes; he yawned and, smiling at the woman, ignored her gift.

'What's your name?'

'Ang Semo. I come from Sollar Kein.'

'Thanks then, Madam Semo. I have to sleep, or get some air — '

'Dr.' Stiff as her suit. 'It's dark outside now – we'll escort you back when the time comes. I have to take your name and details.'

'Loy Sen. Loy. You must've seen it on the vans when you were down at the beach.'

'Yes. "The Democratic Travelling Circus. Proprietors, the Artistes. Artistic Director, Loy Sen", all beautifully lettered in three languages.'

'We like to be prepared.'

'I'm Artistic Director here,' she announced and roused him again, made him stare and sit up in his hard chair: she was the freak. The tumbled hair of Crinon M'una escaping from its plait as she worked at her clown paintings, the obscene figures on the wooden walls of the Shack, Shiron's chivs like sunbeams cutting the air – that was Art, the past, the City.

'You?' What art could live in this stifling plastic tomb?

'"Greed" is my chief public work – the construct saga, the ultimate soap opera.'

This time his gaze must have beeen a real blank.

'Computer Art. Advanced Graphics. Fractal Painting —'

'I used to know some painters,' he offered, 'Lock and na Faraja – they were desperately poor.'

She had spread a form out on the table. She began to bully and insist.

'You will have to satisfy mainland Immigration Control. We can't find your ship.'

He smiled his sad clown's smile. 'No ship,' he said, 'That's right. There is no ship.'

'Come, come, Mr Sen. You can't have came by air. You would have been spotted. How did you come?'

He cleared his throat. He felt he should stand up before he spoke, stand up and gesture like a conjuror, open a box of endless ribbons or bring forth the ubiquitous white dove from some concealed place about his compact and supple person.

'I told you,' he said. 'We came by courtesy of Time herself, across the years without a ship or starship. By our Lady – by magic, if you like.'

'Do you mean you come from somewhere else in the galaxy?'

'Not so far. Our last landfall was Ineit. A little place full of dust and sunbeams called Verzyon. Year was 3,099, Alcuon. We gave the townsfolk a show.'

She tapped ash from her cigarette into the empty coffee cup; some, which missed the receptacle, fell on the floor, and she tutted and rubbed at it with the toe of her shoe.

'I think I should warn you, Mr Sen, that there is a lunatic asylum on Salmo – it's minutes away by skimmer. If you've got any sense, you'll answer all these questions correctly. Immigration doesn't like jokers.'

When he had gone, lithe as an otter beside the uniformed guard who was to take him back to Toul, Ang sighed. She folded the form and carried it away with her, home to her unit, that familiar den which was her haven from the breathtaking lie of her existence. She poured liquor into a glass, a good measure. Here were more lies which her secretary would databank tomorrow. She squinted at her stylish hand and pulled down the lamp. The pool of light shone relentlessly on the page like a police lamp. In the box headed Class she had been forced to write 'uncertain': his lifestyle fitted none of the predefined categories, based as they were on thirty-year-old parameters. There was no niche here for a male artistic director. Status: Clown. She had read about itinerant performers, seen a few – a conjuror bemusing the shoppers in Sollar, jugglers in Ros and Roakn's markets. Their fecklessness was legendary. If she could not make sense of the clown's story, she would have failed him.

He was neither lame nor stupid: he did not need her. And Gaby, despite her friendliness that afternoon, and their doubled concern for the dead owl, did not need her either. Being accorded the role of mentor burdened her. The thought that it was she, Dr Ang Semo DCA MCSy SCS, who needed them made her reach for her cigarettes. She read the clown's biography and found the shadow of his long face with its high cheekbones and dark and knowing eyes behind each charmed word.

When she had made up her mind, she would not deviate from her conclusions – about both of them, clown and Fisher woman. It took four days.

Ang watered the cacti she had brought from Sinein. So far from daylight, so far from home and springtime, they looked sick and had not put on any new growth this year; she cleaned her cameras and repacked the bags they travelled in, to be ready when her time came. The dry compost around the cactus roots had sucked the moisture up, greedily; and she was greedy for refreshment. The air-conditioning and the heat of Traumesse dried her skin: immersed in salt water, it would become pliant again and she would find a temporary freedom in that fluid medium where like an otter she could roll and dive, where like a seal she could fly. Her mind darted at the problem of the circus and the challenge of the Folk. If she believed the clown, then life *was* inexplicable and she could hide no longer; if Gaby was her friend, the barricades were crumbling: not only she, but Traumesse must change. Oh, Lalla, she prayed, What should I do for the best? And, Should I call her on the satellite link, or even write a letter?

Nanket whispered to her terminal, her soft voice giving the clown's bizarre statements a spurious authenticity. For an hour, the voices of the two women wove a skein of sound in the office; afterwards, they sat together at one station and laughed at the machine's responses. It had great difficulty in locating Verzyon where Loy had given his last show but at length came up with discomfiting words: Verzyon, former regional capital, Auter Terrain, pop.10. When it accessed the birth registers in the Sacred City Ang screamed shrilly at her astonished secretary:

'5 Bey in Udan – that's Fall, Matoq here – 4489, 44 eight nine!'

'It's probably a different man,' said Nanket coolly.

The entry fitted his facts: there were Uncle Mel and all the cousins, including the acrobat Amita who had killed herself for love so long ago. Why should he have freely given her so much detail unless he remembered them all?

'Ask him what system he accessed,' said the practical Nanket.

But the machine could not find his dead wife. It knew nothing about his daughter; in its auxiliaries and satellites she did not exist and neither did the old man, Cantor, nor the midget, Florian.

Where had they come from? She thought of prisons and spare-part mortuaries, of cryo-surgeons grafting corpse-skin, and she felt the dead fingers of Grandgrand Pike touch her.

She shivered. She had a report to file.

Float Gaby, she remembered, was about to marry her brother-in-law – who had fathered three children before his wife died. Pak was Needle Cait's cousin – it was impossible for the Folk to learn or practise privacy.

Glosit, they called the custom. Eda Voran had written a paper on it, discussed and examined it in full. The primitive practice disgusted Ang. Soon, the bloated organ which had penetrated one sister would push its way into the next to perform the same loathsome office at the centre of her being. Gaby had invited her to the wedding.

They did this willingly, the Fishfolk, passing spouses one to another as readily as cups of coffee. It was their custom, insurance once against death and the cold and meant the dead could bear children. It made record-keeping difficult, but it seemed to encourage breeding and, of course, it spread the genes around. The Folk matrons knew exactly who fathered their children and genetic fingerprinting only proved them right.

She had drawn her legs together and closed tight her eyes and her mouth; all the gates of her body were shut. Nanket, the good secretary, waited for her next instruction.

If she gave Gaby a better job it might compensate her for the dreadful violation of her integrity.

'He's a good man,' she had confided, 'Although he smells like a dead devil fish.' Her laughter bubbled over. 'I'll get used to him: he's a good man.'

For these and other reasons, her own thirst for a child would never be assuaged. No one knew of her infirmity but herself, Tobin, and Pior who was free of her because he was dead. She and Tobin were permanently linked by their intimate, unarticulated knowledge, their guilty consciences separated only by distance.

The raw smell of men alarmed her. The primeval odour coming from the body of Loy Sen, the clown, had made her stiff, awkward when she would unbend. It was not the clown's body, not that obvious decoy but the glamour, the mystery, which surrounded him, and all the circus people that drew and mesmerised her. Vair were said to entrance their prey by dancing and acrobatics, narrow bodies tumbling across the fresh summer grass. A clown who was not; no oaf but a man of integrity and intelligence, his humour and exuberance bitterly learned: a professional loon. His neat body had attracted her as a coloured still might; he was Jannl in the flesh – almost, for Jannl's proportions were perfect, the equations which made him derived from the finest of fine art. Loy Sen was born of woman. She groped after the common denominator.

Ten, thirteen, twenty-one, twenty-five, twenty-eight; signposts in her life, these were her marker years, all marred by experiences with men. She had seen her father naked and, three years afterwards before the memory had been submerged, her brother: their embarrassment had been like shame. The medics swam in the lake and shouted for her to join them. Tobin and Pior sought her out. The men she had refused to love were as distant as ghosts and she would never know this newcomer, Loy, because she could not accept what he was: a man.

She began to compose her invitation to Gaby, its tempting phrases ephemera in her head, winged messages of consolation which she could never write down.

The offer, when Nanket had finished rephrasing according it to Folk custom and the Ethic, was formal, stiff as her own suits and body. She consigned it to the network for transmission, sat up straight and began to voice her report. So be it: he had not lied. Next day, they were all going to the circus. They should exhibit her there, the woman who would, and could not.

The ice, whose patterns had been as various as the landscape, ridged and peaked upon the sea, traceries on rock inland, was melted. Except in herself, the thaw had passed. The wind had a new voice, warmer, persuasive, for the daylight season; if it gusted at all, it was but to remind them of the harsh seasons: hunt now, and gather, before night comes. It was the same, the north wind, but the Folk called it Annasi, the Summer Visitor. The ice deer gave birth amongst Hairete's flowers and, in the valleys of Sowash, tussock mice built their nests amongst the brood courts of the vair. The wind sighed over them.

This was how the circus had come, softly, to fill the imaginations and hearts of the Folk. One minute it was not there, the next it was, illuminating the grey hollow at Toul with its gaudy colour, its strange animals and perdue people.

Hands were diverted from the ferries to build a fence. A strand of low-voltage wire would have been enough, but they erected metal posts and began to stretch wire panels between them. They worked hard to enclose the phenomenon and, a new instruction relayed, abandoned the job before it was finished. Some people said the tough ferryhands could not bear being laughed at. The wire nets sagged.

The red and gold circus tent lay across the valley head like a sail blown ashore, a beautiful wing sheltering its secrets beneath it. Everyone had seen the elephant through the scopes of the Viewdome; everyone wanted to stand beside her monstrous legs, look up into her face and wonder. The horses wheeled about the boulders; sometimes the tiny figure of a clown was seen, running from van to tent in a frenzy of preparation. Other tents began to mushroom beside the gorgeous striped nautilus of the big top. Lights were seen to dance at night and people out walking the Perimeter heard the thin and faraway song of a fiddle.

It began. Gaby clutched her programme tight and forgot about the hard seat. The gold-starred lucky number on the programme burned its way into her heart and her pulse throbbed out her fortune, 022, 022.

It began with a fanfare, high notes cracking, and the crescendo was a raucous squawk, but it did not matter. She had never heard such music, raw, immediate, live: she had never heard anything like it.

The blue edging of the ring below her was masked by two galloping animals, a thunderous passage of hooves which tossed the mingled smells of sweat and shit up to her. Two horses circled there, all the animals and legs its small circumference would hold. No one instructed them, nor cracked a whip: they galloped free and their long manes tossed. She knew now why Ang sometimes called the running waves white horses; and one horse was white, a great beast with a back as flat as a tabletop. The other was spotted and delighted her. He seemed to smile and the spots on his forequarters were white on black, but on his broad rear end they reversed their random pattern and became black on white. His tail was pied and tied up with a big red bow; a smaller bow of the same flaming scarlet ribbon nodded in the hair between his pricked-up ears.

Suddenly the ring was full of tiny figures which made her feel like a giant and she stared down at them from the third tier, hypnotised. Were they children or adults? They wore strange clothes, jackets that were too big for them, tiny tight shirts and ridiculous hats. They were not frightened of the horses and ran boldly in and out between the racing legs. Now, two were swinging up to the white one's back, using her mane as a rope to gain the slippery plateau of her back; a third ran after the spotted horse, grabbed his tail and, zipzing, was aloft. She realised that the clowns were only three in number; their speed had made them seem a crowd.

Ai! Her own voice joined others. The third clown had fallen suddenly to the ground, and lay stone still. There was utter silence in the audience. She heard the horses breathing as they came to a halt and the other little people were on the ground, bending over their comrade.

Not until a dwarf dressed like a physician ran in and wielded an enormous cardboard knife, did she realise that the fall was part of the act. Bren's raucous laughter almost made her cry. There could have been a dreadful accident. She looked at Pak and her nieces and was relieved to see that they laughed too.

The clowns were pouring water on their fallen companion, dirty brown water from a flower vase which had somehow appeared. The victim struggled and, while they seemed to help him, they only held him down. The physician started to cut off his clothing with her flapping knife. The blur of antics and colour got to Gaby: she laughed and, hearing her own crow rise above the noise of the crowd, was infected by her own merriment, and could not stop. Around her the Fishfolk, hearing their own clown, doubled up.

This was circus, this clumsy and imperfect entertainment, conjured magic in a cold tent, humans and animals the entertainers who, between them, held on to time and wrested joy from its swift and cruel passage, turned the canvas-covered ground within their magic circle into pure gold.

The drum rolled, tarrrum! Someone needed to be kept in order because a man as big as a stinkbear carried in a huge whip. All at once, the child on the ground (for such he was, his head too big and his limbs too delicate for adulthood or dwarfishness) leapt up and left the soaked and dirty chrysalis of his discarded clothing on the ground behind him. He was clad in light, or so it seemed: the mirrors on his close-fitting suit reflected every lamp in the the tent. A tall hat appeared in his hand and he put it on. He took the mighty whip in one small hand and cracked it with so loud a report that the clowns and horses took fright and ran away, pitching and tumbling in a confusion of limbs and tails, to hide behind the torn blue curtain beside the ring. A thin, clear voice rang out. It spoke her own language.

'Do you know what I am going to tell you now?'

'No,' truthfully answered Gaby and the rest of the audience.

'Nor do I,' said the child. 'But perhaps you know what I am going to tell you now?'

Several replied, and the rest quickly imitated them: they would not be caught out again.

'Yes!' they yelled.

'Then I don't need to tell you,' said the child, cracked his whip and turned his back on them. He whistled two bars of a plaintive tune into the hush, and turned back. 'Do you know what I am going to tell you this very minute?'

Confusion seized his hearers, and some·said 'No,' while others boldly shouted 'Yes!'

'Good for you,' the vexatious child cried, 'because the ones who do know can tell the ones who don't.'

He let them laugh a little before he cracked his whip again.

'I expect that all you little Fishfolk are frightened of elephants,' the imp taunted, 'So we won't have to disturb Garissa today. Are you frightened?'

This time, they knew the answer pat, and 'No!' they roared in unison.

'All right then, I'll call her. Sure you're not frightened?'

The animal was mighty like a whale and like a beached malpog, massive. She moved deliberately, slowly: you could see what terror she would inspire if she chose to run. In front of her wide face, in which the eyes were alert, hung the long tube which was her nose and hands. It moved delicately in time with her stately walk. The wrinkled hide of her legs and belly was black like the soil of the land where she had been born, but the remainder of her body was a whirling galaxy of colour, intricately patterned like the treasure at the bottom of a kaleidoscope and her tusks, smooth and straight unlike the spiral horn of the narwhal they had seen last year, off Wirra, were tipped with knobbed bosses of gold. Upon the crown of her head sat another child, a girl dressed like her fellow in mirrored silver. A star floated in the air, a foot above her golden hair.

She made the elephant kneel down, lightly touching her head with one dainty hand, and ran down the side of her face as if it were a wooden ladder. The animal reared, awkward upon hind legs which had become unstable pillars – but the child was safe beside the other, the boy with the whip. One insignificant gesture with that whip, and the elephant stood once more upon four legs. The boy reached under her trunk to slip a reward into her mouth.

Gaby relaxed again, leaned into the hard wood of her seat and glanced behind her, looking for the percipient face of Ang Semo, hoping to find comfort in it and approval, confirmation that they were all, audience and performers, quite safe and really seated here in a tent in the sparse valley of Toul by Traumesse. But Ang was nowhere to be seen.

The elephant picked the child up in her trunk, coiling it around her slender body, lifting her high in the air; she shovelled her up with her tusks to lie still as a corpse across the two ivory scimitars; at last, the elephant set the child on the trampled cloth and the child lay down and stretched her elfin body across the canvas folds. With infinite care, and all the patience in the world, the big animal lowered the flat plate of her right forefoot until it rested on the child's golden head. The captive star still gleamed, close by the fragile skull, the black skin and horny toes.

No one dared clap, lest the elephant should be alarmed and crush the eggshell beneath her foot; wild applause came later, when both children were safely mounted on the elephant and leaving the ring to vanish like a half-remembered dream behind the tattered curtain.

Strange new music filled the tented auditorium with thin and foreign sounds. There was no sign of the lone and lonely player; the blue curtain hid all but the forlorn notes which spun from his fiddle and plucked at the sleeves and the hearts of his hearers.

When the music ceased, everyone was ready for relief; this time it did not hurry in with anarchy and noise.

The white-face clown, Loy Sen, walked slowly into the ring, his slender arms and hands poised before him as though he brought his audience gifts. Coloured balls flew upwards from those dexterous hands, dazzling spheres continually in flight. It was impossible to count them: every colour of the rainbow, they rose and fell, and at last they all flew one way, a folding fan of colour, and the clown caught them and was still. The painted tears ran down his face, and he bowed.

He, too, wore a suit of many colours, a tight skin of spangle and shine and on his feet were soft shoes as white as his face. His head was covered, the black hair hidden under a black cap, a second skin covering his skull. He tossed the prismatic balls high in the air, one following another, caught them and threw them in a cascade from the ring.

Now, he was an acrobat, balanced on one steady hand, as

easy upside down as on two feet. He reached into the neck of his glittering garment and pulled out a mirror, studied his face in it for a long moment, and stood up. He held the mirror behind him, craning his neck, held it before him, still plaintive, still full of grief, for he could never be rid of melancholy, painted as it was upon his face. He stretched his red lips and tried to make them smile; he tried to make himself laugh, tripping and tumbling, walking on his hands and turning somersaults. Thoughtfully, he lifted both arms high, gave his supple body a shake and was upside down again, balanced on both hands and bent in an arc as pliant as the thin trunk of a wind-cut birch; and still his body bent until it found its feet and was turning, turning in the air as fast as a whirlpool while the applause rang out.

The clown bowed, his body hanging motionless from the waist, the movement of his chest the only sign of his recent whirligig motion; and while he caught his breath and the audience clapped, a child got up from her seat in the front row and ran into the ring. She carried a rose in one hand, a rose which was red as blood against her short, white dress, and she gave it to the clown who knelt and held his head on one side, so that she could kiss him. Then he picked her up and hugged and kissed her and the raucous music blared while he carried her from the ring.

Tears, Gaby supposed, had come into everyone's eyes, echoing the long black teardrops upon the cheeks of the white-face clown. She understood the message of the circus and the clown. It was love. She looked round and there was Ang Semo, right behind her, face in hands and elbows on knees, craning forward as if she could never see enough of Loy Sen, her firm Nenian features contorted and sad.

She remembered the rest of that first performance as a climactic blur, the penultimate excitement the interval, through which Fenner strove with a cloud of sugar cotton, capturing wisps of it to stuff precipitately into her hungry mouth; her nieces were impatient; Ial, Pak and Cait chattered, anticipating the show, and Bren was silent like herself, stunned with the colour and inspired movement he had seen. The chance delight which completed her happiness that night was the appearance below of the diminutive ringmaster shouting out her number, 022: her lucky programme had won the prize. So, with a smile from fortune, her assignation with the magic-makers had been made and she would return next day to take tea with them. Surely the conversation would be as mad and lively as the jokes which were told in that last, whirling, comical Act?

'When you tell lies, tell big ones. Lies, kisses and steaks must be big.'

'Hush!' the dwarf told Loy Sen, 'You cry when you catch sight of yourself in the mirror: I've got to look at you all day.'

'Where can I buy a cap for my knee? A key for this lock of hair? Who is walking across the bridge of my nose? Have you got a grindstone? I need to sharpen my shoulder blades.'

'So you laughed when I stumbled?'

'Come here and sit in the shade of the palm of my hand —'

And into the ring ran a girl in a chequered dress. She carried a bunch of flowers and was quite clearly lost – and much too tall to sit in the shade of the palm of the dwarf's hand. She had run away, she cried a lot, she danced and could turn somersaults and cartwheels like the rest of them; she could pirouette on one toe, turning as slowly and as gracefully as a clockwork doll. Her lover was the acrobat with the red mask and the lath; her father, who ran on in a long coat with his hair on end and a candlestick in his hand, was cruel.

'So you want to get married?' said the dwarf; and they played their play, which was farce and knockabout with words in a foreign language and visual jokes anyone could understand. The girl danced, white and graceful as a gull; her lover made rude gestures with his slapstick, hit the clowns with it and stole gold from her father whose continual rage was a sight to see.

At the end, after theft, tomfoolery and murder, the play was played out. The lovers kissed and the white and the spotted horses circled, their riders, a woman in a rainbow dress and the silver child, poised on tiptoe on their backs; a man flew in the roof of the tent, catching his falling body on a narrow suspended bar, turning and tumbling through the air so that they all held their breath in case he should fall. The small clowns came on again and the spotted horse and the patterned elephant, Harlequin and Columbine and Pantaloon, and the musicians marching and playing their trumpets, drums, flutes and gongs. Then – at last – Loy Sen returned, his sad white face for an instant splitting in a grin when he felt the acclaim; and the performers were clapping the audience without which there could be no performance.

It had ended. Gaby bowed her head to clear a space in her senses and saw the bare ground beneath the scaffolding which supported the seats, sweetpapers and candyfloss sticks littering it, the coarse tussock-grasses crushed into the salty earth, brute tokens of the circus's ephemeral hold upon the enduring north.

Cait nagged her; Fenner too, querulous in frustrated curiosity.

'What is a tea party?'

'Dry,' said Bren, his voice brittle.

They drank tea in the City, that was all she knew, a thin and bitter brew of hot water and herbs. She supposed it gave them the courage to ride horses and swing from narrow bars of wood, the same sort of recklessness that she had seen Bren, Pak and Ial display after a liquor party.

'He'll be along in a minute, dear,' said the fat woman in the booth by the abandoned fence. 'He's just stepped over to Sierra's to see about provisioning the Rat.'

Gaby waited, agog. The rain fell sweetly, brightening the shy greens of Toul, sleeking down the thick tangle of her untidy hair. She smelled the strong spice of elephant dung and reached inside her coat to touch her crystal beads. The fat woman peered out of the booth.

'Step inside, my love. You'll get wet.'

Inside, neat piles of coins made rows upon a table: the Sineinian decads the Folk had been given to pay for their tickets. Beyond the boulders and the gravel the magic

106

tent was moored against the valley-side, sea-smell and mist drifted in through the doorway and mingled with the woman's cloying scent. Something hairy lay across her shoulders and coiled about about her thick neck; a head and bushy tail hung down over her silky dress and the padded coat the Sineinians had given her.

'What's that?'

''s my fennec fox – poor thing, he's going bald.'

'Poor thing!'

'He ain't alive, my dearie – died long ago. Stroke him: see his big ears and his sweet little teeth and his glass eyes? He keeps me warm— 'Like some caley?'

She proffered a crumpled paper bag. It contained sugar crystals like bits of yellow glass, edible gems which lay in dense confusion like the beads. They were difficult to grasp, and the woman tilted the bag, so that a glittering stream ran into Gaby's outstretched hand.

'They're my last,' said the woman sadly and Gaby saw the soaked and forlorn valley through her eyes, who was used to foreign suns and thick vegetation; whose thin silks did not keep out the cold.

'Thank you,' she said and, 'Never mind', thinking while she ate the sugar of the perpetual and clinging warmth inside Traumesse and of the transparent stars and hearts full of candy which they sold in Floraliy.

The woman laid her piles of coins down in a grooved tray, picked up another tray, or frame, which was strung with wire and beads and began rapidly to flick them left and right while Gaby, taking her in, looked at the limp fox nestling against white fat and greasy curls, at bright lipstick and brass earrings set with big blue stones. On the woman's left wrist was a tattoo: a stiff little mannikin which seemed to bow and dance as her fingers flew.

Loy Sen was walking towards the booth. Today, his usual colours were reversed and he wore pink dungarees patched at the knees with sky blue stuff. His gift-coat flapped. He wore nothing else and she could see that his body underneath was strong and fatless. A grubby cloth hung out of one pocket and on his dark head a broken straw hat, to shield him from bright sunlight, keep off the rain. His tears had been wiped away with his greasepaint but there were faint furrows in the brown skin of his face, which was long, sad and suffering. Yet he whistled as he came, unknown melodies. He noticed her, remembered her: she saw his expression alter instantaneously and become one of welcome. His rare smile shone.

She held out her precious talisman, the lucky programme.

'Did you feed the rat?' she said.

'Not yet.' He did not smile again but a flicker of amusement animated his face. 'Vixen?' he said, and the fat woman nodded and clicked the beads on the frame in a last, rapid tango.

'Four hundred clear!' she cried, 'Whatever shall we do with it?'

'Give it back to them in exchange for Garissa's feed,' the clown said sadly, then, 'Come on Gaby,' as if she were an old friend. 'What do you want to see most?'

She swallowed, she wiped her sticky mouth with the back of her hand, in the first act keeping back the rush of love and good humour which rose in her and in the second acutely conscious of her appearance, rained-on and sugary. She let out a helping of friendship. 'The horse,' she replied 'The spotted horse.'

'Old Spooky? Sure? Right then. He's over there, in the shelter.'

Her smile escaped then and broke upon her flat face in successive waves of delight, so that the clown was not deceived.

In the shelter, where the air had the warmth and motion of a fine summer's day, they stood between the elephant and the horse.

'I lose sleep over her,' said Loy. 'She eats so much.'

Garissa looked bigger than ever for she stood in straw on a wooden platform to keep her from the cold and wet. Her tough black hide was a hilly and furrowed map; contour lines marked her limbs and valleys meandered across her vastness: she had been born old and creased. You would have to scrub her with a stiff broom to get her clean, and such a scrubbing had taken away the summertime tide of flowers and whorls which had adorned her in the ring.

'That's really her,' said Gaby. 'A land-whale, not that painted lady I saw. He looks painted now.'

The horse snickered, laughing at her. His eyes were huge and moist, dark brown mirrors. He shook his head, let the shake travel along his body until his spotted skin undulated. He puffed and blew, sending wisps of the hay he held in his mouth out to spiral in the air and fall. The red ribbon was a gay token in the magpie whisk of his tail.

'He's still wearing his party clothes.'

'Just the ribbon,' said the clown 'It's his Mark, like my teardrop – see?' He pulled back the sleeve of his coat and showed her how the City matriarchs had written his destiny on his left arm. 'Spooky kicks,' he said. 'The ribbon's a warning.'

'What if you don't know the language?'

'Doesn't red mean danger everywhere? Gash snakes, the For Hire lights in the Quarter, spilt blood, Temple dancers that eat men – there are red signs and switches on the stairs and walkways in your underground city.'

'It means love, too,' said Gaby, and the clown stared at her.

Now that she had seen the horse, she wanted nothing more than to sit upon his back, higher than the top of Loy Sen's head but still weak and lowly beside the great elephant.

'Could I —' she began, although there was no need; the clown had anticipated her and was himself beginning to speak, while he gently touched her back and guided her to the correct place, on the horse's left.

'We got him in Alut,' he said. 'He was pulling a coal-cart and all his white hair was black; but Tash had seen how broad he was and how strong. . .'

He had elevated her, with a lift and a push, and a shove to her left leg: she was up, aloft, mounted on the horse; riding Spooky, whose ears flicked back to hear Loy's voice and went forward again, pricked up with the expectation of exercise.

'Hold his mane.'

The hair was coarse and long, wiry to touch like sea-worn rope. She looked down through the broken hat on the black top of Loy Sen's head. He had undone the horse's tether, to lead him; the tight turning circle unbalanced her and she was glad to be anchored by the strong mane.

'Sit up,' he said. 'Speak to him.'

When she said his name, Spooky woke. He had been plodding, ears up, awaiting her call. He gathered himself and stepped out, beating the hard valley floor beneath the canvas shelter with his four strong hooves, and Gaby sat tall and felt her legs grip his solidity and her hands relax in his mane. She could not stop smiling.

The clown led them across the cold and windy valley and into the great circus tent. The air beneath its flapping roof was warm and still, though the wind tried to creep under the walls and stir the grass and scattered sawdust in the uncarpeted ring. The trapeze hung forlorn but the white horse, Bluebird, was there, circling the ring at a slow canter. Her gilt harness had been replaced by plain leather tackle and her small rider stood on one leg on her rump. An old man and a boy looked on. From her living perch, Gaby watched the unvarnished rehearsal.

The old man had a grim expression but, after three more turns, he lit a cigarette and seemed satisfied with both its dry flavour and with the little girl and the horse. He spat, a great white gob which sailed across the ring and landed on its blue coaming.

'Toshtoys,' he said.

The child beside him grinned. He had teeth as white as cuttlefish bone and his sungold skin brought outlandish light into the gloomy tent.

'Gajos? Rais – tonight?' said Loy, and the old man answered him in Nenian, 'Nah, Vixen'd have told you else. Third night, counting this one.'

She felt the emotion which flooded from Loy Sen, a great ray of panic and dread. Spooky had felt it too, for he laid back his ears and shifted his feet uneasily so that she had to cling to the mane. She was surprised to hear the clown snarl at him in a voice raw and laden with fear. She did not want

110

to know what the foreign words meant. Perhaps she should excuse herself; go home. Something which troubled them, which was not hers to know, was happening.

The white horse, the old man and the two children left the tent. They looked natural together, easy: pupils with a loved teacher or brother and sister with a dear father. The boy looked back and made a face at her, a friendly face like those she pulled when she was bored and hopeless on the line. His mouth hung open and his teeth shone; in his twinkling eyes appeared the mischief he had displayed before, for he had been the tall hatted pilot of the show, the child-Ringmaster; the infant with the whip. Nor had she recognised the girl, the elephant-rider, without her yellow hair.

'Cantor, 2-Cute, 2-Sweet,' said the clown, 'Sorry, I meant to introduce — '

'Shall I get down?' she said, anxious now as he, wanting to be away from the worries and intimacies of this life which was not hers. 'It's over, isn't it?'

He looked up at her then, and smiled, something that was not quite irony just creasing his lips. 'It isn't you; it isn't us,' he said, 'It's Them.'

'The Sineinians?'

'Um.'

'They like to control people,' she said, 'They call it helping. But if it weren't for them, we – us Folk, I mean – would be extinct.'

'They colonised the world: Southern Sinein to Shrikand and beyond, Ineit and the Lutreians, Noiro, the starships and Hibornal in the night sky; but they never took Mahkrein and Maralis. The City was never theirs so I'll be fucked if I let them have me.'

'Who is coming?'

'Officials from Sinein, to examine me – and the others. To find out who we are and where we come from. To stop us doing it again.'

'They can't, can they?' she whispered, wanting him to agree. 'But I know where you come from – the City of Mahun.'

He sighed 'So we do,' he said. 'And if we could tell them that, there would hardly be a problem.'

He took off his damp straw hat and laid it on the edge of the ring as carefully as if it had been the magic crown of a soothsayer. 'Between Mahkrein and Noiro are many miles of ocean,' he said 'There was no boat. No means of conveyance for the Democratic Circus. Come here, come down. You won't believe me, but – sit here, by me and I'll tell you a story. . .'

The warm body of the horse was a softly vertical slide down which she slithered, to fetch up on the yellowed grass. She sat beside him on one of the blue blocks, sorry that he had not felt it necessary to help her, to hold out his arms and steady her at the end of her descent. Spooky lowered his head, halter-rope trailing, and began to graze. The sound of his munching teeth, and the rip of the breaking stems as he tore them, was a subdued accompaniment to the story.

'Once upon a time,' said the clown 'There was a boy who lived in the most beautiful city in the world. He grew up at the feet of the tall buildings of his city and he wanted to be an architect and make more of them, garnet towers to go with the black and blue and white and silver ones that were already there. The boy was sad; most of the time he was unhappy and angry and bitter, because he could not be an architect. He had to become a circus performer like his mother, who could keep ten silver balls moving and make doves appear out of the air; like his cousins Belami, the rosinback rider, and Lion, the stiltwalker, and Amita, the girl on the flying trapeze. He had to be a clown like his uncle Mel, the famous and celebrated white-face clown, Meleager, who wore a bleeding heart upon his sleeve.

'Because the boy was unhappy, he made a perfect clown. He could see the beauty and sadness which is in everything and, understanding it, could make other people laugh and forget their fears.

'The city people were the circus audience. Some of them were rich and lived on Paradise Hill; most were poor and clever at making a living; some of them were not in the city all the time, but travelled to and from it in little, crowded

112

boats. They were not supposed to do this, at that time no one was, so they were fugitives and had to hide from the security corps.

'The young clown's family fell on hard times. First, his cousin Amita killed herself and then his mother died. Next, there came a time of war and strife and the order in the city was upset. New groupings rose out of the chaos and all the poor people banded together. They had a great leader, a poor man who had travelled and who had once lived like a slave on the Hill.

'Floods came, not the usual seasonal floods, snow-water rushing from the mountains in the north, but great floods which put half the city under water. There was no room for the poor people, for the circus and the clowns, there was no room for artists and artisans; even religion was cast out.

'So the clever man from the Hill led his people away under the swollen river and under the ground, far beneath the drowning red earth and the water which was flooding into cellar and basement, beginning to fill up the streets. . .

'We came out in Elysium, that's what I thought it was: Heaven, a green valley. It shimmered as if it wasn't quite in time with us. The birds were singing. A green valley full of grasses and trumpet lilies, naias bushes – Cal picked a spray and then he turned back and left us there. He must have drowned, getting back —

'The valley was just the start of it. It wasn't now or then, in that valley. It was a time before, a time when the City was new. From there we went to Hayna, then Ineit and Diold for the first time, simmering and settling, in and out of time. We had no clocks, no calendar, and I lost count— '

'That's your story?'

'If you like; if you believe me.'

'I do, I do; please, Loy, I believe you. But I don't understand.'

'Then we should go, I think – don't you? – and finish looking at this shifting world of mine while it is standing still.' He stood up, and the horse lifted its head.

If he had seemed magical before, a spangled clown who could juggle, stand on one hand, rotate about the centre of his being without once touching the ground, he was now enchanted, a storyteller and a man out of myth, a legendary traveller like Witto and Ikbik.

'You should talk to Salter Bren,' she told him, as they left the tent, her small body solid and determined beside his melancholy grace.

When Spooky had been returned to his shelter, he led her about the camp. The bow-top vans stood bravely on the stony ground, lost yet defiant like the children's building blocks forgotten in the winter garden. That was Hayna. They had entertained the Winter Queen, the Udan Hayla, so long ago; the mountain enclave had been such a place as this, a barren garden, territory where to live was to struggle against harsh weather. Queen Hayla had ruled three months while the snow lay on the ground.

He told her the history of the seven vans, how the green one was bought with a performance, why the yellow cart from Lar had bamboo walls; he pointed out his own, the red and blue cart with the name of the circus painted on it in three languages. He shared it with Peach and Zoe. On cue, she came out, jumping from the top step in her excitement, shouting 'Da!'.

'Curtsey to the lady, Zoe,' he said, parading his daughter as she, in her turn, would parade the dogs tomorrow in the ring.

Red Cheeks was crouching, on a level with the wheel-arches, close to Zoe. Zoe's coat, the white snowman's body the folks below the ground had given her, enveloped her and made her skin look darker than it really was. Wisps of her hair poked from the turned-up collar and, below, where the thick coat ended, her circus dress showed. He stood above them, feeling the alien North wind, wondering what Gaby felt.

'I've got three children,' she said suddenly. 'Almost. They were my sister's.'

He listened while she explained her tribal responsibilities. Zoe's gesture, a small hand slipped into the brown paw of this little iceland woman, pleased him; but the hands of the other woman, Ang-the-photographer, Ang-in-dreamland, tugged at him while he stood there, and prospective desire washed over him. How he wished that Charis had not left him.

'Zoe will look after you till tea,' he said, shrugging off the fantasy, a self-indulgent and unsuitable garment for this cold afternoon.

'Yes, yes!' Zoe yelled, and gambolled as she used amongst the green trees of Lutreia. Gaby stood up and pranced upon her sturdy legs, her red boots flying fast. He left them dancing together and stepped up into his van where lay the sticks of paint which transformed him into the white-face clown.

He ran from van to circus tent, late because he'd tarried to pick up the toys Zoe had left on the floor. It was already growing dark again. Yellow lights within turned each van into a retreat and the tent before him was a huge golden bubble. It is the hot centre of my life, he thought. It is more than Charis was or Zoe is because I know it when it is dim and cold, an arena for rehearsal, a stadium in which I struggle continually.

The circular table in the exact centre of the ring was the perfect imitation of a matriarch's tea-table at home. Vixen had covered it with a cloth so it did not matter that it was, commonly, the elephant's tub. The cloth was patterned with flowers; no matter that they were made of paint and not minute, silk stitches. She had brought all the fine china from her van and borrowed more: the table was set and, upon her fantastic glass tea-trolley, normally the resting-place of her puppets, were plates piled high with the City sugar-cakes she had been baking for the past two days. The sugar mountain ranges which crowned them glittered as much as the many facets on the tea-trolley, but neither suggested ice. It must be forming now, he thought, gathering to obscure with opaque crystal each runnel and puddle outside.

Half his people, a fine selection, sat in a wide circle around the table and the five dogs too had been given chairs. They sat erect with ears pricked and whiskers extended. Vixen was pouring tea for the visitor: precious, hoarded bohea from the City. Its scent made him think of hot afternoons and the dry and trodden ground outside his mother's van. He took his place on Gaby's left and Zoe slid from her lap and climbed on to his knee. He watched Gaby.

She is undiscovered like her beautiful, sparse country; unimaginable to us hasty dolts from the south, he thought. He sought extravagant parallels in water, rocky islands, ice and snow; but she was none of these, not cold or bony; she did not flow like water nor melt like snow. She was small and real, her dark hair tangled and untidy, hanging thick beside her scarlet cheeks; her crystal beads picked up and gave back the same reflected light that enchanted sugar and glass. He would like to discover her and could not: she was no *soi-disant* artist like Ang, and he would soon be gone.

This must be his only private performance for her, this first and ultimate tea at which he was glad – and relieved – to be honouring her and not an unknown Fisher. Worse, a Sineinian —

He watched her politely sip her bohea, unsure of the taste. Peach stared too, as if in her smooth face he recognised an old love, his deserting mother or the sister who, he had once confided, tears in his beautiful doe's eyes, had died of a scarlet fever. Dork, beyond bearded Florian and Shiny in his blue acrobat's costume, was mesmerised by the many strands of her marvellous, chiming beads. He coveted them; you could tell how dearly from the way he pleated and creased the painted net of his dress between his long, pink nails.

Loy lifted Zoe, shifting her to a more comfortable position against his chest, and turned to his guest.

Gaby was glad the clown was wearing his proper clothes. They all were. When she looked at the folk around the brightly-lit table, she saw a circle of singular characters, seven smiling children and five laughing dogs with frills around their necks. The acrobat looked like a blue-skinned snake, the silly old father with his yellow fringe and hairless crown grinned at bold Harlequin and beautiful Columbine. Vixen, beside her, kept filling up her cup and plied her with the delicious cakes. And there on her left, the clown sat dreaming in his sequinned costume, his gingerbread child on his knee, his white face turned from all the wonder to her, Float Gaby.

He told her how many million sequins decorated his suit; how he had sewn them on, a laborious apprenticeship; how he made his own soft shoes and all the shoes the acrobats and riders needed. These practical details, the minutiae of circus life, lit up the enchantment. She imagined him late at night in his van, Zoe and Harlequin asleep while he stitched at his spangled costume and sewed laughter and love into it.

They entertained her with jokes and tricks, with so much laughter that, laughing too, she felt swollen with it. They moved before her like pictures on the screen, episode by episode; yet, if she wished, she could reach out and touch their flesh and humanity. The dogs barked on cue and Columbine danced on the table amongst the empty cups. Loy Sen put Zoe down and she ran around the table to the dogs. He leaned one arm along the back of her chair, bent closer and whispered in her ear.

'With each new landfall I become more fearful,' he said, 'lest that time shift should be the last and we should find ourselves trapped again by mortality and condemned to a single life-span.'

She had no reply to this and was silent, all her laughter spent. His painted tears ran down his cheeks.

Outside in the cold, in her world, he shook her by the hand.

'Thank you,' she said, 'very, very much.' Poor, inadequate words.

He walked her to Vixen's booth while Zoe held his hand. Inside it stood the tall guard who was to take her home, and Ang Semo with her biggest camera bag. She was smartly dressed and looked out of place. A blush coloured her pale face when he looked at her.

'Curtsey to the gajo lady,' he said, and Zoe repeated her dip and twirl Ang Semo smiled and the blush in her cheek deepened. Zoe took the hand of this new lady eagerly, staring at her golden hair and spotless clothes.

Gaby trudged uphill behind the guard. He held his torch at an angle, so that she could find a way through the tussocks and she was too hot and bothered and too much in awe of him to protest.

Loy Sen had followed her from the hut. He had clutched her by the arm. 'I forgot to show you the Rat Queen,' he'd said, guiltily. 'Come back and see it – please come back. After the next performance? Soon?'

He had kissed her – on the top of her head – the way a father kissed his child.

She recalled Ang Semo's unusually pink face and her expensive clothes. She had not been herself; that self was the breathless being who dropped stills, who would stoop over a dead owl; that self was the one who needed solitude and the ghosts of Ulbeg. She loves him, she thought. How stupid. How odd.

'Well?' said Cait and Fenner 'What did you do?'

In the circus tent I fell out of love with my own folk, she thought, and in love with the circus. With Loy Sen. Yet I have to marry Pak.

She told them about the spotted horse and the elephant.

'It must have been wonderful!' they cried 'Marvellous!'

'So it was,' she said.

But there was also hunger and patience, glamour covering dirt, persistence, hard work, intelligence; there was trust.

She described the tea-table and the taste of the tea; she spoke of Vixen who had baked the cakes, who took the money and helped sew the costumes.

'What would you do if you lived independently like that?' she asked, and was surprised when Cait said, 'Fish, you fool,' and 'Mend the nets,' answered Fenner at once.

The two faces of Loy Sen haunted her. His painted lips were parted in speech. He smiled in black and white and wept real tears, tears for his forgotten tribe and her abandoned one. I should have made him laugh, she thought. I can. Next time, I will.

Loy recovered some confidence. On the third day, when he expected the Sineinian interlocutors, he stood on the van steps to feel the cold and sharpen his senses. Inside, behind

118

him, was a fug of stove fumes and night odours. They were running out of coal. They had got it long ago and it wasn't mined any more.

The Sineinian delegation consisted of three women and a clerk with a recorder. When he showed them round the circus, he felt like a president, at home on his ground; they were the interlopers, the ambassadors who must prove themselves good.

The matinée he gave them was based on the children and the dogs. It was a form of the show he had developed in Lutreia, where the people loved their huge families of children and dogs. He hoped it would soften the hearts of the Sineinians. As for himself, he put on costume and paint wearily, turned somersaults outside the tent to warm himself, knowing he must impress.

The applause was not overwhelming; but it was loud and appreciative. Ang Semo clapped vigorously and was at the van door to fetch him while he still had cold cream all over his face.

'Come on, Loy,' she said nervously, 'Let's get it over with.'

He wiped off the last of his clown's face and put on his jacket.

Allowed no companion from the circus, he was unobtrusively guarded, and politely escorted into Traumesse. They must hold him responsible because his name was written on all the posters: Artistic Director, Loy Sen – clown, vagabond, accused. He felt his personality disintegrate as the lift descended.

The Sineinian inquisition sat in the room where he had waited for Dr Wireloom, and got Ang Semo instead. She sat half-way between him and the three inquirers. The seascape hung on the wall behind them and its grey waves chilled him.

They read him his life-story.

'That's right,' he said, and heard Ang breathing in the stillness which followed his affirmation.

He thought they might use a lie-detector on him, but they began to talk about the City. One of them had been

119

there last year. What year? Last year, 4624. In Verzyon, the fortieth century had hardly begun. Now the scientist, whose discipline was beyond his knowledge, wanted to question him. She called herself a Response and Articulation Mapper. She was young, and pretty. He felt older than the proverbial hills.

'Mr Sen,' she began 'Do you take any stimulants or narcotics?'

The reputation of the City as the resort of drug-seekers and oblivion merchants, its very citizens constantly high, had preceded and enveloped him.

'Of course I do,' he said 'Tea, coffee, alcohol.'

The clerk spoke into his machine, a verbal record of everything that was said. He looked at the wave photograph and decided that he liked it. In this enclosed environment, it represented the only stability he knew: constant change, variations on a perpetual theme.

'Do you take husk, or dust?'

The City's drugs, brown and gold, powders which brought joy and peace.

'No,' he said, 'I can no longer obtain them.'

'So you took them once?'

'Don't we all?'

She blushed.

The grey print, he realised, was a wonderful synthesis, a timely and timeless moment in the life of the ocean. He studied Ang Semo's profile. The best side, in which her jaw was firmest and the line of her lashes most seductive, was turned to him. He admired the tattooed line which swept across her upper eyelid and ended in a curlicue upon her high cheekbone. It must save a lot of time, and slap. A pearl hung from her earlobe, an imperfect pearl prized for its irregularities. Lust, he thought, takes many forms.

'Have you any supplementary questions, Doctor?'

With a shock he realised that the chairwoman of the inquiry was addressing Ang, and that the anxious Doctor of Computer Art was a mathematician.

'Haibeg says that time is a variable constant,' she said, her voice low and nervous.

'Speak up.'

'I refer to Haibeg's theorem and, without going into argument and proof in any detail, I would submit that therein lies the true explanation of Mr Sen's story.'

Her photograph – he had known its maker all along – lulled him. He watched the waves beat on the shore.

'Very possibly,' said the chairwoman 'But, while we may *have* the argument, in this case we lack the proof.'

'Ask him!'

The chairwoman frowned and with that grim expression, consigned Ang to the same nowhere Loy occupied. Questionable, inaccurate, unreliable; he hoped she did not risk her career. He waited, while the Sineinians checked the evidence and told him, with great bureaucratic detail, how they would retire to their headquarters in Sollar Kein to consider his case, which would then be laid before the Deportation Committee.

So his worries were not to be ended here. Meanwhile, here was Ang Semo. He caught her eye and winked, enjoying while he watched, horror and relief war in her features; their colloquy became in that moment, a conspiracy.

She had relaxed, to a degree. Because his interest in her was naked and sexual, he felt able to invest her with any fancy. He looked at her photograph on the wall, and then at her and realised that in the washing ocean she had portrayed, some of her desires lay afloat, waiting to be fulfilled.

Ang sought relief in the pool at Ulbeg, its liquidity a balm to take away the heat and pain the clown engendered, its cold a sleeping-draught to banish the Folk. She was hurt and bewildered. Gaby had turned her down: Bren had told – told! – his kinswoman to refuse the proffered advancement. Without his co-operation she could not help anyone and their connivance to reject her was her punishment for making favourites against the Ethic; in defiance of Tradition. She imagined them whispering together, barbed slanders against her. She felt sick, sheltering behind the buttress out of the spray, sick and homesick. The hanging lava curtain should move, she thought, both of us unable to dance, petrified rock and flesh. The mist-cloud enveloped her, this dank interior concealed her: there was no need to shelter behind the rock. Absurdly, she thought of home and the old-fashioned and sooty fireplace, its black metal surround polished clean of its dross, a red fire of resin-scented pine and clovewood on the hearth.

She unfolded her clothes and shook off the mist which sequinned each garment. The mist wet her again as she wiped the salt water from her body, setting pearls in her hair.

In White, no one could draw off so much as a glove without risk: flesh to ice in sixty seconds. Now, the air pinched her nipples and her toes: but she had enjoyed her cold swim. The water in the pool was clear: she could see the craggy bottom and the red weeds, the fish that swam there in a little shoal, always solitary, always one of a crowd. The entry of her huge human body had disturbed them.

A quick plunge, changing a body from warm humanity into a cold and slippery fish was not for her: she liked to slide slowly in from the brink and feel the water encroach. The pool was warmer than the sea beside it, but it had a comprehensive touch; when it passed her knees she had shivered, and the cold rising through her legs brought a clutch inside as tight as the spasm Tobin's hideous and coveted erection had provoked; then the water was round her waist and creeping up her chest. Her breasts had floated and she had become as cold as the sea; so cold that she raised her arms and slid under feeling in that climactic moment of immersion the saltwater fill her nose and mouth, ears and eyes, and slip into her vagina, as innocently and blissfully open as the eye of the camera or her mouth in delight and amazement.

Then, the water had felt warm, for minutes together as soothing as bathwater, deep enough to swim in, lively with subtle currents and violent molecular exchange. It filled her up while she entrusted her body to its apparent neutrality.

While the sea water still grasped her, she had swum about looking down at the weed and the young fish. As soon as the ice melted, every living thing began to breed. Her white body an interloper in the burgeoning weed, she had floated like the passive partner she wanted to be, on her back, and felt the mist upon her. Swimming had warmed her and now she was cold, colder than she had ever been, chill and closed.

If a malpog were to come, surprising her naked amongst the rocks, a malpog like the Great Silkie with a liking for virgins. . . malp never came to Ulbeg now. It was too close to Traumesse, humans, noise and their smell. And the malp legends, they were so old that even the Folk had forgotten them, preserved unheard in the glass coffins of far away archives. Bren might know of them, like a seal himself with his blunt face and big eyes, his thin coating of blubber. She wondered idly if the spirits minded her disturbing their restful solitude.

The pink towel did not warm her but its colour was kind. She had a new bruise on her left leg and a long and bleeding scratch on her right, gooseflesh all over, and she bent, shivering and awkward, for the snap camera and photographed them. Quickly, shaking and hoping that the tremor would enhance the pictures, she photographed all the seachanged parts of her cold body that she could see. She towelled herself again.

In the dark days of White next year, she would take these photographs from their folder and lay them out in sequence on the floor, reminding herself once more of her ever-present and incurable disability. Then, she would turn to her portraits of Loy Sen, and shed tears of regret over them.

But now, the hungry eye of the camera had been propitiated with these narcissistic images, which she would extract from it, grasp and hold with the old magic of retained light and sensitive paper. She had quite a collection, herself as she wished to be, naked and exhibitionist. The camera, always truthful, offered her stripped of coverings but wearing her inhibitions and alone. As she journeyed amongst these other selves and abstractedly powdered her damp limbs, she heard the footfalls which approached her secret boudoir with the ears of her imagination and saw the malpog bull, Salter

Bren and Loy Sen succeed one other, each one rampant and aggressively male. The female voice which addressed her was a discontinuity as great a moment of peace in a monstrous dream.

'Ang!'

Ang fled, clutching her towel, but Dr Semo remained, defensive and undignified, surprised with nothing to shield her but a pair of briefs. Dr Wireloom surveyed her body and her predicament.

'Ang!'

Soft now. The given name: ingratiation, the female equivalent of penetration. She bent quickly to retrieve the towel she had dropped and gave her superior more of her nakedness to view.

'It's true,' said Dorta Wireloom.

'That I can swim?'

The Director smiled, a wan gleam in a hatchet face, took off her jacket and moved nearer. A rough stretch of aa separated them and so they began their absurd race, Ang reaching for her garments as the Director, in her thick shoes, advanced across the scoriaceous pavement, shedding her sweater, shirt, camisole, bodice. . .

'This is your bathing pool?'

'It is.'

Inside her thin underclothing, she felt naked as a baby, vulnerable as a soft-shell crab. The little garments she had taken pride in, selecting them one bright afternoon in Ardrazen's boutique, wearing the frivolous scraps of silk and lace under her tasteful outer garments, knowing how expensive they were — now, they were ridiculous and mute witnesses to her humiliation.

Dorta Wireloom had a good body for a woman of her age. The fitness studio had given it a muscular angularity which went well with her stark face. Her grey pubic hair contrasted strangely with her auburn-tinted crop. Her gold locket glowed in the grey light of the sea fret and on her left breast was a small tattoo.

She stood beside the pool without clothes or shame, jubilant and bubbling with life. 'What pretty undies,' she said, lowered herself into the water and cried out as it raked her. She wet her smooth head and trod water. 'The thaw reveals the strangest things,' she said, 'the oddest urges. Won't you come in again?'

'I don't think so.'

Anyone could swim here – it was not her private beach. Anyone at all. The glass illusion was thoroughly shattered and her indifference was not insulation.

'Did you follow me down?' she asked.

'I left after a suitable interval. I knew where you were: I've always known and I think you should join me now. Your work has been erratic recently, half-hearted at best. You should take more exercise. You ought to take a lover.'

She slid back into the water in her underclothes while Wireloom watched her and made soft noises that were somewhere between laughs and gasps. The threat and the water were both oppressive. She ducked under the surface and came close to meet both.

'I've always wondered about you,' her superior said 'No children, no man apparently, brief affairs with itinerants – Pior Detna was a soldier, Tobin Harmeya a mining engineer. Do you remember the first interview, the short-list? Think of this as natural selection.'

The hands that explored her were necessarily cold, huge and blunt as the gynaecologist's shiny instrument. Their unequal struggle made waves in the pool and the water, splashing over, returned to the sea; behind her the rock was diamond hard and ready to graze her tender flesh.

'And now,' gasped her tormentor, thrusting with her long fingers and her painted nails. 'Let me in.'

Soft as her will now was, Wireloom like iron and with the strength of a mason, a player of team games, a madwoman, her resolute body was still in charge.

'You're frigid,' said Wireloom, withdrawing, pulling out her rebuffed hand. 'You've never had it, have you? Never anything in there ouside the gynaecologist's, not so much as a tampon. It's not on your record – because nobody knows.

This is what you've missed: this is what you should feel like. Come on. It's my turn now.'

All that remained of her communion with the sea was the salt smell of it in her damp hair; she was glad of that, the last memory of the last bathe. She could try to wash away the stains of the attempted rape, the spiritual lesions from her forced pleasuring of Dorta Wireloom, with soap, hot water and liquor. The cigarette she sucked on helped her. 'Mermaid,' Wireloom had called her 'Water nixie, siren, white swan,' breast to breast with her in the dreadful, betraying water. The golden lily locket swung like a pendulum between them, tock, tock, spending time.

But the characters etched on Dorta's sagging breast were now etched on her mind, as indelibly fixed in her memory as in the white gooseflesh. She could not have avoided them, as she could not avoid that empty and wasted gland, close against her face, blotting out everything but its insistent and voracious owner and the overwhelming take-over of her responses.

There were five characters, sub-code signifiers. It was the cipher which gave Dorta access to the entire System and that omniscient computer was hers now to ravish. She would usurp, she would misuse her power: when the time came.

First, she needed Bren and Gaby; those two, she must woo afresh so that she could learn stoicism. And, though she was now branded and criminal, she would take from Loy Sen his knowledge of freedom and his ability to laugh and cock snooks at misfortune.

'I love you,' Dorta whispered in her heat, manic, obsessed, 'Always. Always have. Ice-melt does the strangest things.

'We must do this again. Again and again, without the soft-focus fade-out you give your Siloe. How alike you are: both white, remote and utterly desirable. She is you isn't she? A functioning Ang, Ang cured of her crippling vaginismus.'

Ang woke. It was a dream. Thank Fortune, Oma, Om, the Lady, whichever – it was a dream.

Yet the pictures continued, not dreams but iteration of an endless act which she viewed from every angle, tilting and bending the perspective, manipulating mouths and buttocks, hands and cold flesh, smelling – Mother! – that flesh and the hot sambucus-flower odour that merged with the bitter scent of the sea. She hardly dared compose herself to sleep again.

Although she wanted to seek them out, confide in them and befriend them, she felt that the Folk eluded her.

Deep in Traumesse, when she walked the corridors in the course of a day, she would pass Fenner or Cait, hurrying to or from a shift. She saw Pak, Gaby's promised mate, sitting alone in the Fountain bar. He seemed melancholy and resentful although he wore the piece of malpog tooth which, among the Folk, denoted a betrothal. Normally she passed the gymnasium without a glance: on these sad days, she paused in the doorway, looking for Gaby and Bren. Once she saw him, sculling smoothly on one of the rowing machines; he active and breathing hard, the machine silver, stable, and dumb. Gaby remained invisible to her eyes.

She went upside. The moonflowers encircled the View-dome port, their winter pallor turned to gold. White sennis and madder tinctureheads grew in profusion amongst the coarse grasses. She went like a penitent down the hill to the circus and trembled while she photographed the elephant, lest Loy should appear and demand her company.

A small package lay beside the mute terminal on her desk. It was wrapped in flowered paper, colours of the Kein spring, pallid yellow, bright blue and biting green. Ander again. In these circumstances, she could do without his curdog habits. She sighed, unwrapping it. Too much, this: a jewel case.

Inside it, upon white velvet, lay the big gold locket which had flown on its chain and hammered at her face, the ornament Dorta always wore. She would wrap it and send it back at once. There was also a note, folded small and tucked under the gold. Fastidious in her distaste, she unfolded it carefully and read: 'Even ugly ducklings sing and, once, we sang together, Swan – for the first time and the last.'

The hinge of the locket was disguised as the lily-stem, its stiff fastening a ridge upon the enfolded bud. Inside, there would be a lock of Dorta's hair – an old lock, the colour of an autumnal holm-oak leaf, ebony, corn – whatever it had been. She used her nails as levers and parted the bud. Behind a miniature window lay a miniscule corpse. It was dry and yellowed, pressed flat and lifeless for ever in its small catafalque: a ten-week embryo, toes and fingers still webbed, once a water-baby: someone's hope, someone's aborted child. She stared at it and froze while green waves filled her mind and senses, blotted out her vision; all she could hear was the surf roaring and then her own screams, louder than the tide, and an absurdly small thump as the locket hit the wall opposite and fell to the floor.

BLUE II

Therefore let us spit on our hands!

Knud Rasmussen, *Greenland by the Polar Sea*

Swimming is for athletes whose intelligence is attuned to strife, whose intuition is to pit a well-trained body against all-comers; swimming is dangerous dalliance in the cold seas here, north of everywhere; swimming is perilous, a pastime for the damned at the edge of drowning, perdition, damnation —

Ang examined her fingers. They were warm, not wrinkled or flabby from immersion, and her white-tipped oval nails were smooth, as usual; as usual, the faint ghosts of nicotine and Passion rose from them, her own characteristic odours.

She had swum far, deep down where there are no waves. The sheets on the bed were fresh, patterned with fern-leaves, and a jug of flowers stood on the table. Beyond them on the bedroom chair sat a uniformed Medical Carer, Mair from Second Level, who smiled and asked her how she felt.

'Headachey,' she said and closed her eyes so that she could think.

The thing in the locket had made her black out, the culminating horror. Safe in her own bed with the nurse to hand, she could examine it again. She looked into her memory and extracted the terrifying image. This time, sadness filled her; there was a sense of loss which, although it was not hers, was no less poignant for being lent. The child – which it could have been – was a memorial to impossiblility, interred under glass and made into an icon. It was a boy.

'Where is that locket?' she asked.

'Don't you worry about that, Dr Semo.'

There had been an inscription, a name. 'RIP . Amare': that was it, that was all – child or father? Perhaps, in due time, she might ask. Amare, a good Sollar name for a boy, a disappointed father, an autonymic donor?

She had been given a sedative and the release-patch on her neck itched. Thus the headache, the otherworldly sensations. She slept until she was roused.

Eda Voran and Carey Aleph were there, more flowers in her hands; in his, a gift-pack of cigarettes. Unfamiliarly obsequious, they apologised for waking her. She smiled and opened Carey's package, lit up.

'I'm allright now' (But the dream-child persisted). 'It was the shock — '

'What a curse to hang around your neck,' said Eda Voran, 'I always wondered what she kept inside that beautiful piece of Art-Naïf.'

'Take it out,' said Carey tactlessly 'Get rid of it – I'll do it for you. Then you can use the locket as you like – holos, hair, any memento.'

'But it isn't mine.'

She had slept nine hours: that explained the hunger which fought with her drowsiness. They watched her eat supper from a tray and then they sentenced her.

In the short day between the morning's terror and the evening's peace, Dorta Wireloom had drowned herself in the pool at Ulbeg.

'Obsessive lust, eros unalloyed:the worst sign, my dear. The Northern Disease,' said Eda. 'Nanket found a message when she checked the internal mail. I'm truly sorry you became Dorta's objective.'

Because of me, she thought. Another death to add to Pior's. She wept.

Eda held her hand. 'Maybe better not,' muttered Carey.

'I'm all right.' (Betrayed again by my body.)

Dorta's wretched end had despoiled Ulbeg, annexed it for ever; but her thwarted and unhappy spirit might join the rest, the ghosts of the old unburied Folk, those holy carlines whose minds had been the archives of the tribe. Ulbeg had been fire turnd to stone, forlorn memories, the plaintive cries of the tarunt gulls, mist, waves, ice – she would appreciate its remote solitude. Rest in peace.

'There are personal papers and effects for your attention – tomorrow, when you're ready.'

'My attention?'

Carey grinned.

'You are It now, Ang. You're Establishment Director, my love.'

The intruders waited, filling her neat bedroom with their restless personalities. She must speak: she might let them stay for a while, to talk, to warm her isolation, to keep out the ghosts.

'You might as well sign off, Mair,' she said to the medic, 'I'm fine now. Carey, sit down. Would you mind foraging, Eda? The glasses are in the kitchen next to the booze.'

A little wake, a little night celebration. Cheers and goodbye.

So, Dorta was the victim after all and that blunt assault had been her last attempt to find a hold on life. Swimming was profound employment, the prologue to utter change.

The effects would include that damned locket.

She was no longer sleepy. Soon, she would get up, tidy away the glasses and the empty bottle, lock the door behind her visitors. The shots they had drunk had made Eda garrulous and Carey reckless. He had leaned close, his prurience in his thoughts and eyes; but he had not been foolish enough to take her hand. She felt dauntless. She could confront a vair troupe, a carrion bear, pages of programming, fractal maths – anything devoid of sexuality.

Even Loy Sen, if she remembered her purpose and forgot his gaberlunzie charm.

Naked, she walked to the door of her unit and turned the key in the lock. It squealed at her like a wounded animal.

She dressed. Night must become day; she would work. First, she poured a large drink to carry with her to her terminal. The small screen glowed in its grey shrine and she picked up the voice-control and set its circuits racing.

Nanket had left a copy of Dorta's last communication on her scratch-pad so, beginning as she must go on, she spoke an acerbic reprimand and docked a day's leave from her secretary's tally.

The suicide note was long, five thousand words. Parts of it were logical and coherent, those which dealt with money, property, and duty. Because it was addressed to everyone – 'all our subordinates', the possessive pronoun giving it the authority of a lunatic queen – she read it carefully. It laid Dorta bare, disappointments, anguish, decisions counter-manded by Research Commission in Sollar; it robed Ang Semo in light, elevating her higher than Siloe and with as spurious a motive. Here the language was wild, swooping from lyric verse through classical tag to bathos and back with an eclecticism which made her giddy. Most of the expressions were simple codes: darling, dove, rose-centred heart-of-ice. She understood the woman's predicament, but this antic language, this extended rape of her sensibilities, made her angry. Needing a chemical jolt, she left the screen to brew coffee.

Farewell, wrote Dorta theatrically, fare thee well.

She must use the secret code before Sollar acted, examined Dorta's archives, and issued her with a code of her own. Maybe it was already too late.

The sub-code was not hard to find. She typed, her fingers flying over the touch-pads; deep in a machine-code listing, she found the five symbols and they were side by side.

'You stupid cat,' she said. Someone with an agile and specialist brain, like Carey Aleph, might easily have happened on them. Side by side: the signifiers were burned forever in her consciousness, blue, frostbitten scars on a white and salty breast. She isolated them from their fellows to make sure, and pressed the pads on which their identities rode. Dorta's private menu filled the screen.

To use it then, was child's play. She could make Dorta speak. She set up the speech patterns and listened to Dorta speaking her false epithalamion, an epitaph of heroic proportions. She must not float upon her watery bier unsung. The clown might weep for her, as he wept for every soul.

'Fuck you,' she said, 'Fuck you both.'

It was the worst fate to wish upon anyone.

She silenced the harsh voice and set her hands to work. Hands were speedier than voice, so quick to grasp and undo; and also to create in tandem with an eager brain. She loved the chaste expressions of the computer.

```
let d love a
let a love l
if l loves a go to hell
```

she wrote, and erased the silly instruction, watching the cursor reverse across the screen, blinking as it ate her words. Thus, with hungry jaws, would her maggot devour vast

134

sections of code, inserting others as it travelled through the brains and bowels of the machine. She began to search the system for passwords, composing her petard as she worked. On the scratchpad, her little maggot appeared harmless, three lines of programme which would devastate Traumesse. It began with a model from an old population equation:

$$x_{(i+1)} = r.x_i(1-x_i)$$

A subtle increase in the value of r would force Chaos.

Queen now of Traumesse, robed in Dorta's mantle of splendid isolation and absolute authority, she held them all upon the palm of her hand.

She had read Dorta's secrets; she even knew the sizes of her bust, waist and gloves. She knew that Dr Wireloom preferred to import her liquor from Ineit and her chocolates from Ros Kein. With such absurd and intimate concerns, the Director had filled up her empty life. The saddest record was her file of conquests with its addresses and brief descriptions. She had been the ninth.

They were sisters in this, two secret sharers, one with her verse and lickerish notes, the other with her nude self-portraits: two timid and introverted old maids whose libidos powered their careers. They worked together, the one dead, the other locked in armour.

Ang summoned Siloe and Jannl to the sreen. She copied Dorta's command files, looking for the programme which would provide a route into Siloe's womb for the mutant maggot.

Ang and Loy walked side by side. The Folk they passed in the corridors smiled at them, pleased to see the clown with the new Director.

They ascended in the glass lift and saw the many-coloured levels of Traumesse flash by like accelerated dreams of Paradise. There was no hierarchy in the system of floors and levels and Folk units were mixed with Sineinian. Similarly, the many brains of the computer, major and minor, could be found on nearly every level, luminous with knowledge.

The computer suite, the heart of the mystery where Ang operated, was the base and foundation of the buried community and Loy thought, his stomach in his shoes from the acceleration, what a land of artifice and constraint it was.

Down there, she had smiled often, showing him the ropes without a trace of embarrassment or reticence. Nor had she, in the hallowed and spotless environment of the computer suite, been able to smoke.

He had watched her call her ghosts from the machine, her fingers flying like a virtuoso vitriphonist's. She showed him scenes from episodes, close-ups from scenes, and the strands of narrative with which the scriptwriters made capital from her pictures.

'There must be a story,' she said 'It is the story which seduces the viewer and ensures his addiction to the screen. A properly-targeted narrative can be attached to any set of pictures as long as each episode ends with an unresolved question. People watch 'Greed' without analysing it. There was some anguish when ERRATE sacked the actors it used to employ: many of them had become cult-figures.

'But, in long run, it was a benefit. There has been a renaissance of live theatre and constructs are easier for us to manipulate. They don't have tantrums and they don't have to be paid.'

She showed him vision-bites and frames from mini-sagas. He found it difficult to believe the whole populations in the cities of the south stopped eating to view 'Greed' each evening but, when a wry-faced and tearful little boy, a miniature Pantaloon, embraced a dog for comfort, tears like those he had shed for Charis came into his eyes. He felt that his integrity had been compromised.

'This is a future episode,' said Ang Semo.

On the central screen her hero, Jannl, appeared in outline, a scant Jannl of angles, points, and lines. He appeared to be stepping forward from one insubstantial plane to another, which rocked. His face expressionless. On the lefthand screen was a chequerboard palette of colours which flickered and changed all the time. The altering colours disturbed his vision, but when he looked away he saw the righthand screen

136

on which a sequence played over and again: in a timeless city square, Jannl walked beside lovely Siloe and spoke soundlessly from a perfect mouth.

'Give him some of your colour,' said Ang and took his hand and guided it to the central screen.

'Speak: a colour.'

'Yellow,' he said.

Colour flowed from his fingers: wherever he touched the screen it blossomed, alive with random colour from red through all its children: crimson, orange, apricot, to blue and yellow, green, violet, cyan. Jannl's hair blazed like a bonfire.

Ang laughed. 'It doesn't understand you,' she said. 'It cannot recognise your obsolete accent. Maybe in the Historybank — '

More swift movement of her fingers produced a graph. She told him it was the voice-pattern of a dead man.

'Speak – anything.'

'This,' he said, self-consciously, 'is Loy Sen.'

His voice made another zig-zag pattern on the screen. She studied it intently.

'The vowels are the same,' she said. 'He was from the City too, fifth millennium – but he wasn't a Clown. Now you must teach my graphics system to recognise your voice.'

It took less time than putting on his clown's face. The machine imitated his emotive voice exactly: 'Ruby, garnet, madder, rose, amethyst, almandine,' the deep and burnished colours of his imagined towers. He heard the catches he knew lurked somewhere in his speech and the warm tones of his broad gypsy accent softly issue from faceless metal, glass and polymer.

'Beryl, malachite, emerald, apple-green.' He read the colours from a printed card.

'That's enough! You can paint Jannl now.'

He chose the reds and watched them fill and animate the pale outline; and sky blue, happy colour; black, to delineate – when he took his hand from the screen he saw Harlequin, elegant and graceful, honest and open without his mask.

'Thank you.' said Ang. 'I shall remember this.'

Jannl stepped from one boat into another. He was crossing a river in a wide and horizonless landscape, the black boats strung out to make him a bridge.

Ang Semo magnified the picture then and showed him the endless tips of Jannl's fingers which, examined under the mighty magnifying glass of the computer, became other fingers, tendrils, stamens, hair. She let him peer into the cleft between Siloe's breasts and find a garden of coiling flowers there; she showed him the jagged edge of her coasts which, magnified, became new and wondrous lands, green neverending countries.

'Why do you want to re-invent nature?' he asked.

'Why?' She had no answer ready. 'I think it is because I want to improve upon it.' she said, and laughed.

He understood how the countless watchers of the sagas became dependent on this eye-enchanting glamour. The circus worked in the same way: illusion replaced reality – except that, in the ring, the horses and elephant smelled and shat and, after every performance, the clowns and the acrobats undressed, wiped of their slap, and became themselves.

'Of course,' said Ang, 'We have to give it a fairly basic storyline and the herd never sees far into the fractal dimension.'

As he explored, a dark red convolution appeared in the depths of the infinity that was Siloe. He asked Ang why she had changed the pure white of Siloe's cells, which signified a purpose sharp as ice and a purity like virgin snow, to the colour of love and violent death.

'She's not well,' said An, and smiled. 'She has a secret infirmity – she's a rose with canker, a crisp and juicy apple with a maggot at its heart.'

Here, outside the narrow door of her unit, he looked closely at her, suspecting that the 'infirmity' to which she had referred, directly in her clear voice (and indirectly through her body language) was really hers, perhaps an anti-social infection or dissatisfaction with the body she kept concealed; if it lay deep in her psyche then her obsession with her work here would keep it forever secret. She could not afford to break down. But she was warm and soft, somewhere inside herself; he had seen the affectionate glances she kept for Bren and Gaby, handing them out when she thought no one else was looking. Her appearance was a decoy, her motley, the face she put on for the world. Now, she rummaged in her scrip and produced a key which she offered him. Too much aware of its symbolism, he held it in the palm of his hand. It might, were it not for infirmity, be the prelude to an act.

The short bar of metal, a real key with wards and a loop, surprised him and brought back his home in an intense flash: shopkeepers locking up, the Security Corps jingling grips and keys, Mel tucking the key to the van away under its flowerpot, the tiny padlock on his mother's bracelet to unlock which, she had told him, you needed the key to her heart. This key turned the future, but it was not his.

The woman struggled to balance her bulging scrip and packages of stills.

'Give me those,' he said. They exchanged burdens and she fitted the key and unlocked the door.

Like the doors of artisan houses, like the door of the van, this one opened straight into a living-room. Her room. The flimsy door, which he closed behind him, was the only barrier between her painful privacy (for it must be so) and the outside world of polished echoing corridors and the disintegrating workforce.

He laid his burdens down on the floor. The simple act gave a false sense of homecoming. The carpet spread away from him like a salt flat, a bleached and dead shore where nothing could live. Upon it, squatted three black cubes, the furniture, functional and comfortless as the prayerstools in a desert nomad's tent. A small outpost of the great computer stood in a corner, all but the screen covered up. The uplighter diffused light but did not give it. There were no books and no pictures; no plants or flowers. She, too, was clad in black and white, the only colour on her the red gash of her lips. He was a garish phenomenon, with his blue dungarees and pink patches.

Beside him was a silvery blind which might be a door and the room terminated in a vertically panelled screen of greys like a printer's tonal scale. The panels were made of cloth and trembled slightly in the current from the heating system. Ang Semo was dumb. She looked at him with hungry eyes which, he saw now, were the cold colour of the sea at dusk. She found a voice in action, pressing switches. More light came on, white lights, nothing yellow or – M'un forbid – pink. He stepped forward and sat down on one of the squarecut couches, disturbing the spotless cloth with his weight. He spread his hands on his knees and saw that every one of his nails were rimmed with dirt – Garissa's dirt, elephant's dross.

The screen rippled and drew aside. There was another room, a black dais plastered with prints, with *colour* on it: as well as the prints, two green cacti the size of Zoe, one of them with as many convolutions as a brain. The other drooped its rounded leaves, a lay figure at rest. He recognised it, for it grew in the forests of Lutreia: the Queen of Darkness. One night it would flower, as Charis had when they first kissed. It would fill this buried room with its waxen colour and stupefying scent. Then it would die. He gave a deep sigh, releasing his breath into the overheated air in a gust, and clapped.

The spell was broken: she spoke.

'Most of the prints are mine, I'm afraid.'

Why the false modesty? he thought, for they were good, very good: photographs of bald rocks in a second millennium style, many of them shadowed and overlaid with moving water. She was not, as he had believed when he first met her, a hollow reed.

'Why the false modesty?' he said.

'Sorry. You'r the only person, apart from me, who has seen them.'

'That's stupid.'

'No, Loy. People used to simulated and animated images would be unable to tolerate these. They'd wait for them to move and when they didn't, walk away. Stillness equals death. Who expects a corpse to speak?'

'You made the waves in the grey room,' he said.

'Yes – the only waves I'm able to make, I expect. And in the chapel there's a picture I made long ago – a view of the islands after rain. The water gleams and there are many tonal values; but they don't change and no one looks at them.

'Coffee? Liquor? I'll bring both.'

When she had gone, stepping up to the silver panel and through the opening it concealed with a new freedom born of the verbal contact, he too moved. He stood up, stretched (imagine her!) and moved forward to study her pictures. She had used his name: 'No, Loy.' She had admonished him, but her dry and anxious voice had become euphonious.

The rest, about twenty of them, were of the sea in her various moods, lapping, idling and raging against abrupt shores. In some, the angles of the light and the lie of the shadows suggested cold weather, and films of ice assailed the ancient rocks, resistant masses which were slow and loth to break up; in others, the sea herself was the object, her shivering light framed by the camera lens and restricted by the frame of the print.

Three pictures were separated from the rest by a blank strip of wall, the first of rocks so different from these frost giants of the North, that he saw for a moment the whole of his world in relief, a blue and green glob turning in the void, a geological tide reshaping its ancient surface. Water had once covered the dry rocks in this picture and great petrified ripples rushed down a slope, few grains of dust upon them suggesting the harsher movement if the wind: Ang was always in a desert, here studying dessication instead of the cold. Beside it hunt, framed in black, a depressing little sketch in charcoal of a bridge choked with weeds, the stream below it dying in a concrete channel. The shallow water was the grave of five empty bottles and a dead cat. The third picture showed another kind of death and he blinked, disbelieving the image. However, it remained, the unbroken body of a young man, perfect in death, half-covered by a sheet.

It was true – as Alluleya said: his body had not been

swept away by the floods. He had died in bed, his unique-
ness held for ever by the penstrokes of the City's painter,
Crinon M'una. CHM: her bold signature told Loy she had
been present at his death. He winked at the dead man,
this pathetic image of his one-time leader and comrade-
in-adversity become art object. Thus art imitates life, he
thought, and winced at the banality. Should he tell Ang Semo
more old tales of far-off things and battles long ago?

He smelled coffee: she was back into the room.

'Where d'you get this?'

'It's a printout from the Artsbank. I found it one day when
I was looking something up – so I got a hard copy. Do you
like it?'

Like? The wrong word, the wrong question. He left me
his children, bequeathed me Peach and the women; the
circus grew out of his imagination. Like? He was silent.
Turning to face her he was relieved to see her pale face
and tailored clothing, á la mode. Ghosts surrounded him
and as he stood there, arrested on the little stage by the
past, his patched clothing, brown face and dirty nails crying
out against the present order, he felt Mahun's hand on
his wrists. She held them firmly. She wanted him to step
forward. Then she was gone and Ang smiled up at him,
fragile as a bubble. When he spoke of the photographs,
he must be careful. He returned her smile. She carried a
tray on which stood two beakers, two glasses, coffee in a
jug and a little regiment of liquor bottles. Hospitality? A
secret vice?

'What will you have?'

He considered the array. There was no rafi. He did not
recognise any of the bottles. 'That one.'

The liquid was the colour of an aquamarine or a leached
turquoise. He succumbed to its clear colour. 'The blue.'

They ignored the coffee and drank alcohol. Her cheeks
grew flushed.

'I don't know much about photography,' he said, under-
valuing himself.

'It isn't difficult – the mechanics of it,' she replied, reluctant to chatter.

'Yours seem excellent to me— ' Because they sat beside each other, he could not see the whole of her face. 'Look at me, Ang,' he said and touched her cheek, feeling, even as he extended his hand, another hand close over it. He spoke into the void.

'I have so much love to give you.'

Loy's touch had been so soft, and the hand so sure, that she thought of her mother gently waking her from sleep.

She was surrounded by flowers. They grew in dense profusion, hot shades of pink like the colours of vulnerable flesh. Birds fed inside the mouths of the flowers.

She was sweating and something which lay against her face irritated it — She put up her hand to flick it away and found another hand, Loy's hand, hard and grimy, with the dexterous fingers and capacious palm of the juggler. His long face was turned toward her and there were tears on his cheeks.

If this is a dream, she thought, I shall be naked: she was clothed. I shall not feel my teeth bite into my lip: her teeth were hard, and cut. They sat on a bank of grass, the long stems crushed beneath them. Loy's strong arms encircled her and she was not afraid.

'I have so much life to give you,' he said.

There was no one in the garden but herself, Loy Sen and the iridescent birds which flew in and out of the flowers. When she held out her hand, they came and perched upon it.

'This is the Fen Forest in Lutreia. In the rainy season it's a swamp,' said Loy. 'I've been here before.'

'What if you met yourself?'

'I never have – I think the Lady would take care; she has set us down in exactly the right place.'

Because, on this bank and under these tall ewer plants, he had first kissed Charis and she, with the same innocent and trusting gesture as Ang, had lifted a hand to the quake swallows and watched them settle on it with the same wary expression of delight.

'It's like Jannl's Garden,' said Ang.

'This is real. It is in our world.'

She rested against him. While the sun moved overhead (what time did they now inhabit, passing like pilgrims onward from crowded city to empty land?) and the lattice of tree-shadows darkened, she dozed, hearing in the warm interstices of sleep Loy's even breathing. He, too, had fallen asleep. Half-waking, she remembered a verse of the old Gaian song her mother used to sing.

> She opened her door and her window,
> And the heart and the soul came through,
> To her right hand came the red one,
> To her left hand came the blue.

She might admit them if she could shed all her fears.

Loy lay wakeful in his bed. The van was quiet and Peach, asleep in the bunk above him, and Zoe, on the truckle bed, seemed hardly to breathe. Once more he rehearsed the afternoon's events. The computer-god of Traumesse which proposed and disposed six hundred lives, rooms as mannered as stage-sets, Ang's shadow play – these were the toys of her time. He could watch her conjure and admire her complex creations, understanding nothing of the method, but every part of the result. She used universal symbols, the everlasting truths. He – and she – had spent an hour or two, or ten, in Lutreia. Impossible to tell how long: no markers had been provided.

He was back, all in one piece. Before leaving her, he had embraced and reassured her. He had kissed her in this, her time; shown her that, in their absence, the clock's hands had not moved. Then, leaving her alone in her neat solitude, he had walked down the hill. There was the circus, undisturbed in the valley of Toul. The evening performance, crowds of eager Folk, had obliterated past sensations until this silent, night hour.

Were those Lutreian hours parable or prognostication? Did the Lady mean them soon to travel on, from present location to the past, or forward once more to fresher woods? Would they come at last to the City and know their travelling days were done? In what distant age would they find the

City again, and must they return to that enchanted moment when, in the green and scented valley of the First City, Cal would turn again, the red naias branch in his hand, turn his back and leave them to another endless cycle?

Was he meant to take Ang Semo with him?

Whose time is this?

When will I inhabit my own?

He got softly out of bed and into his clothes. There would be no sleep now. He lifted the lamp. Peach was in dreamland, lips apart and eyes fluttering underneath honeycoloured lids, and Zoe also walked in her own fanciful world, the river nixie her mother had made her fallen from her arms to the floor. He picked up the doll and tucked it in beside her.

Outside, the sky was already light. He did not know the time here, or anywhere. It seemed blasphemous for one in his blest state to wear a watch. The earliest birds were singing. He crossed the cold and stony ground, feeling its irregularities through his thin shoes, and went into the tent where he disturbed several nimble mice which were foraging amongst the litter underneath the seats. He sat down quietly and presently the mice returned. He watched them, quick russet glimmers amongst the discarded paper. The dusk was thick beneath the seats the mice felt safe and grew bold. One ventured from its cover and crept near his feet.

The mice and spiders, feral cats and cockroaches did not travel with the circus. But fleas did, and lice. He could draw no sensible conclusion from this thought, as much of an enigma as the afternoon's journey beyond time. He stood up and the mice scattered.

At the head of the valley, behind the tent, was a rock wall about his height. He climbed it quickly – there was plenty of light – and realised that, though he had been in Traumesse and up and down the hill which overlaid it many times, he had not once looked outward at the island of Sowash. The sea beating on the beach of Toul had been a backcloth to his active life. Here, in Noiro, he had worked as never before, ignoring his surroundings because of the cold.

And it was no longer so cold – maybe he was getting used to it, just a little. The wind was softer and there did not seem to be any ice. He thought summer was on its way. As in Eririon, the warmest season was heralded by a brave display of fragile flowers and these bloomed all around him. He saw a grey-furred stoat, or mongoose, hasten through the grass, a limp mouse in its mouth.

In the eastern sky, beyond the lumpy hill Gaby called the Old Woman, was a line of rose and gold. By the time the sun was high enough to cast shadows, he had reached a shore where rocky plateaux made vantage points above the sea. He stood on one of them and looked north. Some large birds, whose bodies seemed too heavy for their slender wings, were flying slowly across the water; others – tarunt gulls they called them – were feeding near the shore. Turbulent waves raced beyond the flock and, of the seven islands he could see, only one had any colour. It was carpeted in sombre purples; all the rest were black as silhouettes. This land belonged to the Folk.

He confronted the North. Somewhere out there lay Hiberna, concealed by distance and luminous clouds which looked as if they held all the snow this cold land would ever need. They swelled and billowed on the horizon, the frigid exhalations of the permanently frozen continent at the end of the world. He turned his back on them and walked as rapidly as the thick tussock grass would let him, back to Toul.

Ang, as she woke in Traumesse, remembered that the lovesick jester had forfeited his life in order to give away his heart and soul.

Yesterday, in the forest's warmth, she had dreamed of a solution but, like the illusion of the circus, her experience there had been another reflection of the truth. Here and now was Traumesse, surrounding her with its manufactured warmth, lulling and cocooning her. Somewhere above her, beyond the granite and the permafrost, was Sowash and a wide horizon, where the salt-laden wind blew softer with the approach of summer.

The circus encampment with its tented arena, its varied animals and its brightly-painted vans drew Loy in. The wind

146

whisked the smoke quickly away from their chimneypipes. Inside each one would be an early-morning fug and sleepy people struggling awake. He would see them all together later in the day. Cantor, as was his right under the unwritten constitution of the Democratic Travelling Circus, had called a meeting.

The smell of coffee was strong on the threshold of his van. He looked in, over the half-door. Peach sat on Zoe's bed, nursing one of the chipped beakers. Beside him was Float Gaby, her flat nose hidden by the red rim of Peach's usual cup. They were deep in conversation. He listened for a moment to Peach's nasal sing-song: 'If I were you I'd stay in the warm.'

'It's a cage,' she replied.

'Go on –'sa paradise.'

He wanted peace, and a cup of black coffee. Sleep would be good, but it was too late in the day for that. Also, he was glad to see Gaby. She had not been near the circus since the day of the first performance. Despite his invitation which, given in haste and guilt, must have frightened her off. She had a life to live up there, under the hill.

'Red Cheeks!' he said loudly, as he opened the door. 'Gaby.' He had not meant to let fall the secret nickname.

'It's Nets today,' she said. 'No work. The day for lazing and visiting friends.'

'What day?'

'Nets. The rest day. When we used to mend the nets.'

He shed his coat and sat opposite her on the stool.

'There's never a rest day here.'

'That's right,' said Peach, 'We always have to work.'

He pulled on his threadbare white sweater. It was cleaner than anything else in the van, for he had washed it in honour of the new landfall. The roses knit into it garlanded his slender body.

'You look very pretty today, Ahlikin,' said Zoe from the depths of his bunk, into which she climbed each morning to play. The blankets moved and her nixie doll peeped out and waved his fingerless hand.

'Thank you, Nix.'

147

Zoe's tousled head appeared beside the doll.

'Goodbye, Peach. Say hello for me to Chips 'n Dickory 'n Spot, and the two terrors.'

'Arf, arf,' said Peach and jumped down the steps. He left both doors wide. Loy saw Gaby's mouth open a fraction as Peach inverted himself and waved goodbye with his feet. She closed it again, lifted the pot from the stove and poured his coffee. While he sipped it, his eyelids drooped and his mind wandered. Gaby sat still and Zoe murmured softly to Nix.

The coffee kept him awake. Sometimes Charis and he had been silent together. She, for all her bold appearance, had been modest and forbearing, smiling lips closed to keep in her thoughts and voice. There was common ground. The forest dwellers moved silently in the shadow of the giant irogan trees and the Fishfolk, too, were empathetic, sensible of their surroundings. Gaby did not speak until he put down his cup.

'Nigerdlit, Orquordlit, Avangnardlit, Akunarmiut,' she said. 'Those are the four tribes of the Folk.

'The Nigerdlit lived beside the South West Wind; they were the Summerfolk who travelled from island to island, harvesting the wild hay and the kelp. The Orquordlit – those who live in the lee of the South West Wind – lived in the far North. Their name was a joke. They were the Snowfolk who could have no harvest except of deer.

'We are the Avangnardlit, those who live with Matoq, with the North Wind; that's us, the Fishfolk. And the Akunarmiut, they were the folk who lived between the winds and the Eastern islands until the big boats came to spoil their fishing.

'The Snowfolk and the Akunarmiut all died, and the Summerfolk have sold themselves to the tourists. We Fishfolk are the only tribe left.

'I think that you circus folk are the new Akunarmuit because you live between the winds, outside of time.'

He smiled at her. She had presented her long speech to him like a birthday gift. 'Thank you,' he said.

'So, Loy Akunar, what will you do next?'

'What will you do, Gaby Avangnar?'

She giggled.

'Float Gaby Avang. I'm a woman.'

'What will you do?'

'Bren is working on it,' she said mysteriously.

'But I shall travel soon enough,' he said, sure of the message from the forest.

'When – how?' she exclaimed. 'But, Loy, you can't go now. We're going to have the Fish Supper and then the Race. You must not leave until the sun does.'

'We must leave before it snows,' he said firmly.

'I like it here,' said Zoe. 'The snow's good for making castles. Cricket made a man before it melted.'

'You liked the cows in Eririon and there was plenty of snow in the Queen's garden,' said Loy.

'Didn't!'

He could see from Zoe's attitude, body hunched in the bunk and head near the window, that she was squashing her nose against the glass, pulling faces at the world outside. Suddenly she shrieked and made him start. Gaby laughed at him.

'Da,' cried Zoe, 'Here's the lady coming down the hill.'

'What lady?' he said, to teach her accuracy.

'The lady with the golden hair.'

'That's Dr Semo, the gajo lady.'

'No it isn't. It's Ang. Can she take off her hair like 2-Cute and Dork?'

'Shut up, Zoe. You're beginning to be rude.'

'Dada.' She fell into baby talk when she was thwarted.

'Be quiet.'

He stood in the doorway to watch Ang approach. Zoe, who had climbed down more nimbly than anyone would have thought possible in a child, held his hand. She climbs well, he thought. Shiny might take her up the ladder. She liked to swing. Ang's hair shone in the rare and precious sunlight. She was carrying the tools of her obsession, the heavy bag packed with mechanical eyes and a wooden prison-cell. Behind him, Gaby rattled the coffee pot.

Zoe rushed out abruptly and left him alone in the doorway. He reminded himself that, despite her long and varied life, she was only five years old. Ang put down her bag to lift the child. She kissed her. He felt a dreaful pang of loneliness assail him. Ghosts troubled him and someone from a different time breathed in his face.

The morning ripened. Cait and Fenner were the next to come and, after them, Ial and Pak. They had a new companion, an older Fisher called Kubbu, and Pak had brought his three children. Ribble, Taviak, and Siri took turns to ride in chairs made from the men's interlinked hands. Atluki trailed along. He had abandoned his portable because, he said, he could no longer hear the silence it made and carried instead a broken icedeer horn which Bren had found and given him.

The imported complexities of Traumesse were hidden under the hill and Toul, a stone cauldron of hopes, held them all. The day became a chance pavement of events which interlocked around a small fire of driftwood the Folk built. They gathered there while the circus went on with its daily round of feeding and rehearsal, rest and preparation. Pak's three ran off to play with the circus children and the dogs.

Ang and Zoe walked on the beach. Zoe danced in time with the waves and Ang paced slowly over the flat stones and the glittering, wet shingle, bending to pick up the best pebbles and the scattered, leathery scales of pelagic pike which made instant nail-files when dry.

Thus Loy was able to spirit Gaby away from her companions and separate himself from Ang, who had rushed at him and drawn back in confusion. He had promised to show Gaby the marvel inside the Rat Queen's waggon. He owed her this time.

It was dim in the creaking wagon whose iron bars and timbers seemed to move of themselves, and made a great cage of the old vehicle. The canvas wagon-cover also had a life of its own, and a voice borrowed from the wind.

Loy lifted the latch on the door, and they went inside. Gaby looked fearlessly about her. The lantern in Loy's hand made the shadows deeper, just as Grandgrand Pike's lamp, which she now kept by her bed, had enhanced the dark mystery of her shrine to the memory of the Folk. Some painted planks were stacked against one of the low walls and straw had been

150

scattered thickly on the floor. In the centre, the stalks were drawn together in a low mound.

'This is the Queen's castle,' said Loy, 'See the gate?'

She crouched to peer at it and he held the lamp low.

'There's a tunnel,' she said, pitching her voice low so that the beast inside would not be disturbed. 'When will she come out?'

'Draw back a little and wait.'

She stood in an easy posture, looking as if she was capable of waiting all day. Small chitters and shrill cries came muffled from the mound of straw. They waited and, with a sudden rustle, the Rat Queen emerged.

It consisted of five black rats, sleek, glossy and lithe. They walked sedately in a fanlike formation because they trailed a burden behind them, a huge knot built from the tips of their living tails, a ball of flesh, scale and bone to which various souvenirs of their long life in different locations adhered: sequins, coloured scraps of confetti, straw, grass and shining, water-worn chips of quartz. The knot dragged and caught in the straw. It seemed too large to be made from the tips of five rats' tails.

Most outsiders, confronted by five live and mobile rats, recoiled and Loy was ready to move and enfold Gaby in the safety of his arms. But she was not afraid.

'People pay to see this?' she asked.

'It's extra.'

'They're like big tussock mice. Why are they stuck together?'

'You should ask "How?" They are a great wonder to a great many gajo folk. Their tails are tied in a knot which cannot be undone; yet they live and prosper.'

'They look well fed – you must be able to untie them,' she said. 'Who made the knot?'

'They say that a Rat Queen makes itself,' the clown said. 'The knot was there when Sierra found it. She used to work people's cellars as a ratcatcher before she joined the circus. The tails have probably grown together – we'd lose money and get bitten if we tried to free them.'

Gaby crouched down before the rats and the biggest one

also squatted and looked up at her with bright eyes. The four remaining rats sat on their haunches. One licked its paws and began to polish its face. Gaby made a soft noise like a kiss and held her hands low and still so that the big rat could sniff them.

'You're as happy to be with them as Sierra is,' said Loy, astonished.

'Why shouldn't I be? They're only animals. What are their names?'

'The big one is Thunder, the thinnest one Lightning; those are Ripper, Biter and Loathing. They don't know their names. They respond to food.'

'Like this.' Sierra had stepped up into the wagon. A low-cut bodice covered in golden cord and mirror-sequins was the only sign of her other identity as the man-devouring Mistress of the Rat Queen. She had left her rat-whip in her van and wore loose trousers like many of the circus folk and an open Sineinain snowcoat. Her thick yellow hair had not been brushed.

She offered some dried grapes to the rats which advanced one by one, the big rat Thunder first, and fed. Then, in unison, they stood upon their hind legs to beg for more. Sierra gave each of them a raisin.

'You have to let the show proceed according to their actions,' she said, 'and keep up your patter all the time: Ladies and Gentlemen, my Rat Queen will now perform a prodigious leap – 'cos you've seen old Thunder skip, like that – and you hold out the whip for them to jump. No, I don't hit them. It's for show: impresses the crowd. Look, Loy, I've got to have more meat for them and more too for the dogs. You've got to see to it.'

'Ask me at the meeting this afternoon. We have many more troublesome questions to discuss.'

Once again, Gaby was bothered by her sense of intruding into their precarious lives. She knelt and looked closely at the five rats. 'You are five fine and handsome rats,' she whispered, and hoped that her voice would cheer them. They were sitting neatly down again, alert and ready. The big rat wrinkled his long nose so that his whiskers quivered,

152

and she was amazed to hear him address her in a thin and squeaky voice.

'Thank you and so we are,' he said. 'And Sierra's right: we are in control of the show. By the way, the name's 'Andsome, not starvin' Thunder.'

It was wise to be polite, even in such circumstances.

'Good morning, Handsome,' she said, 'My name is Gaby.'

He dipped his head very slightly and the other rats made similar bows.

'May I present, on my left, Tooth and Nail and, on my right, Velvet and Whisk, the ladies. Bone used to be between Nail and me, Moon between me and Velvet and 'tween her and Whisk was Hinny and Rind. They've died, sadly, and we're what's left. We've still got their tails though, stuck fast in the Knot. She (and he twitched an ear in Sierra's direction) had to cut their corpseses free.'

'But why are you tied together?'

'Cos we are; born to be together you might say. Dunno how it happened. One night we was in the nest, all separate and lively-o; next morning we was Joined. Tried to pull ourselves free and made it worse, hopping around. Only way to go then was to the Circus.'

'Can't it be undone?'

'Nah. It's hindissoluble and you can't untie it neither. Don't you fret. We're used to it and we have a good life. No need to see the world, except from the inside of this wagon.'

Gaby spoke out in defence of her country. 'There's a wonderful country outside. It's Sowash in Noiro. Wouldn't you like to see it?'

'Cold, ain't it?'

'But beautiful —'

'No use to a rat.'

'There's a lot to eat, if you know where to look. Just now, it's Blue and the birds are nesting. Lots of eggs.'

Velvet spoke. 'It's a long time since I had an egg.'

'Yes,' said Whisk, 'They keep the eggs for themselves.'

'There will be chicks soon, and then the malp will come ashore to pup and there will be plenty of caul and afterbirth,' said Gaby.

'Now you're starvin' talking.'

Grandgrand Pike had certainly been able to talk with the owl, Paikwi. Gaby's new wisdom jangled in her head and the crystal beads chimed sweetly. The power she felt rise in her made her like a child who has just learned to walk; she wanted to launch herself across the world.

The adults, their tense conversation over, were ready to pay her attention again.

'So much chittering,' said Sierra. 'I'll feed them properly now. Once a rat always a glutton.'

'I'm off now,' said Loy.

He went down the steps ahead of Gaby, intending to turn and offer her his hand in the old-fashioned and courteous gesture which he, as a clown, liked to use now and again. She would laugh, and jump past him.

He never did turn to her because Salter Bren, small and indomitable in clothes of fur and tall skin boots, was walking along the beach. He walked erect and looked as though he carried history with him. Gaby emitted an excited squeal and Ang Semo, closer than any of them to the Fisher man, turned from her concentrated contemplation of the waves and stared after him. Then she put her gloved hands together and silently applauded.

Later in the day Gaby tried to talk with the horse, Spooky, and was bitterly disappointed when he did not reply.

'Talk to me, Ang,' Zoe demanded. 'Why don't you speak?'

'What shall I say?'

'Say what you had for breakfast.'

'I had ice cream and cactus. Then I had a big piece of seagull.'

'You didn't!'

'What did I have then?'

'You had chocolate and worms.'

Playing this nonsensical game, they walked to the end of Toul's shore and began to climb the low bank which separated it from Noul and the tall rock-stacks. The harsh stone columns were too big for Zoe's notice, whose eyes were fixed on the spring flowers which grew in the salt-stunted grass between the boulders. Ang found it easy to spin and talk nonsense, walking thus, while her eyes and mind followed the prophetic figure of Salter Bren as he shrank into the mist and distance.

'Where do you think he's going?' she asked Zoe.

'Why, to find things on the beach of course. I found a ribbon, and a bottle as well as all these scales.'

The obvious answer, and the simplest. Her heart went out to him and she imagined him bending to examine flotsam and jetsam, selecting and discarding. It was a universal preoccupation, the obtaining of something for nothing. The best treasures were free. Yet he combed the beaches of a world she would always be denied, an enchanted place where to live was to know all. Like the Lutreian fen forest, it was another garden in the world of the dream. Traumesse was not of that world; nor were Siloe and Jannl whose algorithmic skeletons now struggled with another order of chaos. She looked down at her gloved hands. She had hidden the hands which made her constructs and operated her camera in thick wool: they should feel the cool air bite. When she had removed the gloves, she turned her hands palm up and stared at them. Left hand past, right hand future it was said. There were a great many lines on both. She felt melancholy, a pleasant twinge; later, she would feel regret. Loy Sen and Traumesse must belong in the left hand for he would soon move on, and the destiny of the Fishfolk had passed from her grasp to Bren's.

It was not so cold: she did not need her gloves. Loy's small daughter ran happily about in her thin City garments, the white snowcoat open and flapping like wings behind her. Perhaps she was a seagull.

Ang's hands grew damp in the salty air.

'Oh!' she said, aloud,' How I wish I was warm and dry.'

'Pretend.' That was all the help Zoe could offer.

She chose a rock and sat on it.

'There's room for you, too.'

Zoe sat beside her, short legs tucked up beneath a red and green wilderness of patterned cloth. This painted silk must be Artisan work and, in modern Sollar was priceless.

'Hasn't Loy bought trousers for you?'

''Course. I like my maral. It's pretty. I like my circus dress too – it's white and it sticks out.'

'But aren't you cold?'

'No. I'm snug as a bear in her den.'

'A carrion bear?' What could this child of the South know of bears? 'Oh, a toy bear?'

'A bear bear, silly Ang. Da had a bear for ages. Her name was Dasyssa. She could dance and play ball.'

The child knew more of the world than she.

'Where have you been, Zoe?'

In Sollar, when she had asked her cousins that question, they had replied with evasions and lies, wishing to hide the green and enchanted fields of childhood, where were dragons and stardrakes for the slaying, from her adult eyes. Zoe, however, was her friend and it did not matter that there were twenty-seven years and immeasurable aeons between them.

'With my Da – or with my Ma before she went away?' Zoe asked.

'Both.'

'I used to go to market with Ma and she would buy me a ribbon and we'd buy some fish to cook for Da. But after we left the forest there wasn't a market. The Queen gave us all we wanted.'

'What queen?'

'She wore clothes like that man – but she had a skirt. She had a garden with caves in it. It snowed.'

'And?'

'We've been East and West and South lots of times; now we're in the North my Da says.'

Zoe's memory was a child's. She did not use clocks, watches, hours and minutes – how could she? She was innocent of time and guile. It snowed; Ma bought me a ribbon; the Queen wore furs: she observed the events about her but made no judgments.

Zoe got up and began to pick flowers. When she had picked a posy, she brought them to Ang. 'This is a present for you,' she said.

156

Ang took the flowers. Their delicate petals were translucent, and their colour fugitive against their deep gold stamens. Zoe skipped and hopped on restless feet. She wandered away. Ang held the flowers to her face: they had no scent. She wanted to give the child something in return – a valuable gift, a treasure to keep for a rainy day. She could shed a burden easily here.

A gift, by universal custom, could not be returned and the child, not knowing its value, would accept it gladly. Ang called her back.

'Zoe. Look at this flower. Isn't it pretty?'

Zoe touched the golden lily which Ang drew from the neck of her jacket.

'It shines,' she said.

'It's my present for you. But first, I have to take something out of it. Go and play again like a good girl.'

She turned away from the child, bent and hurriedly scraped a shallow grave in the wet earth between her feet. Then she undid the clasp at the back of her neck and laid the locket on her knee. The gold lily leaves curved as artfully as green and growing ones, promising unimaginable wealth and the fulfilment of seductive dreams. She prised the stiff catch open and looked inside the bud, at the dead child.

'What's that?'

Zoe had come silently back and Ang froze with her hand over the locket.

'It's a little tiny man,' said Zoe, pulling her hand away, 'Is he dead?'

This child did not know dread; she had travelled all the forlorn regions of space and time and seen many sights. She deserved honesty.

'It's a very small baby,' Ang said 'And you're right – he died.'

'Like the bear. Are you going to bury him?'

'Yes.'

She gritted her teeth and extracted the dessicated embryo from its case, expecting every second that it would fall to pieces between her fingers. Its dryness had a leathery quality, the smooth, tanned feel of parchment. His mother's

157

body has been burned and scattered yesterday in her home town in Sinein. Pity overcame her and made tears stand in her eyes.

'Was he your baby?'

'No, not mine – another lady's.'

She laid the scrap of human tissue in its grave.

'Put some flowers in,' said Zoe. 'That's what you have to do.'

'All right.'

She scattered flowers from the posy on the embryo. The black earth which she scattered on it spoiled its unrealised beauty: she could not remember one word of the Valediction. She had none of Gaby's patient acceptance of life and its sister, death, and felt drained, as exhausted as if she had been awake all night. The child was still there, quiet as a listening mouse.

'I meant,' she said, 'In the case.'

'There's a flower, left over.'

Zoe retrieved the flower. It had five cream petals flushed with green and fitted the locket exactly.

'Can I have it now?' said Zoe.

The locket hung well below her waist, and bounced against the bright fabric of her maral.

'I'm pretty,' sang Zoe, 'I'm so pretty.'

Loy would chastise you for bragging, Ang thought. I love your boldness and cheek; and you are pretty. You will be beautiful one day. The circus-goers will worship you as you dance with your dogs and your lovers.

'You're supposed to put a picture in it,' she told the child. 'Or two. Of your mother and father perhaps, or anyone you love.'

'Da will get me one,' Zoe said confidently.

The name of the fortune teller was Alluleya. Her predictions had once influenced the temporal and spiritual government of the City State of Mahun; in the circus her function was, like that of the Rat Queen, to earn extra money. She read hands and tarot cards and considered that, since she was unable to foresee the circus's future destinations, her powers had waned: she had become a sideshow.

Nevertheless, she joined the huddle of Folk and performers which met in early-evening dusk in Loy Sen's van. She had felt restless since the last traverse: a yearning resembling the aura which used to precede her oracular trances interrupted her thought, asleep and awake. If she could not successfully read the hands of these northern people, she wanted at least to look into their faces and try to determine what drew them from shelter. She felt their guides and watchful ancestors about her. Dowdy, insignificant and of indeterminate age, she sat quietly on the clown's bed, waiting while her own spirits gathered.

At first the meeting seemed to be an extension of that which had taken place earlier in the big top. There, grievances had been shouted out and opinions given an airing. These occasional forums were therapeutic: while everyone protested with load cries of 'unfair!' and 'Shame!', they knew that nothing would, nor could, be altered. Loy Sen's statement that he could not even guarantee the Rat Queen's next meal was the truth. In the van, Sierra stood near him, still talking of the rodents' diet.

Gaby wondered why they did not hunt, like her ancestors. Here on Sowash in the growing season was a wealth of meat; when Greening came, there would be fruit and seeds. She thought she would test her own new determination and gather eggs as the women used to do. Not bantam eggs, though she had seen plenty laid away amongst the rocks, but tarunt eggs from Ulbeg. She would give some to her mother and some, not to Sierra for her rats, but directly to the chief rat, 'Andsome.

She would show Zoe where to find the bantams' eggs.

Loy lit the lamps. He had stolen fragments of time from the day and used them to return the van to its normal immaculate state: wood, metal and china gleamed. Already, the crowd in the van spoiled his order and made an atmosphere like that of other days, when the performers met here to dress or, further back – forward? – when his mother gathered the family about her in the City:

There was no performance tonight: occasionally the circus rested too. He sat on his bed near Alluleya.

The fortune-teller watched Ang Semo, who observed the company through her third eye, the rapid lens of a small camera. Sometimes, the camera whirred slowly and the click at the end of its quiet recital punctuated the conversation. Alluleya also heard the quiet dissatisfaction which rippled about her.

She had tried to read the hands of her own circus folk, but they told nothing but tales of the old City.

'Dukrame,' she said to Ang. 'I will tell your fortune. Give me your hands, my dear.'

The photographer spread her hands and Alluleya saw phantoms sitting on her right palm. She held the left hand comfortably in her own. The hurt was still present but it was weaker: the deep life-line scored it across and broke it. What would she do with the rest of her life? Sea and rock, warmth and light: Alluleya felt them all.

'You are going away,' she said, 'on a journey to your heart's desire. You will not be alone: you will travel with a dear companion.'

As she spoke the familiar formula, she saw hope flush the pale face of the woman, who turned quickly back to her camera without a word. But she watched Loy Sen through its lens and frowned.

In some measure successful, Alluleya thought she would tell the hands of the Fishfolk and found, as she looked for a hand to try, that there was no need: she could See.

The links between those present were complex, a gossamer network. The reflective filigree covered every head and spread in the air. By following one thread she could trace a link: blood relation, friend, lover. New links were growing and old ones dying. A smooth rope grew from the head of Needle Cait and soared away from her, out of the van; yet within Alluleya's mind there floated a misty cameo, the image of a Fisher man searching the shore. It was a permanent link. The threads which shimmered between Float Gaby and Needle Pak were stretched and worn and Gaby's face below the net gleamed round and red and wet with perspiration.

160

Alluleya spoke: 'I knew her in old age when she was settled and a grandmother and great-grandmother. Her tale sent me up to Sowash to see the place for myself; that and the genetic tie with my adopted folk – but this is her tale and you shall hear no more from me.'

She fell silent, watching them as she had once watched awed worshippers through her heavy mask of gold. She did no try to interpret the words Mahun had sent her tonque.

In the air between the clown, Loy Sen, and the Sineinian, Ang Semo, was a thick blur of bright and burning light.

Alluleya stared into it, looking deep, but it was like looking into a flame: she could see nothing. The light began to spin. She was on a roundabout, spinning on a children's carousel as she used to before the terrible power first visited her. The music which spun with her was the sweetest in the world.

At last, the silver horses broke free from their spiralling poles.

'Fouf!' cried Gaby 'It's so hot in here.'

She pushed the van doors wide to let in the clean, cold airs of Sowash. They would blow away her headache. Away beyond boulder and beck, the sea rushed up the beach. She could see Ikbik swimming across the dark sky and, turning again to the light, the motley company packed into this hot wooden box on wheels. Loy was smiling at her and Ang Semo's face was hidden behind her camera, its one eye blinking slowly. Zoe was dancing with her doll and Sierra's mouth had fallen open beyond, it seemed, her control. No one had understood the fortune-teller's words. She had spoken cryptically, as they usually did, and slipped backward in her place. It was a little while before Gaby realised that she had fainted. She pushed an airway through the crowd.

The fortune-teller frothed and bubbled as if she would dissolve and become one with her flyaway spirits. Gaby had seen it before: Atluki and his aunts had the eye and, afterwards, the falling sickness.

Out there, in the nigh behind her, Bren must still be walking and searching the shore in his brave fur garments while the sky-pike, Ikbik, watched over him. He was brave and wise. Maybe he too, knew the Reason Why and was familiar with the spirits which governed everything.

Shakla's gulls, the brown sweepwings whose primaries were once valued as paintbrushes, made a hunting flight every evening. You had to be sharp to see them for the screaming attack was over quickly and they swung out to sea with their suppers in their beaks. The effects of their raid lasted longer, the tussock alive with bereaved sea-parrots, those unwary parents who had not pushed their chicks behind them into the burrow.

Bren had always identified with the predators. He considered that anyone who pitied the parrots and their chicks was also to be pitied. The fit, and the fitted, survived.

This evening, the attack was loud. The birds swept overhead, five, ten of them; their wide wings magnificent, poised in an arc and ready for the stoop. He could not hear the lamentations of the parrots on the far side of the hill.

Readiness comes before action, he thought. He had never felt more able, both bodily and in the keen tool of his mind. A deed may be an achievement, but somewhere in the doing, between enthusiasm and culmination, lie escapades, actions which may or may not be successful but are always difficult and sometimes perilous.

His was another kind of predation : beachcombing, shorelarking. There was not much peril in looking for a bit of wood. He grinned. Yet there might be, for who knows what dread beasts lay out in the marsh at night? The act of walking through day and night into the new day was adventure. He had twice been out all night, but never alone; he had never planned to walk so far before, half-way round Sowash in search of the perfect spar. Fifty miles maybe, following every inlet and promontory.

Driftwood was chance stuff. They would want a lot for the Fish Supper fires. Sometimes you found dry planks, uncovered after years of burial in the sand; sometimes sodden timbers, someone's jettisoned deck-cargo; occasionally, a treasure, a whole piece of furniture lost from a wreck. He owned a exotic kokkowood footstool. It had come from the stateroom of a foundered pleasureboat.

Cait would be fishing soon. The day of the Catch and the Fish Supper would soon dawn, a holiday like this one and the fourth day of the week. The Folk name for it was Catch. Once, the day had marked a real catch and was not an annual memorial, a few hours' angling under the Sineinian re-education programme. They called the day by another name which he was trying to forget, as he was trying to forget that tomorrow he was due on shift at midday, his night of freedom over.

His people were famous for leaving as much as they found. The marks of their occupancy littered the islands: tent-rings, burial-boulders, the stone supports of old fish-racks, ruined bothies, carvings . . . abandoned artifacts all, ready and waiting to be revived.

Traumesse also took a tax from the island: it had taken his people instead of leaving them to their fate. He could not blame the Sineinians. They had acted in good faith. He knew how much the cosseted folk of the civilised world (as they called it) longed for their own lost roots. They collected and kept the things his people had discarded. They had collected his great-grandparents and put them in their circus, in their warm, illuminated, insulated nest below the permafrost. They had surrounded them with luxury and incentives – clothes, food, money, book-learning, a new religion – sat back, and watched them perform.

Bren walked more swiftly. He whistled softly, sang a bar or two of a popular song, and stopped. This seductive music he must also forbid himself. He breathed in a lungful of air and expelled it slowly over his vocal chords. The noise he made was deep, resonant, and ridiculous. The women were better at it, producing clear hoots and wails, the happy harmonies of the old days, music without instruments – rather, music with no instrument but the voice. The songs of the swan and the whale.

He loped along the shore past the circus. He liked that wolfish word, lope. It made him feel like a hunter. But all he was searching for was that elusive article, the proper piece of wood – something as long and as straight as possible, a spar without any cracks or weaknesses in it. He would make it into a spearshaft when – if – he found it. He was that far from being a hunter.

Noul's beach, beyond Toul, was littered, but not with wood. He found rope and plastic and worn bits of coloured glass, amber pebbles glistening in weed. Everything, but timber.

The stars were pinpoints in the sky. As the dark rose, their size increased. Aanori winked at Bren, and then the rest of the great pike became visible. He followed Ikbik's pectoral fin East, toward the night. He was glad to be a man of the North, and out at night. He thought of his friend, Pike Miy who had died falling from the boat and Miy's great-grandmother, Pike Neemi.

Usht' rose, giving him light to see by and Annasi, softly breathing in her sleep, kept him wide awake and blew his scent out to sea. He hummed a little to keep up his humour. There was no need for silence: wood was deaf.

He heard every night sound, each one separate and distinct, underlaid by the soft drone of the sea. He was approaching the coast beyond Nusseraq which bordered the kjarr. The Sineinians had taught him the old beliefs with a mixture of condescension and tolerance – how could they know what lay deep in the consciousness of the Folk?

Imps and demons there had been, which pulled you into the mud, and a hag; carrion bear. He treated vair with caution, but did not fear them and in any case they were breeding now in their courts inland. He-bear, this season, were travelling and she-bear and cubs were foraging for bees and honey and frightening tourists in souther Noiro, the fortunate islands of the Orquordlit. Near here, upon Loon Point, the spit between Nusseraq and Asimuss, the shore patrol had discovered Float Siri's drowned and half-eaten body —

He wished he had not taken this adventure upon himself and whispered prayers to Mahun, just in case, and as many of the spirits as he could remember.

There was nothing here beside himself, the night, the animals and the wind. He was not afraid of the animals which, even stinkbears and vair, had their own lives to lead, and he breathed more easily and looked ahead.

Like a sleeping giant, the marsh on his left made its own noises, sighing and sucking. The sea, tossing on his right, made a different sound, a perpetual susurrus as it advanced and withdrew. He felt vulnerable, a warm-blooded being between the cold fresh water and the salt.

Sometimes, although no one lived there, lights shone in the kjarr and roamed about it as if to show the way. I could lose myself for ever if I followed one, he thought.

I wish they'd put me on the development programme instead of intensive Traditions. I might have learned logic instead of emotion.

He crossed the narrow neck of land between the shore and the spit. Now, though he had not dared venture out on the spit itself, only the marshes lay before him, sodden land unassociated with recent dread. When the kjarr was behind him and he was high on the rocks near Narroc, he would be absolutely safe.

The moonlight showed him drifts of kelp, the round heads of seal in the water, the dry and dead wing of a goose. There were many lochans and watercourses. Water flowed from the kjarr in wide sheets and made broad streams on the beaches themselves. He padded through them and his feet threw up showers of watery sparks.

He gathered a flock. Birds, animals, ghosts and imps followed him, some treading in his footprints, some walking at his side. He became accustomed to them gradually, sensing them rather than seeing them. If he stopped and turned round, a confusion of shadows fled from him: from the corner of his eye he glimpsed a fur-clad hunter, a wise woman, and something with a dark red face. Siri linked arms with him, as she used to before she married and lost herself. He wished he could see her, whole again after her terrible death and glowing a little because she was a phantom.

'It's so good to see you, Bren,' she said.

If she had not been invisible, he would have believed she was alive. He could feel the pressure of her arm encircling his. He apologised because he must go on looking for his piece of wood.

'It makes me glad,' she said. 'You make me glad, Bren. You look well in your new clothes.'

The past, the present and the future walked the kjarr with him. He knew that Cait had swallowed the spirit that would become his child; he felt the blow Gaby had not yet dealt him.

He told Siri the news, who had died and who still lived, but she seemed to know it all and he pictured her drifting from one place to another, watching the quarrels and the antics, the reconciliations, the kissing and the labour. Once, she had been as beautiful as her sister Gaby, but shy. Amber buried in kelp. Though the moon shone bright, she cast no shadow.

'Prosper,' she said. 'Be thankful.'

He felt her no more and looked about him, in case a shadow lingered. Nothing. The whispers the animals had made on the shingle had stopped. He was alone. The tide was rising. He climbed up from the lowlands, overland to look at Narroc. The day climbed with him.

When he was the islands to the north, low and hump-backed in the water, he wanted to shout. He had seen them many times before; his feeling was not one of awe, or surprise at their beauty, such as someone like Ang Semo might feel. He was overjoyed because they were familiar and because they were his home.

In the old times, one family had summered on one island, Floats on Demender say, Needles on Sair. This had not meant quarrels and seclusion but co-operation. Each family had shown the others the best features of its island, where the fresh water was and the good fishing. When, in the cold, they travelled by sailsledge and across the open polynyas in their skifts, each island was freely open to all comers. He thought Hairete was the Salter's island. As Cait's man, he would have been allotted a space on Sair.

He did not want to own the land; it was his already because it belonged to everyone. It irked him to think that the land also belonged to the Sineinians. People from Ros and Sollar

166

had lived in the North for more than a thousand years. Salter was a Nenian word. He did not know the Avang word it translated.

The islands called him.

Narroc, across reefs and rough water, was an inhospitable place. In Matoq, when the worst winds blew, the sea rose all around it; waves broke over its craggy head. Then the ice came, stilled the sea, and coated Narroc with a film of ice. He had heard people compare it to a cake or a castle; he thought it looked then like a huge diamond lost in a drift of snow.

He saw the animal which had been sent to examine him: the carrion bear approached the reef slowly, sniffing and rooting on the opposite shore. Bren sighed, and was glad the rapids in the strait separated them. Not that he was afraid. Just wary.

Stinkbears could swim like fish and rough sea was no barrier for them. They were at home in water, just as comfortable as if they trod the land. Ice and snow were green fields to them. The unique arrangement of their padded feet and the hollow, non-reflective structure of their hair protected them from any treachery of the climate.

He estimated that, were they side by side, the bear would loom over him, at least one and a half times his height. On its hind legs, rearing in anger, it would be fearsome. Its black fur made it seem more frightful. It had no need to hide; it fed on whatever meat it found, honey and vegetation too, further south. It killed rarely.

Bren hunkered down behind a rock to watch it. This lowly position made him feel less exposed.

The carrion bear kept on coming. It had ceased its nosing exploration of the beach and had turned towards the water. Its forefeet rested on a water-covered stone and its snout was raised. He saw the nostrils open and close.

The bear knew exactly where he was.

I see you too, he thought at it, and the beast sat slowly down upon its haunches and yawned, so that he could clearly see the doubled set of teeth with which it stripped a carcase to the bone. He thought he would stand up.

Am I not Barendidt?

The icedeer Ang Semo had called had knelt to him. So far, he had possessed his secret quietly and Gaby had not told: soon the time to announce it would come and, meanwhile, he might try his blessed state upon the bear.

He rose slowly from his place of concealment and watched the bear across the water lower itself, close and closer to the ground, until it lay still upon the rock, half in the water and half out.

He could not prevent himself from shouting then.

'O–O–U!' he shouted. 'O–O–U–AH!'

He left the bear to its lonely deliberations and walked on, quite certain that he would find exactly the right piece of wood. When he reached the dunes at the back of Forso, below the ness and the burial ground, he dug in the nearest – easily throwing back vast showers of the dry sand – and brought out his spar. The wood, yellowed and oily, was splintery and flexible. It must have come from a tall sailing ship or a wooden liquor-palace, carvel-built, fitted with every convenience from bath to bathing pool, lost on a pleasure cruise. It smelled of resin and the taiga still.

Bren shouldered his embryo spearshaft and began the long walk back to Traumesse.

The hill over Traumesse, the hill which had been there when his ancestors lived in booths on Hairete and visited Sowash to trade salt fish for amber, had greened over and was shadowed with half-open lyng. He had deliberately chosen the steepest incline. He was ready and he was fit. When he had eaten a fish from Cait's catch, and won the Sineinian's race, he would show Ang, he would show them all.

The gate was open, the wide mouth of a comfortable burrow, all its bars, locks and hydraulics hidden in the rock. He walked steadily down the road into the hill, back into the present time and his nursery. He spoke to a plastimorph by the laundry.

'Oh, eight o'clock,' she said 'Early.'

The artificial daylight oppressed him. It had less luminescence than the brilliant light outside. He noticed that several of the lamps in each cluster he passed, usually unfaltering and so well maintained, had failed.

Of all the many names of Noiro, each one more fanciful than the last, Ang thought the invention of the Summerfolk, the Amber Necklace, most apt for this season, Blue; the prelude to brief summer, when the islands lay like brown beads in a still sea. Perhaps it was only by stringing together her island diversities on a rope of words and metaphysical fancies that Noiro's people could begin to comprehend her design. The string of beads looped over the vast breast of Guna, her Northern Ocean. Purple and gold by summer's end, Sowash and her eight satellites lay upon the collarbone.

Amber could be found on the shores of many of the islands. Once, a forest had covered the liquid blue and frozen white seas in between, a temperate dream of palms, pines, laurels, bays and yews, which she could have used in the landscapes of 'Greed' if she had not sown the seeds of death there. Once, too, the amber gatherers had roamed every part of the Northern Ocean, rowing from island to island, collecting their findings to be sent south to Diold and the City, there to be worked into exquisite toys for the rich.

Amber, travelling south, gathered money just as the sea filled up with brightly-coloured fish.

These days, the amber gatherers were a diverse collection of drop-outs, refugees and misfits from Guna's female society. They lived in huts on Longbeach and took to the seas in Blue to seek and gather their living.

They were reputed to have plenty of money, real cash in bags. She had seen no evidence of it and could not understand, visiting them with Pior, why they chose to live in squalor; and squalor in the cold seemed a lot worse than a fly-swatting existence in the tropics where warmth was free. They might be at sea now, or raking and netting off one of the beaches. She looked eagerly for them from her spray-drenched seat in Float Gaby's skiff.

Gaby steered the boat, confident and skillful. This expertise, which Traumesse gave with one hand and took away with the other, wishing its subjects to remain safe below the ground, enthralled Ang. They had not stepped the mast, nor hoisted the square sail — that would have been used, traditionally, to run south before the wind as summer ended and the sea began to freeze. If they had sailed, powered by wind and water, they would have scudded to Hairete, Salmo or Hara.

Gaby's female relatives powered the boat, leaning back and forward as they pulled on the sweeps. Her mother, whose given name was Susu like the Snow-woman in the photograph, but whom they all called Mu, counted the strokes; and her grandmother who, by the same convention, was to be addressed as Grand, sat beside Ang, sorting the already neat and orderly lines and making sure the children kept still.

Never before had she been invited to the Catch. She had been to the Fish Supper three times and her memories of these dull occasions, held under the strict Ethic of ERRATE, had melded together: she retained only images of spitted fish and sombre and purposeful gluttony. This time she would attend the Supper as the Director of Traumesse; but she was inwardly full of glee because she, Ang Semo, would attend also by invitation of the Float family.

'I've been very busy,' Gaby had said carelessly, offering no further excuse. 'So I couldn't come to see you.'

She had handed Ang a string of multicoloured beads. These, required explanation.

'Writing,' said Gaby 'Our writing. Blue for sea, silver for fish, black for the line and these, many colours, are the floats — and the Floats! Then silver for fish again and red for fire. "Please come to the Catch and to the Fish Supper."'

Once again the unrejected friend, Friend even, of the Folk. She had not troubled the girl with her painful memories and the recent devastation of her self: the Folk, Gaby's people, had become infinitely more important to her than a secure and prestigious job in Traumesse.

Gently, Gaby had taken back the beads; but only to spread them in a wide circle and hang them round Ang's neck.

Her colleagues had remarked upon her new ornament, which was at odds with the tailored image she preferred to project.

'The Folk are all wearing beads,' said Eda Voran. 'Clearly, the fashion has spread! The Traditions course is having quite an effect – and you are very lucky to have been given such a fine example of a message-string. They're a bit like poetry, I find, or primitive hymns. Did she tell you what it says?'

'Yes. It's —'

'Oh, let me, do: "Blue sky, silver rain, the black storm, the coloured flowers, Even the water, all are from our Oma" – the Mother, here the sun, you understand? Wonderful isn't it?'

'Marvellous,' said Ang, and smiled so happily that the anthropologist marvelled to see such free manifestation of her Director's inner strength.

This was the only one way to see Sowash, from a boat. It gave a better perspective. Each time that Ang had entrusted herself to the pilot of an open boat, which was seldom, she had found herself filled with a joy so profound that she believed, in the tossing hours afloat, that her ancestors had been sailors, that she owed her elation to the genetic code which also shaped her body. Out here, the subject of the unsubjected waves, she understood how, despite Science, she was frail and mortal. This violent undulation, this old-fashioned way, had all the discomforts and rewards of reality: cold hands and feet, damp clothes, a stiff breeze. Jannl, crossing his cyan river, could know nothing of this, for all that he was, like herself, a creature composed of neural explosions, synaptic tides and subtle chemical mixes who could laugh and love and weep. Jannl was two-dimensional: he had no depth – unless, within the complex minds of the computer there existed new, minus, dimensions; the yard-sticks of infinity, which corresponded with the diminished scale of its components.

The machine computed polychromatics; here, an endless variation played on green and blue and brown; the islands themselves lay low in the sea, broad backs humped like those of the moon seals which, if they were in luck, would follow the boat.

The skifts (for they were part of a merry fleet of the small boats all laden with laughing women) had come out of the same great gate which opened for the ferries. Indeed, they had passed one at the exit, a sprat to a shark, before pulling out into the unstable sea. They had rounded the south-western head of Sowash, passing close in, between the island and high and barren Skaa. With Skaa's skeletal transmitters and receivers behind them there was nothing to obtrude upon the intricate pattern of sea, sky and islands. The ecologically landscaped hill which covered Traumesse looked as natural as the green hump of Hairete away to the west.

They opened Ulbeg: Ang gazed into the black cleft, and felt nothing. Tarunt gulls still rose and fell upon the thermals. The pillow lava near the water was still magical, wet green float glass. She thought she ought to be angry or sad, but she was content because she was here, at sea with the Fishfolk, and her past was ancient history, even yesterday's routine and the circus's heady days: a closed book. Her mind had drawn away from Ulbeg and unhappy happenings, refusing pain as, rushing to greet Loy the other day, she had drawn back, spoken rather than embrace him.

Ulbeg was closed and lay behind. Ahead were Forso's golden sands, but the boat altered course and began to make across the Reach.

Orsa, green and violet this season, beautiful as Hairete where the ice-deer fed on flowers, had long yellow beaches like Forso's. Northern sand, she thought, the same stuff as ours to the south, pale silica, powdered rock; but how it differs! The light here gives it purity and there is so much of it, unspoiled — by beach huts, jetties, garbage, fat swimmers parading their nakedness. . .It is cold to touch yet, like the bustling crescent which is the City's golden shore, holds a footprint no longer than the time between tides.

If you crossed the sand you found a fragile garden: the weeds the sea throws up when the ice has gone, which lie, rot, and eventually break down into a fertile buttress where soft grasses grow and a variety of vivid and short-lived flowers bloom. Behind the bank lay tussock hag, dense clumps of rough and razor-edged grass and deep and hidden hollows and holes. The grass and tussock were too green for belief – yet it grew, there, not a hundred yards away from her, sprouting for all it was worth until the ice returned.

The Floats rested on their oars: they had rounded Orsa's eastern cape and lay afloat between her and her sister island, Wirra, whose many lakes, mirrors of brown water backed with peat, reflected the light. Mewsmere, the nearest, was alive with swimming and diving birds, with rain geese, mergansers, loons, and singing swans whose entrancing harmonies, nests and eggs accomplished, had degenerated into honks. There too, wading into the sea with their weighted nets, was a party of amber gatherers. Their boats were drawn up out of the water and the tridents they used in deeper water were stuck in the sand. They took no notice of the birds, nor did the birds appear to notice them; but Gaby, leaning on her short steering oar, hailed them in a mixed patois of Sineinian, Noiran and Avang.

When identities had been established and greetings exchanged the two groups parted. The amber gatherers settled to the task of dragging their nets through the water and trawling up huge quantities of red hair weed and dark brown kelp. They sorted through it, throwing the tangled stems aside for wave and wind to toss on to the machair. The amber pebbles they found were often very small and a large boss of the petrified resin caused them to shout excitedly and to sing.

The small fleet of Fishfolk women rowed their skifts away from the disturbance, travelling along the kyle between Wirra and Orsa until they came to a reef. The water ahead was white, fast-flowing water from the Sound, which rushed the rocks and broke over them in waves. But here, in the lee of one broad rock, was slacker water, and the women shipped their long oars and the strongest and most experienced in each boat took the steering oar, to hold the boat steady while the rest prepared to fish.

Hareng, colin and dorfish fed on this reef. The Folk called it the Dinner Table. Ang leaned over the side and saw the fish: some darting here and there in pursuit of crustaceans and fry and others kept their place in the water, heads to the north, fins sweeping, just as the steerswomen worked to keep their boats with the shoal.

Gaby began to fish. Her line was long and covered in hooks, which she baited with pieces of the shellfish she took from her box. A string of painted floats, colourful as the beaded invitation, was fixed about two-thirds along its length. She let the line slide ito the water and her mother, following the line with her eye, leaned across and opened the empty cerf which sat in the middle of the boat.

The wind whipped the fishing line and Ang's hair flew from its confinement, scattering pins. She watched the line sink deep in the water, below its pitted, mirror surface. Beneath the ripple and daze, the water was clear: she saw the weights at the end of the line gather bubbles and become luminous diving bells. She saw the heads and legs of the dead shrimps wave, and the first hareng pursue one, snap, and be hooked. The line of floats sank, and bobbed up again. Gaby, fishing, was reflected in the water, a small foreshortened figure of distorted dimensions, changing shape as the water heaved. The floats sank again and Gaby pulled her line from the water. She had to tug and heave: many fish had taken her bait and the line was heavy. When it was all in the boat the women saw that every hook had caught a fish.

She did not leave the iridescent fish to die in the air but carefully unhooked each one and struck it firmly across the head with a piece of driftwood. As the fish died their lustre faded and they looked tarnished, dying shadows of the bright creatures in the sea. She tossed them into the cerf, except for half-a-dozen, which she put in a bucket.

She had caught twenty fish, and her kinswomen laughed because that was one for each of her years: she would be twenty tomorrow.

'Pak should wash and be thankful,' one of them said.

Gaby took the gibe good-humouredly and Ang wondered how she continued cheerful in such straights.

'We all smell fishy now,' said Gaby's mother.

She, Susu, had caught seventeen fish and the older women made jokes about their youth. Float Grand declared herself satisfied with nine: 'one for each of my babes and I don't need a Sineinian medal to prove my worth!' The six children were ecstatic with a total of twelve.

Gaby invited Ang to fish.

The shrimps crawled over each other in the bait box. Ang, picking one gingerly out, reminded herself of the numerous occasions on which she had pulled such creatures – crayfish, stock-crabs, lobsters – apart in the best restaurants of Sollar and Ros. Their pink shells, blushing in violent death, isolated them from anything real: the green garnish on which they were presented was a pretty bed. These animals were transparent like the shallows they swam in and their gangling legs were thin as spiders'. She pulled the head off one.

Then it was easy and she baited all the hooks and lowered them into the water. The line slid gradually deeper. She had no time now to follow its downward progress for she must control it; Gaby showed her how.

When the first fish bit a shock travelled up the line. She felt its struggles through the fine medium of torture and harvest. Another bit. The line was alive, but Gaby would not let her draw it up until it was leaden and fluttering with certain death.

They did not ask her to club her fish.

She had caught fifteen and was applauded and smothered in embraces and kisses, all of which made the boat rock dangerously. The women shrieked in mock alarm and laughed before they sat down. Their neighbours in the fleet shrieked and laughed with them.

She heard echoes of past mirth in this present hilarity: the other girls at academy had found her reluctance to undress in public funny. They had called her Ang Shamo. Maturity had taught her to join in the laughter and, by adoption, turn the joke. She did so now, for the humour sounded harsh and the women laughed with great gusto. Gradually, they drew her into their circle until she was laughing with them, so hard that she could not remember why she had begun and the noise of it became a song of unity, an audible concern, and an embrace of sound.

Gaby's hoot, that irresistible and infectious klaxon blast, kept them all in stitches until they ran out of breath.

The women unshipped their oars and all the natural sounds of the kyle flooded back. Orsa was their objective now: food to fuel them and a rest.

The picnic, Ang was sorry to see, was no Fishfolk banquet of hareng and crab, but a hungry tearing-open of pots and packages from the canteen. Perhaps the true feasting, and the hoped-for reversion to the old ways, would come later when they cooked and ate the blue and silver fish which filled the cerfs and buckets in each skift. Ang ate her own cold meat and shared a tub of the early yellow cherries which had been flown up from Ineit. The women lay and gossiped on the beach; tales of births and illnesses were exchanged and then Gaby and Cait, yawning and protesting that they would soon fall asleep, stood up. They began to choose two teams for a game. Ang, hunched on a stone, watched and waited. It was school again: the awful wait, the anguish and the silent prayer to be chosen soon, not left to the last.

Gaby, of course, picked her. The object of the game was to defeat the rival team, and running came into it and the gathering of stones which were piled in two cairns. It went on for a long time without result. The piles of stones grew higher and still no one seemed to win. At last, the women flagged and left the game unfinished, laughing as they retired.

Gaby tried to explain why the game had not 'come out'.

- They knew no other games. Rhyming and Skipping, The Farmer in the Field, Marry Me Do – these were foreign and far away, the games of Sineinian children. They did not dance in nightclubs, nor play baccarat; this sole and pointless game had been reconstructed for them by Eda Voran but they had delighted in it and played with gusto and joy.

After all, Ang had seen them being themselves, seen more of their inner concerns and true spirit than any anthropologist. They had shrieked a lot and laughed much more; she, too. She would always remember the furs and the beads, the crystal-strung cords round Gaby's neck, Susu's hood with its tassles of vair tails and the worn malpskin drawers that covered Float Grand's sturdy legs: treasures new and old brought out. Their hair also: they seemed — even vain Cait — to have forgotten Sineinian styles, so that their heads were at once wild and suited to their new — and right — way of dressing. They had the kind of wayward beauty wild flowers display when placed beside an orderly arrangement of cultivated blooms. If she was, herself, that cultivated plant, she could no more escape her heritage of learning and restraint than they their fishing and laughter. She saw that Angle Fenner, whom she had heretofore regarded as overweight and, therefore, unworthy of notice, her fat happily concealed beneath the regulation coverall, was beautiful; her amplitude a blessing in this climate and her long, thick hair, neat hands and feet her treasures.

On the way back, pulling steadily across the Reach, they came up with the amber boats and the craft drew together while fish were swopped for pieces of amber. Some of the amber masses were bigger than gulls' eggs, but the gatherers did not now seem concerned with value. They were glad, rough and hirsute men all of them, to exchange gossip with the women and to be allowed to boast and flirt.

Ang found herself the object of their attention, herself and Fenner who boldly smiled. She was given a piece of butter-yellow amber with a smooth sea-gloss upon it. When she held it up to the sun she saw Sowash, Orsa and Wirra in it, dark humps in a flat calm. The man who had presented her with it had retreated into the prow of his boat. He was fair-haired like herself, but his pale, Sineinian skin was burnt brown by ice-light and sun.

'Remember me to the fountains of Ros,' he had said and she had wanted to question and delve, discover what his antecedents had been. She forbore, turning to the fossilised resin and feeling its intrinsic warmth. She turned the fossil in her hand and, looking again into its clear interior, saw three tears there, constant and unalterable like the tears Loy painted on his face; felt tears on her own cheeks. In deceitful Lutreia, he had wept real tears.

The blond man gave her a cheery wave. They were off: they had a long way to row.

The fountains, she mused, the waterjets of Ros, dozens in every open space and park. They surrounded the city and cascaded in its streets; fiddlers and vitriphonists played beside them. Perhaps he had been one or the other.

She wrapped the amber in her handkerchief and stowed the package in her pocket, intending that it should be, in some sort, a consolation prize and keepsake for herself.

The seals had come. Gaby was speaking excitedly to her, pointing them out. They had white heads and huge round eyes. When they rose to the surface of the water she saw their black backs and the pale ellipse of fur which gave them their name: moon seals.

The purpose of the bucket of fish was explained. The Folk liked to give something back to the sea. Less wary than malp, the animals swam close to the boats, pushed up their round heads and wept. They reminded Ang of the big rosinback in the circus: he had the same rocking–horse quality and pied charm.

'Look!' she said to Gaby. 'Spooky seals.'

'I love Spooky,' said Gaby fervently.

The seal's tears made Ang smile. These, too, were false tears: the animals wept constantly to protect their eyes and, when they emerged from the sea, these same salving tears continued to flow. Their whiskers were trembling black wires, sensitive as fingers; their nostrils were open to smell the fish.

The day had been long and there were many delightful hours to come. The Folk and the moon seals played a game of tag and the reward, when the seals rose at the end of the chase, was fish, ready-caught and hand-served. A seal matriarch swam up and took a hareng from Ang. It was the last. The seals rolled and dived and, suddenly, were no longer there. The sea, which was green as a new apple in the flat light, was empty of seals; they had all fled below and the frail boats moved steadily toward Forso against the tide. The wind had turned cold: Matoq's gentle companion,

Annasi, held ice in her mouth at night. Ang yearned for flames and hot roast fish.

Eda Voran made herself ready by dressing warmly and making sure she carried a paper notebook in which she could unobtrusively make notes. She had a feeling that the Supper this year would mark a development in Folk culture. The new fashions amongst them pleased her: it was good to see them adding their own decoration to the standard-issue coveralls. They had understood the chance visit of the herd of hungry icedeer to be an omen. The early thaw had confirmed its status as a portent: thus did myths and legends grow and the powers which should be attributed to physics and geography were attached to animals following their primeval instincts. It would be an odd and ominous sign of her own culture's failure if the Folk abandoned it too soon in favour of the raw, hunter-gatherer existence.

The eagerness of the Folk to depart the edifices of her civilisation had surprised her, but she was not insensible of the honour they did her in expecting her to be at their Supper.

At half-past four, she set out to walk across the island. She wanted to be in good time, to see everything from the start; she went alone because the Spokesman had been to Ang Semo with a curious request. He had asked the Director if Sollar's annual Supper gift of twenty-five cases of liquor and thirty cases of Gatzo could be suspended 'permanently and for ever'. So (because, astonishingly, Ang Semo had agreed) there was no need for the 'morph porters and their chargehand. No need, no alcohol and no fun. Carey and his team had immediately lost interest; Ander had said he was not going to walk six miles to eat a piece of charred fish.

Eda wondered what would be drunk with the smoky, half-burnt fish. Water? It was unkind of Bren to take away the children's pop for the sake of some half-baked principle. She carried two flasks as usual, coffee for warmth, and strong akwit for stimulation.

At half-past six, she reached her goal, the flat-topped knoll above Forso. There was a slight depression in the hilltop which resulted from the collapse of abandoned sea-parrot burrows. Here, the men would build the cooking fires. A few yards away to the east lay an ancient burial ground. It took a trained eye to recognise it. The tussock-grass was no different and the boulders which lay in it were as gouged and grey as the one she leaned on. The ever-present wind stirred the grass and long shadows crept out of the quirks and depressions in the boulders. An imaginitive person might fancy that the dead moved too, but she was practical and inquisitive. She noticed the repetitive patterns in the groups of burial-boulders and thought about the laborious methods the Folk had employed to shift them. The dead were dead; only the quick came here to feast.

The light gave a clear indication of the time. The sun was full in view. When it dipped below the western horizon, it would be ten o'clock and night would last four hours. Behind and all around her were the lovely islands and the wondrous sea; this landscape, so unlike the cultivated acres of Kein, had lured her here:

"A big town is like a bird-mountain made by man; it is well enough for a time, but one soon has enough of the noise, of the screeching auks, the whistling guillemots, the greedy gulls, and from one's inmost heart one longs for the lonely nest of the wild duck by a quiet distant lake, or out amongst the rocks of the ocean where eiderducks ride the crested wave."

Like her colleagues, she had first read Shakla's logbooks in childhood.

The water looked green and deceptively calm. Those black shapes were the boats. On the horizon, the low clouds made fantasy islands. She turned her head and counted the lakes of Wirra. There were supposed to be ninety-nine – if tarns and lochans were lakes too.

It was a bruiser, this promotion of Ang's. She had wanted the job herself: she was the elder and had more experience of running this delicately balanced operation of renewal. Impetuosity and misguided sentiment could ruin it. These Folk, the last four hundred and forty-seven, the survivors of a vanished culture – and the promoters of its future – were a precious resource. They needed protection still, not empathy. Ang Semo, she was sure, had talent – genius, possibly – had all the right certificates and the personality: slightly stern, her private self reserved and separated from the professional; had a pleasing appearance, had stamina. Had axes to grind.

The circus too. Ang had immediately thrown a fence around it and declared it her territory. The order to stop the enclosure had come direct from Sollar – but it hadn't made any difference. The AD – the Director now, my Lady! – had continued to annexe the newcomers with visits and personal favours – and favourites.

Anthropology was the appropriate discipline. The circus performers were human beings, even if they were also illegal immigrants who concealed their true origins. Why hadn't she been asked to attend the meeting with its director? She had had two hurried conversations with him; one of his subordinates, the man called Peach – what an unlikely name – had been deputed to show her around the site.

No use railing: Eda undid her pack. Hot coffee. The wind already blew cold. This pallid sun-of-the-north had little power once evening came. She sipped and watched the shadows lengthen until she saw the first procession of men appear, winding slowly back from the kjarr-edge, where they had been cutting whins and the ropelike stems of dead crayberry bushes. Their children leaped around them, untidy trolls.

Salter Bren was near the front and as conspicuous as always. His hair was wild now and greasy with its own oils instead of imported slicks. The warm colours of his tailored coveralls had gone, replaced by subtle others, the browns and greys of earth and rock. The beads he wore sparkled: water, Wirra's myriad lakes. He was a hunter. He was the epitomic Avangnard, dressed in his Fachuk's nork and lak – GrandthreeFather's chestskin and forks was the literal translation. She had worked hard at Noiran languages and assiduously kept up her studies – but how was it ever possible to think, to reason, with these uncouth syllables?

While she worked the translation out, an old jingle slipped into her mind:

And all he found in his grandfather's chest
Was a redingote and breeks and a tile and a wig
And Jager put them on

The tune whirred in her head line the motor of the old music-box used, broken, decayed and full of ghostly harmonies.

She was wrong – he was inconspicuous, natural as the landscape. His companions in mixed Folk garments and modern dress were in error, unable to decide between upside where the wind blew them life and death in equal proportions, and downside where work and study were repetitive and death an individual ending in the long apprenticeship of the new Folk. The more she stared at him the more excited she became. Because you've never met a *real one*: her thoughts took hold and shook her.

Here he is – but he can't be true to the tradition. He has been taught it. By me. He is as much a construct as Ang's Jannl.

I ought to call him by his proper name: Barendidt Avangnar.

Bren walked up to her, put down the wood he was carrying, and smiled. The smile was open and full of delight. It said, 'You've never seen me before.' Kubbu and Float Fa were close behind him and the three men stretched out their arms and gave her, one after the other, the proper Folk greeting of a loud slap on the hand. A second procession appeared from the direction of the shore: men carrying bundles of driftwood. Scarcely half-dry, it would smoulder and occasionally produce a yellow flame; dried by its own combustion, it would flare and burn quickly, hot and red to the heart. A corn-cob fire. She thought with rushing nostalgia of bonfires and picnics, of her two daughters far away in their own lives at the Academy in Ros.

'Good evening Spokesman, Float Addush, Weightmaker Kubbu,' she said politely. She shook hands with each man. They never made small talk nor condescended to gossip with her. They grinned absently, almost apologetically, and turned away to build the fires. Some of them, Bren and Kubbu amongst them, crossed the hollow and stood silently beside the burial-boulders. She watched them. They appeared to be deep in thought, praying or reflecting upon the mysteries of their controlled existence; or perhaps they believed themselves to be speaking with the dead. They never spoke voluntarily of this annual communion and her theories, like those of her colleagues, living and dead, remained unproven.

Quietly, she extracted a rug from the pack and clambered with it to the summit of the common boulder behind her.

Kubbu lit the two fires with a cigarette lighter and she fell again into a brown study, wondering what compromises would have to be made when the descendants of these Folk were finally liberated into the reservation.

Fire had returned to Noiro with the coming of human beings. The first Folk had carried it north in portable hearths which could be set down on the bottom-boards of a skift or upon the rough surface of each newly-discovered beach. The southern phenomenon, flame, lightning's child and begetter of forest fires, had made life in the land of ice and water possible. It returned to burn on the heads of extinct volcanoes, a symbol of persistence and a reminder that magma and molten rock had dominated Noiro before it had a name.

The flame had been the responsibility of the oldest woman in each family group. Without it, the fish her daughters caught and the flesh her husband and sons brought her would be useless, for only the beasts themselves ate their commons raw.

Time and education had eroded the custom. Anyone could light a fire now.

Smoke poured from the fires above Forso. Ang had begun to feel the cold; food and flame would be welcome but the fires were newly lit and half at least of the two streaming grey clouds was steam. She pulled on her gloves and the woollen hat she had bought from the Vulyara in the Highlands. Its plaited strings tied under her chin; it was soft and warm and it tickled her chin. She felt like a kjarr imp as she helped beach the skift.

Each catch had been gutted and strung on lines. The women took turns to carry the strings and the children ran about, freed from the confinement of the boats, their shrieks penetrating the cool quietness of the evening. Everyone climbed the hill.

Eda was relieved to see Ang Semo in the fishing party. It seemed larger than was normal and the women unusually excited. She slithered down from the rock and went to meet the Director, consciously submerging her envy as she went.

Dr Semo was diffident and refused the akwit Eda offered. She was holding the hands of two children, Float Siri's oldest who would soon, by the ancient and singular custom of glosit, belong to her sister Gaby, and she wore a curious hat — surely another indication of the strain of her unexpected promotion and that awful episode with the embryo in the locket. Recently, the Director had given up wearing the gold pendant lily, and this was a relief to Eda. Partiality was not the Sineinian way. In Dorta's deranged mind, the locket must have become the symbol of her authority, regalia to be passed to her successor.

The children were persistent, demanding to be picked up and perched on the rocks, and Eda resisted the temptation to ask, 'Where did you get that hat?'

Ang lifted the children in turn. On the summit of the boulder they found Eda's rug which they claimed instantly. Wrapping it round them, they subsided and were quiet.

'I will have that drink, please,' said Ang.

So, a fragile bond established, Eda moved close enough to see that the awful woven hat was Vulyar work from the Central Highlands and became, while not envious of it, interested in it as an artifact. Perhaps Ang Semo was going native: it happened sometimes. Or trying to develop a friendlier face to show the Folk.

The flames had taken hold. They attacked the drying wood with an intensity that made the two Sineinian women want to control them. Ang bent to push a branch further into the fire and tried to look as if she belonged. Out there, afloat on the sea which was the hereditary estate and roadway of the Folk, she had felt comfortable; the presence of Eda Voran, reminding her of her status and authority in Traumesse, was unwanted and her friendly chatter like malediction.

Eda studied the two fires. The dense crowd around the nearest was also the largest and the Folk in it least identifiable as educated biotronics workers since they all looked, more or less in the fading light, like the Fishers in the museum diorama. Salter Bren stood beside Ropewalker Aglit, the Spokeswoman; both looked supremely confident. The Spokesman's bride was near him, hanging her fish in the hot air above the flames, and her family was gathered about her. Nearby were Angle Fenner, Needle Pak, Hook Ial, Weightmaker Kubbu and elders of every family. A ribbon of smoke drifted above them like a ceremonial canopy.

Float Gaby was sitting on the ground and a large group of excited children had formed round her, for she was pulling her famous faces. The cries of the children rose into the smoke and the evening and the laughter of Ribble and Taviak rang loudly from their nest on the boulder.

The second fire seemed to burn without the intensity of the first. It had less wood, less fish hanging above it, and less attention from the Folk beside it. The anthropologist tried to determine the reason for the neglect. Most of its attendants were from the Rower family, taciturn individuals at their brightest. Attachuk was muttering glum sentiments – to judge by his expression – into his wife's ear and old Catch leaned on his stick and fixed the expectant company with a baleful stare which said, 'I want my liquor.'

Eda thought she would offer him a tot of her akwit if he continued sullen; but the party was not hers to host.

Hook Ial, whose dark eyes mirrored the fire, broke up a barrel. He was always willing and quick to learn; a little taller than most Folk, his face a little narrower, he showed traces of a different genetic inheritance. His great-grandfather had been an Ineiti ecologist and Eda remembered the deliberations of the Ethnic Determination Council before his breeding permit was issued. Lapsing for a moment from her professional objectivity, she thought she understood the attraction he had for women – not herself, raised in a Ros physician's family, but Fishfolk women, ingenuous girls like Fenner.

To an archaeologist the barrel Ial had destroyed was a valuable artifact; her role, as an anthropologist was to observe and educate but not to interfere with independent action – and many such barrels and other discarded articles littered Noiro and Hiberna, the remains and leavings of failed enterprises, wrecks, and past expeditions. To Ial, it was firewood. He fed the flames with broken staves and they flickered for a few moments up and down the spectrum causing Eda to wonder what the sea-diluted contents had been.

The twins loved (had loved, for they had now turned fourteen) fireworks. She used to buy them in the market, once a month: Fall Candles, which would scatter sparks of red and gold; blue Twirling Dancers and tall Stargazers. They set them off in the paddock once the donkeys had been fetched in. The rockets had soared high, illuminating the quiet garden and the tiled roofs, while they flew in emulation of their great winged sisters, toward the stars.

This was the second time she had thought of the children inside ten minutes. She felt in her pocket. There, under her notebook, was a tiny bag. She burrowed into it with deft fingers and extracted a minute doll.

She could feel many strands of thin cotton, the hair of the doll. This one, draped in her locks, was Little Om, the provider of fish, the Old Woman of the Sea. Little Om had six companions: Earth, Uta; Wind, Little Matoq, cold breath of the north; Fire, Abayzor; Manikwi, the ubiquitous haze owl; Ikbik, the pelagic pike and Ilgolot, the carrion bear, a beast to be feared when all you had to protect you from its scavenging jaws were the thin walls of your booth and a malp spear or two.

They were worry dolls. She had found them herself, in a ruined bothy. The skin bag which contained the dolls had been buried deep in dry moss in the bed-place. The charm was, perhaps, two hundred years old and she had kept it for herself instead of reporting it.

Telling a worry was still common practice with the Folk, but now they used the psychiatrists of Traumesse. You were supposed to put the doll to which had your passed your worry under your head when you slept.

She held the minute doll tightly and thought of Tilia and Nonet, oblivious among their schoolfriends of their mother's lonely career in the north.

Ang saw Eda's concentration. She would want to retire a little way, to scribble in her notebook. It made an excuse. She edged toward Bren.

The cascading colours which flared in the fire as Ial burned his staves made her think of wavelengths and the difficulties of reproducing colour. Her achromatic images were pleasing because they did not address that problem. But there would be only one way to show the Central Highlands, and that was to photograph their warm colours: browns so dense they seemed viscid, and were hard to distinguish from the low-growing and sun-charred vegetation; reds and an occasional and surprising yellow. She had regressed far enough in photography: to make pictures of the Highlands she would have to resurrect the dyes which complemented the silver halide processes. Photolithography, too, had its exponents; she could use old and grainy film, or the salts of the emulsion itself, the negative enlarged beyond its true proportion, overlapping granules like the close-packed crystals in the Bluffs.

The heat of this fire, pecking at her cheek, was very like the warmth of sunlight high in the massif. She touched the strings of her bonnet and thought of its vegetable dyes, Waythorn, Dyers' Rocket, birch bark.

Here was Bren. He smiled. There was no need to say anything. Together they watched the oil sizzle from the spitted fish. His skins smelt foxy, primeval, slightly dank; he would acquire that smell himself, the old odour of the Folk. The bottled synthesis of musk and grass was gone. She noticed his hands and their long, ridged nails. How could she want anything else for him, for them all, but the true, nomadic life? Cait tested the fish with a forefinger on which she first spat. She looked well. They all looked well out here, where the wind was and the sound of the sea.

'Come,' said Cait, 'Eat.'

She took the first fish from the fire and gave it to her mother to divide. Ang looked across the firelit circle and found Gaby and her cheerful grin.

Old Catch thought he had heard enough from the Rower: a pity he had no boat to row away in today. He had once had a wife to complain to like that. When she died they had given her a coffin, and then they had given him a stick. He looked away from Attachuk and his family and saw how pale the sea was now that night was coming. He thought how good it would be to die and be buried here, next to the old ones.

The fish they were eating over there looked good and fat. In a way, it was his name they were eating and celebrating, one of the three surviving memories of this important day. He had never caught a thing. It seemed to him, seventy-seven, frail and nothing to show, that he had wasted his life. He leaned on his stick and made his slow way across the difficult ground to stand near Salter Bren from whom a great strength emanated.

When Catch came to his fire, Bren knew he had won the battle of wits; if Attachuk chose to align himself with 'civilisation' and 'progress' that was his right. He knew he had not been generous or courageous enough to offer this option to those who seemed certain in their dissatisfaction but, in the heat of the fire and the hastening weeks, it was too much the action of a holy man. He needed Catch to give him the sanction of age and wisdom. His desire was no frivolous dream.

His insistence on the sanctity of his project had driven him to renounce alcohol, not only for himself but on behalf of all the Folk. With the same seriousness of purpose, he had invented a personal rite of renuncitaion and dedication.

Last Sailday, after shift, he had built a fire at Ulbeg, carrying the wood to the cove with the purposeful application of a nesting bird. He had then requested (and required, for there was no opportunity for her to refuse) Cait to burn all the contraceptive devices the Sineians had given her so that he, and not she nor the physicians, would control the number of children she had.

It had not occurred to Bren that he had taken the place of the physicians in charge of the breeding programme.

He had shown Cait the diaphanous garment he had bought her, snatched it away even as she spoke her thanks, and bundled it into his sacrificial fire. The love they made between them then, against the green, fluted rocks, had been the best, freed of all barriers, in full contact. She had been more excited by it than he.

He had made her pregnant: he had felt the life leap from him into her. The babe would be born at the beginning of White, in Pack when the pancake ice fused into huge rafts offshore. Before that perilous time came, he would have given her flesh in exchange for the fish she had cooked; he would have proved his worth, and fulfilled his ambition.

Professor Voran was watching him. Her hand moved: she was writing in her little notebook, hoping no one would notice what she did. Her secretive scribbling seemed as useless as any solitary vice, but he could tolerate it now because she would soon have no influence over his destiny. Like the majority of her countrywomen, she was arrogant. She made the most astonishing suppositions. Now she waved a piece of fish at him.

'Thank you. Thank you so much,' she called.

She was the fool whose antics showed up the worth of his people, and all her intricate theories, which attempted to explain the inexplicable and sacred, were like those tediously sexual jokes the Sineinain academics told each other in the Fountain Bar, too good to be true.

He felt a quick surge of anger, as unavoidable as death while drowning; but immmediately, following hard upon it as the fish follow the incoming tide, a flood of joy. He shook his head vigorously and felt his hair whirl.

Cait's mother laughed. 'It would make a good mop,' she said.

'I'll wash Traumesse clean,' he replied and shook his head again and hopped upon one foot. He needed movement. He could not keep still.

The dance came out of the earth, from the fire and the wind. It crept into his feet and agitated his hands. Needle Mu was afflicted in the same way, shifting and shaking. A low thrumming came from her throat and grew in volume until he thought a skein of raingeese must be flying near.

Bren and Needle Mu danced. They danced like the old ones, intricately and solitarily, together only in sentiment. The feeling they generated soon touched other Folk and the lively dance spread until they all tripped and jigged, even surly Attachuk, apart with his family at the other fire.

'May I have another drink?'

The clear voice of Ang Semo came to Bren through the fog of his trance.

She had taken alcohol from the professor. A great sadness overtook Bren because of it. She could not feel the attraction. He wanted her to feel what he felt: someone, some person from another culture, must feel and understand, must take away and keep alive a memory of this first and last Fish Supper.

Ang Semo danced, awkwardly and slowly until the akwit worked; faster then and nimbly: never before and never again.

They were all dancing, all but Eda Voran, who scribbled in her book like one possessed by a recording genius. Bren, to whom the icedeer knelt, danced, and Ang danced, who called them to Sowash and began to change the times. Old Catch danced with his stick.

I have found the right piece of wood, Bren thought, and the right woman; the right child is growing. I shall Hunt and I shall run the Race and then I will begin.

It was necessary now to show everyone how much he loved and needed them. He twitched and shuffled through the dancing crowd, greeting them all and calling them by their real, Avang names: Caut, Yal, Atluki, Kubbush, Pakak, Fennu, Gabuni.

Gaby, hearing her birthname, spun quickly round. She was giddy; as silly as Atluki for whom the world went endlessly round and round without ever speaking to him.

'Barendidt,' she said, 'Or Bren. Spokesman: tomorrow, I am twenty and can make up my own mind. Please tell them all that I won't be asking for Pak. Please tell them I can't marry him. I love the circus and I don't know what to do. I love the clowns and the music; the elephants and Spooky, the Spotted Horse.'

He stood still, dismayed. He wanted them all to build and contribute riches to his new world, and here was Gaby, refusing to tender him the solemnity that was his due; worse, she jested with his idea, played it down. The first challenge had come, not from Rower Attachuk, nor old Catch, but from his closest ally and best woman friend, Float Gaby.

Harlequin Jannl admired his reflections in the water. The new suit fitted him well. The water never moved but his reflections had uncertain boundaries and the tips of his fingers were frayed and coiled: anemone tendrils, fern fronds, dendritic estuaries.

He put on the ruby half-mask. It made the upper part of his face hard; he had a carapace instead of features and his black eyes glittered. He would make mischief.

The boat rocked. Each boat swayed as he stepped from one to another, further from the shore behind him, where Siloe lay on her bed in the garden, and nearer to the grey shore where, in Spiral City, he would wreak havoc.

Siloe's malformation was silent and secret. Roses blossomed where none should be and marred her white beauty with their dawn colours. Barbed thorns, which could never be pulled out, grew internally. His apotheosis would be public: loud and discordant harmonies would wake the citizens; shape and size would become inconstant and cold and heat interchangeable. He would damage the ever-changing fabric of the city. He had ingested the message; it rang his ganglia and circulated in his cells, endlessly requesting oblivion. Before he went, he would hurt the controllers; better, he would take them with him.

Jannl set off along the shore. The silt changed colour as he walked. He paused there for a while, amused at the oscillating trail of footprints he had left. The blue sky made him happy. He stood on his hands and trod the clouds underfoot. Hanging from the ground, he dangled above a black void and felt the stars tickle his toes.

In the orchard, the trees grew steadily, putting out limbs to support him as he climbed, growing apples fast as thought. He burrowed in the reddest, chewing as he went. The tiny cells were full of juice. He swam in it. He was infinitely small: he could not go smaller, yet he shrank. The blind interior of the apple let in the light and the fruit glowed and became a lamp. In the juice there was water, sugars, minerals, atoms, electrons, quarks, and several sub-atomic particles no one had yet discovered. He had reached the end of the known universe. He felt wrung, mangled, squeezed dry. He burst out of the apple-lamp, shedding water, light, rind, sky. The apple had become the world and he sloughed his segmented skin to fly. There, below him, lay Siloe, asleep on a silken sheet and a carved bed of ferns and estuaries.

I wanted Spiral City, he thought, although the thought meant nothing to him. He had ceased to be a character in Ang Semo's mind. The machine had no sympathy with him and was unable to understand his human aspirations. It moved him. He felt it lock into his limbs. He was naked and jaundiced, a winged maggot, a consuming desire. His wings were spectacular, great arcs of ice and light; he floated into Siloe's purview and entered her body while she dreamed, his winged folded and his intentions without honour. He writhed in her flesh and felt her bleed roses, roses, sanguine and convolute.

His admirable character had been changed. He had been reborn to play pranks, to alter the order of chaos. He was the creature of the new algorithms, the child of disorder. Miching mallecho: out of the frying pan into the fire. He would metamorphose again, burying his body deep in infinity; at the end, he would reveal himself in garments of flame. He was random now, as accidental as his computer-generated name – even the musical name of his once-loved, now-abused beloved was a chance arrangement of syllables which sounded like a lovely attribute with its breathy sigh and its dependent, pendant 'loe'.

Before he hid among the endless iterations, he would go on one last quest to find the name that haunted him: L O Y S E N, six letters, a deliberate combination of characters which had unaccountably got into the machine and flourished their significance at his lack of heart and soul. Violence was creation, hate love, construction destruction and birth death. It was impossible to escape the chaos of order.

The heart of the snowflake is the essence of chaos, a delicate balance between the forces of stability and instability as it alternately thaws and freezes.

But the thaw was past, and summer had brought a state of equilibrium as finely tuned as that exemplary prototype, the snowflake's inner logic. A thin layer of soil supported Sowash's indigenous life, from arachnid and coelopterate to bird and mammal. Beneath it the permafrost lay, not dormant, not slumbering, but neutral and ever-present. Beneath the permafrost, insulated from its stultifying coldness and itself shielded so that the heat it generated made no change in the frozen subsoil, was Traumesse, a heart equally without mystery or imagination, an entity which responded only to the stimuli of off and on, minus and plus, no and yes.

The thaw had released new forces of decay and regrowth. Seeds had frozen in the permafrost, the elliptical and hard-cased fruit of prehistoric trees. Each one lay in a nest of fertile and contemporaneous soil and each one, striving toward continuity, had put out a tiny, white radicle. Their success, the growth of their blind ambition, or their failure, death by cold, was undecided; something on which old Om herself would not have cared to lay a bet.

Ang, scanning her screen for any signs of change, felt like the conductor of an apocalyptic orchestra: voracious, charged with the making of a masterpiece, and slightly mad. The players were already out of her control and soon they would leave the auditorium, one by one, and the tune would falter and, after one brief burst from the last player become soloist, die.

She felt that her choice of the title 'Greed' was prophetic. Greed personified, Jannl ran amok in the system, hungry for sensation and new forms, gathering power and identities to himself, harrying the mute hardware and switching off the lights. Random elements, whose origins she could no longer attempt to trace, had given her whim awful fancies and shapes.

She found one Jannl in bed with Siloe. They were gently making love; but it was a scene she would once – being a devotee of the classics where intimacy and violence were not displayed although their consequences were examined in detail – have cut from the finished saga. When it reached the public gaze, beamed across the planet or encapsulated in a cube, there would be an angry response and consequences to face. It was the death of the popular saga. She, the innovator and creator of the episodic drama, would not be permitted to continue her novelties.

Simultaneously, a scarlet Jannl who wore a mask, raped his once-beloved. She had certainly not made this scene and, with her head on one side and an expression of intense interest on her face, she watched the outrage and compared its disgusting intricacies with the details of her own violation at the hands (how apt the colloquialism!) of Dorta Wireloom. Perhaps her psyche, too, had infected the machine. That Siloe resisted was clear: the sound system relayed her inhuman screams.

A third Jannl held a knife to his inamorata's throat and, as Ang's hand moved impotently towards the Delete panel, traced a direct route of red across that perfect white column. Crimson droplets glowed, then gushed: when Ang used the zoom she saw moss roses whose bronze calyxes trailed fibres; in each fibre was a forest and in each forest there lurked a harlequin who, flitting between shadow and sunlight, was nearly invisible to her straining eyes. She did not dare examine his camouflage closely, his patterned skin of diamonds and dapples, for his supple form reminded her of the white-face clown.

She wondered absurdly and incongruously if her defecting construct had met his other selves face to face. Which one *was* he?

In this order without periodicity there was a new and violent creativity. Here, it was not the absolute truth that everything tends toward disorder: an intricate and interdependent society of violence and endless reproduction was being created by and within the machine which obediently demonstrated each new episode to her. The Folk had their destiny, but what was Siloe's, Jannl's, Eda's, Carey's, hers; that of the sad and childlike plastimorphs?

She thought that, if Traumesse broke down, many new orders would arise.

A mole after a worm, she worked hard; but could affect and alter nothing. She could effect nothing. Loy's contribution was unwitting and extra.

Dorta Wirleoom's signifiers had vanished, consumed by their own products. She had her own useless codestring, generated by the computer in response to ERRATE's supremo in Sollar. The computer and herself were the only minds to know the new code, creator and user. Her crime was untraceable, as unpredictable and random as coronal flare and meteor-strike. The computer manipulated the symbols she had given it: her mind alone attached meaning to the pictures. The intelligences of other viewers, attempting to perform this necessary function, would falter; the logic of culpability and blame had been lost and Jannl operated without origin. The system was liberated randomly to explore its every dynamical possibility. It had become its own creator, an artist of supreme genius and terrible potential.

She needed a drink. She needed to be away from this insensate brain which never tired, and among her own kind, cushioned by the mundane and by normal conversation, able and willing to recognise the signals in a human face.

She closed her window on the otherworld, powering down the terminal at which she had worked. She would wait now, until one of her team discovered the canker, spread and spreading in the current work.

Floraliy was cool and the scent of its flowers sweet. She

took a table outside the Fountain and watched the lights. The cephalopod-based pattern had modulations as harmonious as music. She had been delighted with the programme she had derived from the reanimated squid, all those wasted years ago. It seemed now mannered and plaintive, but brimming with promise. Ang sipped her drink and, when she had enjoyed the first pungent mouthful to the full, took out her cigarettes, slowly extracted one, slowly lit up. She viewed the underground pleasure plaza through her customary veil of drifting smoke.

There were plenty of Folk in the square, hurrying to and fro because it was the middle of the working day, busy about the errands of Traumesse. She noticed Kubbu and old Catch, the one abstracted, the other slow and yet determined; neither seemed to have much to do with the fantastic architecture and the date palms. To them, the flowers were decoration and the macaws irrelevant. They rode the escalators because they must, aliens already, transplants in an artificial garden. Catch ascended and Kubbu descended. They passed out of her sight.

For a little while longer she watched the hurrying Folk, before her gaze returned to the pulsating lights and she saw that the pattern had faltered, stuck fast in one dazzling array of silver and red. She realised with a bittersweet pang, and a swift pull on her cigarette, that she was a witness to the destruction of her own poem, the wreckage which must precede the new order of chaos, the new dynamic. While she watched them, the lights changed colour so rapidly she thought at first that the movement of her own eyelashes had interrupted her perception. Now blue and green, they remained static, fixed in the same striped array. Surely, others had seen the fault? She called out to one of the passing women, Salter Mu in beadstrings as garish as the lights and an odd little headdress of gull feathers.

'There is something wrong with the lights. See how steadily they burn!'

'I daresay,' said Bren's mother stolidly, 'it's the weather. There's so much extra energy about, after the ice deer and the dark thaw. It's bound to affect a mere machine.

My joints are behaving strangely, too. I shouldn't worry, Doctor. Maintenance will sort it out.'

Ang, she wanted to insist, you must call me Ang. You must help me find myself, my new self. I may have murdered my dreams but I haven't found a replacement yet.

Bren pulled the spokeshave along the spar, paring off thin shavings which smelled of resin and the sea. The woodworking tools fitted his hands well, natural companions to the chisels with which he worked the suetstone. The rhythmic work soothed his body and drew it into a repetitive pattern while his mind worried away at the rich variety of his concerns. He had faltered in his purpose since Gaby had questioned his right to institute new order.

'I'm in love', she had said, 'in love with the Spotted Horse.'

No one, except Atluki perhaps, could be in love with an animal. Gaby teased him; how she played with him! She loved the circus horse as he admired the wild beasts, recognising its innate grace and variable adaptation, transfixed and held by its instinctive skill. Did she mean she loved the Circus? Did she love the acrobat, the harlequin, or the white-face clown? Or did she merely mean to throw him off balance and make him think?

He was sure of Cait. Especially now. Older signs than pregnancy tests had told her she would bear his child: she had failed to bleed; she held her fullness tenderly, her body become a cradle and a nursery.

'I am twenty and can make up my own mind. Please tell them all that I won't be asking for Pak.'

Gaby insisted, a noisy collection of thoughts in his mind. What was he to do with her? He had a greater task than being a Spokesman now. He was inventor, maker and leader of the new force.

'When we get out,' he said gruffly to his memory of Gaby, and the spokeshave, 'I shall make you marry *someone*.'

Needle Mu had not been pleased to be called to witness the formal rejection of her nephew. Glosit was rarely denied and the denial considered an insult. He foresaw trouble between the Floats and the Needles: in these circumstances a feud was not out of the question.

He planned to have as many couples as there were women. The surplus men would labour and hunt. They could not afford misfits who ate and refused to work or increase the numbers.

Gaby threatened him.

Gaby had set herself apart; Gaby had denied herself and her true kin.

He put the spokeshave down and stared at the wall. A network of fine cracks had appeared in the renewable plastics spreading down from one corner and spiralling out toward his carving table. The carvings sat there staring, just like him, at the unalterable, mute witnesses to his dismay.

Perhaps – but no, he had decided not to desire her that morning in the Viewdome, and she had acquiesced. Perhaps, if they were all sleeping together in some future time and weather, some unbuilt bothy of driftwood and whins, he might sleepily forget and reaching out, touch her.

No.

The cracks made patterns as complex as tangled hair – but the patterns were unstable and changed all the time, hair combed out and tangled, combed and in elf-locks again. He felt his purpose similarly disintegrate and reform. It was a question of who won, which prevailed: the cracks or the new bonds?

There were more anomalies than certainties these days. The lights of Floraliy had gone on the blink, and the other lights, the yellow clusters which lit the corridors in the upper levels. These could not be symptoms, could not be the results of his indecision: the workings of Traumesse had nothing to do with him. The technical framework was Sollar Kein's, a concern of the Sineinians alone.

Perhaps they had decided to ruin the Establishment.

That would make his task easier, and much less satisfying.

He had grown up in the place, and depended on it for sustenance and warmth, wanted the shelter it gave right until the last moment. His dependence was greater then that of the plastimorphs, whose brains had dried up they said, whose circuits were complete but once a month, when they were plugged in and getting the only stimulus they were allowed.

His excursions into the wilder parts of his island seemed, from this cosy vantage point, like vanity. He felt stronger for them and they had added to his knowledge; they had also shown him what he should beware of and when he should be afraid. He might abandon the great idea and stay on, for ever a servant of the Establishment and a slave to Traumesse.

Night had come, creeping into his mind with ghosts and shadows and uncertainties, though upside night was day and sunlit.

'OUTSIDE!' His shout was the summit of his frustration. Outside was where the land was brown, wet and low, and the sea flushed by the sun's light as it dipped an instant below the horizon and rose immediately upon the next day.

The spherical walls of Traumesse pressed in upon him; he would implode if he did not get out; his distemper and the chaos in his mind would consume him.

He picked up the spokeshave, flung it down again, and rushed out, running along the tight corridors, hurrying to be in the open air where he could hear the sea wash, and the sleepy peets of roosting birds; where he could breathe freely in the endless light and think without doubt, without setting foot beyond the icedeers' track.

Toul and Noul, the two sharp indents in the southern coast of Sowash, had indistinct boundaries today, their steep walls hidden in mist. So dense a vapour deserved the name of fog and Loy, climbing above it, saw that it filled each valley to the brim but rose no further. Beneath the nearest grey ceiling the circus, about its daily business, was as invisible to him as if it had fled.

The fog sat in Toul, stifling all sound and vision. In front of Loy, the gradient steepened where the island rose toward its spinal ridge and the hill of Traumesse on his left was covered in drifts of spring flowers all washed by the cold, which drew the deep dyes from them and left translucent petals with the bleached colours of shells. He walked towards them, eager to see them blossom at close quarters and to experience the uneasy feeling of fragile continuity which flowers suggest.

Snow had lain deep in these hollows and hidden these hummocks in the long, dark season the Folk called White. He imagined starlight echoing in the snow crystals. Snow had become water which, unable to soak into the frozen subsoil, had turned the hill into a sponge. He sat down carefully on a large tussock, above the squelching moss.

No sound issued from Traumesse, no whine or purr of buried motors nor the mufffled sound of the Folk making and packing cubed dreams under the earth. The island manufactory was a paradox, so far from the cities and so effectively disguised. On the surface, the only signs of its existence were the three glass eyes, two minor and one major, the domed windows which let some light penetrate the fastness below. The frantic activity and the hive were otherwise as effectively hidden as the feeding and rehearsal taking place in the circus beneath the mist.

The topmost stones of Noul's rocky columns reared above the mist and shimmered as if they would fall; Toul's biggest boulders showed, mountain summits. 2-Sweet stood on one and Cricket on another, their feet in the clouds. They spotted him and waved their arms, their shrill cries faint mews which faded in the air. Loy, indolent yet with a troubled, active mind, lifted one lazy hand in reply and dropped it despondently on the other.

It was a beautiful day. The twin valleys were smooth, grey pelts. Beyond them, the coastline curved and recurved, as crisp as a relief map. Because it was reality, was here and now, he loved it, and surprised himself – at last, so soon and probably too late, the North had touched him and shown him its truth. He thought he could sit all day, alone up here, feeling the breeze on his face, smelling the sea, and staring at that serpentine coast. The fog trembled in the valleys and began to spill out. He wondered if the wind would disperse it or if it would come creeping up the hill to wrap itself around him and take away the prospect he was learning to see.

He was afraid. He felt neglected; no, abandoned, in the midst of all this beauty; unattached; afloat without anchor or oars. He resented every joy and every occupation of every other person.

The Folk, who had been his appreciative audience, had deserted the circus and left it to perform to a sparse audience of scientists and servants from Traumesse while they went off across the island to indulge in curious customs of their own. Gaby had not remembered to invite him to the Fish Supper.

He was afraid that, despite the extraordinary ability of the circus to vanish down the years, Authority (unknown, unseen) might send it back to the City in a ship. Then his homecoming would not be surprising and uncontrolled, but known, examined, constrained and regulated, with forms to be completed and passes to be shown. The Lady was tardy. They should have passed on, by now.

Worst of all was his most terrifying nightmare: that he would be returned to the City within the twenty-eight years of his realtime existence and meet himself there.

He had read much in that sunlit, other life while the stones and people of the City fell, the victims of yet another war. He smiled to think how he, in common with the rest of humanity, preferred to remember only the good times. The books had been mainly volumes of poetry, vast anthologies which carried him along on the tide of other lives. The poets had insisted, repeatedly, desperately, that all lives intermeshed: no one an island, no one without influence or blame.

He looked at the high, light sky, for which the poets had so many synonyms. But it did not exist: it was not a vault, not silk nor velvet, not an airy paradise. The sky was atmosphere, stratosphere, ionosphere, a space occupied by various gases; and then came true space, nothing, a void traversed by light and sound; and deep space where starships and particles moved in unimaginable journeys between the millennia, like himself – he realised it at last with a feeling akin to awe – without time.

The sky owed its colour to the diffraction of light. This pale northern sky was the domain of strange gods whose influence he did not understand. He knew that, even if sky was gas and dust, that Mahun supported and guided him. It was easy knowledge, comfortable as his old dungarees and he had no wish to examine it nor actively to demonstrate it as Aurora, Lucie, Vixen and the other women who had fled with him from the drowning City, did with loud invocations and regular prayer meetings. If he had a spiritual mother, then he was content.

But what if, like his own mother by death and time, Mahun was for ever gone?

He held both hands up to the sky and said, 'Help me.'

Zoe, he remembered, was visiting Traumesse; Peach was washing the elephant; Red-Cheeks had retired from his influence to play primitive games with the rest of her people and Ang, to whom he had stretched out his hands and his heart, had similarly retired, but into her shell.

Born again! As Lucie, Aurora and the others claimed they were when they exchanged violence and carnality for peace and prayer. If he were reborn, he would wish for a quiet life too, one like Ang Semo's with space for thought and the uncomplicated pleasures of food, drink, and walks in the open air: he would ask for a cloak, a garment of obscurity, in which he could hide: he would want to become grey, unnoticed, the shadow of a man.

He became afraid that the circus might have disappeared altogether, leaving himself, the fog, and Zoe behind, and he got up and hurried down the hill. The smells and noises came to him first, and then the colours, muted by the fog. Peach called out to him from Garissa's wet and gleaming back; Cantor came hurrying from the tent.

'Where in creation have you been?' he grumbled.

'Not far,' said Loy.

'Hrumphff!' snorted Cantor, finding in these crushed consonants and vowels a suitable expression of contempt for those who took themselves off to brood on their work instead of doing it.

Loy carried his clubs into the tent and began to toss them into the air. The exercise was rhythmic and customary but he did not lose his concentration. The flying silver clubs mesmerised him and forced his body to respond to their fluent trajectories but, today, he would not tempt fate and try to keep a dozen in the air.

Cricket and 2-Sweet interrupted him. They had climbed from their boulder lookouts some time ago and, wandering in search of better adventures, had found a marvel on the beach. Their find excited them and made them bold so that they rushed into the ring shouting, 'Loy! Loy! Quick, come quick!'

The clown opened his mouth to admonish them but the boys, borrowing his breath, only shouted, 'Never interrupt, never distract! ' while Vision, a late arrival, shrieked, 'Seals, seals, 's seals to see us!'

They poured from the tent, a small crowd by the time Loy, with the maddening slowness of an adult, had put down the clubs and wiped his face on his sleeve.

The malp were coming to meet them, huge, bulky caterpillars humping into the valley.

'Poshrats,' said Loy. 'You disturbed them.'

'Not. They came by themselves. They've come to dinner!' Cricket was quite certain that the visitation had purpose and walked towards the leading malpog.

'Come back!' His mother, Dove, shrilled a warning. She had appeared on the steps of Aurora's van, a slight and determined madonna hovering on the edge of his sight. Cricket stayed where he was, trembling slightly because he so much wanted to touch that shining sealskin and poke a finger gently into that thick flesh to see if it was hard, or soft.

'He doesn't know people. He hasn't been trained,' Dove reminded him.

But the bull, for its sex was obvious from its size, ignored him, and everyone else, pursuing its own peculiar path; and all the malp followed its lead. When the animals reached the open ground before the tent, they stopped, rolled themselves into humps and curves, closed their moist eyes, and slept.

The circus children approached them cautiously. Dove's shrill reminder had brought their senses back and they stalked the bulls as if they were butterflies which would take wing, while the animals, opening an eye or raising one lazy flipper, allowed them no closer than they would allow the playful porpoises which sometimes followed them at sea.

A wide-open mouth was the warning sign. The children learned at once to tread an unmarked circle, just outside the limit of tolerance and, with the clown and Dove, made a patchwork ring of colour about the dark grey giants where they lay, like fallen stones wreathed in mist. Cantor and Peach approached and, after them, many more of the circus folk, curious, cautious, and unafraid.

They stared at the malp and the malp, raising themselves from their slumbers and the ground, stared back.

Many of them bore scars, where orca, or the hooked poles of Ineiti fishermen had snatched at them. Some of them were beginning to moult and their skins were ragged like the coats of beggars: one had lost an eye and another, half a flipper. Yet they were healthy enough because they were alive and, so far, co-existed with the ice and the chilly spring sea, with the hareng and colin on which they preyed and with the delphinids which preyed on them. No human had threatened them for ninety years and they were content to let these odd specimens come so far, and no further.

It occurred to Loy that he, the accidental visitor, was the intruder. These enormous beasts, knew this valley: it was their resting place and they had come ashore to moult as no doubt they did every year.

They had settled in their territory and would defend it. They made a toothed and tushed barrier right in front of the big top and no one dared pass them.

Here was the golden opportunity, a valid excuse to send for one of the Folk: Salter Bren or the tall good-looking one, Ial. They, if anyone did, would know how to make the animals move. Perhaps Gaby would come and advise him and then, with a suitable excuse, and his need of her trembling on the edge of desire, he could detain her and again experience the joy of showing her his tame and tutored animals, while her kinsmen got rid of the malp. Lady, if only: for a moment he was not sure if he stood in the dank valley of Toul on Sowash or in another, sunlit, valley full of promise and empty of memory.

Zoe knew she was good at drawing. Her Da had said so. She selected a red crayon and drew a flower for the elephant to pick. She had given her a background of tall trees, the spindly giants with great, bushy heads which she remembered, dreams from the time her mother had been there.

She had spent a lovely day with Ang, the gajo lady. First, they had played in a room with a forest and stars in the roof and then they had been to the shops, such shops, stuffed with toys and sweets. They had gone into a room which was all window and looked out at the sea, the spiky grass and a ring of yellow flowers. In the distance, she had seen two grey pools and Ang had seemed sorry because, in the bright voice adults used to cover things up, she'd said, 'Oh, it's too foggy to see the circus. Never mind.'

They had eaten a meal in a big cafe and then she had gone with Ang to see moving pictures which talked and then, at last, to this very tidy room where she lived.

And now, to make pictures, she had a pile of paper and a beautiful wooden box full of colours while Ang knelt on the carpet and laid out *her* pictures, the ones she had made with the black box on legs. Some were of rocks and the sea, some of the people who wore furry clothes and beads; and there was a whole row of pictures of the valley she lived in now, only the circus wasn't there, just the huge rocks, the pretty pebbles, and the little, tiny flowers.

Ang picked up each photograph in turn. The last twenty, the photographs taken in Toul, she thought amateur, hazy uncomposed snaps. Loy Sen, the focus of each frame, was missing. The little Folk grinned amongst the rocks; some of them were seated on air and others had levitated, feet firm on nothing. This was the film she had exposed in Loy's van, the two sets of negatives which had puzzled her in the dark room and made her believe, heedless because she could not believe her memory erred, both cameras faulty. She had twenty pictures of Toul but the clown, his van, his accoutrements, his circus, were not there. Nor could she see Gaby anywhere. She should be standing straight upon the vanished steps which led up to the phantasmal van.

Nothing she had photographed in the circus showed on her plates.

The loss of Loy Sen's image distressed her most. She knew his face well and had wanted, throught the medium of her art, to keep and treasure it.

It was a lined face. The white paste he spread on it to make himself into the clown turned each hairline crack into a valley. His face might split apart, a treasured piece of porcelain time had abused. It wasn't real; he wasn't real yet, at the same time, it and he were everything that mattered. He had love, sadness and humour: he was himself, the fool, who, by painting out his features and adding others in the colours of death, or a witch doctor's mask, became more than reality, a representational figure, an icon of humanity.

'Can you draw a picture of your Dada?' she asked Zoe.

The Ulbeg photographs: amongst the rocks or, bent claws on a indeterminate field of white which might be flesh, or cloth, or snow, her hands were as abstract as her memory of that compelling face, and also belonged to the past. The watery patterns she had taken from the sea, petrified here, might be a graph, arabesques of light and dark which marked the peaks and troughs of her obsessional peculiarity.

Loy Sen could not be different from any other man. She had felt his need of her in that other world of the Fen Forest which might have been hallucination or a dream; which might, since she believed in his fantastic power to move between the years, have been reality. She had felt against her the hard physical manifestation of his passion for her. She feared him now, despite the gentleness of his touch and the two short sentences he had spoken – in a voice which had seemed honest, unless he always lied: 'I have so much love to give you.'

'I have so much life to give you.'

The spring madness was over, for her. He must have met and known many more suitable women than her. Her terror at each loss of her integrity, each violation of her own, interior space, would not leave her and would never let her rest and be thankful, secure in love.

The dry heat of the unit had faded and shrunk the old photographs on the wall. Only the holiday snap had any worth. She had taken it in the Central Highlands, standing at the top of the sloping plane of scoriated conglomerates, as full of red and brown fragments as a pudding of plums and cherries, a treasure chest of bright jewels. The sun had beaten on her back and heat had risen from the parched rock to her face: she had inhaled the hot air and waited a long time for the sun to move round so that her shadow did not obscure the rock. She had already taken down the two prints, the numbered lithograph of the City's filthy canal, and the computer reproduction of Cal M'unor's death-portrait. They had appealed to her because of their melancholy: a quality of desperate unfulfilment pervaded them which the firm strokes of their creator's pen could not prevent.

These images from the City had been made at least a hundred years ago. History, when it did not treat of economics and war, was sentiment emphasised by its isolation from the common run of things. Vaguely, because everything that concerned her now must point forward and she must not look over her shoulder at the ghosts and shadows of what might have been, she wondered why Loy had never mentioned those awful, sad pictures; why, indeed, she had not emphasised their presence on her wall and questioned him about their meaning and origins. Too late now.

They lay where she had stowed them, in the bottom of the trunk she was sending home, and the rest should join them. She rose, ready to remove her work from the wall and, because Zoe would demand an explanation, said, 'Perhaps I'll put the new photos up here.'

'Don't,' answered the enigmatic child, without looking up from her drawing. 'The wall is grey like the big rocks by our van. It's smooth as my Rat's fur.'

'Or like the fog?'

Ang, presented by a gently grinning Loy to the five united rats, had refused to recoil – that was what he expected – and thus taken away with her a frightful image of bondage and secret loathing.

'Yes,' said Zoe, 'My Da's hiding in it.'

'We'll have to go and find him soon.'

'I haven't finished,' Zoe wailed.

'Soon, Zoe.'

It was important, so the nursery attendants had told her, to establish your authority with children and this one, wilful and circus-reared, was more trouble than most.

One by one, Ang removed the pins which held up her photographs and soon there was nothing, except for a network of tiny holes in the wall-covering, to show they had ever taken the place of windows in the room.

The rocks of the Central Highlands remained, both in place on the wall and in her memory. She wanted to tell.

'Look, Zoe. These funny plants come from the Central Highlands, too.'

'I know.'

'Have you been there?'

The possibility was strong. Zoe might know the weathered castles of sandstone, the high marble plateaux and the dry riverbeds, better than she did; might have walked in Desolation Wilderness on the rainy side, where veils of moss hung from the trees and the precipices were too steep for anyone, Vulyar, visitors or apes, to climb.

The child had been near the great massif. Or might have been, since it was difficult to spot location, let alone time, from her impressionistic description. Zoe was quite certain that she had once seen an endless castle of rock, towers, pinnacles, keeps and irregular crenellations, in one of the distances: her father had told her that the nixies lived in it and Zoe, perverse as usual in her responses, had wanted to climb there and prove him wrong.

'Because,' she concluded, 'nixies live in water and how could there be rivers in a castle?'

Ang thought: If I have been through time to Lutreia, a river in a castle is a common wonder. But she did not reply, and Zoe took a fresh piece of paper and began a new drawing.

It was a portrait: her doll Nix at home.

The grey fog which they had seen from the Viewdome, was one of Sowash's frequent, peculiar beauties. Often, it threatened obscurity rather then providing it, and today appeared ready to stay covering the circus in Toul and the nesting birds in Noul without rising to envelop the whole island.

Sometimes, if you were up early enough to see it, it lay in a chain of teardrops across the land, and the top layers sparkled with refracted light.

She would miss these, and the other, more spectacular beauties of sheet-ice and snow, which would once more belong – if to anyone – to their rightful possessors, the Fishfolk.

Tense and still before the single photograph, she listened, straining for the unexpected sounds, for the new noises which were the minute pangs of the infected Traumesse. No one but her was able to connect the curious incidents of the last few days: a plastimorph had collapsed; various light systems had faltered or failed; they complained of the heat on the production line; and, most significantly, a marine zoologist had died when her air pack had fed her pure carbon dioxide.

Meanwhile the Folk had become eccentric, dressing in quvit and skins, refusing to attend lessons and meeting in the open air in the long day of the night. Soon they would refuse to programme and pack the plastic cubes, sweet to the mass imagination as sugar, on which her dearly-loved, ephemeral sagas were preserved for the whole world to treasure and hoard.

Eda Voran saw a quantum leap, the discovery by the Folk of their true identity and the early flowering of a future history: a success for her department. She had proved the little people's innate intelligence; they had been quick to learn the Establishment's work, the new ropes of survival; she was ready now to concede, and allow a measure of traditional work, tasks less rigidly technological and more technical. She had her visions and had drawn up her plans: there would be a model village above Forso. The Folk had once built boats:

let them now do so with the future in mind for, somewhere in the world, was a market for their hand-built skifts, an outlet which would earn money and time for them while they finished their education in the ways of their country, the North.

The benefits of Traumesse had been manifold but, like an overcautious mother, Sinein had smothered initiative and the icedeer, walking out of the snowfields, were mysterious messengers of independence and proof of survival to the Folk. Raised underground, in soft surroundings and continual warmth, they had overheated; Salter Bren and herself were the cooks, lifting the lid, stirring the broth.

She looked down at the warm weight attached to her left leg. Zoe had made a pile of drawings, and abandoned her crayons to sidle up and hold the long, white-clad limb in a tight embrace.

The innocent gesture of dependence from this aged little girl who knew too much made her yearn for impossibilities. Zoe, succeeding where all the men had failed, had released a flood in her of mother-love and tears. She connected the rare emotion with her deep inability to offer up her person and personality, allow her body to be invaded and conceive a child herself. She sniffed, wiping her eyes on her hand, her sleeves, anything, and bent to hug Zoe.

'Whassa matter, Ang?'

Nothing? No, everything.

'Oh,' she said, recovering, 'it's what they call the Northern Disease, up here.'

'Then you ought to go away from it,' said the percipient child.

The golden locket swung between them, the toy now of a child. Loy let her wear it all the time, careless or fatalistic, and Ang, standing up and taking Zoe 's hand, said, 'Show me your pictures.'

Like the drawings of all children who have not yet been blinkered by adult rules, Zoe's were masterpieces in which perspective was disregarded and colour paramount. Zoe had drawn as she felt and thus her red flower was the size of a tree and her elephant kind; her home, the red and blue van, had an open door and smoke rose under a yellow sun from its tall chimney; her doll was eating buns and, in the last and best picture Ang picked up, her father smiled with his wide and painted mouth, and the black tears on his cheeks were small. The spangles on his suit were the size of coat buttons and his black skull cap took the place of his thick head of hair.

'Would you like to put Loy's picture in your locket?' asked Ang.

'It's too big.'

'I can shrink it.'

'How can you do that? Can you do magic?'

Ang, smiling, saw herself clad in night and stars and wielding an omnific wand. 'Yes,' she said (for why should he have all the advantages?). 'I can make a little picture out of yours, small enough to fit the locket.

'But now we must go and find Loy.'

'We must.' Zoe skipped and sang as she gathered up the other pictures; so, easily, were children bribed.

'Can I take the crayons?'

'Leave them with me,' said Ang Semo. 'They are yours; but leave them here, with me. Let me look after them.'

The hunter stood erect in the shelter of the great rocking stone which was itself man-shaped, with a massive square head and a bent and crouching body: one erratic balanced on another. His teachers had told him that the ice had made it and he had believed them. He knew now that his ancestors, who had named it the Malp Stalker, had invested it with greater meaning.

He had a wife and soon would have a family; he had his spear and knife and his grandfather's tinder box in his pocket. He was properly dressed for the time, the place and his job, fully dressed in the skin and hair of other animals so that, adopting their colours, he easily became invisible against the brown land. Inside his shirt he wore a long string of glass beads, clear as water and blue as the sea: he believed they would bring him luck.

The recent sunlit evenings had been rehearsals for this, the first full sunlit night, and the second escapade in his journey from the new and universal enthusiasm of his people for their culture toward a culmination, the return to that hard and rewarding culture. Light brought wakefulness and strength; it was hardly necessary to sleep and Bren looked confidently forward across the next twenty-four hours: I am, I will, I can.

The Race tomorrow was all. By winning it, he would prove how much he had earned the right to free his people. By coming first in the last celebration of the Sineinian innovation, he would show good reason for its demise. Folk did not compete, they borrowed and lent; they shared and, after the Race, he would begin the sharing. Nevertheless, he felt hours and events rush headlong into the future as, yesterday, every minute had sped toward the mutual climax which was his and Cait's, the reason for their wedding.

They had dressed impatiently, bride, groom and guests, choosing the best they could find in their grandparents' chests; impatiently, they had sat and stood through the wedding service in the clean, circular chapel, everyone at odds now with the imported religion yet afraid to deny Mahun. At last, they were free, outside, and eating. They ate the Establishment food greedily and looked wistfully across the Reach and the Sound while their minds and mouths filled with ancestral memories of salt and fresh fish, roast malpog and smoked gull's eggs.

The wedding guests had departed, Ang Semo and Eda Voran tall amongst them, leaving Cait and himself alone with each other and the reasons for their marriage.

He did not understand what chapel marriage was. His people did not marry to be for ever exclusive, though they lived in families and wedded man and woman were, more often than not, together.

He had never understood chapel rules, although he had witnessed and lived beside many marriages in Traumesse. Some of these were Sineinian marriages, foreign customs which, beside the ancient and productive coupling of male to female, allowed woman to marry woman, man, man: like the two women who had come with Ang Semo and himself out into the snow. Only the plastimorphs were forbidden the rite and this denial seemed crass to him. Two women could not make a child together any more than two 'morphs.

He understood that he and Cait would live together, at least until one of them wanted to move on; that she was important to him; that, at present, he desired her; that, for this lifetime, she was the mother of his first child. None of these rationalised states-of-the-heart would prevent him from wanting and seeking out other women and he would not prevent her from enjoying the pleasures her responsive body gave her.

On the beach, they had laughed while they fucked because it felt good and because they were happy and would be free. Like him, Cait had forsworn the wiles and traps of Traumesse and no longer spoke of honeymoons, or holidays in the artificial, forcing-house atmosphere of the R&R centre on Hara. The long, light night was their honeymoon, Forso's sand their marriage bed; the sea and the wind had made their music.

He had woken once from the sleep they eventually fell into. He thought they had married in the chapel of Traumesse so that they could repudiate the marriage here, on the ground, beside the sea, and make their own wedding close by the dunes in which he had uncovered the shaft of his malp spear.

A little further along the beach, near the place where Cait and the women had landed with their catch, he had found an old anchor fluke which he had carried home, its dead weight a real burden. It had shown him how strong he was. In the crafting shop he had shaped and tempered it into a spearhead.

Thus it had always been. The Folk had prospered and learned new techniques with the jetsam of other societies. The cord and feathers with which he had decorated the spear, and which served the purpose of tethering the top section, were Noiran: sea-grass cord, twisted double as the Sineinians had taught him, the pied wing-feathers of the tarunt gull and the barred tail of a mew.

He had tested the spear one quiet evening at Forso, throwing it into the hard sand again and again. He had not tried to kill anything with it. That was for now, for his first hunt.

Forso had been his marriage bed: he hoped it would also be his exit from Sowash.

He lifted the spear to his shoulder and found the place where it rested most easily. The ground he had yet to cover was slippery and uneven.

Before the circus came, that stranded community of skilled southerners who, despite their glamour and agility, could not live off this bounteous land, Toul had been a lonely station on the easterly route of moulting malp. To make a living at all from standing on your head and training animals to stand on balls and barrels were abilities to be admired; but no help with malp. They had already been and gone, prematurely, urged onward along the coast by Ial, Pak and himself. The clown had been frantic with thirty-five malp lying in front of his living.

He had had the sense to call on Kubbu's experience and Float Fa's sagacity: encouraged by Ial's moans, which imitated a ready cow exactly, the bulls had moved within the day – just as the older men advised – and given Loy Sen his circus back; given him, the hunter, knowledge of their whereabouts. From Toul, he had traced their passage along the coast; they were ashore now, hauled out at Nusseraq, the Good Beach, to moult.

There were no seals on the rocks here and he was rested and ready. He had reaffirmed his purpose in the world of outside: out of doors, in the open air where he belonged. He had left that false Sineinian concept, upside, the view the worm had from the soil, behind him and could barely tolerate the stuffy heat below, in Traumesse.

At Nusseraq the unsuccessful bulls were hauled ashore to rest and dream, perhaps, of a win and a bevy of cows. A bull was the proper target for his spear, a birthright his peculiar upbringing underground and under control, had denied him; and Malpogak, shaped like a sealskin pegged out, was the proper place to hunt. For him, it had been necessary to make do, and maybe he would start a tradition at Nusseraq. In shaping the spearhead, he had considered its objective and Cait had read him old instructions in old Sineinian travel books. There, he believed, his teachers had failed him again, making him half old and half new, denying him the best of both worlds, books and his freedom.

He walked carefully in the shadow of the cliff, avoiding the patches of shingle and decaying kelp from which clouds of midges and flies arose, remembering with every step how the icedeer had come first, not to him, but to Ang Semo who, for all her odd ways and alien education, was his guide.

As he went, the midge-count increased and he remembered too late that this itch and annoyance was the chief reason they had often remained below in summer, sampling Traumesse's novelties instead of those outside.

The coastline ahead was low, beyond it the kjarr, the demons and the ghosts. He knew them now: the bull was the greater terror. In preparing to retrace his steps here, he had given great thought to the possibility of another meeting with Float Siri. He had wanted to ask her what she thought of her sister's behaviour.

But the hunt was no place for spirit-talk. He must be alert. He must be cautious and circumspect, using the wind and walking where the malp could not smell him. He thought he must be shaking all over and stretched his free hand out before him to see if there was a tremor.

The Old Woman cast her deep shadow over the shore and he moved in it from boulder to boulder and approached the malp.

They snored and snorted, releasing great bubbling sighs in their sleep. He heard the shingle rattle as one rolled heavily over. He heard nails rasp skin as one scratched. They were far above the waterline, amongst the tussocks where there was soil and fresh water to make wallows. They were muddy and nearly as big as the circus elephant. 'The elephant is queen,' the clown had told him. 'Her trunk is her hand.'

The malp had no such organ to grab and hold him. They ate only vegetable matter but, like the elephant, they had two sharp, upward-pointing tushes which he must not discount when he stalked them. They looked hard, impenetrable and tough as winter.

There were three ways of killing a malpog: you had to hit the heart, the lungs, or the spinal cord. The last way was so difficult as to be impossible; with the other two methods there was the risk that the animal would take to the water before it was dead.

Between him and the bull he had chosen was a wide stretch of tall hummocky tussocks. He could use them as cover, and he crept to the first and leaned against it while he wondered what he would do if all the malp took to the water, submerging him in a tide of flesh as they rushed down the beach. He was afraid of so many things, of falling, of failing, of being hurt, or killed, and he remained where he was against the thick clump of grass for a long time while various physical symptoms of his fear came and went. He felt sick, wanted desperately to piss and cough. He considered urinating where he stood: but the malp would hear him.

Midges settled on his face and on the hands he could not use to swat them. He wrinkled his nose and blinked. His face itched and the tickle crawled upward, making his neck and scalp tingle. He was desperate for a scratch.

One of the bulls roared and raised itself on its front flippers: now he had to wait. Eventually, it settled again, supine and indolent, one flipper over its snout.

His fear made him clumsy but he gripped his weapon and moved forward to the next tussock. Now, only a short stretch of mud, marked with the animal's tail and flipper prints, lay between him and his quarry. The bull was mighty; its muscular hide quivered to dislodge and discourage the midges as it slept. Its shadow was long, its nose moist, the nails which edged its flippers hard and sharp. He was not able to think of it in more general terms, and he studied the two long tushes which protruded from its lower lip: shining teeth, whose size bore no relation to the scrap of ivory Cait had given him and which, separated now from the silver mount, vanity and Sineinian values, hung round his neck with the other talismans.

He decided to risk a loss and try to pierce the bull's ringed and columnar windpipe where it divided to bring air from the lungs, close beneath the two ivory knives, whose upward lunge should miss him.

Suddenly, his purpose deserted him. He watched the bull and admired its reposing strength, its dense grey fur and the black skin showing in patches through the moulting layers. He wanted to let it live; he wanted to lie in his family's skift, hung over the side, watching the malp off Hairete as they swam as easily underwater as clouds through the air, raking the weed rafts and dredging up kelp with their tushes.

He lifted his right hand and the spear in it and stepped into the open.

At once, the bull opened its eyes and moved its head to see him better. Now, he must attack – or flee. He ran forward and plunged the spear into the animal's neck. The double shaft came apart; he held the longer section. The free end, and the hard and obtrusive steel head were buried in the malpog's neck. He hung on, the cord looping between him and his prey, dodging while the animal thrashed and roared, feeling the sudden agony which had torn into it. It was a terrible thing, to kill. He knew his power and hated it.

Blood welled from the wound in the malpog's neck. It made several impotent rushes in his direction but could not raise itself enough to run. He had settled into a stupor of horror and dull pride when it pushed all its bulk at him, turned with a huge effort and made off toward the sea.

He had enough sense to let the spear end go and followed the bull down the beach. He heard its futile breathing, gasps which did not bring it air. It had almost reached the water when it collapsed, and he knew it was finally his. He ran to it and wrenched out his spear so that it would die more quickly.

The thunder he could hear all around him was the stampede of the herd, fleeing and taking to the water.

The malpog had more to teach him. It took a long time to die, beginning hopelessly to move again each time he thought it was finally still. When at last he dared touch it, it was as warm as it had been in life and its blood was still oozing and staining the stones and mingling with the piss and shit its mortal panic had made it release. Its soft fur was despoiled with the filth. He was not sure if it lived, even now; and he wiped the blood from the spearhead with the tail of his shirt and fitted the two sections together; he waited.

I need not have done this, he thought. I need not have killed this animal: I am not starving and I have a home and all the food I need.

Then he thought: I have freed myself. I am no longer obliged to anyone because I can feed myself.

He thought he should shout, or sing to celebrate his kill; but he remained silent, learning the right solemn and workmanlike silence from the dead bull and the quiet of Nusseraq in the midnight sunshine.

'I can hunt; I have hunted.' It was already in the past and he had done what he had set out, only half in earnest, to do when he went to look for a spar.

He turned about to look across the beaches at Traumesse hill, saw a mirror flash on its side, and remembered that Pak, Ial and the rest were waiting up there. He waved his arms and his spear to signal for them to come; they had seen the bull's flight and its death through their binoculars. He had forgotten that, forgotten all about his distant audience with its long sight and distance-magnifying eyes which, reflecting the midnight sun and flashing it back at him, told him he had not endeavoured alone.

The men found Bren sitting by the dead malpog. He had been invisible from the sea but when they had jumped out of their skifts and beached them, they were able to round the huge bulk of the animal and see him, hand clasping spear and chin on hands, staring at nothing.

They were able to celebrate, if he could not, the death being extraordinary, the first for over ninety years, and not yet a job and part of a way of life. They carried a mixed and historical assortment of knives and long blubber blades. If they had doubted Bren and found it difficult to follow where his mad dream led, they did not show it, but rushed, all forty of them, at him.

Kubbu raised him to his feet. Salter Fa had tears in his eyes. They saw the bloodstains on his shirt, the pool of drying blood near him and the dirt of his experience on his hands and under his nails, and they thumped him and clipped him in their arms. Bren smiled uneasily, as if the killing had happened by accident; as if he desired none of their congratulation. Only when old Catch threw down his stick in order to embrace him, did Bren begin to believe in what he had achieved.

'This is what must be done,' said Catch, and the men were quiet. They listened to his instructions because he was the oldest man there and the only one who had known those who had lived in the old way.

'This is what Pike Nomo and Pike Har used to do: First, Bren must take his knife and make the first cut in the skin. There is a long mark on the belly where the fur begins: this is the place to cut.'

They had to turn the animal over. It was a giant and they were midgets. They swarmed about it, organising themselves to pull and shove and, when it was over, flat on its back and exposed to their knives, they hummed and hawed and wondered at its ridged and creased underside of stores and deposits of fat, and its lack of sexual organs.

'Inside,' Catch told them. 'Freeze, wouldn't they?' and they all laughed, remembering winter excursions and the inconvenient need to piss in the snow.

Bren bent and put the point of his knife under the malpog's skin. It was tough, but separated easily from the fat beneath. His sharp knife cut through the leathery skin and he felt the firmness of the pink and white fat. The men grasped the skin and started to strip the carcase; soon it was a flayed mountain of flesh. Lice crawled on to their hands, for the malp had been much ashore and they also had started to breed. The animal was more than twelve feet long and the work of reducing it to meat was hard and sweaty. Kubbu found ticks on its flippers and Bren fleas on its head. The flies made local, black clouds. The men were soon covered in blood and fat and had to remove their quvit and shirts to preserve them. The naked head was a hideous, bloody mask but they poked their fingers with interest into the internal ears the flaying had revealed.

Following Catch's detailed instructions they began to section the blubber.

Strange organs filled the malpog's body: translucent sacs, like ghostly balloons, which had helped it float and kidneys with many, dark red lobes; a great heart buried in fat and a liver the size of a baby. Carefully they pulled out yards and yards of intestine and some of them went to wash the long tube in the sea. The brain was spherical and the lungs surprisingly small, as were the bones which had held up the mighty animal and helped it move on land and in its element, the sea. Bren used a wrench to pull the two tushes from the skull. They were his. He washed his hands and chest in the sea. He stank. They all did. The beach was an open sewer and the shallows red.

When the malpog had been reduced to bundles and piles of meat, the offal stuffed in the stomach, the intestines coiled and tied, the flesh cut up, the skin rolled, the sinews drawn and balled, the best bones tied in bundles and the skin rolled up, there was one thing left to do.

Atluki, the idiot, knew, no one could guess how, that a monument should be built, a trophy of flesh, bone and stone. He walked up to the high water mark and examined the line of dead seaweed there. A few large whin twigs were buried in the litter the tide had left behind. He freed them and stuck them upright in a crack in the nearest boulder. He set the malpog skull between them and decorated it with feathers carried from the same water margin, with a strip of skin, a slice of blubber, and some pebbles.

The Sineinians had taught him the custom. He knew well what must be done, but no one ever listened to him, so he got on with it. He remembered the exact words of the Professor, who had allowed him to sit at the back of her class with his portable, as long as he was quiet. She read to them: 'Fishfolk men, when the malp hunt had been successful, often built a trophy from selected parts of what remained when they had flayed and flensed the animals. Sometimes they used other flotsam from the beach, such as kelp strands or shingle. It is thought that the custom originated among the Snowfolk.'

His trophy was splendid. Bren came up to it. He looked pleased and, bending forward slightly before the trophy, removed the string of beads from around his neck and hung it on the skull. He looked strong and fierce with the white malpog tooth talisman hanging against his chest. He walked down to the Salter skift and boarded it.

Bren wished the beasts of the sea, malp, seal, orcs, whale, no ill; he would need them again one day. He heard the icedeer bell. She lifted her old head and roared. He wished she were here near him, on the beach of death, and not an echo and a picture in his head.

The death of the malpog bull had made him a hero, but he felt no pride. He had demonstrated his worth and was free to proceed; he need no longer do the work of Traumesse. The other men loaded the meat into the waiting skifts, but it was he who had made his mark upon Nusseraq.

The tide would soon cleanse the beach and remove all trace of the butchering. Gulls mobbed the skull and struggled with each other to tear the remaining flesh from it. The blubber had already gone, swallowed in an instant by a big sweepwing. It would soon return for the strip of skin. The empty skull would weather and finally decay; it would fall from the sticks and the sticks themselves would lie and scatter on the beach. Everything that remained uneaten would make a violent return to the sea when the storms brought Matoq back in three months' time. His beads would disappear in the waves. The pebbles Atluki had arranged so deliberately were of the beach, and subject to the tide.

When it was all gone, Nusseraq, the Good Beach, would still and for ever be the Place Where Barendidt Killed The First Bull.

GREENING

The fever of travel had seized on us and we had in mind only the idea of getting away.

Knud Rasmussen, *Greenland by the Polar Sea*

Annasi, the summer wind, let the sea alone, content to ruffle the tussock grass, the lyng, and the heads of the people who waited for the Race to begin.

This time the Folk had remembered to invite their companions-in-spirit, the nomadic circus people. The practised time-travellers looked content, almost joyful as they stood in disparate little knots about the lower slopes of the Old Woman, where the Race began and ended and a good view of the entire course to Ulbeg, Forso, and the edge of the kjarr, could be had. The excitement of the Fishfolk was infectious. Atluki waved his icedeer horn and Ang, standing beside Eda Voran upon a knoll, felt again the pull of the impossible and willed Loy Sen to come to her.

He was talking earnestly with Salter Bren. She felt absurdly jealous: Bren's transformation had begun with her and lately he had been secretive about his mysterious and outdoor Folk concerns. Instead of seeking her out, he had sent her a note written by his wife in which he begged her to be certain to come to the Race.

Cait and Bren together was indeed a consummation devoutly to be thankful for: they looked like two halves of the same fruit, both lively and dark, their individuality submerged but not lost in their skin clothing. They were difficult to tell apart: she smiled at the ancient, prejudicial thought. Cait wore many more beads than her husband and he had tied back his long and untidy hair with a cord.

A light flashed, and dazzled her – Gaby's beads dancing and glittering. She felt inside her collar, drew out the message beads Gaby had given her and arranged the strand where it could be seen. She wanted to show her solidarity with the Folk; she wanted her empathy to be visible and on display.

Eda was scribbling in her notebook.

Ang saw Loy leave Bren's side and half turn. He shaded his eyes against the sun and squinted up at her. She wanted to wave, to lift both arms in a happy salute, and she lifted one hand in a limp and characterless reply. He began to walk slowly toward her, taking his time; taking all the time in the world. She thought her absences, her recent coldness to him must have hurt him deeply. He knew no reason for her volte-face; though he might suspect.

The lithe and supple figure of the clown moved lightly up the hill. It was wonderful that he was here, a total anomaly in the northern landscape. Could Harlequin be wronged? Could a fool ever be insulted, whose profession was the taking of every liberty?

'What's up with the little people?' he asked, when he reached her. 'They're jumping like fleas on a dead dog.'

'Summer – Greening's here,' she said. 'That's all. How are you? Are you well?'

He looked tired, as if long, sleepless nights had succeeded his hard working days and the strenuous evening performances when, before the same audiences of Folk and workforce from Traumesse, the circus played a colourful variation on the entertainment of the night before. His harlequin charm disrupted her heart and she thought her inner turmoil must be as great as the havoc which would be wreaked by Jannl in Traumesse.

Eda moved away, tactfully tactless and obvious, out of hearing. She left them the kings of the grassy castle.

'I'm restless,' said Loy, 'There's a new sound in the wind.'

'Annasi is the same wind as the one which blows in the winter. It still comes from Hiberna. It feels warmer because the sun is shining.

'The Folk are restless too. They long to be away.'

'And will you let them go?'

'We can't stop them. There's the treaty: any development is supposed to be mutually agreed; but we can hardly prevent them. That would go against all the tenets, the careful planned co-operation. The project would become a laughing-stock everywhere.'

'What about her?'

'She can't believe her eyes.'

He laughed then. 'At least,' he said, 'they know their destination and the date of their departure. Each leaving is a little death for us – we never know the hour, or the day.'

She was suspicious of his frankness, especially since it obliged her to speak revelations. 'I shall go home,' she said and, hesitantly, voicing it for the first time. 'Then into central Sinein, to the Highlands. I shall work there.'

'We – I will miss you,' he said.

Tobin, Pior and Loy: what was one more failure, one more remnant? He was the more remarkable because she had refused him.

'You should have dressed up today,' she said to avoid more invitations of intimacy. 'The Fishfolk are wearing their best.'

They looked like nixies scurrying about below on the flatter ground; like giant tussock mice in their brown, furry coats. Ang pointed out and named individuals for Loy; she described the traditional costume and told him what was still lacking.

One of the Sineinian gym instructors raised a flag. It was the signal for the contestants to come forward. Soon the Race would start. There were flags everywhere, to mark the course, in the hands of the spectators, and someone had hung up a line of flags on the headland a mile away. Eda Voran glanced at them from time to time, opening her notebook, finding some new observation to write in it.

The contestants included Gaby, Bren, Aglit, Ial and Pak. There were eight in all.

Ang surveyed the spectators. The Establishment staff stood together in a group, all of them, except for her. She had decided, on the day of her appointment, that the Director's position gave her the authority to differ and she viewed the group dispassionately. Ander Vist and Carey Aleph lounged against a rock; they might have been leaning on a bar counter, in Boatswain's perhaps, Sollar's central, market-place bar. It had once been her favourite resort because it was full of what she and her friends liked to call 'characters', the stallholders, sweepers and prostitutes who worked nearby. With the same élitist arrogance, her clique had made much of their knowledge that 'Boatswain's' must be pronounced 'Bussun's', or you betrayed yourself, not a 'local'.

Ander and Carey wore the matching sweaters they had bought as a joke; which, here, had became essentials. Their intricate moss-like patterns and soft greens were much admired. The men were attractive too: in Boatswain's she would have sought their company as they, in this cold, unsuitable environment, had for so long sought hers, both seeking entrance to the same magical and secret passage behind the ever-locked gate. Let them also be nothing more than idle memories.

Nanket, released for a day from the tyrany of her incessant demands, stood calm and neat beside them.

There were ghosts, too, and no doubt there were similar, unseen presences gathered about the Folk. Dorta stood commandingly in the centre of her Staff, red hair a bonfire to tempt loyalties, the definitive Director, everything Ang herself was not. Siloe, Madame Juh and the Nurse, that sinister ministering angel, Little Brother and Spiral City itself, were somewhere near, interlocked within their colourful patterns, quite alien in this wind-stripped world of cool sunshine and open waters. Eda Voran, approaching Carey and Ander with determination, looked the stuff of which ERRATE directors were made.

As for Jannl – Harlequin: he stood next to her, in blue patched with pink, the rips in his dungaress giving glimpses of his strong legs, his beautiful, straight feet thrust into a pair of hand-made cloth shoes. There was tension in his body: he almost stood on tiptoe, as if ready to flee; but she had deliberately stayed with him instead of doing her duty. She wanted to be the woman he wanted; she wanted to be normal, ordinary, average and capable. A thread, which her deliberate absences had failed to destroy, still linked them. If she spoke too warmly or moved too close, he would put his arm around her and take her with him: she would be in the trap she so desperately desired and so ardently resisted. Then she would have to break it, speak it: I dare not admit you.

Choosing her words carefully, she began to speak. 'In the Highlands, they live in wooden houses. I'll need to make a darkroom as well — ' but horrifyingly, her circuits as undermined and contorted as the infected computer's, she heard her voice, breathy and distressed, continue: 'There is no future for us.'

Very gently, the clown took hold of her hands. 'For me, there is always the circus. It is my art. Photography is yours. I give: you take. But neither of us is guilty.

'For you: rocks always, but in a new place with a proper night and day and with the warmth we both long for.'

'The red end of the spectrum,' she sighed. 'Heat always and nothing to quench it.'

'Now listen,' said Loy Sen. 'Today is today. It's here for the spending. I know who will win the race, for Alluleya told me.'

'But I know that! It's obvious.'

'Then let us watch and see who is right.'

Sure that they both backed the same runner, the certain winner, she allowed him to help her climb a rock and sit beside her on its flat top. He was too close, but she could not now escape, unless she jumped. His daughter was below, sitting on a mat of lyng and laughing with the other circus children. They rolled and crushed the purple flowers, punching and kicking each other in a private game. Then they all fell over on their backs and kicked their legs in the air.

Loy's new frankness was as fresh as the wind. 'Charis left me Zoe,' he said. 'It must be a long time since she went. A cattle farmer took her from me: you would not believe what such theft can do. One moment she was loved and lovely, and in the next, as I watched her walk away, hated, the ugliest thing in the universe.

'I was glad I had Zoe. No one could hate her. Between each tick of the clock, there waits a void.'

'If time stopped now, we would never know the outcome of the Race.'

'We should wait for ever. But look, it's about to begin.'

The eight runners waited in a line. They were to start when the instructor dipped his flag and their eyes were on the yellow pennon, their small bodies half-crouched and half-naked. From here, high up on this grey rock where Loy Sen knelt excitedly up and his hand brushed her back, they were dolls, toys no bigger than her finger. But she could not *watch* them without involvement: Bren must win, but Gaby should, because she was also a woman, and dear.

How could Gaby stand there, in full view, without a stitch above the waist and her legs like those of an animal, russet and furred? Bren looked like a miniature marathon runner. One of them was sure to win.

The yellow flag went down and the pennants the circus folk waved went up in a red and blue ripple, so that their printed message, 'DTC. We love you', could no longer be read. The flags had taken her attention and the runners become a blur; now, she searched for them across the mountain foot and was surprised to see how far they had already run. They ran together, in a loose bunch, one taking the lead and now another, no one ready to play his hand. The old nature of the race had gone. There had been no betting. These were not athletes in bright, sparse clothing who ran like deer across the land: they were Fishfolk who loped steadily and were not easy to distinguish from the landscape. It was easy to see how kjarr demons had become a reality: a shock head or a brown limb glimpsed in the mist. On this clear day they had the appearance of a herd let loose. They moved slowly over the tussock, content to let the land dictate their pace.

'They'll soon be out of sight behind Traumesse hill,' she said (and what will we do then?).

Her subordinates had already lost interest and settled to a picnic; not one of them looked in her direction. The circus performers and the Folk peered anxiously at the spot where the runners would reappear.

Zoe, suddenly loud at the foot of the rock, saved her feelings from being brought out to join the display.

'Da, Da! Let me come up. Ang!'

'I'm not stopping you,' said Loy. 'Baby.'

'Not a baby.'

'Come on then.'

Ang watched the child climb nimbly to him up the rock.

'I'm a good climber,' Zoe said, confidently, 'aren't I?'

'Not bad,' he said.

'Wonderful!' said Ang.

Zoe settled between them, a soft barrier, warm to the touch.

Three faces, three minds, three identities, Ang thought: the representatives of the three continents – for no one so described scattered Noiro, and Hiberna was perpetual wilderness.

Zoe was disposed to chatter and leaned against her.

'You're nice. You're cuddly like my mam.'

'Am I?'

'He's not. He makes me work. He's not soft.'

'I'm not your mum.'

'You're a lady. My mam was a princess,' said Zoe and looked defiantly at Loy, who smiled wide at his daughter's loquacity. 'I said, my mam was a princess, Da.'

So it was all to punish him for making her climb the rock herself.

'She was, chabo,' he said. 'A princess of flowers and trees, and a real one too with a band of pretty women who worshipped her.'

'You took her away.'

'So I did. And you as well. So that you could meet Ang.'

Zoe move closer to him. 'It's Alluleya, isn't it?' she said. 'Alluleya who works the magic that makes us travel.'

'No.' He shook his head. 'Not her. Though she might know how it works.'

'Will we be going soon or will we stay here with Ang?'

'I don't know.'

'You don't know anything!' Zoe's voice had tears in it, though her eyes were dry.

'2-Sweet doesn't mind,' said Loy, 'or Cricket. Vision likes surprises.'

'Them! They come from the City. Their mums were whores.'

'Zoe! What would Ma say?'

'Dove was a beggar.'

'We're all beggars, Zoe. We are living here because these people like us enough to come to the show. If they didn't, we would starve.'

Ang watched the child trying to find her way across the uncharted sea of emotion and loss, without an adult to guide her, for her father was as rudderless as she. She reached out and put an arm round Zoe, to comfort her and feel again the comfort returned by the dependant child.

Zoe shrieked loudly from her new shelter, 'There they are!'

These runners, a line of figures silhouetted against a sparkling sea, seemed harbingers to Ang. They were the heralds of Sowash's bright future, abstracts, symbols of humanity, not flesh-and-bone people. Their dance was jerky and they passed and repassed each other. She had no wish to capture them in her camera: the only humans she had ever photographed successfully were herself and, by accident, the Folk in Loy's van. But she tried to imprint the image in her memory so that, basking in Sinein's high, dry centre, she would remember the black cut-outs and the shining water.

A man was in first place and a woman in second; the rest of the runners strung out and straggled behind them.

She could hear the Folk and the circus people cheering together. The Sineinians remained silent and dignified; it was their race, after all, a structured competition inaugurated to test the fitness and agility programme.

Loy stood up and hoisted Zoe aloft on his shoulders. She hooked her feet together on his chest and hung upside-down. 'I can see you, Ang. Your mouth is on your forehead and you've got a long beard – but no hair.'

'And you will lose your locket.'

The golden lily leaves, their dreadful power exorcised, had become the plaything of this little girl. Once, she would have been horrified to think of a five-year old wearing an antique worth many thousand decads; then, to assuage her own pain and the dismay the child's thin clothing had aroused in her, she had given her the gold, ready money, easy to exchange; now, it dangled from Zoe's neck and was nothing more than a toy.

'I shan't. It's pinned on: see?'

She had been wrong again. Zoe would take care of her locket. She would still have it when time stopped for everyone; unless the circus fell on very hard times.

'Put me down,' commanded Queen Zoe.

The precocious and provoking child went to Ang and stood in front of her second subject. She held the locket in both hands and pressed the catch. It opened easily, and there was the cropped photograph, in colour, of a woman who could only be Charis the forest-dweller, her mother, and Loy Sen's faithless love.

'Da found me a picture, just like you said. And he fixed the catch.'

'May I see?'

On the opposite half Ang saw her reduction of the drawing Zoe had made. It was a curious fact that the shrinkage and the photographic reproduction had replaced the original's rough quality with bold line and a polished sheen, and she had put it in the envelope and sent it down to the circus with a feeling of disappointment: the face was now a caricature.

Yet the two faces complemented each other, positive and negative, both serene: he smiling at the foolish futility of existence, she in the knowledge of its unchangeable purpose. His face was friendly and accessible, in disguise yet a revelation, white as chalk, long but happy; hers was exquisite and distant, dead to the present time, strong yet delicate, oval but not vacuous, smooth; the lips were exemplary, the eyes those perfect dark and oval almonds which are admired because few women have them, the neck that of a gazelle, the skin brown like Zoe's and Loy's, cinnamon, new bread, bistre. RIP Amare, the loved one. The inscription, which Loy could and Zoe could not read, remained an epitaph.

If Charis had been the hierarchical ruler and deity of some forest tribe, it must have been a far distant past in which Loy found her. Ang's secular mind recoiled, but her soul allowed that it might indeed be an aspect of the truth that royalty was regality: the face fitted this conclusion. Charis looked intelligent and sensual: whole. How could she have hoped to reinvent such a paradigm for Loy? How could Charis have deserted the white-face clown for a farmer?

The answer, she realised, was simple: it must have been to find mortality again. She had tired and left, before the endless travelling frayed her beauty and put ugly hollows beneath her wonderful eyes, preferring these marks of experience to accumulate with age, not timelessness. She had left her daughter to console the clown with innocence and hope. As for Zoe, what could be more delightful than eternal childhood?

'Isn't she pretty,' said Zoe, 'My mam?'

'Better than pretty!'

'Show her your secret,' said Loy.

The child turned the open locket over and pressed the hinge. A leaf opened out of the cluster about the lily bud and 'Oh!' Ang exclaimed, her own intelligence and curiosity called into question for she had not discovered this second, secret compartment.

Inside it was a thin glass wall and, peering close, she saw that it must be double, a sandwich edged with gold which now enclosed the dry flower Zoe had picked and a tiny picture, the portrait of a white woman – herself!

'Oh!' she said again, again confused, and Loy and Zoe laughed. 'Where did you get this?'

'Peach made it,' said Loy. 'He's not always the fool he appears to be. We were amused because you never noticed him drawing you.'

She examined her face. It was hardly a likeness: this woman too, was lovable and her features had the kind of vulnerable beauty she liked to portray in the sagas. She, Ang Semo, was harder than that; when she looked in the mirror she saw composed features, the face of a woman who was in control, the face she had made with her creams, pencils and pigments.

This was a face unmasked; it had Siloe's fragility and undeniable attraction.

She worried then. Peach might have seen her soul: in Traumesse, they might have watched her performing every day, dressed to the nines and qualified to slay and seduce, like Siloe. She gave the locket back to Zoe and helped her fasten the safety-pin. She stared at her feet and forgot the wind and the sunshine while she delved in her mind. It was a long descent, beneath the quick and dead, to the caverns where she was buried.

Loy brought her back, with his ringing shout of, 'Bren! Bren! Barendidt!'

The little man was in the lead, by a long chalk. He was approaching the kjarr, downhill, fast. His pace was such that she expected him to fall but his sure feet kept him up as he bounded from tussock to tussock. His head was up too and he did not need to look behind him. His rivals were a hundred yards behind.

By the kjarr, where the lyng and tussock ended and the reeds began, he veered south and followed the unmarked line around the marshes. One of the conditions of this race was that in following the pre-set direction, a competitor had to make his own route. Once Bren had left the kjarr, he must head west and climb the Old Woman's flank to the finish.

He looked fresh and confident. He had increased his lead. As he turned west, the Race and the glory his, a great cheer went up. Even the apathetic Sineinians hurrahed and Ang shouted with them.

Bren looked up, at the head of the Old Woman it seemed. The spectators with binoculars saw him smile. He stopped running and sat on the ground.

'He's hurt,' screamed Zoe.

'He's given up,' said Ang, incredulously. 'He was winning – he's given up.'

The Fisher man did not seem hurt, nor winded. He sat still on his tussock looking north, toward the other runners. He might have been waiting for them, or waiting to see who was next; and when the second runner came close enough for everyone to see that it was Ial, Bren stood up. When Ial was abreast of him, he began to run again. The two kept pace. They spoke to each other, slowed, and laughed; they strolled home.

No one knew whether to cheer or boo and there was a bemused silence when Bren and Ial walked across the winning line together, arm in arm. They slapped each other on the back.

Bren broke from Ial's embrace, turned about and spoke to Eda and the cluster of Staff with the vehemence of a political agitator: 'Fishfolk don't compete with each other,' he said. 'We work together. We fish and hunt together. We must always be close, in harmony, or we would perish in the cold. Please don't award the prize.'

The other competitors came in slowly. Gaby kissed Bren and Ial and began a round of hugs and kisses amongst the Folk.

'We don't need prizes,' she said. 'As Bren told you, we're Fishfolk.'

'That's right,' said Cait. 'We are Avangnardlit.' The two Folk women advanced on Eda Voran, their hands lifted to gesticulate better, Cait's fur coat and Gaby's nakedness not symbolic of domesticity and wildness, but honest expressions of the two interrelated Fishfolk states of mind.

'How can she?' thought Ang, looking down upon the disturbance from her remote and godlike vantage point. 'How dare she let everyone see her like that, without her shirt? How can she forget herself?'

The men, she knew, would be eyeing Gaby, weighing up her sexual potential; enjoying the involuntarily inviting movements her breasts made as she argued. They were all like that, beneath whatever mask or veneer they chose to don. . .

Eda, in the press, was forced backward by the onslaught. Carey and Ander were standing upright now, ready to face any trouble, man to man – or small, enraged woman; and the aloof position of ERRATE's Director on her rock was no longer tenable. There could be blows, dissention, a riot, if she did not intervene.

'I have to go,' she told Loy and scrambled at once down the rock, not looking back and no longer probing the wounds of her memory or delving in the hurtful past. Violent reality waited for her contribution.

She tried to walk quickly but stumbled against the tussocks and arrived out of breath. The situation was not as bad as it seemed: an animated argument which, from the rock, had looked like ugly confrontation, was taking place. Cait and Gaby both spoke loudly and waved their arms in the air; Bren and the others stood close behind them, but they looked relaxed. Indeed, Pak had a broad grin on his face.

'Gaby,' Ang said, and was surprised to hear authority, Dorta's legacy, frost her voice. 'Put on your shirt.'

Their laughter soothed her. Who was she, after all, to insist upon Sineinian proprieties? She was surprised to see the ochre birdskin shirt passed, hand to hand, to Gaby, who dressed herself and smiled all the while. She turned her brilliant smile upon Ang: they had to be friends, allies.

In after years Eda Voran, immobile yet sentient, recording her memoirs with the aid of a sensory processing unit, noted her surprise at the ease and good humour with which Ang Semo had quelled the little rebellion.

Ang and the Fishfolk laughed together.

'We speak as equals now,' said Salter Bren. 'She and I have both been visited, she by the herd mother who also knelt to me, and I by Ilgolot who showed me where to find my spearshaft. He came in Brine. I made my spear then and yesterday, I hunted. But the mother came first to her and began it, began us, Avangnardlit, once more. Ang Semo has given us back our lives.'

The Staff listened quietly. Each one, even while pursuing the lengthy and interventive rehabilitation programme, had been trained to listen patiently to the Folk. Eda Voran, glancing toward the sea, realised that the flags strung out upon the headland were not squares of cloth but pieces of meat hung up to dry in the wind and in the smoke of cooking fires which now, on timely cue, sent up their thin smoke. They signalled merriment and new sights; she thought herself, them all, so lucky to be present at this early renaissance, about to witness a malp feast. Bren had spoken of hunting and the making of a spear. There had, in such circumstances, to be meat.

Ang felt her pride in Bren and her interest in his pursuits return; and yet – she had given the locket to Zoe to be free of Dorta Wireloom and had forgotten that the office of Director would, in itself and by its very nature, influence her. The first words she spoke were hesitant and then, feeding upon themselves, they built quickly into an oration as fine and verbose as any heard in Sollar Kein.

'I believe that the Fishfolk will return to the Wild; I believe my own experience with the icedeer in White will influence that return. Salter Bren also encountered the deer and has further supernatural and natural experiences to recount. These experiences have made him what he is today: Barendidt Avangnar, dressed in quvit and sark. He is keen to leave Traumesse although ERRATE is neither ready nor happy to let him go.

'We have no power in Traumesse or, at least, only the elusive power of allied nations and the good will of the Council of Nations and Noiro whose members meet to confer together and to confer upon their various nationals the responsibilities of being members of the human race.

'If Barendidt wishes to leave us, he may: we cannot prevent him. If Barendidt's wife and friends wish to accompany him, we cannot prevent them. If all the Fishfolk, women, men and children, wish to leave Traumesse and embark upon a cruel sea to find their fortunes, we cannot prevent them.

'The Fishfolk are as free as they have always been, yet we of ERRATE and Traumesse, the great experiment, are chained – we shall never break free because the experiment will not have run its course. There will be no result and no sense of achievement. We, the interlopers, will have failed.

'I appeal to the Folk – to Bren and Cait, to Gaby, to Ial, Kubbu, Aglit, to all of you. Please stay with us until the best time for leaving comes.'

There was a spontaneous surge of applause amongst the Staff. Carey Aleph began it, pleased to think that, in clapping the Director, he was able to praise Ang Semo. He agreed entirely with her sentiments and thought her speech at once graceful and forthright. The bad start she had made at the job was eclipsed.

The circus people looked on; some drifted away and small groups began to make their way back to Toul. Loy Sen, reaching the edge of the crowd around Ang, thought how beautiful she was, and how remote amongst the furclad bodies and shaggy heads of the little ones.

The Fishfolk themselves were silent.

Thus any truth can become the truth for somebody, Ang thought and looked about her, not daring to confront Bren again. In speaking as Director, she had not declared herself. That was right: the correct way. She felt huge and clumsy, a full head and shoulders taller than the Folk. Carey and Ander were giants. She wondered what curious experiment God – call Her Mahun, Oma, Om, Him, Matoq, what-you-will – had devised in creating such diverse beings. It must amuse, maybe delight, Her to look down upon the tall Sineinians and the little Folk, upon all people, malp, spiders, elephants, horses, the sloth, the ant: the supreme judge at some kind of universal beast show.

Bren had been kicked, in the kidneys, in the groin, the places which would hurt him most. He almost felt the bruising. All sense had gone. She said one thing and then, in public, something different. He had watched her closely, as if he would feed upon the words which issued from her, taste and savour them. The hard words had tasted bitter. He spat them out. There! Now let her try to stop him. I am wild now, he thought, no longer a tamed aboriginal. He stood up straight, as tall as he could make himself. They were waiting. He cleared his throat.

'There is a malpog,' he said. 'I killed it. Come, Dr Semo, Professor, Ladies, Gentlemen: eat flesh with us.'

The bitterness set hard as he spoke. It became a lump in his throat. It formed itself into a goad. It was as good a purpose for continuing as any. He lifted his left arm and beckoned to them, to follow.

Atluki, the horn of the icedeer smooth in his hand, saw the old, dead ones clearly. They filled up the spaces in the crowd. His grandmother smiled at him as she rocked his sister in her arms, and between the Doctor and the Professor was that terrifying, red-haired woman, the Boss. Yards of seaweed enveloped her and a sea-demon crouched on her shoulder. The Professor was hers already: they held hands.

The Doctor would follow: she would take the other hand. How big they were, towering over Bren.

Atluki felt giddy. He went behind the nearest tussock and sat down gladly on the solid and comforting earth.

The women's words followed him: 'Well done, my dear,' said Eda Voran. 'And now tread canny. Bren has undertaken a rite of passage. He feels strong and, when he has eaten the meat of the malpog, will think himself invincible.'

'Thank you – but I hardly knew what I was doing. The words came of themselves.'

'I assure you, Dorta herself could not have handled it so well.'

Blood ran from each portion of the butchered malpog across the hot cooking stones, and the headland smelled of smoke, charring and death. Men knelt with their heads in the smoke and turned the meat. They had draped the dark grey skin of the animal over one of the drying racks. It hung limply down beside thin slices of hardening meat, but this grisly juxtaposition of the external and the internal disturbed only the Sineinians whose cultured minds had long ago severed the connection between a carcase and a dinner.

Everyone had followed Bren eagerly. Now some hung back as the Fisher men removed hunks of half-cooked meat from the stones and pressed them upon the would-be feasters. The outside of each piece was sooty and too hot to hold, the inside cold and completely raw. Ander swore and dropped his portion; Eda Voran ate hungrily, dissembling, and damning the consequences: the pharmacy had plenty of remedies for enteritis, back in Traumesse. Old Catch bit slowly through the crisp and blackened outer layers into the fragrant tenderness within: here was the youth he had been denied, given him in a flavour. He closed his eyes, the better to see: his father, younger and fitter than the silent operative he remembered, stalked gigantic, basking malp.

'This is *good*,' said Float Susu, wiping her greasy chin. 'This is what my grandmother talked of whenever we went to the canteen for a steak.'

Ang looked at her generous serving. Its hard black coating had cooled a little; she no longer had to pass it rapidly fom hand to hand. It was heavy and dense. It sagged upon her palm and she poked a finger through its charred and brittle skin and exposed flesh of such a dark and intense red it would match the Highlands' crusted almandines.

'Eat!' said Bren, beside her. 'Eat!'

His allocation, the hunter's share, had been enormous. He had eaten two thirds of it and paused to urge her on, the remnants of his gluttony viscous and shiny in the coarse stubble which was all the beard a Fishfolk man grew.

'It's good!'

She tried, to please him, and bit off a mite of flesh. It tasted rancid and she chewed many times before she could swallow the fibrous mass. She was accustomed to eat colourful salads and the daintily-sliced white flesh of poultry or fish, to eat with knife and fork.

'Good?' said Bren once more, the fierce set of his mouth making a question of the word.

'It's – different.'

'Aagh!' he cried, and caught her hand in grease-stained, grimy fingers. 'Come with me.'

He pulled her along with him; he was very strong and, as she suffered the enforced tour he gave her of the drying racks and the malpog pelt, she felt the gap she had opened between them widen. The gulf between their two cultures yawned.

'Feel!' said Bren. 'Stroke his fur.'

The hide of the malpog was pliant and small slivers of muscle and blood vessels still clung to it. This suety blue skin had covered the animal, been intimately joined to its flesh. The fur side was better. She could touch it without cringing from dumb implications of life and death.

'I killed him,' said Bren. 'Next year his brother will wait for me at Nusseraq.'

He chewed as he talked and showed his teeth and tongue busy about his meat. Ang brought her free hand carefully down to her side and dropped her meat quietly on the ground. Here, in his country, there could be no cheating, and a waiting sweepwing pounced and carried it off.

Bren laughed openly at her. 'This is meat, not canteen soup,' he said, transparent, triumphant and obvious, drunk on the flesh in his stomach and the deed in his memory.

They came to a neat array of entrails set out on the ground. Bren pointed at a swollen, pink sac.

'The stomach. It's packed with heart, liver and lungs. Tomorrow, it will be ready to eat – when it begins to look blue.

'These are the guts: a good seventy feet of rope.'

Bren picked up a thick cylinder of flesh.

'Look. He had a good length to please the malp-women.'

He gestured at her, the wind-dried pizzle stiff in his hand. She knew she should laugh. Gaby would laugh, sure of herself and her reactions and attractions; open, free and unashamed.

She was completely helpless, manacled by the small, strong hand and forced to look at herself. The gentle touch surprised her.

'Come away,' said Loy Sen, 'Leave him to play with his trophies.'

He did not lead her although she followed him, until they reached a clear patch of ground where tussock mice had fed and nibbled the tall grasses away, leaving only low brown clumps. He sat on one of them. She took another. He had come to take his leave, to make a final farewell.

'In the long run,' he said, 'and mine is a very long race, both performance and life – friendship is best, cleanest: the love of parents for children, of brothers and sisters, of the clown for his audience. Carnal love is chaotic and hurtful, always changing its coat or its colour. Be for ever true.'

You can't ask me that, she thought. To live upon remembrances until I, for you will not, die. To live another fifty years alone with the fading memory of a clown.

'True?' she said.'I have already betrayed the Folk.'

'They will forgive you when they understand your speech. They'll be true to their first memory of you.'

The bright sunlight shone upon the clown. He stood up and swung into a handstand, arched his body and was again upright.

'If I had brought my clubs, I would juggle for you,' he said.

'Thank you.'

'I must go. I'll see you at the next performance.' The words were casual, bagatelles. He tossed them up in the air.

'Yes, at the circus.' She would not see him again, not ever; she would stay in Traumesse and begin to remember. She watched him walk away, become a distant stick-figure silhouetted against the green and violet hillside. He stopped on the skirts of the Old Woman. Perhaps he was looking back.

Then two small figures appeared, descending the slope below the headland, making their way to him: Zoe, tiny and scarlet in her silken wrap and someone rounded in outline, and furry: Float Gaby.

'Oh,' said Ang, 'Harlequin. . .'

She was the clown. His tears lay on her cheeks. As for Loy Sen, he had already changed his colour and his coat and hung out his heart upon the sleeve of it.

Before he died, coughing blood and sweating like an overworked horse, drenched by and drowning in his own bodily fluids, Meleager had passed Loy some nuggets of his wisdom.

'Every proposition. Take a good look. Then leap.'

The words were a kind and gently humorous remembrance of the old days when Ma had been alive and his own physical needs so pressing that everyone in the circus, Mel and Ma included, had referred to him as 'that young lepper.'

He was fourteen and too eager; he used to run and turn somersaults, pitch-poles and handsprings, without thinking about it, and usually ended with a fall. He did not stop to work the distance out. Nor, in affairs of the heart and genitals, did he work out the penalties. He fell in love instantly, for ever; then it was over and he had suffered another fall and deep bruising was the result.

He was cautious now, and very old at twenty-eight, the age at which he had left the City. No one could tell how old he really was. He had been around so long in this supple body which never aged, that he knew every inch, hair and quirk of it and, so had reached a spurious maturity which would last for ever. It was like a curse, eternal experience without conclusion. It had been wished on him when he had no lover and keeping one thereafter was harder than the triple somersault. Despite the legends, few women wished to run away with a circus. Getting sex was easy, but he liked to be in love although he found it hard to fix on one woman, to be true. Charis had come and gone, her beauty a past and pleasant holiday. Ang, with nightmares of her own, had torn out the root she had fastened in him and left a raw wound.

Gaby, little Red Cheeks, touched his heart and made it ache; but they all had and did.

He moved slowly across the green and violet landscape toward the Democratic Travelling Circus beached in Toul, and Gaby and his daughter followed him.

He was a consummate clown, acrobat and juggler, at the everlasting summit of his skills, yet he still made leaps in the dark and suffered the pain they engendered; it was double pain now, from the liaisons themselves and the eternal memory of their heights, depths and nuances.

Charis had left him Zoe. Ang had left him nothing at all and Peach had given Zoe her picture, locked away inside the golden lily which, when he had examined it cursorily without attempting to guess its value, he had handed back without a word: gift-horses were usually aged. Ang had given *Zoe* the locket with its engraved message of love and remembrance.

This heat was what the City enjoyed in winter, in Hibornal after the rains stopped: such a gentle warmth it was cool. His body remembered more than he did of the moisture of the true southern heat, a force that lay against the skin, made it sweat and uncovered heads hot. Shade, sea, water, ices, straw hats, had not been enough to cool certain tempers which, like his own, would willy nilly leap into any dark breach for the chance of a fight or a fuck.

But he did not believe that climate caused violence or its counter, love.

He had once been able to hold a steel spring shut; and supposed he could do so still. His arms were strong from the endless years of juggling, his legs flexible braces which held him lightly up upon the smooth surface of the rolling ball. He could move like a cat in and out of shadows but now the abject posture of the world-weary clown had taken him over and his shoulders drooped as he walked across the island towards Toul.

His state of mind was reflected in his gait. He stumbled from tussock to tussock like a drunken man.

Memories of the City were strong this afternoon – if that was the time of day: in the continual light it was not easy to tell. He used them to drown Ang Semo and the ghosts which, deeper in the body, perpetually revolving in the brain, were as persistent as they had ever been. If he thought too often of her true face, the unpainted one, and of the white body she hid from him, she would not leave him peacefully. He hoped he would never see her again; he knew he must see her again because she was the arbitrator who would prevent the Sineinian authorities from returning him, with his bulky baggage and train, inside time to the City; a City which, in this year of 4625, knew nothing of him, save as the record in the Archive of a disappearance and presumed drowning.

Both Ang and Professor Voran had spoken of the City and there, upon the grey wall of the photographer's room, were Crinon Hinoor's two pictures: Bania, City canal, bleak summary of filth and degradation and Cal M'unor, City boy and man, the soul of beauty and a different kind of degradation – poverty, luxury, enslavement, death. She must still exist, yet he wondered sometimes if she was the same City of blue and black towers that he remembered. She had become a destination as hazy and desirable as that perfect heaven which, his religion promised him, would be his when – if ever – he died. Once or twice, when there was no food left for the elephant or Peach had been especially stupid, he had asked himself whether suicide might be the way out; if, by cutting the loop he was bound to, he could escape it altogether and find his own way home, back to the beginning, to Ma and the old original: Madam Sen's Circumcentral Circus and Hyperlative Hippodrome.

Sometimes, he thought he might have died in the floods which had overwhelmed the lower City a hundred years ago, and he did not want to die again. He felt as good as dead, tripping over these rough tussocks as if he had the palsy.

Zoe's plaintive wail claimed him and he turned, exasperated and guilty, to wait for his child.

He had forgotten about Gaby, hand-in-hand with Zoe, children together, two for whom the circus was, in his mother's grandiose definition, central. Was it not also the core of his personal universe? Gaby's red cheeks were heated to a high degree, a dark, glowing red, and the white hair of her jacket floated, a soft nimbus, on the wind. She looked as round as she was short but now he knew what she was. She had a lean body like that of the acrobat, Dove, and he, in common with every runner and spectator, had seen how her brown skin glistened after the Race with sweat and how her young breasts supported those petrified droplets, the many-stranded crystal beads.

'Come on, Zoe,' he said lightly. 'The party's over.'

'Didn't like it anyway.'

She was still in her obstructive mood and would continue so until he gave her a token of his love, a kiss or a candy. He decided not to placate her now. There would be no promised treats, nor even the comfort of a piggy-back. He was too soft with her. He turned his back and made for the circus.

Zoe ran ahead across the open ground before the van and disappeared inside. She did not seem unhappy, but she banged the bottom door. Probably, she had chipped the paint again.

Loy felt intensely sorry for himself, never free of problems, always beset, forever required to present the clown's acquiescent face to the world. His own needs were discarded, stained and crumpled papers hidden in the undergrowth, the messages written on them made illegible by forces greater than himself. Each day the rain fell on someone; whether it was regarded as blessing or malediction depended on indecipherable, inner scripts. Here he was – in the middle of nowhere, at the back of beyond – engaged in a game he thought long ago played out, instead of applying himself to his work and the circus's predicament.

Ang's countrywomen would allow him no more grace. They were on the island now, a merry party no doubt after their slow summer cruise from Habin, Sollar's port, but, nonetheless, a party of officials which had come finally to assess and rematriate the circus. Real time was running out; he might no longer be immortal.

Here was Cantor, the perfect balm for a suppurating sore. But, instead of uttering one of his perjorative queries such as, 'Was it worth the walk?' or, 'Another day past its prime and what's been done with it?', he smiled – a horrible sight in itself – and said, 'you've brought Gaby.'

'I've brought her back for tea,' said Loy, suddenly inspired with reason enough. 'She likes to visit the rats.'

'Well,' said Cantor, reverting to type, 'You'll have to count me out. I've work to do.'

Loy heard Gaby snort as she suppressed her ready laughter.

'I don't even like your thin and scented tea,' she said.

'You had better learn to like it,' he heard himself say while the kettle, which Zoe (he was amazed to see) had set on the stove, began its shrill, ascending scale inside his red, blue and vagrant home. Peach looked up from the shoes he was mending and smiled at Gaby.

Zoe poured the tea and, when the four cups were full to the brim with the pale greenbrown liquid and its ethereal smell likewise filled the van, Peach lifted his cup. 'To the City!' he said.

'When She chooses,' said Loy, unable to keep the preoccupying dread out of his mind.

Zoe rattled the tea tin at him. 'There's not much left.'

'Well Zoe,' he said. 'If we're unlucky, we'll soon be able to fill it again.'

He wanted to see what Gaby was doing with her cup: drinking from it like any normal person, or sipping it because she really could not bear the taste. Gaby, he knew, was incapable of daintiness and dissembling. She drank her tea steadily and put down the cup.

'On the whole,' she said, 'I think it's better than malpog meat – just.'

He remembered, a flash of summer lightning, a sudden lifting of the cloud, how she had immediately taken on the useful role in the cluttered and sleep-scented van the other day, brewing fresh coffee against Ang's approaching invasion of his space and soul.

'This is not a tea party,' Gaby said. 'It's a tea break. Is there a circus tonight?'

'There's always a circus,' said Peach. 'Those Sineinians are coming again.'

'Which ones?'

'The women from Sollar.'

'People often come here from Sollar,' said Gaby. 'You mean the Deportation Committee.'

She was so practical, thought Loy, and how comfortable she had seemed, deep in easy talk with Peach, whose sympathies were with both sexes and whose thoughts, in whatever ungrammatical language he chose to use, were accessible.

'I'm hot,' Gaby whispered to Peach.

'Take off your dead deer.'

She answered him by lifting the hem of her long jacket and showing him an inch of bare skin.

'You can borrow my sweater.'

She turned her back on Zoe and the two men and, with the astonishing speed of a time-lapsed photographic sequence, shed her skins and covered her brown underbody with white wool. She arranged her beads outside the sweater and pulled off her boots. Loy smiled to himself. The furry trousers she was wearing had as many patches as his dungarees and ended just below the knee.

In here, foreign territory, the City's migrant Embassy, she had lost her bold Folk identity and become what they were, embarrassed refugees. He reached for his hat and lobbed the broken straw cone gently on to her unkempt head.

'What are you doing, Loy?'

She sounded plaintive and annoyed, like Zoe. He laughed out loud. She could not resist that and laughed with him. She stood up and paraded her rags around the small area of floor between the beds and the stove.

'That,' said Peach, between his shouts of laughter, 'used to be a hill tiger's sweater – pure white wool to cover up a rich dosser's deeds. 'S made of goat wool too.'

'Hi, Nix!' said Zoe, holding up her doll to compare with Gaby.

From the boulder-top, frustrated and involved with Ang Semo, he had seen the little Folk scurry about like small furry animals, or the sprites they believed lived everywhere. Here beside him now, a few hours later, was one of them, Float Gaby escaped from the solemn commitments of her fellows into humorous parody.

'Red Cheeks', he said. Her cheeks were scarlet, aflame with pleasure at their delight and her own audacity. He captured her easily and sat her, secured by the tight bonds of his arms, upon his knee, while Peach enhanced her colour with a stick of bright red greasepaint and gave her the scarlet, exaggerated lips of a clown. He let her wriggle while he gripped her and released her with regret.

'I can stand on my head too,' she said, and did so there and then.

'We can always do with an extra clown,' said Peach, and fell back into his bunk to enjoy another bout of laughter to the full.

'Yes,' said Loy, the dormant idea rooting, 'you can ride Spooky into the ring tonight. We must put on a good show for the Sineinians.'

He stood up and stretched. His spangled suit and fiddle hung ready on the wall. It was time to prepare.

They sat her on the horse, put a child hardly larger than Zoe, 2-Cute, in charge of Spooky and herself and left her to perambulate the ring while the trumpet and drums played and the clowns and acrobats tumbled. 2-Cute was dressed as a little old woman. It was some time before she realised that the crowd was laughing at her as well as at the other clowns and, falling into her tatterdemalion part, she clung to Spooky's mane and pretended to be afraid. This, the first parade, was called Meet the Circus. She grabbed at Spooky's mane and slipped and slithered on his broad back, while she marvelled at Dove, turning the like a wheel of fire in the centre of the ring.

She stood in the wings, abandoned by the busy performers and full of curiosity, her strangely modified clothing giving her courage and a different self. There was a table nearby, with a mirror on it. A few sticks of paint lay in a scatter on the tabletop. She could see this new self smiling slyly and she touched her extra-red cheeks and the huge and friendly mouth which Peach had given her.

Harlequin walked up to the table and looked into the mirror. He picked up a white stick and mended a darker patch upon his pale face. He put on his mask and swung the club he carried threateningly.

'Look out!' he said, and made a hideous face at Gaby.

Peach, she saw, was also transformed into someone who went far beyond the bounds of his kind and sympathetic self. Red Cheeks did not giggle as Gaby did, but skipped and hopped half-a-dozen erratic and joyful steps of a crazy dance.

Columbine had come up and linked arms with Harlequin. It was still difficult to see where the fragile girl ended and foul-mouthed, handsome Dork, who sulked alone in his van, began. Together, Harlequin and Columbine were the most beautiful couple in the world.

Cantor too, the gruff man who stank worse than Ang of cigarette smoke had become silly and frail. Those strong arms and hands, which she had seen lift horses' hoofs and great big bales of hay, looked thin and wasted. A red dressing gown hung limply about him and he carried a candlestick – though, in the evening daylight, the inside of the tent was bright.

Gaby watched the Harlequinade and saw how the players

winked and smiled at each other while they played out their sad comedy of life.

She watched Shiny hang upside down by his teeth and saw how careful he was, and how controlled about the risks he took.

She watched 2-Cute, Cantor and Bluebird make a spectacle together in which the girl did handstands on the horse's back and the man spoke timed commands so that nothing was left to chance.

The clowns gathered and drew her into their throng. She was the tallest, except for Loy who towered above them all. Florian the dwarf took her arm and told her to dance. They all went into the ring and laid siege to Loy who tried, in vain, to toss his clubs and balls in arcs and rainbows in the air.

The clowns retired. Gaby watched Loy Sen concentrate upon his juggling and then, for the magic was not diminished by being understood, draw tears from the audience with his fiddle and bow.

In the interval she stood still and looked at the tiered crowd.

'Come on!' said Peach, pulling her away. 'No time to stand idle.' He thrust a tray of sugared cakes, those sweet delights she had eaten at tea with the circus, into her hands and sent her out to sell them.

She was excited and also filled with chagrin, for no one out there recognised her. She wanted Ang there, to share her anonymous triumph; but she was not in the audience. The line of well-dressed Sineinian officials was in the charge of Professor Voran, whose precise voice could be heard explaining the meaning of the circus to her captive hearers.

'Two tenths please, ma'am' she said, and put one of the sticky cakes into the professor's hand.

'That character,' she heard Professor Voran explain as she moved along the row, 'must be another of Gaian ancestry. Not from the Commedia – probably a debased version of the Green Man, one of their fertility gods.'

The band struck up, the elephant performed, and Aurora and Zoe brought on the dogs which begged and bowed and walked upon their hind legs. One of them could count. Dove and Shiny walked a tightrope. They wore soft shoes like Loy's and counted quietly as they inched along the wire with beautiful and practised smiles upon their faces. The She-Devils of Hy Shrikand charged into the ring and shot arrows at each other: she could unearth identities by now and saw Peach, Dork and Tash riding Spooky, Bluebird and one of the van horses. The men were dressed in silken draperies and armour made of painted leather. Their arrows went wide of the mark and struck the ground; but they rode energetically and the horses were only still for the instant when a rider spoke, 'Now!' and loosed his arrow.

'Red Cheeks!' Loy was there, reaching out for her hand. It was time for the Grand Parade. She ran with the white-face clown, into the trampled ring, and saw the audience standing up to clap. Loy lifted her for an instant high in the air, and set her down on the edge of the ring to curtsey and bow. He held out his arms to call Zoe from the audience where she sat with the silk rose ready in her hand.

The people in the front row, close enough to see, wept when Zoe gave her rose to the clown and all the children who, like Zoe, had waited for their moment to come, rushed into the ring to dance with the performers. Gaby danced unrecognised in the elated crowd until, moving from one child to another with smiles and laughter, Loy came to her and handed her the trusty scarlet rose. She took it from him and saw desire in his eyes. Then he was gone from her side into the throng again.

The children's pleasure was audible and visible. They were reluctant to leave the ring and Loy watched them trail away, back to their parents, with regret. If only the climactic moment could continue, the multicoloured, whirling pageant go on – but the Sineinians were approaching him with expressions which concealed their true purpose, the Professor of Anthropology and Ethnography at the head of the line. They grouped themselves about him, staring like a ring of theatre critics at his costume and paint.

'We wanted to say how much we enjoyed your performance,' said Eda Voran, 'And the entire show, of course.'

In the City he had learned to fear academics. The destinies of countless citizens had been theirs to tend or throw away. Here, it must be the same.

'Thank you,' he said gravely. (Where had Gaby gone?)

One of the women was eager to speak to him.

'That little girl,' she said. 'The one who gave you the rose. She must be part of the circus?'

'I'm afraid so,' he said apologetically. 'She's an important part of the illusion. She's my daughter.'

'Oh.' The soft sigh of disappointment showed him again how important it was not to talk shop with the customers. (Where was Zoe?)

'Excuse me,' he said and turned away.

There they were, Gaby and Zoe together, peering at him from the concealment of the curtain. They wiggled their fingers at him and disappeared.

He turned back; the women were still their. Some of them, he saw, wore military uniforms. He thought of Sierra strutting in her tunic and boots; but these were real. A few more minutes and they would invade.

'If you are interested,' he said, 'I can arrange for a tour of the circus tomorrow.'

'Before our meeting or afterwards?'

He smiled. He deferred to them and their superior judgement.

'Before,' said Eda Voran, anticipating the concensus. 'It will help to put you in perspective.'

'Then,' he said, more boldy while he wished them all in hell, 'I'll see you tomorrow, Professor, Colonel, Major, Ladies.'

Anxiety made him run when he was safely out of sight. Tomorrow afternoon or the day after, he was certain to be summoned to Traumesse. Last time they had made him come alone and, casting about in his mind for a companion, he rejected every possible candidate. Peach with his City accent would never do, nor Dork who had plied the catamite's trade in the Quarter there; Cantor came from Roakn which had quarrelled with half the world; Mel was dead and Alluleya, unobtrusive in the circus, had once been such an eminence she could not be revealed. He, when he had followed Cal M'unor into the Land Beyond, had conspired with him to shelter the City's oracle.

Gaby had made a pot of coffee and cleaned her face. Akunarmiut, she had said, those who live between the winds. He was buffeted, assailed on all sides. She calmed him by simply sitting still and drinking her coffee. She had given Zoe a bottle of the aerated cordial they had sent down from Traumesse; she understood children – she had a host to practise on at home. She had given Nix, the doll, a bottle too.

He told her about the coming interview. She would not allow him to frighten her with tales of what might be.

'Something'll turn up,' she said, 'and I had better go home.'

'No – not yet.' He must salvage a little time of his own from the long day. 'You came for Rats and Rats you shall have.'

'They won't mind. I'll come tomorrow instead.'

'Please stay.'

'Very well.' She smoothed her furry trousers, prim as Ang Semo. She was fully dressed, a Fisher woman once more. The yellow birdskin shirt and the thick jacket, with its fluid and animal surface, hid the desirable shape she had twice shown him. This time, he followed her to the beast cage and watched her kneel down in the straw and whistle to the rats. They came sedately out and sat down in the fan formation their knotted tails forced them to adopt. Gaby whispered to Thunder and stroked the great, untiable knot. Loy watched her almost fondly, remembering how the women of the Quarter and his mother's circus, two fearsome groups of performers, used to whisper sentimentalities and secrets to puppies, kittens and the like. This cage, with its gilded bars, was another of the circus's illusions: it had been the home of Dasyssa, the tamed and dancing bear and beneath its floorboards, in the well of the cart, was the circus's secret coffer and treasure hoard.

Gaby conversed with the rats.

'You've grown yourself a fine fur coat,' said 'Andsome.

She did not like to tell him it was made from the skins of dead animals. 'Thank you,' she said. 'It's a magic coat.'

'Well, well, lets see if you can magic any more of them eggs you brought us before.'

'I've got a cake.' She took it from her pocket.

The sugary spikes which had crowned it had broken off and the cake itself was squashed, but the rats viewed it greedily. She could see their noses twitching as they sized it up.

She had stolen the cake from her tray and she had cheated with the eggs when Ulbeg's precipices had frightened her and the restless spirits of old ones had spoken to her. The eggs she rolled last week into the Rat Queen's castle had come from the grocery store in Traumesse.

Tooth took a bite from the cake and retired as far as his tail allowed him, while the other rats fed.

'Thank you, Red Cheeks,' he said. His tinny voice was faint; perhaps it was the voice of Loy Sen she heard. She looked round. The clown was smiling at her.

'You like animals,' he said.

'Yes. There aren't many in Traumesse – some macaws and lovebirds, and two pools with fish in them. There was an owl, but he died before I got to know him properly.'

She looked bright and perceptive, a small quick animal herself, crouched on the floor. She was very much alive. Ang would never get on her hands and knees to talk nonsense to a pack of rats: she was buried in the underground city, making up more dreams. He had interred her there with her tortuous, mathematical fantasies whilst he enjoyed his pleasant, idle fancies under the sky.

'If I can't have one, I'll have the other,' he thought.

The Director of ERRATE in Traumesse had issued her first directive: she was not to be disturbed. Nanket kept guard in the outer office; within, in the copper-coloured inner sanctum which had been Dorta Wireloom's and where certain decorative objects, a dwarfed lime tree, a stuffed gecko and the dried skin of a scorpion fish, testified to a perverse taste, Ang woke the dormant terminal.

And we shall have music, she thought, her warm fingers dancing a jig upon the cool chequerboard through which she could speak with, and command the demons of Traumesse.

On the tenebrous wall above the beautiful, blank screen whose non-relective surface mirrored nothing, was the profile of a strange attractor, an old snap of Chaos. It looked like the two wings of a butterfly or the inscrutable face of an owl. If you could step upon those wings and follow the coloured tracks which formed them, if you could follow the spirals inwards, you would never tread twice in the same space.

Jannl had disappeared into the system: she could not locate him in any of his mutated forms. She could speak to the computer with both voice and touch, have its music – thin, abstract disharmonies like the voice of the whale – or silence. He was no longer listening.

In the Panlands of the Central Highlands the guides had shown her fossilised drought, great fissures in solid rock which were the rigid memories of a time without rain and an age when saurians and theropods had lived. She felt herself splitting under the strain of the parting from Jannl and Loy. She sat still, with her hands on the terminal and her gaze on the permutating pictures, interactively excommunicated by her hidden creation.

Though she was no longer a factor in the history of the Folk, who were now their own makers, shapers and ambassadors, she wanted still to care for Gaby and for Bren, whose lives lay before them. They would be parted by time and distance, but she belonged with them and was forever Loy's: Gaby might take him in her stead; then Gaby would bear the children she could never have, his daughters and sons, while she was released to dream amongst the highlands and red rocks of Central Sinein and to play with their images instead of with her children.

It was possible, if time in the circus truly was suspended, that Gaby might remain pregnant for ever, an immortal foetus eternally weighing her down, never able to be born.

It was more likely that time there trickled through the hourglass in slow motion. Thus, every experience was heightened, the audiences ecstatic and the performers sublime; every anguish was prolonged: the breach at the heart of sex, its product a heavy stone in the gut.

It would take two clowns to accept existence under those conditions.

He had been funny and full of anguish. He laughed and wept. As with her, love and hate met in him in equal proportions. In clowns, angels and demons could live together – and every day, she put on her own motley of black and white suit, purple-lidded eyes and perfect red lips, an involuntary Pierrot. But not by the light of the moon, my friend – in Traumesse's lamplit confines. Here was necromancy, magic of changing body-shape and colour, the mask and masque of life. Soon, Dr Semo would be no more, her chrysalis abandoned and dead, while Ang went forth.

There had been a magician at one of the performances, just another clown with a magic cauldron made of tin. His companion, a zany in a pierrot costume had besieged him with demands and the magician, stirring his cauldron with a huge wooden spoon, had conjured for him. She could remember their dialectic precisely:

Magician: Do you want her white or brown?
Clown: Red.
Magician: Do you want her to have large breasts?
Clown: Yes, very large.
Magician: Eyes blue or brown?
Clown: Large.
Magician: Do you want her to be musical?
Clown: Large, large.
Magician: Clever?
Clown: Large, very large.
Magician: Rich?
Clown: Large, I tell you, large.

And a huge red form had burst from the cauldron and beaten the clown for making a monster of her.

Another classic routine, which had made the Folk double up, was called 'You can't do that here.' Whatever the clowns attempted, be it music-making, cooking, painting or simply sitting down, was interrupted and forbidden by the minute and dictatorial ring-master. At least the Folk and her staff had given up that game and so, soon, would she.

When the sea began to freeze and Matoq's bite replaced Annasi's kiss, she would be free.

The terminal chirruped at her, a friendly sound of the kind one would associate with a small, furred animal and not a complex and massive artificial brain.

Anything might happen now.

Ang touched the five letters which summoned her demon: JANNL.

She looked into a furnace. She knew he was there but she could not distinguish him from the redhot coals of the fire. So this was the intent: looking about her, feeling her own body hot with excitement, she clearly saw the network of cracks which covered the cypris-hued walls of the room like spiders' webs. Most of the walls of Traumesse had developed this fault: in the last month. The engineers she had consulted had spoken of uncalculated stresses and looked for someone to blame. It was a cosmetic fault, they said. Nothing structural, just the tinted dermis. She must complete a requisition document and apply for an allocation from the Repairs Fund.

Fire was swifter than decay.

She cleared the screen and, calling up another doomsday, lost herself in the infinitely deep and tortuous streets of Spiral City, which the scriptwriters had named Fairmile but which she privately called Pandemonium. It was a place of fallen angels and the resort of the grossly deformed, a rest and recreation centre for constructs endowed with beauty, ambition, huge amounts of money or something to sell. She imagined it always as a city whose fluid spaces were filled with the sound of voices shouting and the grotesque noises of lives being vehemently expended but, when she listened to its transmuting structures, she heard the same, thin, whalesong which was Jannl's voice. She wanted to hear the violin.

He would return to the violent milieu which was Pande-monium: infinity is always an attractor. She played with the colours of the fractal city for a while and left it bathed in a melancholy afterglow of lapis and violet. Chaos was one of civilisation's oldest concepts, the burning ladder by which humanity hoped to escape into order and domination – of pain, disease, unhappiness and death; but then it was found that chaos had ecapéd the pit and was the order everyone believed made their clocks tick and the tides and seasons recurrent, predictable and safe.

It had no sense of adventure, the human race: it did not like surprises unless they were well-wrapped in pretty parcels and labelled 'Open only on your Birthday.' Humanity feared the jack-in-the-box.

She saw marvels in the empty streets of her mind: laden skifts hastening over a wintry sea; a circus tent in flight; two clowns walking hand-in-hand and herself sitting in the sun and the warm winds of a new landscape. She saw Siloe and Jannl die.

The circus folk must not be transported across the seas of this world, like unregistered aliens. There must be a supernatural solution to Loy's anguish: the circus would, before the time for transportation came, surely have moved in it own inexplicable fashion, leaving only memories behind it. She hoped that its people and the Folk would both remember her and that she might retain, for her new horizons, a trace of Bren's strength and a little of Loy's grace as, in her pocket, she kept the piece of raw amber which contained the clown's three tears.

It was the viewing hour. If any still watched her saga, few might care to see the destruction of Siloe and Jannl by the cancer of her imagination. This maggot, born of revenge and nurtured with unrequitable love, had escaped into infinity, exceeding both its dictionary definition and its original, spiteful purpose. It was crooked, perverse, fanciful, pandemonic and ultimate.

The blue room looked soiled and grimy. Cait hoped she had not left the burden of her fantasies of true love and endless riches there, to haunt the place. All the moulded surfaces, her old bed, the chest of drawers, the picture-frame surround of the screen, were covered with a rich overlay of mould. It had happened once before, when the air-conditioning broke down. She rubbed at it with the furred cuff at the end of her sleeve and found that it was ingrained: mould growing in a filigree of tiny cracks which seemed to spread and multiply as she watched them.

She and Bren spent long hours out of doors. Often they did not even return to sleep but lay on the ground in their warm skins and covered themselves with the pale sky in which the moon and the sun rode together. She had returned now to find out if she still needed her old diversions and toys: she had told Bren she was going to fetch the useful gear: knives, fishing line, floats and a hussif of needles.

The betrothal gifts were still in the drawer. She laid them on the bed, a compehensive and useless collection. The suit she had worn in chapel was white like Ang Semo's best, and thin as tissue paper. The china was painted with flowers. She set it out, cup on saucer and saucer on plate. She set aside a small metal pan, some knives and spoons, a pair of scissors and a solar lighter: those could go with the family's goods, up, out – away!

With the useless articles, she put the perfume the ferryhand had given her in exchange for ten minutes behind a refuse crasher, and opened the middle drawer. The fanzines looked yellow. She did not want to look at them, ghosts of the never-living that they were, and she dumped them upon the satex wedding clothes, beside the pretty china.

The room was stuffy and, despite the lighting, full of shadows, a synthetic gloom which crept from the grimy walls. Cait took two steps toward the screen, hesitated, and reached out to press the activation panel. The blank window filled at once. She saw her old heroine and role-model, Siloe, in a wondrous, overgrown garden.

She was surprised by the location. The sagas told how Jannl's garden was imaginary, the safe refuge he wanted and could never have, because of his hopeless poverty. His only hope had been Siloe's love.

Maybe, for it was two or three months since she had last watched 'Greed', Jannl had found riches at last.

A bonfire was burning, although it was not the season of bonfires: the garden was full of flowers and sunlight. Red and yellow flames licked roses on the fire – not leaves. Some curious change had taken place in the garden, for this was not the only anomaly. The birds were singing their hearts out – black and white birds with cruel beaks – and Siloe's white cats and rabbits had died and lay, stiff and unlovely, on the tesselated paths and in the flower beds.

Yet the story was the familiar soothing fable, told in soft voiceover with musical interludes.

Cait touched the interactive query panel and read the message it flashed upon the screen: Now showing, 2551st episode of 'Greed': Siloe and Jannl Explore the Secret Garden (c.) ERRATE, 4625.

So it wasn't his garden, and the dead animals and burning roses would shortly be explained. She watched, entranced as ever by the sentimental narrative and the rapidly-changing picture on the screen, conscious that this was the last dose she would ever take of a dangerous and addictive drug.

Siloe was asleep on a daybed in an arbour. Cait watched her yawn delicately, stretch her graceful, white arms and wake. The construct put her feet on the patterned marble beside her couch, and stayed there, unwilling to move. Her legs, clear of their concealment under her gown and the cloudy draperies that always hung and shimmered around romantic action, had changed shape: she had horny yellow hooves like an icedeer and dark brown hair grew on her perfect calves. She examined her new feet, smiled, and raised her head. Jannl appeared. It seemed as though he came out of the fire.

He ran to Siloe and a close-up showed their faces as they kissed. Hers was pale, and full of clefts as deep as the Sound. She kissed her lover greedily, while the music played her tune, a fine and melodious rising scale, a ring of glass bells.

Jannl had also altered. His brown skin had become as white as chalk, paler than the graceful column that represented Siloe's neck had ever been. He wore a patchwork suit of cyan and madder and his kindly expression had gone. The two white faces flowed into one another and became one (while angelic voices sang), a lucent sphere in a sea of red; and then the gross shape divided, and they were two again. Siloe spoke.

'Ah, Jannl,' she said. 'I am dying.'

She touched her stomach. It was distended, a hard globe beneath her gown: she was pregnant with her own death.

'I will help you to die,' he said, and the voices pealed a crescendo while the credits rolled.

In her room in the Angle family's unit, Fenner had already switched off her screen. She gorged candies with an urgency and greed which far outstripped the lovers' kiss. These were her last, one pound of soft-centred, creamy sweets coated in lustrous, dark brown chocolate.

'Lying garbage,' she muttered, through the sticky mouthful. 'How I used to love it!'

Jannl was a composite of chemicals and electrons, the picture of a man who did not exist. Yesterday Ial, who was flesh and blood, had agreed to be her man. She worried that, without Traumesse's ready supply of candies and cakes, she would grow thin – he would no longer want her. Pared down and – perish the thought! – slim as Gaby, she would no longer please.

'Fat,' she said, 'Suet, lard, blubber, grease.' In the mirror, she watched herself pinch a rounded arm. 'Plenty of malpog; plenty of hareng and saithe.'

She had eaten the malpog meat hungrily, finding meaty echoes of her beloved chocolate in its fatty richness. She turned about before the mirror. The furs became her and she felt complete. Ial would get her better skins than these old things of Grand's: white wolf pelts, a black stinkbear hide, blue vair. . .riches poor non-existent Siloe never had. But, by fish and fowl, she was hot. When she had helped Mu pack the rest of the clothing, she would go out and walk upon the Perimeter above Traumesse to think out her goodbyes – though, in a year or two, she and Ial would be back off Sowash for the fishing. From the Perimeter, she would be able to see Hairete and beyond the double humped island and, sparkling in the long, sunlit day, the Northern Ocean, where they would first try their luck, Ial and she.

'I love my man,' she thought.

She combed the tangles from her long hair and went to find her mother.

Conception, Fine Artwork, Original Pix: Ang Semo.

The Director had at last succeeded in showing herself and, thought Cait, had overplayed her hand. She cancelled the intrusive credits and silenced the screen. Like every piece of equipment in Traumesse, dedicated or multi-purpose, it could not be isolated from the continuous circuitry behind walls, floors and ceilings. It would hang there on the mould-covered blue wall, a blank frame waiting for a viewer and she, Needle Cait, would carry the symbolic, shambolic episode away with her, one of the last memories of the time in Traumesse.

The episode was Ang Semo's homage to Loy Sen, a scarcely covert version of her unconcealed desire for the alien: her version of what she dared not do with him. Cait, newly-wed, was full of scorn for the unpaired. It's easy, she thought: all you need do is lie down and open your legs, though I, Barendidt's bride and the mother of his first child, know a few more tricks. . .Loy Sen and his circus in Toul also explained Gaby's absence; both she and Dr Semo had been seduced by the glamour of the white-face clown. She hoped Gaby would not give him more than adulation. The man would soon be gone, into the deep south, deported from Sowash along with his motley company to entertain different audiences.

Siloe's intensity of being had entered her. She longed to be with Bren. The room had grown warmer, heated by the radiation from the screen. She felt sick: it came to her not in the early morning but after noon, and she took one last look at the presents on the bed, at the bed itself whereon she had spent so many hours asleep or dreaming, at the dusty furniture, the efflorescent walls and the black screen. She left them all without any regrets.

MATOQ

The cause of their journey is chiefly a desire to come at a place where conditions are better than those they enjoy at the moment.

Knud Rasmussen, *Greenland by the Polar Sea*

The sea had silver in it and other shiny lights, like the glint of moonlight on a knife blade. The wind was cold but it did not trouble Atluki, snug inside his new suit of furs. He could only count up to five but he nevertheless tried to count the new, white islands which had appeared beyond Wirra and Orsa in the Sound. He had learned the Nenian name for them, which was *icebergs* and also the word Bren used, which was *tapla*. He knew they were made of ice. Another thing he knew was that they moved along in the water like a boat.

The tabular bergs were floating islands of great and dazzling beauty. They had been calved when the sun came to high Hiberna and, retracing the routes of the old explorers, drifted in the strong current named for Arne Shakla until they reached the shipping lanes of the mid-Northern Ocean, where they began rapidly to melt and add their burden of fresh water to the salt sea.

From the air, they looked no bigger than rafts of ice upon a pond; from land nearby, the north coast of Sowash where Atluki stood, they were giants' dinner tables or the petrified decks of the broken bridge to heaven, moving past the small, low islands with the stateliness and dignity of an ocean-going liner. You expected someone to appear and cast down a hawser end, to bring them into berth.

They were dangerous and unstable. Bits broke off them as the sunlight wore them down. Their surfaces were as treacherous and deceitful as those of the glaciers which had given them birth.

The Sineinians sometimes boarded and measured them, but always from the air. The Folk avoided them and watched them go by, relieved that they were both transitory and migratory, and glad to have seen them, for their appearance marked the end of summer and the coming of the ice, when they would take the ocean road out.

Only poets, idiots, and travellers with a romantic bent, saw them as castles of frost, or outposts of the palace empire of the Snow Queen. Only seal and malp, which understood their instability, could use them, as short-term sunning-places or as temporary boats.

Atluki had a boat. It lay beached on the shore below, at Forso where the wind lifted and whirled the soft sand and shaped it into hills. Bren had left the boat there instead of returning it to its dock inside Traumesse. It was a good boat with black, tarry sides and six oars beside the steering oar; like every Folk boat, it had no name: it was just 'the skiff', the two words spoken in the same casual and familiar tone that was used for 'the sea' or 'the snow'. Boats were tools, not the living entities which required eyes, names, and blessings that they were in the south.

Atluki was pleased to be standing here on Forso Ness at dusk, the long night before him and lots of new and empty days ahead. There was a friendly quietness full of soft noises and the constant boom of the waves hitting the rocks below him. They whispered on to the sands, or shouted when there was a storm. He no longer needed to listen to the music in the box, nor to its silences. He was glad to have his deerhorn with him and had washed it in the sea until it was clean and white again. The sea had swallowed the blood which had stained and spoiled it.

He was like Bren now: a hunter. A man. Traumesse and its imprisoned noises were gone for ever.

He had been in the marshes a while and had not seen any demons. The only animals he had seen were kjarr rats, and he had known where to find the last of the crayberries, the ones Gaby and Fenner had missed, and the late clutches of kjarhen eggs which never grew into chicks. He knew which coves and bays had the best and juiciest crabs, and he was an expert at dislodging cone shells from their rocks.

None of his people had come to look for him, though he had heard them banging about in places no one would use for a hide. When they had gone, he had found some bread on the boulder above Toul.

A skimmer had flown over the island; but he had been in his cave under a pile of boulders.

At first, he had made for the circus, but the dogs had barked and frightened him away although the lights, which burned a lot now that the cold and the dark were coming, had called out to him. He had gone to Noul and walked about on the rocking stone. It would tip so far and then begin its seesaw motion, backward and forward, up and down. He had waited there, laughing to himself, until the moon rose.

Atluki picked up his deerhorn and walked down the long slope from Forso Ness to Forso Bay.

Although Bren's boat was light, it had been pulled right up the beach, above high water mark and further, until it lay almost in the dunes. It took Atluki a long time to drag it down to the water and set it afloat.

He climbed into it and, when he had carefully stowed the deerhorn with the other things in the central cerf, pushed it off with one of the oars. Bren's boat floated well, high in the water and lightly because it had only one person to carry. Atluki rowed steadily across the bay, the bowpost of the boat toward Orsa and its stern and his gaze toward the ness upon which he had waited for the ending of the day. As he rowed, a great surging wave rushed from the fast waters beyond the smaller islands, where the bergs floated, across the Reach and into the bay. The wave caught his boat and tossed it around as mercilessly as if it were made of cork. Atluki's excited shouts echoed on the shore.

And then the kanel, which the bergs had displaced, passed Atluki and, breaking against the sand, spewed up the tangled mass of kelp, hairweed and fish it had collected as it ran. Atluki rowed on and was swallowed by shadows and darkness.

Eda Voran's comatose body lay on a bed in Intensive Care and was attended by the Medical Carer, Mair, who had watched over Ang Semo after her collapse. She waited calmly and, from time to time, checked the instruments which monitored the professor's condition. One permanent death in a year was unfortunate; two would indicate a gross deficiency in the intricate and carefully synchronised programme which had created, and now ran, Traumesse.

There could be no link between the two deaths, the first the suicide of a stern woman at the end of her aggravated tether, finally and irrevocably lost to the madnesses of love; the second a brutal murder by a person, or persons as yet unknown. The place was getting to her – this new feeling that time was running out: her dream last night of ruin and decay; the bacteria on her fingers which would not wash off; the limp and wasted feel of dead flesh under leathery skin – the job, too, was beginning to take its toll.

Next month, she would be free. Her leave was due and then, heighho, the skimmer down to Ros. . .

Without her recorder and notebooks, the Professor looked as fragile as a geriatric. In off-hours, she had been likable: cheerful, a friendly sort. Now she resembled a plastimorph before its programming sessions, dead but living, her brain traumatised and its responses erratic. Without her extensive certification, diplomas, degrees, and proofs of motherhood, she would certainly have become a plastimorph. None of her systems were at present her own, to work independently. Each one was linked to a biotronic substitute and, through these, to the CPU. The deep coma became her because it emphasised her womanliness: no signs, here, of her once-formidable brainpower and wealth of knowledge about vanished cultures: all, most likely, forever lost.

'We're competent engineers,' thought Mair, 'but not yet miracle-workers.'

Beside keeping vigil by the sick professor, she had also to wait for the Visiting Carer, Élis Tailler, who was absent collecting and collating data for her submission to Sollar Kein. When she reported back, whatever the decision at Command, Mair could proceed: call the neurosurgeon, or switch off the subsystems and transfer the body to Cold Storage.

Eda's skin felt cool and smooth. It was pale gold, the legacy of old holidays in the south and judicious use of the sunspa in the gym. The golden threads of her hair added extra lustre. She had daughters, a brace was it not? Academists or freshers. Were they adoptive, donative or natural? – Élis's researches would tell and it would be her job to contact these next-of-kin.

The body was in good order and would probably function as a separate entity again. Although her role was secondary, a siter of probes and stimuli, Mair was impatient to begin upon the restoration of the brain. The new Eda Voran lay asleep upon the bed, ready but not able to function by herself, as Traumesse lay in Sowash, isolated from external concerns, linked to life by supply-lines, optical fibres and pulses travelling near the speed of light. Blood, nutrients and air for the body; food, water and intelligence for Traumesse. The disposal systems were in figurative juxtaposition: a catheter for the body; for the buried city, an anaerobic sump into which the catheter's contents, via pipe and drain, eventually flowed.

When the traces faltered on her screens, Mair stood up, ready to apply manual resuscitation; but the glitch was brief, a hiccup, no more. The life-support systems of the intensive care unit had transferred themselves from the main circuits to standby, but she was a nurse and failed to notice the faint glow from the indicator light. She sighed and fetched a cup of coffee from the dispenser. She might wait here, on extra shift, all night until Élis came.

The entrance to the Folk Museum was guarded by two face-less figures carved from wood, a Fishfolk man and woman. They had been clothed, and their stiff arms extended to hold spear and net, keepsack and line. Their garments were replicas of Fishfolk summer clothing, the woman in bead apron, birdskin shirt and leggings, the man in malpskin drawers and a sark of woven parrot down. Pike Neemi had sewn the garments at the request of the Traumesse Anthropological Unit, in her middle age fifty years ago: their colours had faded but were otherwise almost as good as new.

The dusk which filled the museum after closing time obscured the figures and gave them souls. Near them were more of Pike Neemi's things: her belongings arranged in a special display which had been opened in honour of her long life in the service of her people. She had been the link which bound them to their past, a child of seven when the Folk were taken in. She had been able to remember the fishing in Blue and Greening, the berry-picking, egging and plant-gathering; the main hunt, the butchering and skin-preparation in Matoq and White: all with a child's-eye view of enormous boats and mighty seas, giant malp and huge, blood-stained men. She had been able to remember the detail, too: how to thread crayberries on stalks of grass; how to work with beads, and the names of the three different ways of stitching them on clothes; where to find shrimp, crab, and the best sand-eels. She had known the name of everything in her young child's world, and many tales.

Pike Neemi came into the museum and sat down on the attendant's chair. She tucked her bead apron neatly round her and stroked the cherry-red sleeve of her blouse. She could not rest comfortably and felt thin, and hazy: she could remember little except the forlorn sight of her empty room and the awful indignities to which the anatomist had subjected her old and worn body.

So this was where her bits and pieces had come to rest. Locked away in glass cases. From her hard seat, she could see the mop of real hair which crowned the Witto mask. Where was that owl?

'Paikwi,' she called. 'Chee-rup.'

The white owl floated out of the dusk, and settled on her shoulder. He preened her thin hair and chirruped to her.

The old woman stood up painfully and slowly. Death, it seemed had brought no advantages such as a new, young body, or an insubstantial form which would let her float freely from air to water, or into the very rock. She leaned against the case which housed her suetstone figures and wished the Sineinians had not insisted on cutting her up before they gave her back to the Folk for burial. The figures under the glass stood still and she thought how like her husband was the model of the carver carrying his block of stone. The floats her family had collected over the years had been arranged in a circle on the wall but they too were covered with glass and untouchable. She did not see the kjarr sprite which peered at her from beneath the case, a bald and slimy thing no higher than her knees, but she noticed that some of her dry simples, locked in the case, were looking moist and green, and she could smell rain and flowers, as if an enclosed and internal Blue had come to Traumesse. A tussock mouse and her children sat in a row by the wall, each one washing its face. They liked to hide from the cold, whether in their own tunnels beneath the snow, or in the myriad tunnels which carried air and cables about Traumesse.

'The snow will fall soon,' she thought, 'and beneath its cold blanket, life will out.'

The words danced a jig in her mind: 'Snowfall, lifeout, coldfall. Soon.'

The museum was no longer quiet, but awake to subdued noises: animal chatter, grunts, and soft inspirations. The shadows had feet and hands. Float Siri stood beneath a skiff which, itself, sailed on air and Pike Miy, Neemi's great-grandson, who had fallen from the bow of such a boat and drowned, waited beside a case of fishing tackle. Her husband, Har, came to stand beside her. She was comforted; she was happy to see other, older ancestors. Floats, Salters, Angles, Needles; Ropewalkers, Splicers, Careeners, Hooks – they all came, a legion from the past. Pike Neemi welcomed them all.

The small creatures which had come from the kjarr hissed at each other and a red-faced figure as stiff as the guardians at the entrance squatted in the centre of the polished floor. Witto had come to look for Gaby.

The spirits and sprites had a common purpose and were prepared to be patient while they waited for Bren to act. They wondered if he had sufficient courage. They waited patiently, but none of them were prepared for the change the next comer brought with him. Fur and feathers moved in a cold breeze and every dry pelt rattled as the north wind himself breathed on them.

He was wrapped in fog and smelled of the sea. He tried to be still and quiet, but his smallest breath lifted the hangings and rattled the glass in the cases. The room held him close but it could not withstand the pressure of his occupancy. The walls began to crack and brittle shards fell from the ceiling to shatter on the polished floor. The locked doors shook.

'It was meant to be a pantisocracy, a society in which everyone was equal and had an equal voice; like Folk society itself,' said Carey Aleph.

'That's hopelessly idealistic,' Ander Vist responded. 'You can't have equality if you call people Professor and Spokesman. The seeds of dissent are built in from the start.'

'Sown,' said Ang. 'Traumesse was a field, ploughed well and harrowed ready for any megalomaniac to seed – Dorta, for instance, or poor Eda.'

The men ignored her speech and she looked at the static emblems in her office: the butterfly map of the outskirts of Chaos; the mutilated linden tree; the suetstone carvings, ancient and modern – work without provenance and Salter Bren's distinctive New Sowash style. The squatting woman, which she bought at the Potters' Fair in Habin, was meant to be a joke. She reminded herself that it was she who was called Director. Carey and Ander clearly could not accept her as that alone for, when one or the other remembered her and smiled, she saw the twin wells of invitation and invasion in their eyes, deep, dreadful, and so vainly desired.

The liquor bottle was nearly empty. She refilled her glass.

She *would* have a response:

'What a tragedy,' she said. 'Do you think Eda will come through?'

'Why not?' said Ander. 'I saw worse cases in Alut.'

(Alas, poor Pior – I knew him none too well.) She knew which was the sensitive one: Carey shuddered.

'I don't like to think of her,' he said. 'The Dorta business was bad enough. But I bet the attack has something to do with this sodding renaissance. It has to be one of the Folk.'

'Why? Why not a ferryhand? One of us?'

'Come off it, Ang.'

So, deliberately, they returned her to her place in the corner, out of the action, out of the way.

'The System must have had a fault built into it, right from the start,' Carey said, reverting to the burning question. He drained his glass.'Look at Dorta's terminal – Ang's terminal, so-rry. It's dead as a doornail. You try and wake it. Go on, have a go. See if you can log on.'

Ander took his glass with him. He made a few vain passes over the board, a magician without virtue. He rested his hands on the colourful, tesselated pads and his face assumed a concentrated expression, as if he hoped pure will-power would get him a response from the machine.

'I tried to disinfect my sector,' said Carey, 'before the thing went dead, of course.'

'It's still running Traumesse.'

'After a fashion. The vital systems are running off the standby supply. How many lights are left in Floraliy? Fifty? A hundred? The lamps are going out – we'll soon be in the dark.'

It was an apt metaphor, thought Ang, for the way her colleagues had tried to run Traumesse, thinking themselves illuminated while they groped in darkness. They had never learned the inner language of the Folk. They spoke all the dialects, made long lists and analyses of the vowels, verbs and sentence-patterns, but had been deaf to the real sounds, unable to understand the voice of the North. They had used the Folk to fulfil a dream, in an attempt to retain, vicariously, a heritage like the one they had lost to science, the arts, medicine and technological growth.

To punish Dorta Wireloom, she had stolen the secret code written on her breast. Her simple act of theft had taken away her colleagues' auxiliary speech and intellectual function.

'Ghosts in it, bloody ghosts,' said Carey. 'It's made a hash of everything. The sagas are full of junk, the programmes are garbage. And it's still running the place. It's a bit warm, but the air's still clean. How the hell can those old generators cope?'

She blamed the circus. It could not all be the result of her tiny maggot: something from Loy Sen had entered Traumesse and taken hold, just as the circus had taken hold of Toul and made a warm haven of its bleakness. The circus! she thought, and held her glass high. Precariously now, a poor tenant awaiting eviction, the circus sat in Toul where the wind was gathering its winter strength together and gusting in the canvas. If he had received his deportation papers, Loy would have been unable to rest, a clown without a laughing audience to make him weep, a homeless beggar. He must, for ever, carry his home upon his back and be followed by his strange crew of animals and performers. She would not be the one responsible for imprisoning him in time: she had folded the papers tightly together and tossed them into a passing refuse cart.

The wind dropped, died altogether, and left a warmth like balm upon the air. The icedeer basked in it, the fawns grown big enough to walk frozen seas, the hinds relaxed and lithe, their udders thinner after a summer's suckling, the two stags only half on guard because there was no threat.

The herd mother tasted the air. It was sweet, the last of the benevolent season, honey in it, a little pollen, and a cold, salt tang. She would not leave Hairete. She was too old to travel again and her work on Sowash with the tall white woman and the little brown man was done. Her successor lay beside her, attentive, good at finding the juiciest lichens and the tender grass; ready to lead the herd. When the wind came back, it would bring the ice and the snow. The herd would move out, over the frozen sea, to walk and seek food in the lee of the wind; but she, alone and patient, would remain on Hairete until the lichens had shrivelled and the bright yellow moonflowers turned white; until she herself was as cold and dead as the winter landscape.

Bren carried his spear into Floraliy. He kept it in a corner of the double unit which was his and Cait's, a cosy set of rooms whose apricot walls were now spoiled by the mould, by the spreading cracks on every surface and besmirched by his activities with the moulting malpog hide and hers with its transparent gut, which she had made into a long rope. Apart from these new and significant sights, there was little in the unit to indicate the profound change of direction which had come to the Folk. He had removed most of his possessions to the cache at Forso and those he considered superfluous, he had dumped in a crasher. The best things had gone for ever, out of his control: knives, nets, lines, hooks, skins, a fire dish, all had been in the boat Atluki took, his big, clumsy footprints and the mark the boat had made when he dragged it down to the sea clear in the sand. He must replace the lost necessaries. Cait had gathered the women together and he, after calling Ial, Pak, Kubbu, Fa and the rest, had picked up the spear. They would have what was theirs by tradition and right: there would be no opposition.

The twilight in Floraliy comforted Bren. It reminded him of winter and the beauties of the night. He walked steadily with the Fisher men past the dark and shuttered Fountain Bar and the shadowy trees and tubs of flowers. The macaws and lovebirds were silent, roosting high in the palms.

The Folk were surprised to find the doors of their museum open, heavy touch bars dangling, and Bren suspected a trap. He made the others wait, a close, conspiratorial crowd, too great in number to go quietly, unnoticed by the Staff, and went alone into the museum.

The lights burned dimly in ones and twos: there was something desperately wrong with Traumesse. At first, he thought the museum had been wrecked: the gallery door had been blown as wide as the other and glass and plastic from the ceiling lay everywhere. It cracked as he walked on it. None of the cases was locked. Here and there amongst the wreckage he found black stalks of Noiran lyng and the fallen, rounded leaves of skaa birch, dry pieces of kelp and sea parrot down, trails of sand deposited on the floor: the diverse litter the North Wind carried in his arms. The room felt damp and cold. He was not at all sure, but thought that some things, some creatures like the ones which had followed him in the kjarr, lingered in the shadows. Here was an area of blue dusk, there one of grey and there, a redness, hot and blurry like a sunspot in the eye.

Someone trod behind him with a loud crunch like a boat grounding on shingle. He turned and saw, not an ancestor, not the men, not Cait – but Float Gaby.

'There might have been security guards,' he said.

'This – is beyond their ken. This is our business.'

She took his arm and led him to the broken cases. The contents were intact. In the half-light every artifact looked new, and ready for use. He examined articles as he went, a carved kist, a woman's knife, a netting needle, a comb of malpog ivory with a handle shaped like a tarunt gull, wings folded, long bill closed. . .in this case, plants were growing. He remained still for many minutes, looking into a miniature garden of mosses, lichens and summer herbs. Gaby was standing in the shadows. She glowed, so warm, so much alive. Again, he had and enjoyed his regrets. He heard her laugh and then, her lively voice: 'I don't need you now. I've learned to do it myself.'

'You must follow me if you want to amuse the Folk.' The second voice was robust and boomed as the waves did at Ulbeg or the wind on the ness.

'No. I will not follow you.'

'I am Witto: you and I together will make the Folk laugh.'

'I am Red Cheeks. I make everyone laugh.'

His spine tingled, the back of his neck was alive as if midges crawled – he had an impression of heat in the air and of laughter all around him, a circle of flame like a red mask pierced with eyes, nose and mouth. When it had faded, or passed him, he saw Gaby smiling confidently, alight with her own fire, and sparkling like her many strands of crystal beads.

'Who was that you spoke to?' he asked.

She did not answer, but made her own tour of the cases, touching a group of floats here, a suetstone lamp there.

'The Old Ones have all left,' she said. 'Call the Folk: let everyone come in.'

When they were gathered, and they came gradually, slowed by the bottleneck of the door, they stood shoulder to shoulder, closely packed amongst their ancestral belongings, four hundred and forty-six Fishfolk men, women and children, filling the museum. The artifacts their forebears had made hung from the ceiling and were displayed upon the walls and in the shattered cases. Each piece represented many hours of careful work, not only in the making, a tool to do a job, but in the decoration, a beautiful object made to love. Bren felt his zeal vindicated: here they all were, ready as he had been when he went out to find the spearshaft, and keen to continue – even Rower Attachuk. He climbed the spiral staircase to the gallery: each varied step was made of stone from the islands and he stepped up from Salmo via Malpogak, Clash and Demender to Wirra, Hairete, Longbeach, Skaa and Sowash on pegmatite and diorite, from olivine and surturbrand to hornblende, dolerite and basalt. He thumped the floor with the butt of his spear, and spoke to the Folk below.

'Arrange yourselves in families,' he said, and waited while they made intricate progress in the aisles. 'Now let each family take what belongs to it, and only those things,' said Bren.

They rushed from case to case, seeming rash and without discipline, but they had listened to his instruction and carefully read the labels on each specimen before it was taken or passed, with many shouts and complex messages of direction to its rightful owners. The Rowers pushed past him to reach the wires from which their skift hung, Attachuk himself manhandling mast and sail; women ransacked the trays and drawers in which Arne Shakla's priceless collection of Fishfolk jewellery was laid out, the Needles laid claim to an array of shuttles and netting needles and the Hooks to several large boards in which hooks, barbed, double and triple, were carefully fixed like skeletal entomological specimens. His own father claimed the sailsledge and he saw his brothers hurrying to lower it to the floor. In the doorway, he saw a posse of security guards and Carey Aleph, as immobile and dumbstruck as the two wooden figures and, opposite him, across the void above the littered floor and the scurrying Folk, Ang Semo and the Theorist, Vist, latecomers at a feast. They, too, watched the frantic repossession but did not intervene.

Bren felt his heart fill with an irrational love for the woman who, after supporting and encouraging his lonely and difficult rebellion, had denied him in public with her turncoat speech. He tried to catch her eye but she was intent upon whatever Ander Vist was saying to her, his hands flapping, clearly wanting to reach out and take hold of her. She shook her head. He saw her laugh and then she looked across the room, at last acknowledging his presence and his leading role, and she spread her hands, shrugged expansively, and smiled a warm welcome for him and the Fishfolk.

Now, above the hubbub, she was shouting. 'Get *your* things!'

Vist, he was glad to see, was ignored, as useless as a glass of liquor to a dead man.

Bren ran down the stairs and went among the cases and displays. They had left him some property to claim: a rifle with a cracked barrel, a sifting basket and a shovel, several preserving tubs and a stone bowl full of the dry mineral which had given him a trade and a Sineinian name, salt. Cait was helping her mother, both women laden with the goods the Needles had claimed. Gaby stood by him drawn, he thought, by the force which had begun the rebellion. She had claimed nothing but a bead bracelet and a feathered apron, and when he asked her what else she wanted, 'Nothing more,' she said. 'I already have Pike Neemi's lamp and her blessing. These are for Red Cheeks.'

He stared at her. Those round cheeks were always ruddy: he had not seen them enhanced by the greasepaint, glowing with the ardour of the clown.

'Come with me!' he said, against all reason and the agreement they had made to the sound of the icedeer munching and the drip of the melting snow: in the Viewdome in White, before she was enchanted by the circus, before he hunted and became truly Barendidt.

'Spooky's waiting,' she said. 'I have to say goodbye to him and then: who knows? What *is* your marriage worth?'

'One malpog and one child, so far,' he said, and began to laugh: it had great value, and none. 'Who knows?' he said in his turn.

'There will be great hardship, and death in the snow,' said Gaby.

'Some may starve,' he said. 'I know what may happen. The thing to have, is the courage to live out there from day to day.'

'You can't see drifting snow or sastrugi, nor feel the blizzard or find polynya to hunt in when you are shut up like a caged animal. But summer's best, in Greening the living is easy — if you find me on Sowash next Greening, I will come with you. Goodbye, Bren.'

She left quickly and he, stacking his new belongings in the basket, considered her airy promise. It wasn't vain but it was not likely that she would remain another ten months on this island. He wondered where she would go. Her family had no claim on her since she had refused glosit with Pak. She had freed herself from all obligation to the Folk.

The museum was emptying. One of the security guards had found a broom and was sweeping up the glass. Ang Semo hurried down the stairs, as if she was afraid that Bren would suddenly leave.

Without the Folk, Traumesse could not function. Ferry-hands and plastimorphs had their place but none of them was trained to handle dreams: they were workers, pure and regular, and had no ambition beyond a simple life, and no desires greater than the tokens due at the end of each week.

Ang looked fondly down on Bren, who smiled. She put her hands on his shoulders and they hugged each other. The tears they needed came to both of them.

'To the islands and the seas!' she said.

'To the Highlands!' said he, both aspiration and destination in this final salute, which was also a goodbye. They waved to each other, she firm upon the wooden deck of the museum floor, he departing under his own steam, a small and strong vessel with a long voyage ahead.

'Goodbye, Barendidt.'

'Goodbye, Ang.'

They parted friends, all the rules broken, free of the Establishment's constraining Ethic. They had selected the next episode of their lives. Ang was glad to find Ander and Carey close by, ready to talk — about the consequences, about what was left: anything, to keep her mind upon the Folk and away from the error she had sown for the machine to compound and multiply.

The Folk Museum no longer existed. Save for the broken relics of imprisonment, the elegant cases of glass and fine woods, the Folk had taken every single thing.

Matoq moved over the island and whatever he touched, or breathed upon, froze. The tussock withered where he trod and the pools of water which lay upon the sodden ground were swept into sudden activity before his ice stilled them. Below, in the valley of Toul, the red and gold of the circus tent and the darker canvasses of the bowtop vans stirred, hardly strong enough for roofs and too thin to keep out the cold. He carried the spirits with him, sprites, ancestors and ghosts; even Arne Shakla whose soul had never left Sowash, so strong her love of it. They hurried on to the circus, a stream of frost and swiftly-moving limbs, and Pike Neemi hobbled after them, wishing herself alive and in the warm, with a cupful of hot soup to drink.

The cacti had not flourished this year, the Queen of the Forest drab and flaccid and her new leaves tipped with brown, the spiny cerebellum dark red and hungry for daylight. In the forest the big succulent would have mist, dappled light and cool nights: in the Central Highlands, the other would have a hot season in which to shoot, and a dormant season of renewal. Deep in Traumesse, where it was always warm and the air always too dry, they kept trying to grow and weakened even their tough constitutions. Ang watered them in the summer and kept them dry all winter, in reverse simulation of their true environments. She had tried them in different situations in the unit, but they had ceased to thrive. Now, dribbling the last water they would have this season into their pots, her attention was caught and held by a singular trespass, and the trickle of water ceased as she tilted up the can.

Like all the plastic surfaces in Traumesse, the grey wall where her pictures had been displayed was covered in pits and cracks, through one of which the intruder poked a pallid and fleshy tendril. She put down the watering can and went to examine it. From a distance it looked like the limb of a deep-sea creature, a squid or the end of a ribbon worm: when she peered close, she saw the hairs which grew out of it in all directions and searched vainly for some soil in which to bury themselves.

It was a root. In the garden of her mother's house, she had turned up stones and been surprised to find white roots beneath them: more surprising was the verdant growth of nettles and docks from old concrete and brick in the slums and then, home again after a photography foray, a third example of the tenacity of life: the spiny branches of a young conifer breaking through the stone of the terrace itself.

This root too was vigorous and hungry for growth. It had found its way into Traumesse from above.

She sat between the cactus plants to consider what it meant.

Inside the hill, there must be other roots which would extend themselves along every duct and conduit. They could not grow in permafrost, therefore they must have found a way down through the thick insulating layers which covered and surrounded the underground settlement. Indigenes, they flourished where the cacti would not.

Soon, the cold itself would enter and take over Traumesse.

That, or the heat the settlement generated, no longer separated from the frigid earth, would bring a subterranean thaw and water, running down to sea level, would end the great experiment.

Ang stood up and began carefully to search every surface in the unit, looking for more roots. From time to time, she paused in her task and called herself ridiculous. Once, she stopped for a long rest and several cups of coffee. She found six more vegetable invaders: two in the kitchen, three in the bedroom and one more in the living room. On the whole, she felt pleased at her discovery. The place was alive and no longer cut off, divided from the outside world by stone, infill and artificial membranes. She thought she would fetch Bren and show him her discovery; and remembered that he had aleady left.

Surely Gaby, who had been so concerned over the death of the owl and who had laughed with the moon seals, would want to see this evidence of the subversive action her world had been forced to take. But she, too, had left. Her warm body might sleep, resting for one last night in Traumesse, but her heart and soul was outside under the stars and the canvas, close by Loy Sen.

Outside, in the circus, they had few anxieties compared to hers. The future of her lieutenants, so lately recruited to her cause, so touchingly loyal, was not at stake – she was so far ahead of them. They would find another system to tend, other experiments to involve them, mind and soul. They had become what Bren and Gaby once were, dependents, no longer mere colleagues, no longer mere names on ERRATE's payroll. Carey was calm enough, looking forward to resolving his problems with the silent computer. Ander was full of panic at the loss of the facility, his surrogate faculties of vision, speech and computation. He knew of vacant posts in Mahkrein, in the City herself: 'Let's go down there,' he had said. 'Let's go together – both of us. They won't ask any questions, they're still an underdeveloped power and glad of what they can get.

'And you could do worse than me. I'm worth more than the sum of my earnings, and my intelligence rating's high. I'm twenty-eight, active, not so ugly.' (A sly smile.) 'I can give you a good time, maybe even keep you happy.'

At this, she had laughed. He was so far from the mark and she, with her incurable infirmity, not the prize she appeared to be. Neither the warmth of Loy Sen nor the heat of the Central Highlands had the power to thaw her lifelong coldness. In the pure form of the world-religion she denied, to feel love and refute sex was a cardinal sin. She could never be made happy and would not relish a 'good time'. Above all, she would be a misfit in the temple-dominated, chime-haunted City of Mahun.

'Ander, dear,' she had said. 'You're very sweet, but it must be obvious – think about it – that I'm not too fond of men. Except as colleagues, of course, and you and Carey are a joy to work with.'

Thus, with flattery and a downright lie she had killed his rambling speech, his hopes and sentiments.

'Ah, I understand,' he'd said. 'There was some truth then – Ang, I do apologise.'

She had caught sight of Bren at that point, powerful, masculine, and full of pride in his people and joy in his achievement. Ander had retreated into the background as she saluted the brave Fisher man.

It had been a merry party; and now all the historical artifacts would be copied, treasured, and repaired.

One last task remained, the dying cacti watered and the day examined and put out of mind: she laid her hand on the touchpad of the small terminal in the room. Silence equalled death. It hummed still, although it would not respond to any of her strokes: somewhere, the system was awake. She wanted to view Jannl once more, to see what his last act would be, as he pulled the pieces of the jigsaw in over his head and made his own pyre of bits.

She had turned in frustration from the machine when it called her. The notes were faint and had a dying fall. If music be, she thought, and turned back to the blank screen. It played her Loy Sen's plaintive fiddle music, but so quietly she had to strain to hear it. The screen filled with a universe of coloured pixels and Jannl himself emerged from this nightmare mist, a sunrise figure in orange and red. He bowed.

The inhuman figure was five inches tall and yet it terrified her. It mopped and mowed with dreadful irony, imitating and distorting the graceful gestures of the white-face clown. It was hard to separate it from the shimmering background which, like the aurora in the real world outside, hung scarlet banners over a berg-infested sea.

Jannl laid his two hands on his chest and opened it up like a garment. He pulled his red heart from the dark cavern and offered it to her, scarlet and quivering upon his hand. She had reached out to take it when the picture vanished. She looked at the blank screen and was bereft.

The vision had been so brief and the sound of the violin so faint, she hardly believed in it. She wished she had imagined it, but knew she had not. The terminal was dark and had ceased to hum, although it still felt warm. She went to bed, dog-tired and no longer caring what the next day might bring.

Two hours later, for she looked at her luminous watch, she woke: in another two hours the day would break. When the birds woke, they would gather to migrate. She wanted to hear the swans sing once more and, dismissing the idea of further sleep – for why spend a third of these amazing days unconscious? – reached for the switch of the bedside lamp. It clicked but the room remained in darkness.

'Shit!' she said. Maintenance dealt with such deficiencies, but it was both unfair and impractical to call them out by night: she might fetch a bulb from another lamp and so have light to dress by. She picked up her cigarette lighter, struck a flame, and made her way from the bedroom.

None of the lamps worked. The golden lighter grew hot and she moved it from one hand to the other as she tried switches and touch panels. Ridiculous – but it was she who had begun the decay. She had not thought it through. Now it was clear to her that the breakdown was real, permanent and affected everything the system controlled: air, heating, cooling, lights, Eda linked to her life-support – best not to think of her. . .

She was as deaf and dumb as Eda, the transoceanic link out, all signalling at an end.

She stood still to listen, the small flame throwing her shadow behind her. It lowered on the wall and bent over her, a giant caught out. There are no sounds in the tomb, she thought. Silence there is the desired outcome, eternal peace.

But might one not – if buried alive – hear the worm crawl and the beetle tunnel, hear water moving between the grains of soil?

She listened hard, and heard a slow trickle. Somewhere water was running and finding its own level. That level was the sea's, far below the safe hilly height in which Traumesse had been built; and once the water had found its brother it would not rise to fill the buried city up but would flow away into the ocean. Inside the waterfall then, a small trickle which might become a flow, a cascade as the permafrost melted.

Those roots had surely grown another inch, their long shadows preceding them into the room.

She had feared the weight of water frozen in the soil, but in White it had been there for ever, a certainty, predictable and stable. How much did an acre of water weigh? Was an acre of frozen soil heavier? Had all these stresses been calculated when they built?

She felt reason desert her, while her fingers burned.

A lamp. She must have light, and something to keep her sane. She found her cigarettes and lit one, sucking hard upon its comforting butt.

In the kitchen there was a bottle of salad oil. A saucer and five or six threads pulled from the towel and twisted into a rudimentary wick made her lamp. She was surprised because it worked. It worked well, giving a clear yellow light as bright as the birthday candles she remembered from home. The light from it made her shadow firm. The soot the flame deposited on the saucer was thick and black. It made her think of cave paintings, hunting rituals, protohistoric life, and Bren setting out. So easily was Traumesse turned into a gigantic cave and its inhabitants into troglodytes, refined and sophisticated though they had thought themselves. She tore a strip of cloth from the towel in case she needed to make another wick and, as she did so, saw the bright-eyed tussock mouse which had come into her unit.

'It's all yours, my little friend,' she said, and went to make herself ready for escape.

Thoughts of Eda would not flee. It was she who had insisted upon mechanical locks and keys for living units. Such doors, independent of the System, were perversely more secure, and a key was a symbol to each Folk family, speaking with its steel tongue of home and the comforts locked therein. Ang collected her camera bag, her jewellery and her key. She fastened the message beads Gaby had given her about her neck, put in her earrings and unlocked her door. The corridor was black as pitch. She held up the makeshift oil lamp like a beacon in her hand.

Gaby awoke in darkness and heard the gentle sound of water running. Someone had forgotten to turn off the tap.

She roused herself and, reaching out to turn on the light, felt drops of moisture on the wall. The light would not work. In her room it was darker than winter. No stars down here; but Grandgrand Pike's stone lamp would be her particular guide. She struck a match and, as it ignited and the forbidden flame took hold, saw her room transformed into a garden. Things were growing in those cobwebby cracks: she was inside the earth, where all the plants began.

'Mu!' she cried, 'Fa! Light the lamps!'

The family gathered quickly, grouped like an ancient memory of Folk working together, lit by their ancestral suetstone lamps. They helped each other to shoulder the burdens of the new life.

'We must leave now,' said Float Susu, and Float Addush agreed.

'Ribble, Taviak and Siri; you girls, ' he said. 'Keep close: hold hands and don't let go.'

The smooth tube of the corridor which, only yesterday, had been a green pathway decorated with flowers, was black, uneven and full of pitfalls where sections of the floor threatened to drop into the level beneath. Water streamed on the walls, and made pools where the floor was undamaged. The invading roots had multiplied here: a few more hours of growth would make a jungle. The Floats looked upon it as a miracle, an act of Sowash herself who, tired of the irritation deep within her, had decided to destroy it. Gaby, hurrying ahead of her parents and her sisters, thought sadly of the scarlet macaws and the neat blue lovebirds, of the orchids, naias, lilies and palms in Floraliy and the shining fish in the pool beside which her journey of discovery had begun. Creatures of the lovely and fabled tropics, they would die when exposed to the blunt and chilly temper of the North.

Ang moved slowly. This was Chaos. The roots curved and spiralled through the void between ceiling and floor, following their own patterns and paths. She did not know which way to go: this was not her order. In that, she had tidy hair and fresh clothes, and everything was in the place she had chosen for it, herself most of all, clean, neat and closed. These vegetable probes broke apart anything in their way. The walls were bursting with their energies; the ceiling sagged. She tried to avoid the dangling runners, ducking away from them, imagining them in her hair. When she touched the wall, to follow it, her hand became soaked and dirty.

Here was a stair, and a notice: 'Entresol'. She climbed. From the half-floor a passage led upward, past the office suite, and out. Only when she stepped out on the mezzanine did she remember the depth of the pit, that fantasy-land above the nursery floor, full of fake trees, animals and birds. She gripped the glass railing and crept forward, her lamp lighting the treetops and finding echoes in the reflective stars embedded in the roof.

Someone lay still, halfway along the floor. Many needed to escape. Beside the Folk who still remained, were Staff members, medics, ferryhands, Eda, the guests. . .the deportation committee, abandoned in the dark. She should have gone to rescue them.

Stupid. If this was someone she knew well – she could not cope. She would fall or faint. She came to it, and passed quickly by. 'It' was correct, a plastimorph, no longer functioning without its weekly dialogue with the System, its mental refurbishment. That the dead thing was a reconstructed human being somehow made its dying worse.

She had not thought anything through. She had killed it.

The sky was light and faint offspring of the bright aurora borealis chased each other from the sky. This was life and whatever had taken place below, the creation of the sagas and the death of the imported and the artificial, the conception and birth of many more Fishfolk, were preparations for this moment. The adults gathering on the hill were far outnumbered by the children, running, tumbling, and shouting to one another of their adventure in the night.

Her Staff were present; correct too. The medics clustered about the stretcher on which the mortal and maybe

irredeemably damaged remains of Professor Voran lay.
The committee members made another group. The Major
looked dishevelled and the Colonel hot. Carey and Nanket
were organising a head count. Those ferryhands who had
climbed upwards instead of taking to the boats and sailing
out below, sat on the smooth grass of the Perimeter, and
nonchalantly smoked or ate the food they had brought
out with them. The Folk were busy, collecting themselves
and their belongings together. Parties of those who had
already begun their journey came hurrying with a welcome
as messages were carried and the light increased. Only the
Floats seemed disturbed by their experiences.

'Where's Gaby?' they were crying. 'Where is Gaby? Has
she left already or gone missing like poor Atluki? Is she still
inside?'

Tears ran from Float Susu's brimful eyes. Her husband
made to return, back into the dark, when Angle Fenner,
smiling and confident beside Hook Ial, spoke: 'She went
ahead, didn't she? She'll be at the circus: that's where she'll
be, saying her goodbyes to the horse and the clown.'

The sun shone and the bergs passing in slow procession
along the Sound were translucent, like Hiberna's icy mountains or impossible dreams of a fantastic country far away.
Yet summer had gone and, in Ulbeg, the sea looked grey,
forbidding all contact and banning immersion with the
promise of fatal cold. She had heard the swans fly over
with their unforgettable melody.

She had dared return at last, near the end, the three hours
she had spent collecting and rallying her staff, giving encouragement and organising them, comforting the discomfited
committee, reason enough her solitary choice. The Folk had
drifted away, gone down, she supposed, to Toul to satisfy
themselves that Gaby was safe.

The ghosts had fled and the tight inlet felt empty, more
desolate without its familiars, the ghosts of the old unburied
Folk, although it was no longer a fearful place. It remained
a remarkable example of the power of water over fire, its
glassy pillows and columns the petrified memorials of the

volcanic age. She could take nothing away but her memories of Ulbeg: the photographs were all destroyed, left in her trunk to drown with Traumesse. The roots of the liberated prehistoric yews, the laurels and red pines, would pierce and destroy them.

Dorta's ghost had also left Ulbeg. She had been present, a presence at the last Race where Bren, despite her rebuff, had come into his own. Perhaps she would drift now with the other past and finished lives, with Float Siri, Pike Neemi, the haze owl and the malpog Bren had killed about Sowash until she found her peace.

Ang dipped her finger in the water of a rock pool. It was colder than Dorta's heart. Traumesse too would die. The reason for her life here had gone. She could no longer make sagas nor direct the affairs of a place which did not exist: she could not superintend a failed experiment. She was as free as the Folk to go. For this, the last and happy day, the circus was the focus of their desires, a powerful magic which had ceased to work for her.

They were no longer her responsibility and the circus must stand or fall by itself. She had done what she could and was released until the ferries came. Tomorrow the Folk too would be on their way.

She sat against the green pillar, where the sunlight was warmest, and fell thankfully asleep.

Aurora could not sleep. She stood in the doorway of her van and watched the natural display (better than any City firework extravaganza or Erirean dawn) after which she had named herself in the wild days, thinking the bitter North more exotic than her own tropic South. She was reformed now: she dressed herself fantastically and performed, but only upon the wide back of old Bluebird; no longer in the mazy lanes of the Pleasure Quarter, procuring, seducing and robbing the unwary. She lifted her hands to the rain of light and prayed thankfully to the supreme being and most ancient life force, Mahun. At half-past two, when the night was at its coldest and the northern lights giving their most brilliant show, descending cascades of blood and viridian green, she called Vixen and the two women stood close together for warmth, each one wondering at the sight.

Neither could Loy Sen sleep. Soon, the officials would come, to take the circus away. He had been deserted: Ang, and – who should most care – Mahun, both had turned from him. Gaby would be leaving, tomorrow or the next day, with the Folk.

The nights were cold. Garissa was beginning to suffer. He felt the north wind hammer at the roof of the van and got out of bed. The tent canvas too, he saw, heaved under the wind's assault, rattled and shook. Much more and it would rip: unless they took it down, gave up, gave in, and went with the Sineinians in their ship, back by temporal means to the City of their onetime birth.

There were lights in one or two of the vans. He stepped down to the ground and walked about amongst the silent vehicles. Vixen and Aurora stood on their steps, gazing at the fiery sky, and he called out a greeting as he passed.

It was warm in the straw with the rats. They were glad to see Gaby and welcomed her with rodent squeals and also with, she was glad to hear, words which did not fade or seem to be the projected voice of a human being. In any case, she and the rats were alone together, safe and cosy in the shelter of the great cage. She told them how she had escaped from Traumesse.

'I don't hold with it, neither,' said Tooth. 'Imprisoning folk, that's what it were: like us.'

'Andsome, as far as his tail and the knot allowed him, tried to sit on her knee. As usual, his concerns were gastronomic.

'Got any treats for us?' he asked. 'Some cake, an egg or two, a bit of bacon rind?'

She produced the candies she had saved against this looked-for time.

'They do stick up the teef!' complained Velvet daintily, continuing nonetheless to eat her share.

'I came especially,' Gaby told them, 'to free you. If that's what you want. We are all free now, except you.'

'And the helephant, the 'osses and the circus folk. We're bound to go where we are sent,' said Nail.

'But you need not be tied together. If I untie the knot in your tails, you can choose what you will do.'

'Awright,' said 'Andsome.

'Go on then,' said the other rats, 'Do your worst.'

She had been careful to place her lamp where it could do no harm, what with the dry straw and wooden carcase of the wild beast cage, and it shed a sparse light from its place between the cage bars, eclipsed by the brilliant show in the sky. Now, she took it in her hand and held it so that she could see exactly how the knot was tied. With her free hand she began to pick the looser fragments of dross and scabrous filth from the crust around the knot. She replaced the lamp upon the transverse bar and softened the knot with water from the rats' drinking bowl, probed and worried at it with her strong nails.

'Ouch!' said the rats. 'Ow! Lay off that bit a while.'

The knot, when it was uncovered, was a complex multiple of many loops and nodes. The tapered ends of the nine tails were not visible and Gaby explored the intertwining, scaly muscle with her fingertips. She found an end, dry and flexible as a strand of old seaweed. To touch it at all made her shudder, for it was the cut end of one of the still-entwined tails of the four missing rats which, after death, had been sliced free. But it was her clue to the maze, and she traced its path in the knot and worked to free it.

At last, it came away from its fellows and she held it in her hand for an instant before dropping it on the straw.

'That was Hinny's,' 'Andsome declared. 'I can tell by the kink.'

Gaby glanced at the discarded tail, which had several kinks set in it.

The knot was looser. She worked on the mummified tails of the dead rats first, but before she had removed them all, she saw that Velvet was held by a single loop. One pass and, 'There, Velvet. How do you feel?'

The she-rat sat up, took her tail (new it felt and beautiful, her own) in her paws and stroked it.

"'S mine,' she said. 'My tail.'"

The knot fell apart, and the remaining four rats freed themselves by walking in different directions. They capered and pranced, and groomed their stiff tails. Only 'Andsome's was damaged, the last third of it projecting at an acute angle.

'Does it hurt?' Gaby asked anxiously.

'No. It drags a bit. Reckon it got twisted long ago. It's all mine, though; adds a touch of class, having a broken tail. No one won't trifle with me now.'

'There you are then, Rats. Free to go.' She straightened up, and flexed her aching fingers.

'Andsome peered through the bars. 'Looks cold, out there,' he said. 'And windy. Where can I find them eggs?'

'They've all gone now, turned into birds and flown away.'

'What?' said the disappointed rat. 'Well, then: where are we to live?'

'Under the snow when it comes, I thought. Like the tussock mice.'

'Mice? Are they any good to eat?'

'I suppose so.'

The consequences of her compassion came flying now to Gaby.

'What price freedom?,' Tooth was saying. 'That bear that once lived here. She knew what was what, and who buttered her bread.'

'I think I like it here,' Velvet said. 'It's warm. There's plenty of straw and Sierra will soon bring our breakfast.'

'I'm just nipping out,' said Nail. 'Come with me, Whisk. I fancy a bantam's egg.'

Someone was coming. Gaby looked out through the bars and saw that it was Loy. He came like a gift, an unexpected benison to be welcomed with joy. She rushed from the cage to catch hold of him, to hide her face against his chest, expecting rebuttal, expecting ire —

Loy had seen, with some surprise, two rats slip down from the cage and run across the open ground to the nearest cover. Next came Gaby, precipitately from the door, straight at him, straw-covered, clothing and speech awry: 'What will Sierra do to me? I've let them all go — '

He steadied her and held her; let her talk. Afterwards, they sat together in the cage, three rats washing contentedly beside them, while she related her tale of the tails once more. At intervals, he laughed, his fancy taken by her daring and by his predicament in the marooned circus where freedom was no longer timeless, but measured out by the Sineinian deportation committee.

'I saw two rats running away,' he said.

'Um – they'll be back.' She did not want to tell him how Nail and Whisk had instantly become thieves.

'How do you know? Perhaps these three will leave soon.'

'They won't.'

She seemed so certain, so sure that what she said was right, he left it there. Time, as with everything, would tell, and if he had lost one money-spinner, he might have gained another: or why had she come here?

'I haven't told you,' she said. 'Something else happened in the night. It's not just the rats who are free.'

Thus, after the second tale, he understood. Everyone was leaving and Gaby had come to say goodbye.

'Where shall we begin?' he asked her and, anticipating her reply, 'With Spooky?'

The spotted horse was lying down. He had only just woken and needed words of encouragement from Loy to make him stand. Spooky performed his perfunctory toilet: beginning with his ears, he shook himself until every bit of his skin quivered. He neighed a complaint to the day. It was almost light outside, very early, and he had not had his oats. Loy gave him a small handful.

'There now. You've plenty of hay.'

A few strands of the aurora were left in the sky, red and green ribbons hanging down and fading as each moment passed. The flush in the east spread across the bowl of the sky, and Loy stepped out of the shelter to see day dawn. The face of Traumesse hill was shadowy but he saw movement there and soon, the little people appeared, a crowd of them, hurrying towards him.

'Here come the Folk,' he told Gaby. 'What can they want?'

She laughed. 'Well, they are homeless now. Perhaps they are coming to live in the tent.'

Susu, Gaby's mother was in front, her father and sisters not far behind. They waved to him, and shouted. 'Where is Gaby? Where is she?'

He pirouetted on the rock he had chosen as a vantage point and pointed to the shelter where his Red Cheeks, as intent and serious as any clown upon his work, was combing out the long tail of that notorious kicker, Spooky the circus horse.

Susu rewarded him with a hug and a kiss.

'*I* didn't save her life,' he said. 'She says she has come to say goodbye.'

'We all have, and to applaud you for the last time.'

Vixen ran up. 'What's happened? We're being invaded.'

'I think they want a performance.'

'Now? They all look as though they need a cup of tea: pity we've run out.'

And so it came about that the Folk sat in the damp and dim circus tent while the performers lit the lights, and brought cakes and candies to be divided amongst the children, and prepared themselves for a performance. The Folk were delighted. Ropewalker Aglit stood up and gave an impromptu recital of throat music while the children clapped their hands.

But it seemed to Bren, impatient to be on his way, that the tent was already full with the ghosts of his people and of others who belonged to Sowash. He sat by Cait, waiting for the time to pass.

Gaby was left in the shelter with Spooky. She gentled him and, when she had finished combing his tail, began upon his mane. Presently Cantor entered and started work upon the elephant.

'We're giving a performance,' he said. 'Four in the morning and we're going into the ring. He's taken leave of his senses, at last.'

Loy had never seemed more sensible, nothing had ever been so right as those past minutes when he had held her in his arms.

'It's to say goodbye. The Folk are leaving Sowash.'

'Oh yeah? I'll give 'em a goodbye.'

His bark, she knew, was worse than his bite. She continued to groom the horse, brushing his coat until the spots gleamed on his dark quarters like new snow. Cantor had finished with the elephant.

'You on?'

'Not this time. I want to watch.'

Prenta hurried in with her brushes and paints. Deftly, she painted yellow blobs upon Garissa's rough hide, and set multi-coloured petals all about them.

'Does it in no time,' said Cantor to Gaby. 'She's a clever girl.'

He leered at Prenta, who took no notice, and came across to fit the bridle on the horse.

'Now for Bluebird. You helping or hindering?'

Gaby entered the big top when everyone was seated and awaiting the parade. It was packed. Many places had two occupants: a smiling, fur-clad Fisher and another, fainter spectator, not quite in focus, not exactly defined. She was glad to see Siri with her family, young Siri unaware upon her lap; and the old ones, the ancestors from Ulbeg. A few Sineinan spirits sat at the back: they looked happy, too. She smiled to see Grandgrand Pike and her owl, which sat on her shoulder and preened her hair as if they had never been parted. A stranger sat next to Pike Neemi, a tall woman dressed like one of the Folk. There were other strangers too, some in furs and some in padded snowcoats. They must be the explorers, who had so loved the North that they had travelled far to discover it for themselves and who, finding their own white paradise, had died there but still could not bear to leave.

The wind howled, and tore at the canvas. It put cold fingers into the tent and the Folk smelled their future: snow.

Gaby waved to the living, to her friends Cait and Bren, Fenner and Ial; to poor Pak, beside her nieces, his daughters, and their aunts, her sisters; to her mother and father. She sat down at the end of the first row, not quite in the audience and not quite in the ring. She clasped her knees and listened to the fanfare. When it ended, the circus would begin.

Fire came in, long, flaming torches carried by Florian, the dwarf. Perhaps he had snatched it down last night from the red sky, and brought it in here to amaze the watchers. He was dressed in the skin of a striped animal and, alone in the ring with his flames, looked bigger than he was, and immensely strong. He had bulging muscles and thick hair. His beard flowed down his chest. 'Give me my dinner!' he shouted, tilted back his head and thrust the torches into his mouth one after the other. The flames died as he swallowed them, and roared to life again in the air.

Some in the audience cried out: none of the Folk had ever seen the dwarf eat fire. Why did he not burn or become a living bonfire in the ring? Someone clapped and cried, 'Bravo!': Arne Shakla, who might years ago have seen the circus perform in her own country of Maralis, before she travelled north. To Gaby, she appeared quite solid now, as Siri had in the atrium.

The horses came galloping into the ring, Bluebird and Spooky together, and the other horses behind. They all had riders on their backs. The elephant, Garissa, walked round and round, carrying Harlequin and Columbine, while the mad old fool ran after them and the clowns pursued him in his turn. The acrobats tumbled and Dove and Shiny swung on the trapeze.

Loy Sen entered the ring and stilled the rout with one note of his violin. He played for the Folk, old southern melodies and sad and forgotten tunes, dances they would never hear again. He handed the fiddle to his daughter who curtsied and took the rose he plucked from the air. He sprang forward and cartwheeled across the ring. Zoe threw him his silver clubs, one by one by one, and he caught them all and threw them up in a dazzling display, faster, quicker, until they looked like shooting stars.

The five dogs ran on, and barked at him. They chased him from the ring and, when he returned for the crowd's applause, he brought back the clowns and the entire company, even Vixen, the ticket-collector, Sierra with her five free-running rats, Prenta who made up the faces, Lucie, who made the costumes, and Alluleya, the fortune-teller.

Gaby sighed. What now?

Loy stood on the blocks that edged the ring. He beckoned to her and bowed, the white face failing to conceal his own underneath, the grin on it wicked and welcoming. 'Red Cheeks!'

She took the hand he offered her, jumped up, and went with him into the ring. Everyone was dancing with the spirits. The sawdust flew up about their feet and Zoe and the circus children shouted with excitement. It was not every day, nor every century, that they were able to dance with the dead, to skip with wise old men and women and hold the hands of Arne Shakla and her imitators and followers. They seemed familiar with the departed, and unafraid; perhaps their ease came because they were also living outside life.

2-Sweet danced a jig with Pike Neemi while the others formed a ring about them. Gaby danced with everybody and so, was able to speak once more with her friends, and laugh.

Then Loy was back, and the music was slowing, had stopped. The clapping drowned the sound of the wind, and the Folk and their ancestors, demons and sprites, turned about and slowly left the tent, the spirits fading with each step they took into the daylight.

Loy took her hand again, so that she left by the performer's exit. They stood close and watched the Folk leave merrily, laughing as they recalled each time-worn joke and piece of business, wondering at each feat.

'Magic,' said Gaby. 'That's what it was.'

He bent and kissed her to obliterate her view of the exodus, not caring how much paint he transferred to her lips: they were both clowns and he, the older and more adept, was an expert at hindering and deception. He was determined that she should not leave him to follow her people.

Ang Semo came over the hill from Ulbeg: too late. She pushed her body into the wind, hurrying as if a troupe of vair pursued her. The Folk had dispersed, each family going its separate way to the skifts which had been left upon the beaches, north and south. She saw them restored, small animals busy in the huge, cold landscape where they belonged. The circus lay below her, a three-dimensional plan, its people moving between tent and vans. There was Harlequin, Peach still in costume; there Columbine, half herself and half the superlatively handsome, sulky Dork; Cantor led Spooky to his shelter, 2-Sweet sat high on Garissa's back and there, before the circus tent, his spangled suit catching the light, his skin white as chalk and his cap removed to show his soot-black hair, which the wind tossed about, was Loy Sen, the white-face clown. His strong arms were wrapped around the small and indomitable figure of Float Gaby.

As she watched, the valley blinked, a huge lens closing and opening again, and the wind died. She saw into the fourth dimension: a glimpse of a wide and deserted plain. The colours of the circus melded with those of the land, red and gold, pink and blue into the greys and the greens. And then it was gone, forward into the unknowable future or back into the past from whence it came. This was

THE END

except that, and she smiled and began to run, a small and frantically-waving figure in a frilly white dress remained in the empty valley. Zoe had been left behind.

ENVOI

Ang and her child, Zoe:

She walked in Toul, holding Zoe by the hand. Zoe held Nix in her arms. Apart from their three selves, the boulders were the only sure things to be seen. The mist rolled down about them from the hill.

They walked on the beach. The sea hardly moved, creeping slowly forward into a field of white blossoms at its margin, flowers made of ice. They had crystallised from the ice and were, Ang thought, the tribute of the North to the circus.

They had all left: the acrobats and clowns; the rosinback riders and the brave dwarf, Florian; the rats, horses, dogs, and the great black elephant with her painted patterns of coloured flowers; the children. Columbine, the counterfeit inamorata, had left, and Harlequin with his slapstick, his parti-coloured clothes and his half-mask – Harlequin, Hellequin, Arlecchino, Mezzatinto, Pulchinella, his names as many as his moods or his loves, clues to his nature and identity hidden in them, whether you saw him as a devil, as the leader of a troupe of demons like himself, as a playful clown dressed neither in one colour or another, as a strutting male emblem. . . Loy Sen, painted white to disguise himself, was all of them, lucky and unlucky in love, without Charis or herself, with his new beloved, Gaby; without his cherished daughter.

Horses, vans, tables, chairs, buckets, the flock of bronze and green chickens, would fly from minute to minute. The tent would sail the sea of time like a starship with sails tilted to catch the solar wind, or a paper nautilus adrift upon a world of water, and might have made a landfall already, in someone's time, or else be drifting between the hours.

The Folk had left, to embark upon the next tide in their little boats. She had nothing to remember them by, except a string of beads. They would live in hazard for her, and for all cowards like her, to satisfy a romantic and inaccurate ideal of freedom. She had gone with Salter Bren to meet the icedeer, fished with Float Gaby, danced and feasted with them all, but she could hardly imagine the life to which she had condemned them. There was snow in it, and death on the ice and birth in the bitter cold. If the Folk survived their first winter, there was continual labour for them all, from elder to toddler, finding food and building shelter, building more boats and sledges, and travelling, always travelling with the wind.

They might return to this place when the malp came back. It was theirs. Because of this, they had left nothing in the stony valley. They had no need to mark it to remind themselves of what was theirs.

Gaby, who had gone with the circus, had put the string of beads around her neck. She felt it, to remind herself.

They had all left, even the ghosts. Arne Shakla had loved the valley and spent many summers in it but she, Ang felt, had also departed, sad as herself at the breach and yet looking forward to the next adventure. Toul was deserted, with only its stones and its thin cover of seasonal vegetation to look after.

The wind was getting up. It would blow the mist away and reveal the miles and miles of tossing sea which she would soon pass over. The valley of Toul became slowly visible and all its grasses shook in the wind.

She bent to lift Zoe and to shelter her inside her warm coat. They would go first to Sollar, where she would show the sights to Zoe and show Zoe to her mother.

'We'll go to the shops and buy you some new clothes. We'll take a carriage and a picnic and ride out of town. We'll climb the Peace Monument: it's higher than that mountain, there.'

Zoe held her locket tightly, as if she realised that the picture within it, of the white-face clown, was all she had left of her father.

'We won't see Da, will we?'

'No. He has gone with the circus.'

'And I'm to go with you?'

'Yes. We'll travel into the country, to the farm to see my Aunt Murali.' (She would be amazed to see Ang with a child and would mother Zoe.) 'We'll go out on a cultivator in the fields and see how they plant the seeds.' (Over the bare wintery fields, riding back into childhood.)

'When spring comes, we'll set out, take a skimmer south – but not too far, for you can only explore the Highlands properly on foot.' (When I am thirty-three and Zoe's six, for she will grow now and age in the world.) 'We might get horses from one of the herdswomen. Horses will be useful in the hills, faster than oxen.'

'I can ride a horse,' said Zoe.

On horseback then, they would skirt the arid Stuk until they came to the pine forests. They would ride up the track which at first was wide and well-trodden and which became, later and higher, past the wooden houses of the Vulyar, narrow and stony. They would enter Desolation Wilderness with its mists as fickle as these of the north and its perfect, circular lakes rafted with lilies and full of dark red fish. They would cross the first ring of mountains and, entering one of the deep and shadowy defiles, continue upwards until they came to the top.

From the ridge they would see the red mass of the Central Highlands, which Zoe had glimpsed once, and Ang seen twice; which was the objective of her quest and which would be Zoe's warm nursery, more or less in the centre of Sinein. You could travel no further than this from the sea.

Here, in a valley with red cliffs, a yellow foot and a fringe of green along its tumbling stream, they would build a house: a wooden house, equipped with the usual conveniences, a darkroom, and plenty of paper and books. Then they would wait and see, and maybe photographs would grow or paintings; perhaps a story or two. If they tired of living so far from a city, they would call up some transport and fly out, back to Sollar Kein and her cool streets and wide and open parks, her university and civilised talk. It was easy for them, not forgetting Nix, to return to a secure and orderly culture.

'Now, Zoe, let us say goodbye. We have a long way to go.'

The circus had set its ephemeral mark on Toul. Plants had already grown and perished in the mountain of elephant dung at the valley's end; there was litter where the rake of seats had been; a scattered ring of sawdust; elongated pits where the vans wheels had rested and countless footprints which led from one van to another. A scrap of red and blue colour stirred in the ruts where Loy Sen's van had stood: a handbill. It lifted on the wind and blew past them before it was hurled away, out to sea across the gathering ice:

'The Democratic Travelling Circus. Proprietors: the Artistes. Artistic Director: Loy Sen.'

He had gone, with his white face, his tricks and tears. They had all gone. Now she and Zoe would go, and leave Toul to the long months of darkness and ice. Next, and every year, the sun would return and begin again the delicately balanced cycle of the North.

What would the world be, once bereft
Of wet and wildness? Let them be left
O let them be left, wildness and wet,
Long live the weeds and the wilderness yet.